SISTERS
of the
HEART
THE TRILOGY

By Shelley Shepard Gray

FAMILIES OF HONOR

The Caregiver
The Protector
The Survivor

SEASONS OF SUGARCREEK

Winter's Awakening
Spring's Renewal
Autumn's Promise

SISTERS OF THE HEART

Hidden
Wanted
Forgiven
Grace

SISTERS
of the
HEART
THE TRILOGY

SHELLEY SHEPARD GRAY

AVON

INSPIRE

An Imprint of HarperCollinsPublishers

FIRST EDITION

Designed by Diahann Sturge

ISBN 978-0-06-211485-3

12   13   14   15   16   OV/RRD   10   9   8   7   6   5   4   3   2   1

HIDDEN

Sisters *of the* Heart

BOOK ONE

To Charlie and Cindy, Dale and Nancy, Cathy and Don and Janice. And Tom! Thank you for letting me learn from you, grow with you, and most of all . . . be myself.

Let anyone with ears to hear listen.

Mark 7:16

When the Holy Spirit comes to you, you will receive power. You will be my witnesses.

Acts 1:8

If you admire our faith—strengthen yours. If you admire our sense of commitment—deepen yours. If you admire our community spirit—build your own. If you admire the simple life—cut back. If you admire deep character and enduring values—live them yourself.

—*Small Farm Journal* (Summer 1993)

Prologue

Rob's right fist hurt more than she'd remembered. That was the first thing Anna thought as she tried to focus through the pain. Tried not to cry in front of him.

But that didn't stop Anna from cupping her palm protectively over her cheek, just in case Rob decided to hit her again.

Rob was sitting across from her once more, his crisp Brooks Brothers dress shirt hardly wrinkled. He scowled. "What, Anna? For once you have nothing to say?"

With a force of will, she dropped her hand and clasped her palms together. Resolved to stay calm. Yet, one more time, her mind played back to what she'd seen in his office earlier that day. How he'd been cashing checks for personal use from his campaign funds. And, worst of all, the realization that he'd spent some of that money on her. "There isn't anything to say. Not anymore."

"That, my dear, is where you're wrong. I don't ever want to hear that disbelieving, sarcastic tone in your voice again. And once more, you will never even think of mentioning your opinions about my business when we're in public again. Do you hear me?"

He was yelling. Of course she could hear him.

But now she believed his threats. After she'd questioned the receipts she'd found in front of one of his closest staff, Rob had been livid. Less than an hour later he pulled her out of the party, saying they had things to discuss. He'd barely spoken a word to her the whole way home. She had a feeling this was coming. And yet had hoped that his anger would subside, that it wouldn't come to this.

"Anna, answer."

"Yes." Unable to help herself, she nodded. The movement swayed the diamond drop earrings. When she'd first received them, she'd loved the sweet tinkling noise they made. Now that she realized they'd been bought with money from Rob's supporters, their weight merely intensified her piercing headache.

Rob's eyes followed the flash of the diamonds against the shadows of his living room wall. Anna knew the look that glinted in his eyes. It spoke of satisfaction. Ownership.

How had she been so very wrong about him?

Color returned to his cheeks as Rob leaned back against the cushions of the cream-colored couch. "Don't forget who you are talking to. We have a future together, Anna. We have plans."

She didn't even try to hide the bitterness in her voice. "I don't date men who hit me."

"That was an accident."

"Rob—"

His voice hardened. "It was an accident, Anna."

She knew it hadn't been. Instinctively, she knew he'd planned to hit her from the moment she said too much at the party. "Are you sure?"

Almost smiling, he raised his brows. "Come on. We both know I'm not the type of man who would hit a woman. But I'm also not the type of man to let a woman walk all over him. You need to learn your place, Anna. Learn your place and not forget it."

Unfortunately, she was slowly learning her place. She was just sorry it had taken her so long.

And that was the problem, wasn't it? Rob Peterson was all polished veneer. He was smooth talking, gift-giving, perfectly handsome and extremely well-mannered. When he'd first asked her out, Anna had been foolishly excited that he'd even noticed her.

And though he'd seemed possessive and at times controlling, she'd pretended it was only natural that a man like him would want everything to be perfect.

After all, he was running for a seat in the House of Representatives. He was an important man. A lot of people thought so.

As weeks turned to months, she'd quit her job and took another one—a silly position at an insurance company where she didn't have to work full time. Rob had asked that she'd be available at a moment's notice. To attend fundraisers and society galas.

When he took her shopping and paid cash for a closetful of designer dresses, skirts, and shoes, she'd pushed aside her own feelings for the clothes, even though she would have usually never worn skirts so form-fitting, necklines so low, or heels so high. After all, those things were important to Rob and the clothes were so much nicer than anything she'd ever owned.

But now Rob wasn't going to let her go. She knew it, and he knew it. Now her cheek knew it, too.

She was trapped.

As she sat across from him, felt his gaze on her, noticed that her cheek was swelling, Anna knew there was only one thing to do. She had to get away.

She tried to smile. Let him think she was just going to shrug this off as she had the other times. Standing up, she smoothed the jade green silk sheath around her hips. Stepped toward him on four inch heels. Close enough to smell his cologne.

Close enough for him to touch her again if he wanted to.

Tried to think of a lie he would believe. "I'm sorry about everything, Rob. I had no business saying a word about your finances, especially since I love your gifts so much. The truth is, I . . . I've been nervous about our future."

His dark brown eyes turned languid. "What are you nervous about?"

She picked a reason he would completely accept. "I saw how you were talking with that girl at the party earlier this evening. She was flirting with you nonstop."

"Who?" Rob leaned forward. Ran a finger up the expanse of her bare arm.

"The redhead?" Anna pretended to almost forget the woman's name. "Sammy?"

"Oh. That was *Samantha*, not Sammy." Oh, so gently, Rob pulled her down next to him. "Don't give her another thought. She's a nobody. You have nothing to be nervous about, baby. No other girl is like you. I get compliments on those pretty green eyes of yours almost every day."

Anna looked down so he wouldn't see the emotion she was trying so hard to conceal. But just as firmly, Rob tilted her chin up, so they were almost eye to eye. Almost tenderly, he wiped away a stray tear from her cheek. "Don't cry, Anna," he murmured, frowning. "I'm just doing what I have to do."

Inside, her nerves were warring. Fear and regret churned together, making her feel faint and nauseous. Anna knew she couldn't continue the charade much longer. "I think I better go home."

"Already?" He glanced at his gold watch. "It's not even midnight."

She tried to smile. "You're forgetting that I'm a working girl. They're expecting me at nine a.m. sharp." She pulled away and reached for her coat.

He followed her to the door. "As soon as we're engaged, you can quit," he murmured as he helped her slip on the black wool coat over her shoulders. After fastening the top button, he leaned closer and grazed his lips across her ear. "Then your time will be all mine."

Her heart was pounding. "I know it will. I'll see you to-morrow, Rob."

Just as he leaned close to kiss her, his cell phone rang. Looking at the screen, Rob grimaced. "I've got to get this, Anna. Sorry."

She slipped out.

There were twenty steps to the car. She just had to make it twenty steps. With every ounce of effort, Anna walked slowly, her back straight, her head high. Just as if Rob was watching from the window.

Ten more feet.

Two more. She slid into her sedan, turned on the ignition. Placed the car in reverse. Slowly edged the car down the driveway. Switched to drive. The front curtain fluttered as Rob finally walked away.

As she drove down his street, Anna dared to lock the doors. Safe. She was almost safe. The tears came, fast and furious. There was no doubt anymore, she had to get away.

Everyone loved Rob Peterson. They loved his smile, they loved his promises. Her parents thought his commanding manner was just what she needed. So far, no one had believed her when she tried to tell them he was dangerous. No one believed that he could hurt her, that he would hurt her. Especially not his brother-in-law, the sheriff.

Yes, as far as everyone was concerned, Anna Metzger already belonged to Rob Peterson.

With a ragged breath, Anna knew what she had to do. Before it was too late, she had to go someplace where no one could find her. She had to hide. By morning, she would have a plan. And then, to almost everyone who knew her . . . she would be gone.

Chapter 1

"Anna! This is surely a *gut*—a good—surprise," Katie Brenneman said in her all-too-familiar lilt. "Come in out of the cold, wouldja?"

Anna breathed a sigh of relief. For a moment she hadn't been sure she'd be welcomed by her childhood friend. Hadn't been sure of anything anymore.

Katie clucked. "Anna, come in. You're lettin' in the cold."

Obediently, she stepped into the foyer of the Brenneman Bed and Breakfast and was immediately surrounded by the smell of beeswax, spiced oranges, and crisp cotton. Behind her stood a finely woven basket filled with beautifully hand-carved canes of different woods. To her left was an antique table and chairs, each piece finely crafted and shined to a polish. A simple staircase curved upward to her right. Rag rugs in twirls of blue, dark green, and blood red decorated the wide planks.

On those planks, she placed her small suitcase. Well, maybe it wasn't so small.

Katie noticed. "You here for a spell?"

"I hope so. If you don't mind."

"Why ever would I mind?" Katie, dressed in her simple cobalt blue dress, gathered her into a warm hug, the kind of acceptance that only a friend of ten years could offer. "You're as cold as I've ever seen," she said, looking Anna up and down with bright blue eyes. "But something's wrong, ain't it now?"

Anna knew there was no way to sidestep her problems. Something was, indeed, very wrong. "I need help, Katie." Did her voice sound as desperate as she felt?

Katie's cheeks brightened with color, and she was just about to speak when Anna heard another voice, one that she'd tried hard to forget.

"Katie? Who's here?"

Anna turned to find Henry Brenneman filling the doorway, his expression guarded and full of distrust.

Katie stepped closer, as if her slight build could offer Anna protection from her brother's probing eyes. "It's Anna, my friend from *Mamm*'s quilting class, Henry."

"I see."

Anna was sure he did. From the time they'd first met, he'd always seemed to find her lacking.

Gesturing to her bulging suitcase, he said, "You here for a visit?"

Anna flushed. Against her will, she felt her composure falter. But that was always how Henry made her feel, unworthy. So . . . English. "Not exactly. Actually, I'm not sure why I'm here. I was just going to speak to Katie—"

His suspicious gaze cut her off as sharply as his words. "Why?"

Piercing brown eyes scanned her without embarrassment, leaving Anna to feel like the interloper she was. "I need somewhere to stay for a bit."

Katie motioned her silent with a finger to her lips. "We're due for a visit. I, for one, am delighted you're here. We have two bedrooms open. You're welcome to one, if you'd like."

"They're paying rooms."

Katie playfully pushed her brother's shoulder. "Get along, now. We'd never charge my *gut* friend Anna here for her company."

Anna stepped forward. Though it was kind of Katie to attempt to smooth over her appearance, Anna was done speaking—or acting—in veiled ways. "There's a reason I need a room."

Katie gripped her hand and pulled her into the kitchen, finally pressing Anna down into a wooden ladder-back chair. To Anna's dismay, Henry followed, though neither she nor Katie had invited him.

"I'm in trouble. I've been in trouble." Picking up the linen napkin on the table, Anna gently rubbed it against her cheek, doing her best not to wince as she did so. Little by little, the thick makeup she'd put on just a few hours ago came off, revealing her bruise.

Katie's eyes widened appreciatively. Henry, too, must have been struck by the discoloration on her cheek, because he sat down as well. Then, as was their way, neither said a word.

Anna remembered the wonderful sense of privacy that seemed to surround the Brennemans and their Amish relatives. Though part of the New Order, so not quite as strict in the ways of the Old, where electricity and modern conveniences were always forbidden, the Brenneman family adhered to many of the tenets of the Amish way of life—and that included an extreme respect for the privacy of others.

That respect made what had happened even more uncomfortable. "I . . . I should begin by letting you know that I've been dating Rob Peterson. For six months."

Blank expressions met the news.

They had to be the only people she knew who weren't fazed in the slightest about that. "He's kind of a famous man in Cincinnati. He's a former lawyer. Now he's running for the open spot in the House of Representatives." When still neither said anything, she added quietly, "He has a lot of influence. Money."

"And this matters to you, Anna?" Katie said.

Anna knew it didn't matter near as much as it used to. "Rob and I had already gotten serious when I started to notice how controlling he was. Prone to bursts of temper. The first time he hit me, he swore it was an accident."

"And that?" Henry asked.

She gingerly fingered her swollen cheek. Swallowed. "This happened late last night."

If anything, Henry's gaze hardened. "That there was no accident."

Henry was right. "No, no it wasn't. He, uh, now seems to think of me as a possession. He's taken to following me, or to having someone who works for him do that."

"Have you gotten the law involved?"

Anna almost smiled. Katie's knowledge of the outside world

was sketchy at best. "I've contacted the police, but they seem to think I'm just clumsy. No one wants to go against him."

"Not even your family?" Katie's voice was full of wonder.

For the moment, Anna had forgotten that her mother and Katie had formed a relationship. They'd gotten along very well, especially when Katie revealed that her cousins owned a dairy one hour north. Her mother claimed that the Amish products were the finest she'd ever had.

"My mother thinks I'm just having second thoughts about marrying Rob. She's always felt I didn't take anything very seriously."

Something flashed in Henry's eyes before he hid it—but Anna knew what he thought. It was the same thing everyone thought—there wasn't much to Anna Metzger. She'd made mediocre grades, had hardly ever kept a job more than six months, and had more than her fair share of boyfriends.

Her mother had plenty of examples of Anna not taking things seriously.

"So you've run?"

Henry's voice was full of accusation. But still, she couldn't deny it. "Yes. I ran."

"And in doing so you've put my family in danger?"

"No. I would never do that."

"But you did."

Anna sought to explain. "First, Rob doesn't even know about you. We didn't talk of things beyond his work and our social calendar." She paused before continuing. "Second, I'm sure I wasn't followed. I took a taxi here."

"But you canna be sure, can you?"

"No."

Henry folded his arms across his chest.

And made Anna realize she'd been a fool. Again. Scooting out her chair, she stood up quickly. "I'm sorry. I'll go."

Under her white cap, Katie's eyes were bright and questioning. "Where will you go?"

"I don't know."

"Maybe you shoulda thought—"

Katie turned to her brother. "Enough, Henry. Go tell *Mamm* and *Daed* that we have company, will ya?"

Henry put on the straw hat he'd been carrying and left without a word.

Next, Katie glanced at her. "Sit down. Now, I'll make you some tea, dear Anna, and you can tell me how else you've been hurt."

"There's not much else besides my cheek." *Not at the moment, anyway.*

"Inside though, I'm guessin' that will be another story."

Katie's eyes looked so caring that Anna almost broke down. "Oh, Katie, thank you for being here."

"Where else would I be? This is my home, *jah?*"

Anna sat still while Katie busied herself with a pot of tea, carefully spooning the loose leaves into a strainer and boiling the kettle on the kerosene stove.

Katie then carefully cut off a thick slice of apple bread and served it to Anna on a piece of oatmeal-colored crockery.

After her childhood friend seated herself again, Anna spoke. "I'm scared. I'm scared of Rob. And just as frightened to look in the mirror and truly see what I've become. *Whom* I've become. I never thought I'd be the kind of woman to hide from anyone."

"Sometimes we all hide. Even from ourselves. But, the Bible says we must seek shelter with the Lord."

"I suppose."

Katie bustled with the tea again, pouring and straining. With easy motions, she brought a jar of honey to the table. When she was settled again, she smiled. "Whatcha been doing, otherwise?"

Anna chuckled. "I've been working for an insurance company sometimes."

"And you like this?"

"No. I took it because the hours were flexible and I never had to get too emotionally involved. I could leave when I needed to help with the filing at campaign headquarters. Or when Rob wanted me to go out."

Katie blinked, telling Anna quite simply that she found the idea of being emotionally distant strange. "Will they be lookin' for you today?"

"I imagine so, though I did call and tell them I was taking some time off."

"I see," Katie said, though it was evident she didn't see at all.

"I spoke to my mother yesterday, but when all she did was laugh off my worries, I knew I had to leave. The disastrous episode with Rob late last night just confirmed I made the right decision. I purchased a plane ticket to Miami and parked my car at the airport. Then I left a message on my parents' home phone, saying that I was taking two weeks' vacation." With a shrug, Anna added, "I don't know if it will buy me much time, but I'm thinking it might."

"And then you came here."

"I went to the taxi stand and paid a small fortune for a ride out here. I truly didn't know where else to go."

Maybe because the Lord was guiding you?"

How could Anna describe completely the things she yearned for? Peace, tranquility. Faith and simplicity. Steadfast love. All were things the Brenneman family had shown her on numerous occasions over the years.

All were things that seemed to lie on the outskirts of her existence.

"You were right to come here, Anna."

"I don't think everyone feels that way."

"You talkin' bout Henry? He doesn't trust you."

There was the fact, said boldly and without rancor. "I know. Because I'm an Outsider?"

"Maybe. I think it might be something more, though," Katie said cryptically.

Mrs. Irene Brenneman entered just then, saving Anna from deciphering that message. "Anna, my dear. What a sight you are. Henry says you have need of shelter."

"Yes."

"Then you must stay here."

"If you're sure."

"Of course we're sure," she said, bending down and placing one soft cheek next to Anna's.

"I'd like to earn my keep. I can pay for my room and board and help out in any way I may."

"If you help, no money will be necessary," Irene said briskly. Turning to Henry, who was once again hovering near the door, she said, "Show Miss Anna to the room off the kitchen, would ya?"

After receiving a wink from Katie, Anna hastened to follow him, his hand already gripping her luggage.

"I can get that."

"It's no trouble."

She followed him down a wide hallway, the walls covered with a few carefully framed quilt squares. Anna recognized two of her favorite designs, the Bear Paw and the Monkey Wrench, the former icy white and indigo blue.

Finally, they stopped at the last room on the left.

"This is a small room," he warned.

"It will be fine."

He opened the door and set her bag just inside. "Well, then," he murmured. "I'll be seeing you, I suppose."

"Does my being here upset you?"

Instead of answering, he volleyed a question her way. "What would you do if it did? You arrived, bag in hand and marks to show. We didn't have much choice in the matter, now did we?"

"I didn't make up my circumstances."

"I didn't think you did." Finally he turned to her, his eyes piercing. "I think you're a selfish woman, Anna Metzger. I think you've chosen to run and hide and put my family in danger instead of facing your own consequences. And, I'm sorry, but I don't have much respect for that. My mother and sister have a soft spot for you, so I'll abide their wishes, but I don't like it."

"Thank you for your honesty."

"You're—welcome." With a last look before he shut the door, Henry added, "Honesty, I'm bettin', is something new for you."

Chapter 2

"I'm mighty disappointed in you, Henry," Katie said the moment he entered the hearth room in back of the kitchen. "The way you acted toward my friend Anna was terribly rude."

Henry fought to keep his expression neutral as he met the questioning looks from his sister and parents. He knew he'd been harsh and inhospitable toward Anna Metzger, but he hadn't been able to help himself.

Anna's appearance in his life had rattled him good. Not that his brash little sister needed to remind him of it. "I wasna being rude—only saying the truth. Which, I might add, is more than we are hearing from Anna."

Katie set her sewing to one side. "The bruise on her cheek looked mighty real to me."

Taking a seat in front of the blazing fire, Henry shook off

the cold look of his sister. "*Jah*, but I think there's more than what she's told us."

"I reckon there is," his father said as he peered at Henry through his reading glasses. "I fear there's far more to Anna's story than what she's shared with us."

"All the more reason to be circumspect, don'tcha think?"

After sharing a glance with his *daed*, his mother reached out and clasped his arm. "Oh, Henry. What has happened to you? You used to be far more accepting of others."

He spoke with more force than he intended. "Just because I don't immediately put my trust in an English girl who shows up for the first time in years doesna mean the problem lies with me."

"You couldn't have been any more discourteous, though." Katie picked up her sewing again, the bright yellow fabric shining bright against her dark skirts.

"Any ruder than arriving for a visit unannounced and un-invited?"

Most likely in a lather, Katie presented her shoulder to him while she spoke as sweet as molasses to their mother. "*Mamm*, thank you for allowing Anna to stay here."

"No reason to thank me, it's our Christian duty," her mother replied as she picked up the spool of thread that had just rolled off of Katie's skirts. "It's not our place to judge, Henry. Our Lord takes care of that just fine, without any help from us."

There, in the back room off the kitchen, one of the few rooms reserved only for family, Henry knew his mother was right, which made his cross feelings toward Anna even harder to understand. "I'll try to do better."

His father nodded and picked up his Bible. "I'm pleased to hear that."

Feeling too restless to remain seated by the fire, Henry stood up. "I'll go out now and check the horses."

"*Danke.*"

He'd just put on his black hat when his mother spoke again. "All women are not like Rachel, Henry."

Rachel. It was truly amazing, just how easily the woman's name could cause him grief. "I know that."

Katie's hands stilled. "Do you? Rachel was my friend once, too, you know. Sometimes I think you've forgotten."

He'd forgotten nothing. He'd been courting Rachel Baar for two months when she met an Englisher who was visiting the farmer's market. Lightning fast, Rachel left their community and married the man. Henry had watched, hurting but unable to do a thing to stop her journey into the outside world.

For many a day, he'd worked hard and long hours in the fields surrounding their inn . . . anything to divest himself of Rachel's memory and the hurt feelings she'd left him with.

He'd thought he'd accomplished his goal. He'd been sure of it until he saw Anna with her thick blond hair and bright green eyes at their doorstep.

Anna brought back memories of the first time he'd seen her, seven years before. Now, as before, he'd been struck by her beauty. "Rachel is not the problem here."

Katie raised her chin. "Neither is Anna."

"I don't agree. She should have sought shelter somewhere else. It is not our place to harbor her."

"She's my friend."

"She's English. And she could bring trouble with her. Maybe she already has."

"Henry. Katie. Quieten, now," their father ordered. "Your sharp tongues will lead you to trouble, mark my words."

Not ready to apologize yet again, Henry just nodded before slipping into the kitchen, then finally out into the bitterly cold January frost. Glad for the warmth of his thick wool coat, he made his way to the barn and their four horses. From the moment he entered his sanctuary, Henry felt right once again. Stanley raised his head in Henry's direction, neighing a friendly greeting.

From the back room, Jess carefully padded forward. Kneeling down, he took time to rub his old dog behind the ears. "Jess? How are you, my friend?" Warm brown eyes softened with trust as a fluffy brown and white tail wagged. "Did you eat? Let's go see."

Jess stepped alongside him, walking to his water and food bowls, which were still full. After taking a sip of water, Jess sat down on his favorite blanket and watched Henry with bright eyes. That Jess wasn't eating made him sad—there'd been a time when the dog would sneak bacon and pancakes from the kitchen counter with lightning speed.

Now Jess preferred the quiet of the barn and days filled with sleeping.

Henry sank to the dog's side and leaned his back against the rough wood of the barn.

Just for a moment, he remembered the past. Remembered how he'd always assumed things would be.

Rachel.

From the time he sat next to Rachel in their one-room schoolhouse, Henry had known he'd found his heart's match. Rachel had been everything he'd ever wanted.

Though nothing had been said, Henry—and everyone

they knew—had assumed that when Rachel turned of age, they'd marry.

But she'd cast her eye on another man and left everything she knew with little more than a backward glance.

And now he was faced with the only other woman who'd captured his attention, and she was everything he shouldn't want. An outsider. Far more educated than he. Far more worldly than he.

Her hair, so full of curls, so thick and pretty it captured his imagination from the time he'd seen it hanging down her back in a loose ponytail. Green eyes, so sharp and filled with expression that every emotion was written plain on her face. A bright smile. Creamy skin.

And never more than a cursory glance his way.

Over the course of the late January afternoon, the Brenneman Bed and Breakfast filled, leaving Anna no time to discuss things further with Katie or her mother.

Instead, she kept herself occupied in the kitchen, carefully rolling out dough for the evening's batch of apple dumplings.

First thing that morning, Mrs. Brenneman had handed her a simple blue dress, woolen stockings, and a crisp apron, offering it to Anna as a way of keeping the rest of the guests from observing her too carefully. Anna had gratefully slipped and pinned on the garments, appreciating how the well-worn cloth felt against her skin and kept her warm.

Voices, loud and boisterous and foreign, filled the inn's halls. Anna hid a smile as she overheard Katie discussing the nearby general store with a couple from Tennessee. Over and over, Katie patiently answered their questions concerning the Amish way of life.

When Katie entered the kitchen again, Anna raised an eyebrow in her direction. "All those questions! Do they ever bother you?"

Her friend looked surprised at the thought. "Oh, not at all. People come here to be a part of our way of life. Given that, there's always questions."

"Sometimes it seems too intrusive."

"If we found it such, we wouldn't open our home," she replied softly.

Anna stewed on that as she carefully brushed a layer of butter on the top of each cloverleaf roll that she'd just fashioned into the tin. "I know you're right."

"I am."

"I'm sorry I've taken up a room. I'm costing you money, I'm afraid."

"You're important, too, Anna. You mustn't forget that."

Anna ducked her head, realizing with some surprise that she was carrying that sense of unworthiness from Rob. "I'll do my best to be helpful. Just tell me what to do and I'll do it."

Katie gently touched her cheek. "If you do your best to heal, that will be enough."

"The mark isn't so bad."

"We both know better, Anna. The mark is a symbol of many bad things."

Anna's hands shook as Katie was summoned out of the kitchen. Katie's words were very true. Her relationship with Rob had been unhealthy from the very first—she'd just never been strong enough to see that.

No, that wasn't true. She'd hadn't been strong enough to take control of her life and change things. But now, she was slowly changing and determined to use the time at the

Brennemans to grow both spiritually and in maturity. Though living with the Amish was proving to be full of long days and hard physical labor, for the first time in her life, Anna wasn't afraid to commit.

It truly seemed as if her friendship with Katie and the Brennemans' hospitality was a gift from God. Anna just hoped she wasn't destined to hurt the very people who were giving her aid in the process.

She frowned, thinking about the outside world. What was happening at home? With Rob?

Did he even realize she was gone? A number of scenarios ran together in her head. Rob knowing immediately that she never left the area. Rob searching through her belongings and finding some careless note that Anna had scrawled on a scratch sheet of paper.

Rob coming out to the Brennemans and reclaiming her . . . and she going with him because she had no choice.

No matter what Henry said, she wouldn't put the Brennemans in danger. She owed them too much. Was too appreciative of their kindness to her.

But what if she already had?

Digging her hands into the dough once more, Anna prayed.

"Florida? Are you sure she flew to Miami?"

Meredith Metzger clutched the phone, biting back the sharp worry that engulfed her as she scanned her daughter's note again. "Rob, that's what she said. Anna also left me her itinerary. She decided to go with some girlfriends to the beach for two weeks. Don't worry."

"Who are these girlfriends?"

"Jennifer and Linda," Meredith said, making up two names from the top of her head.

"I've never heard of them."

Taking care to put the right amount of amusement in her voice, Meredith chuckled. "Rob, please don't tell me that you and Anna spent your time together talking about her long list of friends."

"This trip seems sudden. Too sudden."

"Maybe it wasn't," she ventured. "Now that I think about it, I believe Anna had this trip planned for months and I just forgot about it." Doing her best to keep the conversation light and easy, Meredith laughed. "That sounds like Anna, doesn't it? The girl would forget her hands if they weren't attached to her arms."

"Maybe you're right," Rob said after a moment, his usually silky voice sounding stilted and rough. "Though that doesn't explain why she hasn't answered her cell phone. Every time I call, it just rings before going to voice mail."

"She's probably just not taking it to the beach with her."

"Maybe. When you talk to Anna, tell her to call me. She should have never left without contacting me first."

True worry settled in Meredith's heart. Had the man always been so controlling and she'd just been blinded by his wealth and good looks? "I'll do that, but I doubt she'll call home today." Summoning a girlish, artificial laugh, Meredith said, "You know how Anna is—always out for a good time."

Still no humor infused his voice. "Tell her to call me as soon as you do—no matter what the time."

After she hung up, Meredith stared at Anna's hastily scrawled note one more time.

Mother,

I'm going to Miami for a few weeks. Sorry I forgot to tell you about it earlier. I'll call you in a few days.

Anna

No matter what Meredith told Rob, taking a trip on the spur of the moment was not like her daughter. Neither was forgetting about it.

Something wasn't quite right.

Meredith quickly climbed the staircase to her daughter's room. Lifting up the powder blue dust ruffle, she noticed all of Anna's suitcases were still neatly stowed under her bed.

Pulling open a drawer, she saw it was filled with shorts and bathing suits—too many if Anna had really packed for a trip in the sun.

She investigated further. Sunscreen was in the medicine cabinet in the bathroom. Sandals rested on her closet floor. Her camera sat on her dresser.

No, something wasn't right at all.

Neither was Rob's anger.

Foreboding filled Meredith as she wondered if maybe— just maybe—her daughter might not have been exaggerating when she said that Rob Peterson was a dangerous man.

"Please be with her, Heavenly Father," she prayed. "Heaven knows I have not."

Chapter 3

The air was icy cold and its breeze bit into her cheeks as Anna crossed the well-worn path from the main house to the barn where the horses were stabled.

And where Henry Brenneman had seemed to be more often than not. Hearing the clang of his hammer, Anna wondered if he was still as angry with her as he'd been the evening before. She certainly hoped not. The last thing she'd meant to do when she'd sought refuge at the inn was cause distress.

Her steps faltered. Who was she kidding? She hadn't thought of anyone but herself during that hour-long trip from the airport to the Brennemans'. In many ways, Henry's accusations were not far off the mark.

After knocking on his closed workshop door, she called out, "Henry? Your mother wants you in for breakfast."

After a moment's pause, the workshop door opened. "I'll be right out."

For a moment, Anna couldn't help but stare. Henry's cheeks were flushed from exertion, and his sleeves were rolled up. Beads of sweat dotted his brow and neck. Under a worn leather apron, broad shoulders and an iron-hard chest peeked out. Henry Brenneman was gorgeous.

How had she not noticed that before?

It took her a moment to remember to close her mouth. "You're working out here awfully early."

He almost smiled. "Me and Jess here do best in the morning," he said, gesturing to the old dog sprawled on what looked to be a discarded horse blanket.

She peeked in further, smelled leather and wood oil, dust and horse and . . . Henry? She swallowed. "What are you working on?"

"Only a chair that needed fixin'." As if her proximity made him nervous, he took a step away, broke eye contact. "As I said, I'll just be a moment."

Anna nodded, and took a step back as well, lengthening the distance between them. Though a little voice inside her said she might as well turn and leave, Anna decided to wait for him. She needed to make some kind of peace with Henry, if for no other reason than to ease the tension in the Brenneman household.

With easy motions, Henry untied his apron, righted the chair, and put each tool in its proper place. Anna watched him with something close to surprise, as if she'd just seen him for the first time.

Why was that? How had she never noticed how handsome he was? How steady? How much he cared for that old dog? Had she only been concerned with herself?

Or had she only thought of him with a label firmly attached? Amish. Foreign. Different. All the tags she'd never pinned on Katie.

As if surprised she was still there, he frowned. "Tell *Mamm* I'll be right along."

Offering an olive branch, she said, "I'll wait for you, if you don't mind."

"*Danke.*" Wariness filled his brown-eyed gaze.

Anna leaned against the doorframe as Henry knelt down to Jess and gently patted the dog behind his floppy ears. He whispered something to him, then straightened and met her at the barn door, resolution in his eyes.

As their boots crunched over the fallen leaves and stones underfoot, Anna offered, "Will your dog be okay out here?"

"*Jah.* He's happy as long as he can stay put here."

The cold air made her eyes water. "You've had him a long time?"

"Thirteen years. Long ago he used to keep me company when I worked in the fields."

"Now Jess has earned his retirement."

Once again, Henry almost smiled. "Retirement? We Amish don't believe in such things."

Anna wasn't sure if he was teasing or not. "You just slow down?"

"We follow God's will, Anna Metzger. That's what we do."

Anna stewed on that as Henry held the door open for her and they stepped inside the bustling kitchen.

"There you both are," Mrs. Brenneman said, holding a platter full of eggs and sausage. "I thought I was going to have to send Katie out for you, mark my words."

As Henry sent a superior look Katie's way he said, "It's lucky we came when we did, then."

After a moment of silent prayer, Henry started eating. Anna served herself a smaller portion while she stewed on Henry's abrupt change in manner.

She mentioned it to Katie later when they were clearing the table and preparing for the guests, who would start coming down for breakfast at seven thirty. "I don't understand your brother. One moment, he seems angry at me for everything I've done, the next, he seems almost sociable. I hardly know how to act around him."

Katie chuckled. "It's because you make him nervous, Anna."

"Me? I don't see why."

Mrs. Brenneman stirred her coffee. "Don't fret, my dear. He'll find his way."

Find his way around what? Her? "Do I make him nervous because I'm English?" That didn't make sense. Most all the guests in the bed and breakfast were English, weren't they?

Katie chuckled. "You make him uneasy because you're *Anna.*"

"What is that supposed to mean?"

"We've all caught him sneaking a glance your way a time or two over the years when you've come visiting," Katie explained, her eyes twinkling.

Anna felt her cheeks heat. "I had no idea."

Mrs. Brenneman clucked. "That almost makes it harder, I think. My *buwe*, my son, is having a time of it, preparing for his future. His Rachel fell in *lieb* with an Englisher and left us all. Your appearance brings back memories."

"Makes Henry think of things that are not possible—at least not for him," Katie added matter-of-factly. "He's made it really clear he has no need to live outside of our ways."

"And here I was, pushing him to accept me. I'm sorry."

"Nothing to be sorry for," Mrs. Brenneman said with a warm smile. "You being here is wonderful *gut*."

"Thank you."

Katie's mom clapped her hands. "Now, dear, you did a fine job on the rolls yesterday, but I have a different chore for you this morning, if you've got a mind for it."

"What is it?"

"Sewing."

Sewing and quilting were two of Anna's favorite pastimes. So much so, it didn't seem like work. "Wouldn't you rather I did something more helpful? I'd be happy to help clean the guestrooms."

After pulling out a finely woven basket filled with indigo cloth and white linen from a cupboard near the kitchen door, Mrs. Brenneman placed it in front of Anna. "This chore would be most helpful, if you don't mind doing it. I've cut the cloth for a new shirt for Henry and a new dress for my eldest daughter's baby. If you could work on them, I'd be mighty happy."

With a kind smile, Katie added, "The sewing room is in the back and has a nice rocking chair and fire. With the morning light, it's a peaceful place."

Looking at the platters of food still needing to be washed, and the plates of muffins to serve to the guests, Anna still worried. Though she'd come to hide, she certainly didn't want to shirk the many jobs that needed to be done. "If that's what you would like me to do . . ."

"I would," Mrs. Brenneman said, gently cupping Anna's sore cheek. "Today's a time for resting. Tomorrow's soon enough for more."

"I'll join you after I finish helping the guests get organized for the day and washing the walls and floor of the kitchen," Katie promised.

"I'd be happy to sew, Mrs. Brenneman. But first could I help with the dishes?"

"Yes, dear Anna. First, you may help with the dishes."

The day had been fulfilling in a way that working at the insurance company had never been. After helping with the dishes, Anna carried the sewing basket into the back room and inspected the fabrics for the dress and shirt. Both cloths were finely made and soft as the finest materials in expensive department stores.

Luckily for Anna, there were also patterns to follow. In no time, Anna was working at the trundle sewing machine stationed in the corner of the room. Time flew as she painstakingly pieced the garments together.

After a time, Katie joined her for a bit, then left when it was time to prepare two of the rooms for new guests. Anna helped with some baking, then went to her room to prepare for the evening meal.

As she approached her room, the discordant sound of her cell phone interrupted the quiet tranquility of the house. Quickly, she hurried to her room and had just picked it up when Mr. Brenneman loomed in her doorway.

He eyed the small silver phone with distrust. "Anna?"

"I'm sorry, I didn't know this was on."

"If you're planning to stay here a length of time, I trust you'll think twice about using your electronics." Waving a hand at her dress and cap he added, "Especially seeing as you are hoping to blend in."

"I'm sorry, I forgot to turn it off." After quickly seeing she had two missed calls, Anna ignored the temptation to check to see who had contacted her. Instead, she quickly pushed the power button and turned off her last link to the outside world. In seconds, the screen went black. "It's off, now. I won't use it again while I'm here."

"I thank you for that."

"If you don't mind, I'd be obliged if you'd take this," she said, handing Mr. Brenneman the thin silver phone.

He balanced it on his palm as if it were about to explode in his very hand. "That isna' necessary. It is enough that you give me your word."

"I know, but I want to earn your trust."

"It's not my trust we should be concerned about, Anna. When all is said and done, it's all really about us and God, don't you know? Our personal relationship with Him and His word is what matters."

Our personal relationship. How funny that her childish faith had fled to the background as she'd stepped farther and farther into the brash culture of Rob's place in society. "I'm sure you are right. But if you don't mind, I'd still appreciate you putting that phone away. I don't want to be tempted to use it or to leave just yet."

Mr. Brenneman looked alarmed. "Truly, Anna? You'd go back to a man who so terribly hurt you?"

"I don't think I would, but I can't always trust myself anymore," she said softly, thinking about how topsy-turvy her emotions had been lately. "I'm afraid if I speak to my mother, she might convince me to return, and I'm just not sure if that's the right thing to do."

"I see." As if that settled the matter, Mr. Brenneman closed his hand around the phone and slipped it into the deep front pocket of his heavy wool shirt. "I'll put this away for a time, for safekeeping, but it's always yours, Anna."

"*Danke*, Mr. Brenneman."

Her awkward pronunciation brought a true smile to her host's lips. "You're welcome, dear Anna."

When she was alone again, Anna wondered what would have to occur to prompt her to ask for the cell phone back. Something very good . . . or very bad.

Hands shaking, Meredith Metzger watched Rob pull his Mercedes away from the curb and speed away. When he was out of sight, she pulled the blinds down tight and sat on the couch, doing her best to ignore the urge for a cigarette.

"You okay, dear?"

"No. Calvin, I'm scared to death. Rob was nearly violent."

Sitting down beside her, her husband rested his hands on his thighs. "Nearly? Rob 'nearly' tore Anna's room up and took a box full of her personal items to examine. I 'nearly' called the cops."

Meredith swallowed hard as her eyes pricked with tears. "That wouldn't have helped, would it?"

"No. Anna said she'd called the police before and all they did was advise her to calm herself. Between Rob's prestigious family connections and his current office as county commissioner, I don't think there's a person here in Ohio who would easily think ill of him."

"We did the same thing two weeks ago. She told us how worried she was about Rob's controlling ways."

"I know." With bleak eyes, Calvin said, "She wanted to break up with Rob."

"And I told her she was throwing her life away."

"How could we know things were different? To our defense, our daughter was never one to hold onto a commitment."

"Not even a little bit. Three colleges."

Calvin held up two hands. "Seven jobs, last time I counted."

"At least that many 'serious' boyfriends. Oh, Calvin, Lord help me, but I thought she needed discipline."

"We can't blame ourselves for seeing Rob's heavy-handed ways as nothing more than a way to encourage her to grow up."

"And now she's out there. Somewhere. I hope she's okay."

One more time Calvin picked up the phone and punched in Anna's cell phone number. Meredith watched anxiously. When he frowned and hung up, she leaned forward. "What happened? Why didn't you leave a message?"

"This time I didn't even hear a ring. Either her phone's been turned off or its service has been disconnected. Meredith, I hate to admit it, but I'm afraid we have to face the truth. Anna's gone."

Closing her eyes, Meredith prayed for her daughter's safety and health. And that wherever she was, she was well and hidden from Rob.

Otherwise, Meredith was afraid that even the Lord wouldn't be able to save her from the man's temper.

Chapter 4

The voice reverberated through the near empty office suite, clattering in Rob Peterson's head and making it pound.

"Rob, you need to forget about that girl and get back on target. We're charging two hundred a head for the dinner tonight. For that kind of cash, people are going to expect their money's worth."

Rob looked hard at Bill Williams, his campaign manager and right-hand man, and wondered why he'd ever thought he was worth the salary he was paying him. "Don't pressure me."

Bill lifted his head in surprise, before returning his concentration to what he did best—shuffling folders. Bill always organized folders like a gigantic deck of cards, his hands in motion. The nervous gesture betrayed his jovial oh-gosh-oh-gee way of speaking. "Don't pressure you? Rob, you pay me to me to pressure you."

"The dinner will be fine. I'll do what I always do, tell them what they want to hear."

"These people are a little savvier than that, Rob. They're going to want to know what you plan to achieve as their new representative. This is the big time. The majors, you know? A whole different ball game."

Bill had always enjoyed over-stating the obvious. At the moment, he was getting on Rob's last nerve. "Stop the whining, Williams. I've never not done what is expected of me."

"You have recently. You were late for the luncheon at the women's club."

That had been because he'd stayed too long at the Metzgers', looking through everything and anything to find a hint of where Anna had gone.

He'd found nothing. The box he'd eagerly removed from the Metzgers' only contained patterns for quilts, maps, and notes about the Amish, of all people.

Who knew Anna had even thought of such nonsense?

His irritation at the Metzgers had almost caused him to lose control when they had stood at the door, as if they were attempting to fend him off.

It had taken everything he had not to grab Meredith Metzger and shake the information out of her. She had to know where Anna was. Had to.

Because he needed Anna back. *Nobody left him.*

Nobody made a fool of him.

"Rob, are you even listening to me?" Bill's voice turned whiny and loud, burning deep and annoyingly shrill.

He'd had enough. With almost more force than he intended, Rob slammed his hand on the desk. "Don't question me again. If you're not careful, you won't have a job."

"Sorry, Rob." Bill's eyes widened and his hands stilled for a split second. His face paled enough that Rob felt a burst of satisfaction rise through him. Satisfaction, and the niggling disappointment that the only thing that ever seemed to work was the hint of retribution.

It had been that way with Anna time and again. She'd only become obedient after a reminder of his power. Only then would she look at him with respect, with fear and submission.

It was a shame mere words never seemed to work.

When Bill still looked at him warily, Rob did his best to shift his expression into something close to patience. "Did you bring me notes about the attendees?"

Bill deposited a folder in front of him. "I did. It's mainly going to be a bunch of bigwigs from the north side of town." Grinning broadly, Bill added, "Get this, they believe a portion of the dinner will be benefiting the Leukemia Society."

"Ah, yes. One of my favorite causes."

Bill chuckled. "They're all your favorites, Rob."

That was true. Long ago he'd learned to do and say anything to get his way. As he opened the folder and began to skim through the selection of notes written out for him, Rob's mind drifted back to Anna. Anna, with her perfect figure and green eyes. Her full lips and bright, easy smile.

Everyone loved Anna. People noticed him more when she was there. Looked at him with respect, like he must be something special if a girl like that wanted to be by his side.

He needed her back. He needed her in his life. Maybe he should hire an investigator?

"Rob, about the—"

"Go away, Bill. I don't need you right now."

Relief floated through him when the front door opened and shut, finally allowing Rob to sit with only the silence of his thoughts for company.

"You're up even earlier than usual," Anna said after she got dressed and sleepily wandered into the kitchen. The morning sun had yet to make a bit of an appearance, but already Katie looked neat and pretty, her cap securely pinned on, and a black apron over her pale blue cotton dress.

"I'm going to the general store today," Katie announced. "We need supplies."

Something about the way Katie was talking about the store made Anna take a second look. "*That's* why you're so excited? Because you're in a hurry to purchase flour?"

"And for other things, maybe."

Before Anna could comment on that, her friend poured them two cups of coffee and spoke again. "I'm helping *Mamm* today with washing and ironing, so I thought I'd get some of that done early. Would you care to help?"

"I'll be happy to. What would you like me to do?"

"Begin the ironing?"

"I can do that. I'll go heat up the irons."

"*Danke.*"

Though Anna had watched Katie or Mrs. Brenneman iron many a time before, their calm, cool manner made the chore seem easier than Anna found it to be. Anna felt ironing in their kitchen to be anything but easy. The heated irons were heavy and hard to get used to, and the heat emanating from them made the hair on her forehead curl even more than it usually did.

But she was diligent, and before she knew it, Anna was

carefully smoothing fabric over the ironing board, taking her time to smooth out the wrinkles from the cotton fabrics that had dried on the clothesline near the hearth room. By her side, Katie maneuvered the fabric with practiced ease, having no trouble judging the temperature of each iron.

After Anna finished her third shirt, Katie broke the quiet. "I must tell ya, Anna, you have surprised me."

"How? That I haven't scorched a shirt yet?"

"Maybe. Also the way you are adapting to life here." She set the iron down. "I've always thought of you as a fancy girl."

Anna would have described herself much the same way. Well, maybe not "fancy," but spoiled and used to her conveniences. And, no wonder. Most people no longer ever thought twice about where their power came from, going to the giant supercenters or considered the untold electronics they assumed they needed just to prepare for the day.

Here at the Brenneman Bed and Breakfast, life was much slower. And though there was electricity for the guests' sake, the Brennemans, by and large, took little advantage of it.

As she hung another shirt on a wooden hanger, Anna said, "I never would have thought I'd be happy right now, but in some ways I am. I appreciate the silence, and the lengthy time it takes to do things I once hardly realized I was doing."

"You'll accompany us tomorrow for our services?"

"If your parents don't mind, I will."

"*Mamm* and *Daed* will be happy to have you with us, for sure." With a sweet smile, she added, "We're going to the Kringles'. My sister Rebekeh will be there with her family. I canna hardly wait."

"It's been a while since you've seen her, hasn't it?"

"Almost six months. Too long."

They worked in silence for a while longer.

"What makes you so excited to go to the store today? Is there someone you'd like to see?

Twin spots of color decorated her cheeks. "No."

"Oh, okay."

Like a child, Katie stepped forward, words bursting through her. "Well, if you must know, there's a man I sometimes see at McClusky's."

"Who's that?"

"Jonathan Lundy."

"Have you known him long?"

"Not so long." Peeking around the kitchen, Katie lowered her voice. "As a matter of fact, we don't know each other too well at all. But he's a widower, has two daughters, and he lives on a farm not far from here. One time we spoke."

"Ah." Anna struggled to keep wistfulness from her voice. Contrary to what Katie might have thought, Anna didn't find her friend's fascination with Jonathan Lundy silly at all. Instead, she felt more than a little bit jealous.

It had been quite some time since she'd been a part of something so innocent and pure, something opposite of her life with Rob. When had she last felt infatuation? In high school with Mark, her first "real" boyfriend? Just thinking of Mark and the butterflies she used to feel around him made her smile. All he'd had to do was smile for her heart to pound.

But then he'd found someone else, and she'd become jaded. Her love life had slowly spiraled downward until she'd ended up with Rob.

His toxic demeanor and way of looking at life had poisoned the rest of her innocence. Now, she sometimes felt incapable of seeing the best in people. She instead wondered what they wanted, why they did the things they did.

"One Saturday, three months ago, Jonathan asked how my family was."

"And you said?"

"We are well."

"Sounds like an appropriate response." Anna could picture it now, Katie with the elusive Jonathan Lundy, both too shy to say more than a few words to each other in greeting.

When was the last time she'd felt like that?

"I suppose. Jonathan's wife was taken to the Lord a year ago July."

"That had to be hard."

"*Jah*. I'm afraid he needs a new wife."

"Why are you afraid? Is he mean?"

"Oh my goodness, no." Shyly Katie focused once more on her ironing. "I just fear that any wife will do, you know?"

"You're worried about being just a replacement."

"*Jah*. Maybe if I do catch his eye, it will be only because I can care for his daughters, not because he fancies a life with me."

"He'd never see you like that. No one in their right mind would."

"I don't know. Well, no use counting chickens, as they say." Clasping her hands on the edge of her apron, Katie said, "Please don't tell anyone about this. I'd be so embarrassed if Henry found out."

"I would never share your secret, especially not with your older brother," Anna said. Reaching out, she squeezed Katie's hand. "Thanks for trusting me with your secret. And, who knows—maybe everything will work out. You just have to believe in yourself, Katie."

"Well, right now, I believe I'm needed here at home. The Lord will guide me with Jonathan, I suppose. His timing is always right. And, in truth, Jonathan Lundy and I hardly know each other."

"I hope it works out," Anna said, carefully slipping an apron on yet another hanger just as Mrs. Brenneman entered the kitchen, her familiar smile lighting the room, though it was barely six in the morning.

"Anna, Katie, how industrious you two are today."

"Yes, *Mamm*. Just getting some chores done before we go to town."

"Who's going to take you?"

"Henry will when he's done taking care of the horses and Jess."

Anna turned to Katie in surprise. For some reason, she'd thought the two of them would go by themselves.

Katie explained. "Henry said he had a few things to get as well."

Irene pointed to a neatly written note on the counter near the back door. "I've written a list down, don't forget. Oh, and I've another chore for you both, while you're out and about. I want you to deliver some bread to the Lundys."

Katie's eyes grew into saucers. "Really?"

Anna kept her eyes on her iron so she wouldn't be tempted to share a smile with Mrs. Brenneman. If Anna wasn't mistaken, Katie's mother knew exactly who her daughter had a fondness for—secret or no secret.

"Really. Jonathan's sister Winnie is in town, don't you

know. She won't be able to come to services tomorrow, but I wrote her and told her I'd let her try my cherry bread and pass on the recipe."

"Sometimes Jonathan is at the store when we go. We might see him there," Katie said.

"Wherever you see him is fine," Mrs. Brenneman said easily before pulling out a cast-iron skillet. "Now we best get a hot breakfast ready for our guests. Otherwise, they'll be wondering what they're paying for."

Three of them in the open buggy was a snug fit. Henry glanced again at Anna Metzger and wondered why she was accompanying them, anyway. Wasn't she supposed to be hiding from the English?

Now, here she was, dressed Plain, and accompanying them just like she had every right to.

She was also looking at his horse Stanley with something akin to worry. "Will he be okay? It's a big load, the three of us."

"Stanley's a workhorse, not a lapdog. He could carry your weight or even more without taxing his strength."

Katie playfully nudged her brother. "Oh, Henry, you always say the wrong thing. You're supposed to tell us that with our light weight, we're no trouble at all."

Henry felt his cheeks burn as he realized his sister was right. He didn't have any soft words or coy remarks inside of him. Instead, all practicality ran in his head, leaving no room for sweet phrases or flattery.

Maybe that was why Rachel had left his side without a moment for looking back? Because he'd never done much to keep her close?

"I hope it doesna rain," he muttered.

"I hope it doesn't, either. We'll get soaked."

They moved along the old road, only having to move aside for a few cars.

Half an hour later, they arrived at the store. Katie and Anna clambered out of the buggy easily.

"I'm going to leave the bread here, just in case we don't see Mr. Lundy in the store."

Henry nodded absently as he guided Stanley to the side of the tall clapboard building and hooked up the buggy to a small hitching post. Then, he nodded to a few friends who were unloading carts of finely made toys before entering the McClusky General Store.

"Henry, good to see you," Sam McClusky said in greeting from the back of the store. Once a successful salesman, Sam gave it all up about ten years ago when he longed for a simpler life, one where he could spend more time with his children. Now he owned the store and ran it exceptionally well. Mennonites, Amish, and English all frequented the vast building, mingling with each other with the ease of years of practice.

"*Gut* to see you, too."

"You need something special?"

"I need some nails and a package of sandpaper, but I can take care of finding what I need."

"Very good."

As Sam went back to his business, Henry scanned the aisles, then found Katie chatting with a lady near two large quilts.

Where was Anna?

Finally, he did spy her . . . sitting by herself, looking pale and uncomfortable as a family of tourists stared at her and pointed. For the first time since she'd arrived a week before, Henry allowed himself to feel for Anna. The girl was in a difficult predicament; that was for sure.

Stepping closer, he pointed to the door. "Would you like to wait outside?"

"You don't mind?"

"I don't. Let me just tell Sam to charge my account for this." When he returned, she looked extremely grateful.

"Thanks so much," she said, already walking to his side. She stayed uncomfortably close as they wound their way through the narrow aisles and stacks of goods. "Leaving your home wasn't a good idea, I'm afraid. There are too many people here."

After telling Katie that she could take her time, Henry fought against his better judgment but lost as he walked Anna down the grassy hill to a set of picnic tables.

Luckily, the morning's clouds had passed and no rain was in sight. Instead, the cold, brisk air held a hint of sunshine, encouraging him to breathe deep and catch a taste of spring.

Turning to him, she smiled. "Thank you, Henry. I really needed rescuing back there."

"It was no trouble."

"All right . . . but no matter what, you escorting me out here is certainly appreciated."

For a moment, Henry let himself meet her eyes, felt the warmth of her gaze burn through him. Let himself imagine that she wasn't English and that he'd never heard of Rachel Baar.

And for that split second, with the sun shining and Anna

Metzger looking so fresh and pretty, Henry almost felt content. Hopeful.

But then, as she turned away and he spied the yellowish-purple remains of the bruise on her cheek, Henry knew that contentment was just as false as the paint she'd worn on her face . . . fleeting and covering up what they knew to be true.

Chapter 5

There was something in Henry's eyes that made Anna turn away. As she did, a rabbit hopped into the clearing and grabbed her attention.

Henry smiled with pleasure when she pointed it out.

After wiggling its ears fretfully for a bit, the rabbit settled in and relaxed. Doing much what she and Henry were attempting to do—enjoy a clear blue sky and wan rays of sunshine on an otherwise very cold day.

Seeing how Henry's brusque manner had finally softened, Anna dared to smile at him. "You have a way with animals, don't you?"

Henry shrugged. "I don't know if I do or not. I just appreciate them, maybe. All Amish do."

"Why is that?"

"The Amish believe we are as a part of our God's creation

as the berries on the trees, or this rabbit here. It's why we take such care to work the land, why we excel at work in the dairy, why we treat our horses like lifelong companions. It's what we've always done."

The pride in his voice made Anna realize that she'd struck a chord with him, and a good one at that. "The only times I've been to Amish country was to see Katie, and we talked mainly of quilting and the inn. I realize now that I've never thought about your work outside in the fields."

Henry's gaze remained on the rabbit. Almost like he was afraid to meet her eyes. "No reason you should," he mumbled.

"Well, I appreciate it now."

"Because it's cold outside?"

"Because I'm realizing that being outside with nature is where you were meant to be."

"I'm glad, then." Slowly, he added, "If you ever care to learn more about the hills and such around the inn, I'd be willing to share what I know with you. I've spent many an hour of free time walking in the woods near our home, enjoying the peace and quiet. "

"I'm trying to imagine your mother letting you do such a thing. You are a very industrious family."

"Work is not a burden."

His voice had hardened. The rabbit's ears trembled and Anna felt herself stiffen as well. Obviously, no matter how pleasant Henry was trying to be, he still didn't think much of her work ethic. "I didn't mean anything negative by what I said. I meant it as a compliment."

Henry waited a long moment, his body almost motionless

as the rabbit hopped a little closer, its nose twitching nervously. "I didn't take your words to heart, Anna. As a matter of fact, I wasn't thinking of you, I was remembering me as a boy." Miraculously, a red stain appeared on Henry's neck. "When I was younger, I'm afraid that I did have a tendency to wander a bit too much. It was in my nature, I suppose. Sometimes, not in my best interest or my family's."

The idea of the strong, steady man beside her dodging responsibility made her smile. "You? Goofing off?"

"I didn't do that. But sometimes maybe I took too long when it could have been completed fast, in half the time."

"Such as?"

Henry frowned. "Weeding my mother's garden. My sister Rebekeh always fussed, saying I took too long because I was studying the bumble bees or some such thing."

"Your stories always make me wish I had more family."

"Are you an only child?"

"I am, but not by my parents' choice," Anna said, realizing with some surprise she was finding it so easy to speak with Henry. "My mother was diagnosed with cancer soon after I was born. Though she had a complete recovery, she and my dad decided against any more children."

"So you grew up alone and afraid you'd lose her?"

His directness took her off guard. That, and the way he'd pinpointed her worries in a way that hardly anyone ever had before. "Alone, yes. Afraid, sometimes." Nudging a rock down the hill, she added, "I was terribly afraid the cancer would come back."

"But it didn't?"

"No. Well, it hasn't yet."

Henry swallowed. "I must admit I've been guilty of imagining your life and thinking that it had been too easy, soft. I was sure you'd never known hardship, had never concerned yourself with things that mattered."

"My life was different than yours, but not perfect. And not completely aimless, either."

"I'm realizing that now, as we've gotten better acquainted. When Katie would talk to us about you, after a visit, or a phone call, or a quilting class, I never thought about anything other than how different your life was. How fancy your clothes were, how fast and free your existence was. Even during my running around year, I never did the things Katie said you did."

Stung, Anna stared at her feet. "I don't know what you think I've done, but I promise you that my life hasn't been as full of sin as you make it sound."

A hint of a grin lined his mouth. "Let me finish, now, wouldja? What I'm trying to say is, I felt that no matter how much I might know or learn about you, I was sure that we'd have too many differences to ever have a friendship. I thought our differences would prevent a connection."

Henry's honesty, as always, made Anna wish she'd learned to hold her tongue a bit more. "I've done the same thing," she finally admitted. Stealing a look his way, Anna slowly added, "But now I'm coming to the conclusion that maybe we have more in common than I had previously thought."

"Maybe we do, Anna."

A rush of voices filled the parking lot behind them, making the rabbit freeze in midmotion, then scurry away. A mere rustle in the bushes was the only clue it had been there at all. In spite of herself, Anna held her breath, waiting for the rabbit to reappear—even though she knew it was silly to wish for such a thing.

"And now you're here. With us."

"Now I am." As more voices carried on the wind, Anna felt yet another burst of apprehension. Wariness engulfed her. Caution made her want to shrink and hide. Just like the hare, maybe if she was motionless, no one would see her, or guess where she'd come from.

But despite her attempts to blend in, she still stood out. Her posture was wrong, her eyes too aware. Fingering her dress, she whispered, "Henry, I shouldn't have left the inn. Seeing everyone here, both the Amish and the English, it makes me nervous. I feel like I don't look Amish enough, that I'm catching everyone's attention."

He'd noticed other men and women looking at Anna, but Henry felt it most likely had to do with the fact that she was a stranger, not an imposter.

But her nervousness made him curious. "If you're so sure you don't look 'right,' why did you want to come, then? To get away from your chores for a bit?"

After all they'd just said, did Henry still see her as a nuisance, nothing more than a lazy woman with a multitude of sins? "I was thinking of Katie, if you want to know the truth."

"Katie?"

Anna wasn't sure how much to share. "She was hoping to see some people she knew, and when I agreed, I thought it would just be the two of us going together. I knew she needed the company."

Henry's open expression shuttered and a soft look of

amusement flicked across his face. "People she knew, hmm? Well, now I understand."

Anna doubted it. But if he did, she sure hoped she hadn't given too much away.

"No matter," Henry said. "I or my parents should've thought those things through. It isna wise for you to be here—it opens up the world to too many questions." Looking behind him, Henry stood up. "My sister's done with her business now. Perhaps we should go deliver the bread and return. I've work to do."

"I think that sounds like a good idea," Anna said as Katie approached, though she couldn't prevent a certain amount of frostiness from peeking out. Henry could be so maddening.

Looking from one to the other, Katie frowned. "Have you two been arguing again?"

"No. Just talking," Anna said.

"Oh. Well, then." She cleared her throat. "Jonathan Lundy wasna in the store. I suppose we'll have to deliver the bread to his homestead."

Anna fought to hide her smile. Thank goodness Katie didn't have dreams of being on the stage, because her acting left a lot to be desired. Her voice sounded wistful and surprised, all at the same time.

Henry, on the other hand, scowled. "Are you sure that cherry bread has to be delivered today? The Lundy farm is five miles beyond our place."

"I am. *Mamm* asked us to deliver it, Henry," Katie replied as they walked up the hill and each took a box of supplies and loaded them into the back compartment of the buggy.

When that was done, Anna and Katie stood to the side while Henry checked Stanley's bridle and the buggy's hitch with steady, confident motions. Finally, he gestured for Anna and Katie to climb in. "I still think it's a waste of time, I'll tell you that. We'll see him at church tomorrow."

"It would be rude to hand him a loaf of bread to carry around all afternoon."

"He could put it in his buggy. That's what we are doing today, after all."

Katie frowned. "Henry, stop being so cross."

"I'm not cross; I'm just reminding you two that I have other things that need doing besides taking you on fool's errands."

"This errand is not foolish at all. Besides, *Mamm* asked us to do this." With an exaggerated sigh, she said, "Why Henry, you're acting as if this was my idea."

Henry opened his mouth, like he was tempted to say something about that. After a second, he pursed his lips and stared obstinately forward. Silence followed.

While Katie looked to be either stewing about her brother or eagerly anticipating their arrival to the Lundy homestead, Anna felt a different set of emotions wash through her.

They were leaving the crowded confines of the store. She felt safer, more hidden.

But by her side was a man who had almost seemed like he could be a friend . . . but instead had closed up again. She felt uneasy around him again and a slight disproval emanating from his posture.

It was like their conversation on the bank of the creek had never happened; the feelings of friendship that had begun to spring forth abandoned.

Old worries and the vague feeling of not ever fitting in surged forth, capping her earlier optimism.

Reminding her that she was getting no less than she deserved. One day she really needed to learn to stop trusting people.

"I'm going crazy just waiting to hear something, Calvin," Meredith said on Saturday afternoon.

As had become their habit, the two of them were standing in their daughter's room, looking at Anna's wide array of photos on her desk and wondering if anyone in them was their clue to Anna's whereabouts.

"There's not much we can do. Maybe Anna really did pack a bag and leave for Miami."

"I'm going to call some of her girlfriends and see what they say."

"Do what you feel is necessary, but I have to tell you, I think you're rushing things. We may be overreacting."

"You don't think it's strange that we haven't heard from her?"

"I do think it's strange, but not completely unheard of. She's a twenty-four-year-old woman, not a teenager on spring break. She doesn't need to call us every night."

"Calvin, you are deliberately being difficult."

"And you are deliberately forgetting that everything between our daughter and us is not all right."

She knew he was right. But that didn't mean she was wrong. "Things weren't that bad."

"They might be. Remember, we had quite a few words with Anna the night before she left. She may be in a snit. She may be even angrier than that."

Meredith sank to the edge of her daughter's bed and felt as if she would never forget that last conversation. Anna had been frightened and asked for help. Instead of listening and offering advice, she had done the complete opposite. Yep, while Anna had sat there, stunned, Meredith had pointed out every flaw in her daughter's life.

No, she hadn't forgotten a single one, had she?

Meredith had mentioned the price of college tuition wasted on degrees never earned. On interview suits bought for jobs that had lasted barely a month. Of lost opportunities with men who wanted a steady companion because Anna kept protesting those men—a long line of successful and attractive men—weren't special enough for her.

Anna hadn't thought she could love any of them.

Meredith's temper had snapped. She'd said almost unforgivable things, even going so far as to give her daughter a timeline. Told her it was time to grow up and take charge of her life and move out. That she and Calvin had had enough of her foolishness.

Anna had stared like she'd been slapped.

Then, the very next day, her dear daughter was gone. Crossing the room, Meredith walked to the desk and stared at Anna's note once again.

Mother.

When had Anna ever called her "Mother"? It had always been "Mom."

Only "Mother" when she was really angry.

Only "Momma" when she was really upset and scared.

Opening the top drawer of the antique cherry desk they'd given her on her seventeenth birthday, Meredith decided to hunt for a clue. Anything was better than just sitting and waiting.

"You sure you want to do this, Meredith? Anna won't like you going through her things."

"I need to find her address book. She needs me to get involved."

"Rob probably took everything of value."

"Not this." Meredith pulled out a spiral notebook. Underneath lay an old address book, the outside pale pink and decorated with purple stars, the edges frayed. She'd bought a new one in tan leather for Anna just last Christmas, but Anna had said she didn't want to transfer all the names and addresses. Not yet.

She'd thought it was yet another example of Anna not wanting to give up her childhood. "I'm going to start calling everyone, to see if they know anything. To see if she told them about her plans."

Calvin placed a reassuring hand on her shoulder, the warmth of his easy comfort sustaining her and giving her peace. "You sure about this?" he questioned again. "If we discover something and Rob finds out that we kept it from him, he could make things worse for Anna."

"Or us. That man obviously has no problem hurting anyone or anything standing in the way of his wants." When her voice started to crack, she paused for a moment to gather strength. And strength was what she needed—strength to continue in the midst of guilt and lost opportunities.

Strength to accept guilt and responsibility but to soldier on instead of hiding in the shadows.

Calvin rubbed her shoulder. "There might be another way. We can call the police again."

"We can do that, but I don't feel that it will do as much good. Besides, I need to do something besides wring my hands and wish I could do things over again."

"This isn't all our fault, Meredith. Anna has had a history

of being impulsive and not thinking things through. There've been plenty of times in the past when stepping into her business has helped her a lot."

"I know."

Calvin continued. "And, we didn't find Rob and make her date him. The two were in a very real relationship by the time we met him. Anna told me she thought she was in love."

"I know, but I'm slowly learning not to look at our daughter's life in plain black and white. No, Anna's problems are not our fault, but they aren't all hers, either. Something could have happened to her, something far worse than we could ever imagine."

"We'll pray and call, then."

"That does sound like the most reasonable option. We don't have a choice, do we?" Meredith picked up the address book, and clutched it to her chest as they exited Anna's room, then headed downstairs to the kitchen. "She may already be worse off than we can ever imagine."

Calvin filled the kettle with water, then handed her the phone and a pad of paper. "If she comes home next week with a tan and a smile—"

"I'm going to hold her close and be the happiest mother in the world."

Calvin laughed. "Go to work, then."

Meredith didn't laugh much two hours later. No one had heard from Anna. Most hadn't spoken to—or even e-mailed—her in months. That was surprising. Anna had always had a large circle of friends and appreciated a tight, long-lasting bond with them for years.

When Meredith had conveyed her surprise to Julie Gowan, Anna's good friend for years, Julie wasted no time mincing words. "It wasn't my fault, Mrs. Metzger. After I met Anna and Rob one evening for pizza, Anna called me the next day on the verge of tears. Rob had forbidden Anna to see me."

"What?"

"I felt the same way," Julie said wryly. "Rob didn't like my look. He didn't like my pierced nose, my tattoo, or my job."

"But you do so much good!" Meredith said, amazed. Julie's job at a halfway house for troubled teens was something to be proud of. "Anyone would be honored to know you."

"Not Rob. He was afraid somehow someone would sneak a photo of me and Anna together and connect it with him."

Hands shaking, Meredith tried to make sense of it all . . . but there was no sense—none whatsoever. "I don't know what to say."

"There's nothing you can say. Rob's refusal to look beyond my tattoos didn't bother me, Mrs. Metzger . . . I mean he didn't know me from any other person off the street. And, well, if you want to know the truth, I didn't care for him any more than he did me. But that Anna didn't even think twice about moving on? That hurt. I mean, we went to kindergarten together."

Resisting the impulse to apologize to Julie for her daughter's behavior, Meredith murmured, "I'm beginning to realize that there were a lot of things that happened with Anna and Rob that I didn't know about."

After a long pause, Julie said, "Look, I've been pretty upset with her for a while, but I'd never wish anything bad to happen to her. Tell Annie to call me if she wants to, would you? No matter what, I'm still there for her."

Meredith smiled at the old nickname. "I promise I'll pass on your message."

After she hung up, Meredith shook her head in wonder as she shared the story with Calvin. "I never thought I'd see the day when Anna and Julie weren't friends."

"Did Julie say she understood?"

"Julie said that she understood why Anna was doing what she had to do . . . and that she'd always be there for her. No matter what."

Tears filled Meredith's eyes for what had to be the hundredth time in a week. "Why didn't I say those things, Calvin? Why didn't I share my love with her more openly? Why didn't I ever make sure she realized that no matter what our differences, I would always be there for her?"

Instead of answering her, Calvin squeezed her shoulder. "You're only on 'G,' dear. You've got a whole alphabet of people to ask about Anna. Don't give up."

"I have fought a good fight, I have finished my course, I have kept the faith." The Bible verse from Second Timothy floated to her, giving her strength.

Chapter 6

"Do you think I was too bold around Jonathan Lundy?" Katie asked Anna three days later. They'd spent most of the day on the second floor, washing walls and dusting furniture until it gleamed.

Now they were in the attic guest room, cleaning it top to bottom in preparation for the next pair of guests, scheduled to arrive before supper.

"I don't think you were bold at all," Anna stated as she flicked a crisp cotton sheet onto the down-filled feather bed covering the mattress. "In fact, I don't think you said very much to Mr. Lundy at all."

"I spoke to him about the weather."

Anna conceded that. "And you asked if his daughters were happy with their teacher."

Katie nodded, her dust rag hanging limply. "Those are reasonable questions, don't you think?"

"They *were* reasonable," Anna said dryly. "I don't think they could have been any more reasonable."

Not catching Anna's slight teasing, Katie stewed some more. "I hope he didn't think me too forward. I'd be sorely embarrassed if Jonathan thought I was being too personal." Her eyes widened, shining blue like the pansies around the barn in the summer. "What if he thought I was hinting?"

Katie had lost her. "Hinting about what?"

"About his home life, of course. And his personal wants and needs. I mustn't act like I know he needs help." Katie swiped the windowsill, then turned to Anna again. "Should I?"

"I'm the wrong person to ask. Every relationship I've had has ended badly." And every relationship probably could have used a little more of Katie's thoughtfulness and consideration, too, Anna thought. Maybe then she wouldn't have drifted alone and lost for so long. Maybe then she wouldn't have ended up with Rob.

Together they unfolded the vibrant quilt that Mrs. Brenneman had hung on the clothesline during the stretch of sunshine that afternoon. Anna caught the scent of fresh air as they smoothed it onto the feather bed, the bright white, velvety violet, and indigo blue Ocean Wave pattern turning the otherwise spare room into one of beauty.

As she fluffed two pillows and carefully set them on top of the quilt, Katie ventured, "So you no longer care for your Rob Peterson?"

"No." She was puzzled by his actions, wary of what he might do next, and frightened of what would happen when they did meet again.

"*Daed* said you asked him to hold onto your phone, just in case you thought about returning to Rob."

"A few days ago I was afraid I'd give in. Now I feel stronger and surer of myself. It would also be true to say that he wasn't the only thing I'm hoping to hide from at the moment. I also need a break from my job and my life. I need time."

"Even from your family?"

"I love my parents, but we don't have the close bond you all do here. Plus, I haven't been as mature as I could've been this past year. Sometimes I think I've reverted back to fourteen again, only thinking about my hair and appearances," Anna admitted, remembering how concerned she'd been about looking "just right" by Rob's side.

"And then Rob hurt you."

"That tells you just how mixed up my priorities have been, don't you think? The Bible speaks often about honoring and caring for your friends and enemies. Lately I've been putting my trust in false idols . . . in money and privilege and things that don't mean anything." Pressing a palm to her cheek which was now void of any discolorations, Anna added, "I guess we could say I've learned from my foolishness."

"Do you really feel you deserved Rob's marks of anger? Surely you're not shouldering all the blame?"

Anna speculated that she hadn't been shouldering enough responsibility. She'd been charmed by Rob Peterson, even knowing that the things he believed in weren't things to be proud of. She'd encouraged his attention, even when her conscience told her she would regret leading him on.

And her conscience had been right. If she hadn't been mesmerized by Rob, she wouldn't be hiding from him now.

No longer could Anna wish things were different. The truth was, she'd been impressed with Rob's money, affluence, and power. When she'd been in his company, she'd allowed herself to forget what was important, what really mattered.

"I've made a mess of things in my life—my hiding here is certainly evidence of that. But right now, everything feels so overwhelming. I don't know how to fix anything."

Katie's concerned expression turned confident. "With prayer, of course."

"I've been praying." With some surprise, Anna added, "I know He listened, because here I am with you."

A look of sheer happiness floated over Katie's expression. One of innocence and love, pure and all-encompassing.

Had she only prayed for protection? "I have been praying for safety. I think I need to expand my goals. I need guidance, don't you think?"

With a soft laugh, Katie reached for her hand and clasped it. "Oh, Anna. Haven't you felt His guidance all along?"

Anna was prevented from replying when a door opened and slammed shut down below. *"Mamm? Daed!?"* someone shouted.

"That's Henry," Katie said with a start. Quickly, they left the guest room and started down two flights of stairs.

Below, Henry continued to yell for help. "Katie? Are you here?"

"I'm here!" she called out as she skipped down the stairs. Anna followed her closely. As if they were in jeans and tennis shoes instead of barefoot and clad in long dresses and aprons, they tore down one flight of steps, then another.

Anna barely caught her breath when they finally skidded to a stop.

"Henry?" Katie called out again.

"Here."

Anna felt as if her heart had stopped when they finally came face-to-face with Henry. Cheeks pale, eyes red rimmed, he was visibly doing his best not to cry.

"Henry, whatever's wrong?" Katie asked, running to his side.

After catching his breath, he replied. "It's Jess. He . . . he's dead."

Katie's face crumbled as a single tear fell from Henry's eyes. Without a word, she wrapped her arms around him. Henry hugged his sister close, burying his face in her shoulder.

Anna stood by the doorway, reeling from the news. With some surprise, she realized that she, too, would grieve for the dog she'd only seen a few times.

And then it hit her—the pain she felt was for Henry. Because he loved that dog. Because he was hurting. Because she felt helpless.

Irene came in. "Whatever is going on here? Henry and Katie, you two know better than to cause such a ruckus."

Anna spoke quietly. "Henry just found Jess—he's dead."

Pure sympathy entered her blue eyes. "Oh, now. That is a terrible shame. God bless that dog. Henry, what happened?"

Henry raised his head. After wiping his eyes with the corner of his fist, he said, "I don't know. I went to the barn to finish working on the chair and saw that Jess hadn't eaten. I thought he was asleep and reached down to wake him up." Henry's face became carefully blank. "That's when I knew that something was wrong."

"He was an old dog, Henry. He's lucky to have passed his way where he was happiest, in the barn on his blanket."

Katie nodded. "He was a *gut* dog."

"He was a *gut* friend." Looking almost embarrassed by the expanse of emotion, Henry glanced at Anna before leaving out the back door. For a long moment, only the echo of the whoosh of the screen door filled the kitchen.

"Poor Henry," Katie finally said softly. "He loved that dog. And Jess loved him."

"Jess was hurting." Irene laid a hand on her daughter's shoulder. "It was his time."

Spying Henry walking resolutely to the barn through the kitchen window, Anna asked, "What's going to happen now? What's Henry going to do?"

"He'll most likely decide where to bury Jess," Irene said. Walking to the window, she, too, gazed through the thick pane. "Perhaps Henry will choose the back field. Jess always did fancy the rabbits that nested there."

Anna realized that Katie and Mrs. Brenneman were prepared to let Henry take care of Jess all by himself. And Henry was prepared to do that as well.

Anna's stomach clenched as she realized she couldn't let him do that. She couldn't let him be alone. "Mrs. Brenneman, I'd like to help."

"With what?"

"Bury Jess."

"Oh, dear, you mustn't fret so. Henry will shoulder this burden without complaint."

But Anna didn't want him to have to carry that load on his own. "I'd like to help so Henry won't have to be alone."

"There's no shame in mourning a creature of God, Anna. Henry will do just fine."

Words failed her as she tried to make them see that she needed to be there for Henry. Needed it in a way she hadn't needed anything in quite some time. "Would you mind if I went to the barn?"

"I don' mind, but Henry may not want you there."

"I'd rather he sees me and refuses my offer than for him to think I didn't care. Please, Mrs. Brenneman, may I go to him?"

"Of course."

Anna was halfway to the barn before she realized that Katie had been conspicuously silent, only looking at Anna with a new understanding in her blue eyes.

Why?

Henry had wrapped Jess in the blanket she'd seen the dog lay on and had placed him in a wagon. He was holding a shovel and pulling on gloves when she entered.

With a jerky movement, he looked up. "Did you need something?"

"I thought I'd offer my help."

Henry looked genuinely puzzled. "With what?"

"I . . . I wanted to walk with you when you buried Jess."

She thought he was going to refuse. However, after a long moment, he nodded. *"Danke."*

She removed the shovel from his hands and hooked her cape securely around her as they walked out into the elements. Beside her, Henry pulled the old wooden wagon, the wheels creaking, signaling their unaccustomed use.

As the wind blew into their faces, they turned left and walked slowly onto the worn path, through a maze of fields that had been tended by the Brennemans for generations.

A sense of peace flew through Anna as they plodded along. For the first time, she felt Henry's longing for things to be different.

Maybe Henry's stalwart temperament didn't always serve him well. Maybe he wished he could sometimes ask for help or admit to disappointment and grief.

Their path grew steep. With a grunt, Henry adjusted his grip and lifted his arms a bit higher, easing his load, though Anna sensed it was not too heavy for him to bear.

The cold air bit into her cheeks, making her grateful for the black bonnet on her head. The brim shielded her face from the worst of the wind, and the thick woolen cloth helped to keep her head warm.

Finally they reached a thicket of woods. A few rocks and stones jutted out, keeping company with the maple and oak trees. A sharp scent of pine floated closer, making Anna think of Christmas.

Henry carefully set the wagon to rights. "This'll do, I think," he said softly, clearing a small spot of leaves.

Anna passed the shovel, then watched him use his foot to help pushed the blade into the hard, frozen earth and scoop out a patch of dirt.

Again, he dug, doing the same thing for almost an hour, removing his coat as the hole got bigger and deeper. Finally it was big enough.

Tears pricked Anna's eyes as she saw a wave of emotion fill his gaze as he bent to pick up the dog. His hands trembled for a moment before his arms braced to hold the load. Anna rushed to his side and supported a little of Jess's weight.

Together, they knelt and placed the dog's body in the earth. Anna was amazed at how small it seemed now.

"Would you like me to recite a psalm?"

Henry shook his head. "No. The Lord knows Jess was a good companion to me. I will miss him."

Yet, Anna was sure he still did say a prayer. Unabashedly, a tear tracked his cheek as he briefly closed his eyes. A moment later, he stood and picked up the shovel again. Anna pulled it from his grasp. "Let me," she whispered.

Amazingly, Henry complied.

Anna carefully set the first clump back in the ground, her heart breaking for Henry with each scoop. After a bit, Henry finished the job. And, when everything was back in place, he stepped back.

Around them, the woods seemed to come alive. In the distance, a jay squawked, closer a trio of branches rustled from the breeze. Overhead, the clouds broke, and a slim ray of sunshine filtered through, offering a band of warmth.

Henry cleared his throat. "I don't know why you came, but I thank you."

"You're welcome." Afraid to contemplate exactly why she'd had to be by his side, she held out her hand. To her relief and surprise, Henry clasped it right away.

The touch was combustible. A pulse beat through them, an awareness that had nothing to do with their differences and everything to do with a change in their relationship.

His face lifted, capturing her expression.

Then Anna knew what she had to do . . . she stepped into his arms and hugged him. Henry's arms folded around her, holding her tight.

His chin rested on the top of her head, and she placed her cheek on his chest. Even as she sought to comfort him, it was impossible not to be aware of how finely toned his torso was.

Of his scent. Of how warm and secure he made her feel on such a cold day.

Later, as Henry's shoulders shook and he dared to cry, Anna rubbed his back, as she would a small child, and murmured that everything was going to be all right.

Rob Peterson almost lost control at five o'clock that afternoon. It took every bit of willpower to keep his expression impassive as his sister's husband, a country bumpkin sheriff, spoke in circles yet again. The man's meandering statements and refusal to stay on topic reminded Rob exactly why he'd usually done everything he could to stay away from him. Axel Grant was maddening.

Irritated beyond belief, Rob interrupted him again. "What do you mean there's no way to check to see if Anna is in Amish country?"

"I mean if she's staying at someone's house, most likely, we wouldn't know it." His brother-in-law shifted a wad of chew from one side of his mouth to the other. "Most don't have phones, you know."

That was inconceivable. "How do they communicate?"

Axel dared to smile. "The old-fashioned way—they talk face-to-face."

"And in emergencies?"

"Some folks do have phones that they share with neighbors. We could try to track down some of them, but it's going to be like looking for a needle in a haystack."

Grant was a real fan of clichés.

As the sheriff spit into the plastic cup he was holding, worry coursed through Rob as he imagined the things that Anna would be telling strangers. His misuse of campaign contributions. The times his temper had gotten the best of him. He needed to find her before she spoke to someone who actually cared, who actually would do something with the filth she would most likely be spewing about him.

If he lost the election, he'd lose more than just a job. He'd lose his power.

Where had he gone wrong with her, anyhow? When they'd first met, she'd seemed so impressionable and dim. She'd taken his gifts easily enough, slipping on the diamond earrings the moment he'd handed them to her.

Smiling brightly when he'd placed the heart locket around her neck. She hadn't done more than blink when he'd glided a finger along the smooth skin of her collarbone after fastening the chain of gold around her neck.

She'd gone into his arms easily enough after that. In fact, she'd been so pliable, Anna had never done anything but what he'd asked her to.

Until he'd lost control and hit her.

It was then that everything changed and she began to question him more. Every so often, she'd not look pleased to see him when he picked her up at the insurance company.

Once she almost refused to help him answer the phones when his office had been particularly busy.

And it was then that the light seemed to go out of her eyes whenever he touched her. He'd known how she acted—like she was only putting up with him. Dealing with him.

Suffering through his advances. Her genuine love for him had turned and become fake and full of lies.

He'd hated the changes. And hated that it was almost too late to claim her. And he'd intended to do that, no matter what.

He'd dreamed of her. Buying her clothes, showing her off, having other men look at him in envy.

Now she was about to remove herself from his grasp and ruin his reputation. It wouldn't be tolerated.

"Where is this area? I'll go there myself."

"I'm telling you now, don't expect to see a bunch of Amish standing around in the middle of the road, congregating. They've got things to do, I tell you. Why, they're the busiest folks I know, from sunup to sundown." Resting a scuffed, dirty boot on his opposite knee, Grant nodded complacently. "Yep, those Amish are real hard workers."

Rob glared. He hadn't asked for the Amish daily schedule. *When would people ever learn to listen to him?* "Axel, I need information, not advice. Please."

Stung, Axel looked at him with widening eyes. "If I was you, I'd go to the Brenneman Bed and Breakfast. You can use that as a home base for a few days while you look around."

Like he was going to spend the night with some backward hillbillies. "I can't take that much time off."

"Then I suggest you wait a bit. Your woman most likely got cold feet, and decided to assert a little independence. Don't fret, she'll come back to her man . . . they always do."

The reminder of ownership made Rob almost happy. "You think so?"

"I know so." His brother-in-law plopped both feet back on the ground. "In the meantime, you might want to go take a spell at McClusky's hardware. If they've seen your blonde, they'll let you know." Pointing to the professional photograph Rob had taken of Anna just the month before, he said, "A girl like that will stand out anywhere."

"I hope you're right."

"I do, too, Rob. I do, too." Replacing his hat, Axel left, leaving Rob with too many questions and no way to get answers.

When the phone on his desk started ringing and no one was there to answer it but him, a wave of frustration hit him hard. Rob cursed again. Anna was such a disappointment.

As was his infatuation with her.

The phone rang again. "Peterson," he barked. "Oh, sorry, William," he tempered his voice as he realized that one of his bigger campaign contributors was on the line. "I just burned my hand on the coffee pot."

"You, pouring coffee?" William Scott's laughter came through loud and clear from his end of the line. "There hasn't been a time we've met when you haven't had someone standing around you, seeing to your needs."

Rob struggled to keep his voice calm and steady. Light. "I do all right on my own, William. It would be a sad state of affairs if I couldn't handle even the simplest of chores."

"I'll second that. Where's that pretty girl you had in your office last time I visited? She made us a good pot of coffee. Seemed to me you two were getting along just fine."

"Anna stepped out for a moment, but she'll be back soon. I can promise you that."

"The two of you still courting, then?"

Rob winced at the ancient language. "We are."

"Good. I've spoken to quite a few people on your behalf, Rob. We like you—and are ready to do whatever it takes to see that you're elected."

"I appreciate that."

"I'm glad you do. I must warn you, however, that a great majority of the folks I've talked to are a mite concerned about your bachelor status."

The old man sounded more blustery with every conversation. Rob struggled to keep his patience. "I'm not the first bachelor to hold office, William."

"That may be true, but we'd like to see you looking more like a family man." He paused. "As a matter of fact, everyone likes the sound of that woman I told them about. What was her name, Amy?"

"Anna. Her name is *Anna*."

"Ah, yes. Let me know when you decide to make your arrangement with her a permanent one. We'll throw you a party."

Rob slowly sat down. "Are you giving me an ultimatum?"

"No, I'm giving you the honest truth, Peterson. If you want my support, and others' as well, you're going to need to do as we say. We don't want even a hint of impropriety being linked with us, and that will surely happen if you continue to go on as you have, squiring around a different lady friend every week."

"Is there another reason you called, sir?"

Scott didn't catch his sarcasm. "As a matter of fact, yes. I'd like you to look into the possibility of encouraging some big businesses our way."

Rob pulled out a pen and poised it above his paper. "Tell me more," he said, writing down William Scott's directives. But all the while, he was staring at the door, willing Anna to walk through and make his life the way it had been just two weeks ago.

Chapter 7

Chopping wood had never felt so beneficial, Henry thought as he once again raised the ax over his shoulder and let it fall. The blade hit the thick trunk with a reassuring *clack*, raining splinters of bark and wood to the grass below.

In no time, the tree would be felled and he could then begin the painstaking job of chopping it into firewood.

As his muscles strained, Henry welcomed the feeling. It enabled him to concentrate on the job at hand instead of the other thoughts warring in his mind and making his head spin. Jess. Rachel. Anna.

Anna.

As the ax met the wood again, Henry swallowed hard. Anna had surprised him yesterday when she'd joined him in burying Jess. She'd also surprised him by putting his needs before hers. It was now hard to imagine how he'd spent so many years only thinking of her as selfish and self-serving.

Of being merely frivolous and concerned with outward vanities instead of inner integrity. Nowadays, those thoughts shamed him. He was enough of a man to find fault with himself and wish he'd been better. He should have recognized his faults where she was concerned. He should have expected to find only the best from Anna . . . like he did of himself and the other members of his order.

After all, wasn't that how the Lord asked him to behave? "Whatsoever a man soweth, he shall also reap."

If he were honest with himself—which he found hard at times—Henry knew he would be best served by remembering that it was not just her character he was concerned about . . . but also his.

How was it possible for him to be thinking of the curly-haired beauty in any terms other than the ones that were in the most general way? They could never be a match.

Never have a future—not unless one of them was willing to change their lifestyle completely. He most certainly did not plan to do that.

From the time he was old enough to look at the world around him, Henry had known he was happy where he was. The Amish were his people, and he'd never felt alone or out of sorts, the way he'd heard other men speak of at Sunday socials. He'd hardly spent any time in the outside world during his *rumschpringe*, his running-around years. And though he enjoyed reading the city paper every once in a while and counted many English as his friends, their way of life and modern conveniences held no appeal to him. In truth, Henry felt far more interest in *The Budget*, the Amish newspaper.

He was far more at peace in his own community . . . and

in God's world. He was content to follow the traditions of his father and grandfather and the many generations who had worked the land before him. He'd looked forward to marrying Rachel and working the land near the bed and breakfast. To abiding by the principles they both had held dear.

Anna Metzger did not fit in with his past, his way of life, or his dreams for the future.

And, contrary to what she might think, he did not begrudge her for her beliefs. Everyone had the right to live how he or she saw fit. There was nothing wrong with each person following his or her given path. Anna's path was far different, that was all. She'd grown up with different expectations.

Their paths shouldn't have ever crossed for any length of time. They weren't expected to. Later, when Anna was no longer using their inn as a safe haven, she would be gone, most likely to never return.

So why did he find himself thinking of her expressive green eyes when he closed his own each evening? Why was he remembering her smile of encouragement when he sanded the piece of maple he was working on? Or her laugh when he drove his buggy to the market just the past afternoon?

Why was he reliving the feeling of hope that had filled him when she'd walked by his side, lifting his spirits, making him realize that Jess had been a good companion, but that it was his time to go . . . just as it would be his time one day as well.

More chips fell to the ground as his ax cut into the wood. Above him, the branches trembled, signaling that his work was almost done. Soon, the tree would come tumbling down, bringing with it years of growth, birds' nests, and insects' homes.

Just like he feared his life would be, if he continued to let

Anna play a part in it. Yes, the tree was about to have another purpose in the Lord's creation. One of good use . . . firewood.

But just like his life, his path, Henry knew that use wasn't what God had intended. God had intended for the tree to grow tall and strong, supporting years of growth and change. To be homes for the multitude of animals in the woods. Not to be burned for fuel in a matter of minutes.

Crack! The noise caught him unawares as the tree shook, then broke. Henry stepped back in a rush, watching the tall limbs above him come tumbling down. With a sharp rustle, branches broke and leaves crunched as they met the floor of the woods. Birds squawked and wings flapped as they flew to safety. Then, all was silence.

Henry used that time to pray for guidance . . . and to pray for Anna. He prayed for her safety.

But, to his consternation, he also prayed that she would see that her path in life was far from his. That they were not supposed to find any common ground.

And, to his complete shame and consternation, he prayed that she would leave very, very soon.

No longer did it feel strange to get up before dawn. As Anna splashed water over her face and hurriedly got dressed in the dim light from the kerosene lamp, she realized how easily she'd accepted the Brennemans' way of life in the last three weeks.

Now, first thing every morning, she accompanied Katie to the henhouse to gather eggs and then got to work making the day's bread and rolls. Little by little, as the sun rose to start their day, other Brennemans would stop in the kitchen. Mr. Brenneman came first, always taking the time to wish her good morning. Never much of a morning eater, Anna would serve John a bowl of oatmeal before he went to the barn to tend to the cows and the milking.

Next came Irene, bustling with lists and information about the night's borders. Katie would sip on a cup of coffee before going into the main dining room to quickly shine everything free of dust and set out plates, silverware, and napkins.

Anna would do her best to help Mrs. Brenneman prepare the breakfast meal. She'd gotten quite good at making scrambled eggs, if she did say so herself.

And finally, always as if he were waiting to the very last minute, Henry would appear, his tawny brown hair damp and the blanket of sleep still seeming to surround him. A mumbled *gut morning* would be followed by a complete concentration on the food she placed in front of him. Little by little, as he ingested the food and drank cup after cup of coffee, his brown eyes would brighten.

After the first few uncomfortable days, Anna had given up attempting to converse with Henry. Though he was so obviously not a morning person, she couldn't help but realize that it wasn't merely the time of day that kept things stilted between them.

No, there was more than that, and all of it was hard to even speak of. They made do by sharing glances. Though there was no animosity between them, Anna felt an awareness toward Henry different from any other Brenneman.

On some days Anna was certain she could feel his eyes on her, watching her every move. Vanity would kick in, and suddenly Anna would wish for even the smallest bit of makeup. Mascara or lipstick. Anything to brighten her eyes or face, to have him think more of her.

Which was wrong and she knew it. They had no future, and she should have been learning to care less about her vanity.

Of course, that was just one of the ways she still had trouble fitting in. She stumbled on the simplest of Pennsylvania Dutch words, still managed to offend at least one Brenneman a day with her desire to help in all the wrong ways.

To her embarrassment, she'd also spoken a time or two without thought, complaining about the scratchy dress or the pins in her hair, or her desire to just sit and watch TV.

No matter how hard she tried, it was obvious that she would never fit in. Or, she wouldn't fit in without a lot more trials and errors on her part.

That morning, after the men had been fed, Katie and Anna were in charge of placing warm Danishes and plates of eggs, homemade sausage, and bacon out for the guests.

"You take the juice out first, wouldja, Anna?" Katie asked. "I need a minute or two more to get the eggs to rights."

"All right." To her surprise, a number of people were already standing in the dining room, sipping coffee from the pot Mrs. Brenneman had placed out just moments before.

Seeing the curious eyes regarding her, Anna stumbled slightly, almost spilling the juice over her pale lavender dress and black apron.

One woman stepped to her side. "Want some help with that?" Her voice had a New York accent, and it sounded jarring to Anna's ears. She'd become so accustomed to the distinctive lilt of the Amish.

"No. *Danke*," she whispered. After righting the pitcher she carried, Anna placed it on the sideboard. Worried of being seen as an imposter, she kept her gaze down.

"Oh. No problem," the lady replied before joining the other eight or so people in the room, merrily discussing their rooms and some of the many Plain crafts they intended to buy at the flea market that they were preparing to visit.

After wiping off the side of the pitcher with a dishcloth, Anna turned toward the safety of the kitchen. Being around so many strange faces did make her feel uncomfortable. With some surprise, Anna wondered if it was because she was becoming used to the confining lifestyle of the Amish. Or was it something else?

Something didn't feel right. The same feeling had risen when she'd known it was time to hide from Rob signaled that she needed to be aware. Conscious that there was another in the room besides just tourists. Wasn't there?

"Miss, do you have any tea?"

Her heart pounded. *"Jah."* Oh, she hoped they wouldn't notice how strange and awkward she sounded! Or how nervous! Struggling to sound more nonchalant, she said slowly, "Herbal?"

"Yes, please. Thank you."

"All right." Anna had just turned when she caught another woman's eye. That lady was staring at her in surprise, tilting her head to one side as if she couldn't be sure what she was seeing.

Anna felt like doing the same thing. She knew that woman, those red curls, beautiful rosy skin, and tawny-colored eyes. Miriam Whitney. She had been a friend of her mother's since high school and had been a frequent guest at their home, especially in the summers when Mrs. Whitney and her mother played golf together.

For a moment, Anna was afraid she wasn't going to be able to breathe.

Miriam's eyes narrowed for a moment. Anna tried to look as serene and distant as possible, then hurriedly turned to make her escape.

Anna quickly pushed open the swinging door and launched into Katie. "There's someone out there I know."

Katie's eyes widened. "Really! Who?"

"The lady with short red hair. She's a friend of my mother's. She was staring at me—I think she recognized me, too. I can't go out there again."

"You think she might know your Rob?"

"I don't think she does, but I can't risk her telling my mother. By now my mom has probably figured out I never went to Florida and is wondering where I am."

"And then your mother could tell Rob and he'd find you."

Feeling tears of stress fill her eyes, Anna proclaimed, "I'm so sorry. I'm a mess right now. For a while I thought I was safe."

"You are safe," Katie said soothingly. "Don't worry so much. You mustn't borrow trouble."

"I can't help but worry. I know I can't hide forever." Hands shaking, Anna pressed them against her thighs. "For the last couple of days, I'd almost thought I could."

"Don't fret so, Anna. Sit down for a moment."

"A lady wants tea." Anna closed her eyes, hearing the desperation evident in her voice. "Herbal tea."

Katie patted her shoulder comfortingly. "That's no problem. We fix herbal teas all the time."

"If I prepare it, will you bring it out?"

"Of course I will, Anna."

Henry came in just as the tea was steeping. "Taking a rest already, Anna? When will you ever do your fair share?"

Anna almost lashed out at him until she heard the teasing note in his voice, saw the amusement in his eyes. Finally, Henry Brenneman felt comfortable enough around her to joke. And tease.

This final acceptance of her felt like a hug . . . and made her want to burst into tears. She had become attached—had started to feel real friendship toward him.

When he gazed at her a moment longer, Anna knew he was waiting for a reply. "You know me, always lazy," she said brightly, though her voice cracked and effectively ruined the pert comment.

True concern washed over his features. "What's wrong? What happened to you?"

"Hush now, Henry," Katie chided. "Anna knows someone out there. In the dining room." Brushing past her brother importantly, Katie picked up the tray of tea, the carafe, and a small towel. "Move to the side, please. I've tea to deliver."

In a flash, the swinging doors opened and shut as Katie's bright blue skirts disappeared from view.

Anna's heart slammed in her chest as she heard the guests speak to Katie.

Henry took the chair by her side. "Who do you know?"

"Miriam Whitney. Mrs. Whitney's an old friend of my mother's. I've known her since I was in grade school."

"You sure she's who you saw?"

"I'm positive. She's a nice lady, but I know she recognized me. What am I going to do?"

Henry winked at her. "Breathe, Anna. Even if someone

thinks she knows you, she'll never assume you've turned Plain. You had made a wise decision when you chose to hide here. No one would suspect you to be here, dressed like us and servin' tea."

Put that way, Anna supposed Henry was right. She knew of very few people in her former life who even thought about the Amish more than characters in a movie or quaint people in a postcard. They'd certainly never consider joining their ranks.

"That's better," he said soothingly, even going so far as to pat her shoulder.

She'd just taken his advice and breathed deep when she heard the low echo of Miriam's voice. "Where's the other girl? She seemed so familiar."

Anna couldn't hear Katie's reply because everything seemed to be roaring in her own ears.

Both she and Henry stared at the doorway when Katie appeared again, her face white.

"What happened?"

"That lady asked about you." With a stricken expression, Katie added, "Lord, please forgive me, but I lied! I . . . I told her you were my cousin!"

Henry blinked. "Katie, you shouldn't have told her anything!"

"I tried not to, but she kept staring at me. And, what is worse, I don't think she believed me, Anna."

"It's okay. There's nothing to be done," Anna said, though inside, her heart was breaking. She was going to have to leave—if Miriam happened to say anything to her mother, and there was a very good chance that would happen, her mother could tell Rob. Next thing they knew, he would appear, endangering her and all the Brennemans.

And what would she do then? Leave with Rob? Anna shuddered to think of what her life would be like then.

"I need to go tend to them again," Katie said awkwardly, her arms now loaded with a plate of apple muffins. "They're waitin' for their breakfast, for sure."

To Anna's great surprise, Henry picked up the platter of sausage and eggs. "I'll help, Katie. You go to the barn," he whispered. "Go to my tack room and wait."

"Are you sure?"

"I am. Go now, Anna."

Anna threw on a cloak and hurried to the barn. The brisk air whipped against her face, but while she'd found it invigorating before dawn, she only felt the sharp sting of the wind now. After slipping in through the side door, she headed straight to Henry's workshop. In seconds, she opened and shut the door, firmly closing out even more of the outside world.

Her hands and legs were shaking so much that she sat down on his stool before they gave out underneath her.

Little by little, her breathing slowed, and once again she was able to think reasonably. It was time to think of other people, time to put them before herself, no matter what the cost was to her.

As she recognized Henry's comforting scent in the room, Anna knew she had no choice; she was going to have to leave. She'd been a fool to think that she fit in, that she could hide at the Brennemans'.

Once more, she was ashamed to realize that Henry's dire prediction had come true . . . she had, once again, put her own needs first and in so doing, had endangered all the Brennemans. She'd done exactly what she'd naively promised she would never do. . . . she put the very people who had offered her solace in the grip of danger.

In four hours, after the first round of visitors had checked out and left, Anna would follow.

She had no choice.

"Lord, please help me," she whispered. "I now know that I should have completely repented for my sins weeks ago. I repent now and am truly sorry.

"Glorious God, please help me find the strength to stand on my own two feet and come to grips with all the doubts that fill me. Give me strength to accept my faults and to not run. It's time to begin again."

Closing her eyes, Anna continued to pray with all her might. She just hoped God would see fit to help and guide her—and not see her repentance as too little, too late.

Meredith's hands shook as she set the receiver back on the phone.

"Who was that?"

"Calvin, that was Miriam Whitney."

He coughed, making Meredith recall that he never really had enjoyed Miriam's company. "What did she want? To tell you that latest gossip on her street?"

"Calvin, she's not that bad."

"I certainly think she is! Why, if that woman paid half as much attention to herself as everyone around her, she'd have a whole lot less health problems. She has more ailments than anyone I've ever met. And if she's not complaining about her joints or her hip, she's spreading rumors about everyone she knows."

Meredith closed her eyes and tried to keep her patience. "She wasn't calling to gossip."

"What did she want?"

"To tell me that she thinks she saw Anna."

Calvin froze. Slowly stepping forward, he searched her face. "What? Where?"

"In Amish country."

He rolled his eyes. "Who else did she see? George Bush?"

For a moment, Meredith smiled before shaking her head. "Actually, Miriam said she saw Anna at the Brenneman Bed and Breakfast."

"That place sounds familiar."

Meredith noticed he wasn't laughing now. "It is familiar. Years ago, Anna and I spent a weekend there, learning to quilt. From what I recall, she and one of the daughters have kept in touch."

"Is that allowed? I didn't think the Amish were encouraged to keep relationships with outsiders."

Meredith shrugged. "No, many Amish have English friends. What's rarer, I think, is for two teenage girls from such different backgrounds to keep in touch for so many years—especially through letters! It seems most teenagers only pay attention to who they see a lot. I recall Anna mentioning that she would pay a visit to the Brennemans once a year or so. She sent them Christmas cards, too . . . and that the daughter always teased her about them."

"Would Anna go to them?"

"I don't know. Miriam said that Anna looked Amish . . .

she was dressed Plainly, in their clothes . . . but she recognized Anna because of her distinctive green eyes."

"Nothing to think about, dear. Let's get dressed and go get her."

She laid a hand on his arm. "I'm not sure if that's wise. I've gotten the feeling that we haven't seen the last of Rob. What if he's following us?"

"That sounds a bit paranoid, Meredith. I doubt even he would do something like that."

"A month ago, I would have agreed, but now I'm not so sure. Every time we've been in contact with him, Rob has acted strange and angry. Now I don't believe I'd put anything past him." After a moment's hesitation, she admitted the rest of her worries. "I'm afraid of how he'd retaliate if we even tried to stand in his way."

Calvin slowly sat down. "So what are we going to do? Call the police?"

"Calvin, I think we should wait a bit. If that really was Anna at the Brennemans', then she's safe. The Brennemans are good people, and I know that they will be vigilant about caring for her."

"Even though I'd rather our daughter be back here at home, I'm sure you're right." Her husband of forty years stood up and walked to the fireplace. As was his habit, he brushed a hand lovingly over the mahogany mantel they'd bought in auction years ago.

But where once the gesture brought a pleased smile from him, now it was obvious that all of their material possessions paled in comparison to what was really at stake . . . their only daughter. "What are we going to say to Miriam? What did you tell her?"

"I didn't say much of anything. I laughed off Miriam's hunch and said that Anna was in Florida."

"Do you think she believed you?"

"I'm sure she did. I mean, why wouldn't she? The only thing worse than not having anything to gossip about would be to get caught gossiping with the wrong information. We aren't alone," she said softly. "Anna is in God's hands. He guided her to safety, and I truly feel He's placed His loving arms around her. Maybe we should ask Him for His help, too."

"For us?"

"Definitely. I need His blessings and guidance more than ever."

Calvin murmured, "Do we deserve it?"

"No," she said with a smile. "We don't deserve His guidance at all . . . but that's the beauty of grace, is it not?"

He walked to her and took her hand. "Oh, Meredith. What would I do without you? You make everything better."

"I wish that were true." As far as she was concerned, she'd failed her daughter. She was ashamed. If that girl was indeed her daughter, Anna had taken refuge with another woman's family. And that for whatever reason, they'd seen the need to protect her far more quickly than she had.

Chapter 8

Henry wished Anna Metzger had never come into his life. If she hadn't, he wouldn't be feeling the things he did right at that moment—panic, longing, and resignation.

He was captivated. He longed to hold her in his arms.

He knew why—it was no great mystery. He was pining for her, thinking about a future with Anna. Wondering if there was anything he could've done better in order to comfort her, to give her hope and solace.

And all of it without his family finding out.

These discordant feelings were unfamiliar and trouble-some. Intrigue and secrets were not part of his life, nor were they for anyone he knew. It was the Amish way to speak without rancor, to speak from the heart. With sincerity and frankness. People did not keep secrets. They did not covet things they could not have.

They did not lie, not even to themselves.

Henry slowed his pace as he wondered just how long he could continue to deceive himself about his attraction to Anna. Not much longer, he knew that to be true. There was something about her green eyes that drew him to her. Made his gaze last a little too long whenever she was nearby. Made him dream of things that could never happen. Made him want to protect her, when just days ago, he'd only wanted to protect himself.

Squaring his shoulders, Henry quietly opened the barn door, then walked into his workshop to where Anna was. He cautioned himself to think only of her safety, not his own feelings. Not how seeing her perched on his stool made his heart glad.

She looked up when he closed the door behind him. "Hi."

He tried to smile, but it was hard to find the energy. Anna's cheeks were streaked with tears, and the sight of her sadness struck him like a blow. "Anna, are you okay?"

Wiping a cheek with a fist, she shook her head. "No."

He stepped closer, finally stopping across from her, resting the back of his thighs against the top of his workshop table. Now mere inches separated the two of them. "That lady, she moved on about a half hour ago."

"I thought I heard a couple of cars drive off. Did she ask a lot more questions?"

"Questions? Oh, *jah*." He tried to pretend to misunderstand her. "She asked about milking cows and my schooling. The usual questions."

A hint of a smile fought its way forward. "And you answered?"

"I did answer. I even told her about my carpentry business," he added, seeing how his chatter was freeing some of the gloom from her expression.

"I'm surprised."

"You shouldn't be." He jabbed his chest with two fingers. "Sometimes even I have patience."

Anna finally did smile then, her face lighting up with a beam of gratitude. "Who would've thought?"

"Not I, and that's a fact."

They shared a smile, bringing a warmth to the room that had nothing to do with heat and everything to do with their proximity. Once again, Henry knew what he was feeling was wrong. He tried to focus on the scent of wood chips and oil. On the faint movements of the horses on the other side of the wall.

On anything other than the way that one stubborn curl had sprung out of her *kapp* and framed her cheek, reminding him of just how much he'd been taken with her golden hair.

Anna stood up and put a full foot between them. "Well. Thanks for coming out here. Please tell Katie that I'll be right in to help her with the dishes and rooms."

"No hurry. I came to let you know the woman left, not to summon you to work just yet."

"Is that the only reason you came out here? To deliver a message?"

Her directness with him was new. Usually Anna sidestepped information, talked in half-truths and in vagueness. Usually that bothered him . . . he would far rather she say what was on her mind. But now that the tables were turned and he was the one fending off uncomfortable questions, he wished they could go back to their old ways. Anything to prevent him from saying too much.

"Cat got your tongue, Henry?"

"Maybe I was worried about you," he murmured. "Maybe I thought you'd be in here crying."

"You don't need to be," she replied, though her eyes still glistened with unshed tears.

"I'm afraid I do. You need someone looking out for ya."

"I need to look out for myself a little better, I'm afraid." Before he could think of a fitting response, she went on. "Henry, you were perfectly right in your assessment of me the afternoon I arrived."

He recalled the conversation and regretted his harsh words. "No, I wasn't right at all. I should have held my tongue. I treated a guest in our home shamefully, and that is a fact."

She chuckled softly. "No, I think you treated me exactly how I needed to be treated. I needed to hear your words of truth."

"Not the way I said them."

"The way you said them was fine." After a pause, she continued. "I have been putting myself first and, consequently, you all in danger."

"I don't know about danger."

A firm resolve entered her eyes. "I'm afraid I do. If Miriam talks, and she will, I'm sure of it, word will get around that I'm here. It's time I left."

The statement came so suddenly that Henry wasn't sure he heard her correctly. "Leave?"

"Yep. I'll help Katie and then pack up my things. I should be out of your lives within a few hours."

No longer did his anger and bitterness about Rachel cloud over his feelings. Instead, all things Anna came to mind. He remembered her embrace when he'd grieved for Jess, remembered her quiet company and was grateful for it. There was no way he could live with himself if he encouraged her to leave directly and make her way alone. "I hardly think that's a wise idea, Anna."

"Luckily for you, you won't need to worry about it. This time, all the responsibility for my ideas, good or bad, will rest on me."

Panic engulfed him as he envisioned Anna leaving. Just like Rachel, she'd be walking toward a way of life in which he didn't fit in and never would be able. He would stay where he was, waiting and wishing for circumstances to be different. "You're running scared. Take some time to think this through. Where would you go?"

"I don't know." She pushed back a stray curl again. Henry watched it return to rest upon her cheek as she spoke again. "I have some money. I did remember to take quite a bit of cash. Perhaps I'll travel to Florida, after all."

Henry knew that if she left for Florida, he'd never see her again. And though that might be the best thing for him—out of sight and mind—he knew he wasn't ready to say good-bye to her yet. "You can't keep running," he said slowly, like he was just realizing the consequences her actions would have. "Sooner or later you'll have to stop."

"I know that, but I also know I can't stay here. Rob will find me, if he wants to. And I'm afraid he's going to want to find me very badly. As far as he's concerned, I'm *his*. I also know things about his financial dealings that could ruin him."

"Then tell the authorities."

"They might not believe me. Rob is a well-respected lawyer, running for office with a great many influential people backing him up. I don't know for certain, but I'm very afraid that he's got quite a few other elected officials—including his brother-in-law who's a sheriff—on his payroll. Even if they don't approve of Rob's ways, I know they're not going to risk losing their own livelihoods."

"Perhaps you could make them see the benefits of helping you. Seems to me more often than not, people do care about what is right and good."

"I hope that's true." A bright, sudden smile transformed her features until worry replaced her expression once again. "It won't be easy. I wouldn't even know where to begin."

Unfortunately, he didn't know exactly how to aid her, either. He knew few English. And though he did know a few men who left their order, Henry hadn't kept in close enough contact with them to help Anna in any appreciable way.

But that didn't stop his need for her. Desperate, Henry tried again. "Wait a day or so, then. At least do that, wouldja?"

"Why?"

Awareness sparked between them, making Henry recognize that Anna wasn't as oblivious to their connection as he'd tried to pretend she was.

Amazing how, now that he'd come to know her, Henry realized she was far different and more thoughtful than he'd ever imagined.

Before, he'd turned Anna into a lazy, silly, fancy girl. Now, he knew her to be looking for acceptance and comfort, just like he was. For a split second, he considered asking her to stay with them forever. To adopt their ways and join their order. Then, with God's help, one day he'd have the right and opportunity to pledge himself to her.

But that was as impossible to imagine as wishing Jess to rise up from his grave. Some things were over and done with, and it would be best if they all came to grips with that.

He didn't want to say good-bye. Not yet. But it wasn't his way to voice his innermost thoughts . . . and it wasn't Anna's way to merely listen and not act.

Because of all these things, he stayed silent.

Inadvertently, his silence seemed to answer her question.

Hurt and a sad kind of resolve filled her gaze. "I see."

"You don't." He opened his mouth, to try to verbalize his feelings, but old hurts and thoughts of what could never be got in the way. To push her so wasn't his way, and wasn't the best thing for her.

Thirty seconds flowed into one minute, then two.

Moving toward the door, she shook her head in dismay. "Thanks for letting me hide in here, Henry, but I think we both know it's time I left. I can't hide in your workshop or at the Brenneman Bed and Breakfast any longer."

"But—"

She held up a hand. "But most of all, I can't hide from myself."

It happened before he was aware of it. He reached out and took her hand. Linked his fingers with hers. Stunned, she stilled, her lips parted.

Did she feel the same connection that he did? "Don't," he whispered. "Don't go away. Yet."

Her hand still folded into his, Henry was aware of her soft, smooth skin. The way her fingers linked around his, curved, so delicate and sweet in his own work-roughened hands.

He didn't want to let her go.

The surge of awareness he felt for her was nothing he'd anticipated, asked for, or could control. "I don't know what's happening," he said honestly. "I can only tell you that it's taken me by surprise."

Still looking at their linked fingers, Anna carefully caressed his knuckles with her thumb, the nail cut short and looking pink and perfect. "Do you want me to say it?" She swallowed. Shrugged her shoulders. "All right. After all, I guess I have nothing to lose, do I?"

He shook his head to stop her, but she'd already continued. "I . . . I am starting to have feelings for you. Feelings that are more than mere friendship. I'm sorry."

Inside, his pulse leaped. Inside, his heart pounded with the knowledge that Rachel hadn't taken everything from him. No, instead of stealing his heart, she'd only injured it, and before he knew it, his heart was beating again, strong and true. Showing him that life could go on. And maybe—just maybe—he and Rachel had never been meant to be, if already he was tempted by another. "We're different, you and I."

"I know," she said quickly. "Please don't ask me to apologize. I just don't think I can tell you that I'm sor—"

He cut her off. "I wasn't going to do that. Anna, I was going to say that I, too, feel that way."

Eyes widening, she pulled her hand away from his. "You do?"

"I do." He felt the loss of their connection just as strongly as if someone had removed his shirt. Suddenly, he felt cool and vulnerable. Open to her prying eyes.

As Anna continued to stare, her gaze full of wonder and

the faint feel of hope, Henry hung his head, feeling like a giant load had been lifted from his shoulders, only to land on his foot.

Once again, Anna took the first step forward. "You look upset."

"I am upset. I don't know what to do. I don't know what to do about you and me."

"Perhaps we could just remain friends."

"Have we become friends?" Yes, he did feel more comfortable around her, and he'd valued her companionship when he'd buried Jess, but he didn't feel friendship for her. No, it was more like a very strong awareness, shaking him in his soul.

"I hope so. All I do know is that I could sure use a friend right now."

"Then I will be a friend for you. Only a friend. Just don't leave."

"I'll speak to your parents. I need to tell them just what might happen if Rob discovers where I am."

"Their minds won't change. They'll continue to offer shelter."

"I'll be grateful, but also feel guilty if something were to happen. Henry, I just don't know if I can shoulder that burden now, as well."

He stepped forward. Took a risk and wiped the last tear track on her translucent cheek. The skin there was as soft and feathery sweet as he'd ever imagined. "I'll walk you inside, then."

"Because we're friends?"

"Because unless our worlds change, that's all we can ever be."

Chapter 9

She did wait. One week.

"And so, you see, Mr. and Mrs. Brenneman, there is a very good reason for me to be going," Anna finished, feeling fairly proud of herself because her voice didn't come out as shaky as she felt. "I think it would be best if I left you in peace."

Mr. Brenneman leaned forward, bracing his elbows on his knees. The five of them were seated in the hearth room. "I think it's too late for the peace you're speaking of, Anna."

Irene nodded. "Your presence has disrupted our household mightily."

Katie looked as if she were about to cry. *"Mamm."*

"Hush, daughter," Mr. Brenneman commanded. "Anna has disrupted our home, there is no doubt of that."

Anna felt as if she couldn't breathe. Their stern expressions were repressive, their words as stinging to her person as an ice storm. "It won't take me long to pack my bags."

"We didn't ask you to leave, though," Mr. Brenneman said.

They'd done everything but say those words. Standing up, Anna murmured, "It's not necessary. I'll be out of here soon."

Katie stood up, too. "Anna's my *gut* friend. She's done more than her share of work. *Mamm*, you saw how the guests were mightily pleased with her cloverleaf rolls. And she's ironed—"

"Hush, daughter," her father said again. Turning to Anna, he said, "I think perhaps it's time for you to speak to your parents."

"I would agree, except I don't know if I can trust them."

Irene's gaze softened. "You'd doubt your mother's love?"

"I know she loves me, but I doubt that she completely understands just how bad things are with Rob."

"Give her another chance. Imagine what Jesus would have done if He would have settled for doubt and distrust. Sometimes a message needs to be delivered more than once."

The thought of calling her parents, of asking for their help just to be denied again, was scarier than the thought of surviving on her own. "I can't."

This time it was Henry who stood up. "Give them a chance, Anna. Now you have us. Now you know we can help you. Give them a chance."

As if the whole conversation was settled, Mr. Brenneman walked to the doorway. "I'll go get your phone out of hiding and you can call your parents. I'm sure they're worried about you by now."

When he left the room, Mrs. Brenneman patted her on the shoulder, then exited as well, leaving Anna with only Henry and Katie for company.

Katie's lovely blue eyes were bright with unshed tears. "I'm so sorry, Anna. I thought my parents would surely listen better."

"They have listened," Henry corrected. "And I have to say I agree with their words. We canna move forward until we come to terms with our past."

John Brenneman entered the room and with little fanfare, handed Anna the phone. "Would you like our company while you call or would you rather be alone?"

Anna was afraid if she was left by herself, she'd be afraid to punch in the numbers. "I need all of you here," she said.

"Call then, dear Anna. No use waiting any more."

Four interested faces watched her push the power button on her phone. "I'm waiting for a signal," she said when they all looked at her like it was about to start ringing. When the bands of a good signal came into view, Anna gathered her courage and dialed her parents.

The phone rang once. Twice. Finally, after the fourth ring, the message center clicked on. Though she was afraid to leave a message, especially since Rob could be monitoring her messages, Anna took a leap of faith and spoke. If she didn't step forward into the open, she might never be free to move forward. "Mom, Dad, it's me. Anna. I, um, never went to Miami. I've been hiding from Rob. I'm at the Brennemans'. You know, the Amish B and B we used to go to for the quilting classes. Come out for me, would you? I need you. I love you, too. "

She clicked off. "They weren't home," she said unnecessarily, and feeling more than a little let down. But what had she expected? That her parents would be sitting by their phone, just waiting for her to contact them?

Those days were long gone—if they'd ever been there at all.

Henry, to Anna's surprise, leaped to the rescue. "When they get home and listen to messages, they'll be pleased to hear from you, mark my words. Before you know it, we'll be looking out the window and watching your parents come walking in."

To her surprise, Anna realized she, too, was hoping for that day. "I hope it's soon." Now that the call had been made and with the conversation with Henry so fresh in her mind, Anna was ready to reach some resolutions.

"I'd be mighty surprised if it wasn't soon." With a smile, Katie added, "Then we'll see if they recognize you, dressed all Plain like you are."

"They might. No one has your eyes, Anna Metzger."

There it was, once again. A sudden pull toward Henry that was filled with unspoken words and quiet promises. Quickly, she peeked at Katie to see her reaction.

As usual, Katie said nothing—merely looked at Henry thoughtfully, her gaze knowing and silent.

But at the moment, there were too many other obstacles in the way to think of relationships.

Anna clicked off the power on her phone. "Thanks for encouraging me to do this. I am glad I reached out to them."

"I am, as well."

"If you don't mind, I'll just go put the phone back in my suitcase. I trust myself a lot more now than I used to."

"That's a *gut* idea, dear Anna," Mrs. Brenneman said. "And then you must help me in the kitchen."

Katie rushed out to do a chore, leaving the room empty

except for she and Henry. "Thank you," she said. "I needed to do this."

"I know you did."

"About earlier—"

"Let's not speak of it. I don't want to forget our words, but perhaps we should remember that things need to happen in their own time."

"Having time sounds mighty wondrous."

Henry laughed. "Anna Metzger, just that moment, you sounded Amish. Almost like one of us."

As Anna went back to her room, her steps faltered. This afternoon, she'd been more aware than ever before that she wasn't one of them . . . and to everyone concerned, she would never be.

Chapter 10

Meredith played the message one more time. After a loud *beep*, Anna's voice filtered through the small speaker on the phone. Her pulse raced. *"Mom,Dad, it's me. Anna."*

Turning toward Calvin, she raised an eyebrow. "Well? What do you think after hearing it for a third time?"

"Just about the same thing I did when I heard the message the first. Anna sounds good. Like herself."

Meredith bit her lip they continued to listen to Anna's too-short message. *"I'm at the Brennemans'. You know, the Amish B and B. . ."*

"Do you think so?" she asked. "Do you think Anna sounds nervous? Worried?"

"If she does, I don't know what we could do about it."

"Calvin!"

"Mer, Anna probably is worried. She's probably worried

about what we're going to say when we finally see her." He tapped the machine. "I, for one, would like to wring our daughter's neck. I think I've aged ten years since she took off."

"I don't imagine Anna is sitting around worried about getting in trouble. I think she knows she is still in trouble." She paused. "Maybe things are even worse, and that's why she finally called us."

Calvin walked around the kitchen island and reached for her. "Don't worry, Mer," he said. "After all, she's where she wants to be, where she feels safe."

Meredith heard the bitterness in her husband's voice and knew it came from hurt. No matter what he said, Calvin was disappointed Anna hadn't tried harder to seek their help. "I suppose." She stepped into his arms and finally let herself let go. After over a month of worry, they now knew Anna was okay. Within hours, they'd be with her, patching things up. Developing a plan of how to break her free from Rob's clutches. Everything would be back to normal. How it used to be. With a sigh, her shoulders relaxed.

The horrible, terrible ordeal was almost over.

Cal gently smoothed her hair from her brow and pressed his lips to her forehead. "You know, it's going to break my heart not to go see her."

His statement practically sent Meredith to her knees. "What are you talking about?" she asked, jerking away from him. "She called us. *Finally* called us! We have no choice but to go to the Brennemans and pick her up."

"We can't do that. Rob's been driving by here on a regular basis. I've seen other strange cars parked out in front of the house for hours at night. If we suddenly took a trip out to

Amish country, there's a very good chance he or someone who works for him might be suspicious."

She waved a hand in dismissal. "You're getting ahead of yourself. There's no way Rob is watching us that closely, and even if he was, he wouldn't know where we were headed. I doubt he's going to care. Besides, what does it matter? Once we have Anna, everything will be fine." Her voice cracked but she covered it up with a smile. Someone had to believe everything was going to be okay.

"I doubt it."

Her husband's sarcastic tone caught her off guard. Had Calvin really become so hard over the last month? "You need to have faith, darling. With God's help, everything is going to work out just fine."

He shook his head in irritation—and shook off her hand on his shoulder. "You, Meredith, need to stop being so naive. Rob is watching us. And I don't think anything is going to stop him from trying to get Anna. This isn't just a case of a man missing his girl. She knows something, or else she has something that he wants."

"I know . . . but—"

"We know enough. We just can't risk it, Mer. We can't."

Nothing he said held any meaning for her. She had to go to Anna. "We're not prisoners, and we shouldn't act as if we are. Even if you won't go, I'm going to get in the car."

"No."

"She asked for us." Meredith bit her tongue, holding back the obvious. Finally. She'd finally asked for her parents.

"It's time we faced the facts. Anna must know something about Rob. This stalking nonsense can't just be about some relationship that's gone south. She must know something about his work or his personal life or his campaign." He drummed his fingers on the counter. "There's got to be some information he didn't want made public that she must have discovered. Something really powerful—powerful enough to compromise his bid for the election. She's in danger."

Her mouth went dry. Steadying herself, Meredith said, "If she's in danger, then that's all the more reason that we need to go to her." Memories of a much different time sprang forth. Meredith remembered a time when Anna was in middle school. One afternoon she'd come home with a broken heart, straight into her mother's arms. It had taken hours of long conversation in order to make her happy, to dry her tears. "I can't ignore her, Calvin. I can't let her just sit there, all alone."

"She's not. She's with the Brennemans. They're looking after her."

"It's not the same as her parents."

"No, it's not. We didn't believe her when she told us about Rob, did we?" Bitterness tinged his next words as he continued. "We ignored everything she said and were going to force her to continue to see Peterson."

"You're not being fair. I'm not going to let you win this one."

"It's not a win-lose game here, Meredith."

"I'm not playing a game." Panic rose in her throat as she totally grasped everything Calvin was saying. "We can't ignore her. Anna is going to be looking for us. She's going to be expecting us."

"We can't go there. Not until we know for sure that Rob isn't following our every move."

"But Cal—"

"Right now she's safe." Almost in a whisper he added, "What if *we* put her in danger? What if we unknowingly led Rob to her? *Then* what would we do?"

She wouldn't be able to go on. That's what would happen.

Thoroughly defeated, Meredith stared at the speaker phone. "What are you suggesting?"

Calvin erased Anna's recording. "Let's begin to think offensively. There must be someone we know who will either work around Rob Peterson or not be intimidated by the man."

The recorder beeped, letting them know the erasure was successful. Hearing that made it feel as if they were losing Anna all over again. "Anything else?" she asked.

"Well . . . is there anyone we could trust to go to the Brennemans' for us and relay a message? Anyone who Rob wouldn't be suspicious of and follow?"

That was a good idea. It was just too bad that everyone she was thinking of couldn't be completely trusted to either keep her silence or not get involved. Or, they were in such poor health that Meredith was reluctant to involve them in something so potentially dangerous. "I can't think of anyone off the top of my head."

He reached out for her again, asking without words to trust him. To have faith. "I just had an idea."

"Who?"

"Beverly Lowrey."

"Beverly? She must be almost seventy years old!"

For the first time during their conversation, Calvin grinned. "We both know Beverly would have your head if she heard you describe her as too old for anything."

"She's too old for this. We can't put her in danger."

"But what if she makes that choice on her own? She's one

of the gutsiest people I know. She's also one of the most reliable people."

"But do you think she'd want to get involved?"

Calvin squeezed her hand, gifting her with the first genuine smile in a long time. "I think she'd love to get involved. I think she'd jump at the chance to do a little something other than crosswords and make her weekly trip to the grocery store."

"You may be right. If Beverly wants to help, I can't think of anyone better," she said.

But that was a lie. More than anything, Meredith wanted to be the one to make everything better.

And once again, she wasn't even going to come close.

Tracy Cleese was perky, brunette, and had the type of figure that was hard for a man to ignore. Rob hadn't even tried.

Not that Tracy had been around all that long. After William Scott had delivered his ultimatum, Rob had gotten busy and started making calls to anyone who might know of a woman who was suitable for him to be seen with publicly.

Tracy had been the strongest contender. A recent graduate of Ohio State, she'd been in a number of going-nowhere jobs and living at home. He'd met her at a coffee shop for a first date, then taken her to a trendy spot for lunch the following day. Both times, she'd been pleasant, easily distracted, and had looked fabulous.

She definitely had possibilities, if one overlooked the fact that she was almost too easy to bend to his will and had no conversational skills beyond her hair, her diet, or her miniature poodle, Fluff.

"Rob, are you sure you want me to work here with you?"

She giggled before continuing coyly, "I'm just not sure if we want that kind of relationship."

"I'm sure."

"Okay. But if I do something you don't like, let me know, would you?"

"I promise I will," he said, though Rob's mind was on Tracy's looks and not her words. Her smile was suggestive. Too suggestive and obvious.

The conservative constituents in the county would take one look at that and make a beeline for the door. No one wanted their congressman hooked up with a floozy.

Mentally, Rob made a note to bring in another girl, soon.

Figuring everything between them was peachy, Tracy blathered on about the sale at Nordstrom's before working quietly on some files when the phone rang. "Rob Peterson's office. Tracy speaking. Oh, yeah. Sure." Brown eyes batted as she pushed down Hold. "It's for you, Rob."

As if it was going to be for anyone else. "Peterson."

"Rob, it's Grant."

His worthless brother-in-law. "Do you have any information for me?"

"Not yet."

"Another week's gone by. What have you been doing?"

His brother-in-law's voice turned hard. "I've been working. There are actual cases that need to be taken care of, you know."

"Actual? What is that supposed to mean?"

"Anna isn't even classified as a missing person yet. The Metzgers haven't even contacted their local police. Rob, I bet Anna is sitting on the beach somewhere. I bet she's going to

be laughing her head off when she finds out you've been looking all over for her. She's going to make a fool out of you."

A fool? Every cell in Rob's body wanted to reach through
the phone and punch his worthless relative and tell him what
exactly he could do with his so-called job. He owed every bit
of his power and authority to Rob, and it would serve him
well to remember that. And Rob also knew Anna was nearby,
in Amish country. He could feel it. "Watch it, Grant."

"You watch it, Peterson. I warned you finding a gal in
Amish country was going to be hard . . . especially if she
doesn't want to be found."

Rob refused to give up. He was not a quitter, and never
had been. Not since his dad had told him just what happened to losers and quitters. "There's got to be some sign of
her somewhere. A girl like that wouldn't be missed easily."
Thinking of the way her green eyes were so expressive and
how more often than not, her laughter would carry far and
cause too much attention, Rob added, "I'm sure she's caused
notice somewhere."

"Maybe, maybe not. People don't always look beyond the
clothes. And if she's in disguise, we may never know what
happened to her."

Never? Panic flowed through Rob. With force, he tamped
the unwelcome emotion down. Anna was not going to disappear from his life. Even if she was dead in a ditch, he had to
find her. He had to know.

Otherwise she could ruin him.

"What you are saying is unacceptable. You need to get a
deputy or someone else on this case. Full time."

"Maybe you should contact the local police."

All they would do was delve into things that were none of their business. "Not yet."

"Have you pressed her parents for more information? Maybe they know more than they're lettin' on."

"I've pressed." Anger coursed through him as he imagined what people would say if he actually had to admit he'd chased her away. If she could prove that he'd hit her multiple times.

He drummed his fingers on the desk. Would she have had the foresight to take pictures of her bruises? Had she been that devious?

Of course, even those photographs would be nothing compared to what could happen if she ever leaked exactly what he'd been doing with much of the campaign and charity contributions. If the press got hold of that, with their liberal viewpoints and propensity for stretching the truth, he'd have a full-blown storm disrupting his life. "Just keep trying."

"I already am," Grant said quietly. "You may have put me in this job, Rob, but I take it seriously. Very seriously."

Rob hung up the phone, feeling even more furious than from their earlier meeting. Where was Anna? And why would she be in Amish country?

The cloying scent of roses and honeysuckle permeated his office, followed by the baby-doll sweet voice of Tracy. "How about a cup of coffee, Rob?"

"No coffee."

"You sure? I just made a fresh pot." She patted his shoulder. "I bet it will perk you up." A giggle followed—obviously Tracy was a fan of puns.

"No."

"No? Just 'no'?" A hand popped on her hip. "Well, that's rude. The least you could do is add a 'thank you.' I'm doing all this for you, you know. A smile every now and then would be appreciated."

Tracy, with her too-long nails, too-strong perfume, and too-dumb way of speaking, was driving him to the edge. Gripping the table in order not to dissolve that cloying smile, he said, "I think it would be best for you to leave."

Down went the cup of coffee, most likely leaving a ring on his cherry desk in the process. "Leave? What are you saying? You want me to, like, quit?"

"Exactly."

"Now?"

"Immediately." Quicker if possible.

Ten minutes later, Rob found himself alone in his office, ignoring stacks of paperwork and multiple messages waiting to be returned. All he wanted to do was stare out the window and wish for things that never were.

A loser. He was becoming a loser.

That would never do.

"I'm sure there's a good reason your parents haven't stopped by," Katie said reasonably. "Perhaps they didn't receive the message? Maybe that answering machine you told me about didn't click on like it was supposed to."

Anna tried to match her friend's optimistic tone but it was hard. "That's a possibility, but I kind of doubt it."

"Or they haven't listened to the messages?"

"I couldn't imagine my parents not checking messages the minute they got home." Hanging her head, hating her self-doubts, Anna murmured, "They must not care. You heard my message. My mother knows exactly where I am. I asked her to come here, to come and get me. She doesn't want to come." Once again, they'd let her down.

"I'm sure that isn't the case. Perhaps she's on her way, Anna." Pointing to the long, winding road leading up to the inn, Katie smiled. "I betcha any minute now we'll be seeing your parents driving along in their automobile."

Unfortunately, only silence greeted them from the frost-covered streets and lanes.

"Maybe." They stared out at the road, at the back parking lot for another few moments, then unable to take it anymore, Anna turned away. It was hard to accept that her parents weren't running to her side. Hard to accept their betrayal. She felt empty inside.

Yet she knew she couldn't pass off all the blame. She, too, had acted selfishly. She hadn't tried harder to get them to believe her, merely had run and asked the Brennemans to take her in, no matter what the consequences might be. No small wonder Henry hadn't thought much of her.

Now that the fog of Rob's abuse had lifted from her shoulders, Anna saw more clearly than ever before the danger she'd put the Brennemans in.

The danger Rob was to her, and to everyone around her. Back when she was under his influence, she'd still succumbed to his flashes of kindness. She'd still sometimes been fooled by his movie-star smile and his campaign promises. Now she realized that there was nothing about Rob Peterson under that shiny facade. No, like the proverbial onion, he had no core.

At least, he didn't have one that she ever wanted to witness ever again. "What do you think I should do now?" she murmured, knowing that there was no good answer and not expecting one.

Katie shook out her skirts as she stood up, her whole being projecting a sense of purpose. "I think you should come help me clean guest rooms. *Mamm* said she expects two couples this evening, one a repeat customer."

Anna noticed for the first time that Katie, too, was gazing off into the distance, but not fixating on the paved road. No, she seemed to be looking over the hills. "Does Jonathan live out that way?"

Katie started. "Yes."

"Do you think anything's ever going to happen between you two?" Anna meant to be teasing. Comforting.

But as usual, Katie took her question very seriously. "I don't know. Jonathan is still missing his wife. And I'm much younger than him. Sometimes I think he sees me as a bit of a nuisance."

"I doubt it. No one would ever see you as anything but a pleasure to be around."

Katie's cheeks blossomed from the compliment. "You're a *gut* friend, Anna, but I'm afraid what I say about Jonathan is true." With a sigh, Katie linked her arm through Anna's and guided her back to the kitchen door. "Jonathan Lundy isn't ready to begin again. When God blesses him with relief from his grief, then time will tell."

"That's good advice."

"Is it? Some days I forget what is good and what isn't. Some days I just long for things to move faster, or for guidance."

The stark words struck a chord within Anna. "I guess it's good we have so much to do, then," she said softly. "Otherwise, we'd be fretting all day."

Katie finally smiled. Bright and full of life and hope. "Anna, you are truly a gift to me. God bless you."

Anna hoped God would bless her with a great many things soon. Patience and hope and trust.

And parents who would one day go out of their way to help a daughter who really needed them.

Chapter 11

Katie did know best. After parting her hair down the middle, then fixing it neatly under her *kapp*, Anna realized with some surprise that over the time she'd been staying there, work, and the feeling of pride it had given her, had become important. It was also necessary to not forget that her work was needed. She was being asked to help because her efforts were important to the running of the inn, not just meaningless, made-up chores.

After receiving some instructions from Irene about how to go about oiling the oak furniture in the two west-wing bedrooms, Anna carried the bottle of oil and a pile of rags and got to work.

In no time at all, Anna cleared the utilitarian writing desk and dresser, then carefully poured a liberal amount of lemon-scented oil on the cloth and gently rubbed each piece of furniture.

She'd learned some time ago about the fine workmanship

and time that went into each table, dresser, and chair. Years ago, she and her mother had visited a farmers market and visited with an Amish man who spoke about the various steps he took in order to fashion a superior product.

Anna didn't know if she'd appreciated his patience at the time, or, for that matter, his pleasure in doing one task very well. She'd probably been in a hurry to get to the next stall or to investigate the quilts or, more likely to go home and see her friends and go to the mall.

But now all that seemed childish and foreign. Since first arriving at the Brennemans', the Plain clothes had begun to feel comfortable. The lack of time spent on vanity gave her freedom to pursue other interests. The lack of bombardment from a million vices gave Anna time to dwell on what was in her heart and mind. How strange it was to concentrate on her own goals and dreams instead of what everyone else thought she should do.

A burst of laughter floated upward. Curious, Anna peeked out the window. A woman stood in the parking lot, talking to Henry. She couldn't see much of the woman, her back was to the house, and the large oak in front of the house hindered much of the view from the window.

But she could see Henry. And he, for once, looked relaxed.

A stab of jealously filtered through her. Oh, not because he was speaking to another woman—but because it seemed that he was speaking so easily to her. Even their most earnest conversations had lately been stilted and full of tension.

When he glanced up toward the house, Anna turned away so he wouldn't catch sight of her. It wouldn't do for him to catch her spying.

But as his deep voice resonated through the air and seemed

to catch her heart and hold on. Why did each movement of his create a stir in her heart? Why was his furrowed brow a source of amusement instead of irritation?

She'd begun to think what they had between them was a relationship—something special to embrace, yet not defined, at least not defined in the way she used to characterize past relationships.

As she watched him, her hand barely moving the cloth around over the already polished woodwork, Anna dared to imagine that they had a future.

And for the first time, began to realistically imagine the consequences of such a thing.

Seeking solace, she turned from the window and breathed deep . . . and began to pray. God's will would be done.

Was she finally ready to listen?

"I'll be pleased to pass this on to Anna Metzger," Henry told the older woman who'd lumbered out of her shiny sedan and approached him in the parking lot. In clear, concise tones, she'd introduced herself as Mrs. Lowrey, a friend of Anna's parents. And then, before he could do any more than absorb the fact that Anna's parents had indeed heard Anna's phone call and had sent someone in their place, Mrs. Beverly Lowrey handed him a sealed envelope and announced that she'd be on her way.

Henry stepped in her path, effectively blocking the way to her car so he could claim some information. "I thank you for bringing it here."

"It was no bother, Mr. Brenneman. I care a lot for Meredith Metzger; I have since she became my neighbor thirty years ago. It was a pleasure to do something for her."

In spite of his efforts not to judge, for that was God's business, not his, Henry found he couldn't resist pointing out the obvious. "Mrs. Metzger wasn't able to come here herself? I think Anna would've liked to have seen her." Surely that was a fair understatement. Though she hadn't specifically shared her feelings of disappointment with him, Henry had seen the expression on her face when she'd spoken to Katie.

She'd been disappointed, which made him wish he had a way to ease her burdens.

If Mrs. Lowrey had personal feelings about her errand, she didn't look in any hurry to share them. Her tiny chin tilted a bit up as she replied. "She was 'able.' However, I don't believe she wanted to come this way. I'm assuming she had her reasons."

Henry wondered what they were. What kind of woman wouldn't rush to see her daughter the minute she knew she was hurting? "What would they have been, I wonder?"

"It wasn't my place to ask. Nor yours, either, Mr. Brenneman," she replied with more than a small hint of censure in her voice. "It would do us both a world of good to remember that, don't you think?"

"The Lord gave us a mind to wonder. I'm only doing that."

The lady's eyes remained piercing. "I learned over the years that it never pays to judge or to guess what other people are thinking."

"Or to criticize?"

After a pause, genuine amusement broke through her salty exterior. "Obviously, none of us is perfect."

"I'll take the letter to Anna."

"I'll tell her parents that I completed my errand, then." And with that, she turned and stepped to the left, making her way once more to her silver car. "As I said, this errand has been no trouble." She gestured to the wide fields behind them, one after another covered with a light dusting of snow. "This is pretty. I've always looked for an opportunity to visit Amish Country. I'm surprised it's taken me so long to come out this way."

"You should stay at our inn, then."

She cackled. "Ever the proprietor. Maybe I will one day soon. It's calming, even in the winter."

"Yes. Even in the winter."

Looking into the distance, she raised a hand to shield her eyes from the vibrant glow mirroring off the snow-covered fields. "I do have to admit that I got lost a time or two this afternoon. One must really want to visit the Brenneman Bed and Breakfast. If I hadn't promised Meredith I'd deliver this letter, I feel certain I would have abandoned this chore quite some time earlier."

Henry had heard that said more than a time or two. "The roads are marked, but winding. It takes time to learn their curves and hills and valleys, I'd say."

Mrs. Lowrey grinned. "It takes a bit more than time to learn this part of the county. It takes a good map and the patience of Job. I suggest you print out a better map for those of us who are not gifted with never-ending patience."

Henry couldn't help but appreciate her quip. Time and again, he'd ridden in folks' cars, directing them to the highway after their attempts had gotten them nothing but a half tank of gas. "Now that you're here, would you care to come in for a cup of tea or coffee?"

She looked longingly at the front of the house. As her gaze feasted on the wide-planked porch and the fine quartet of handmade rockers, Henry felt a burst of pride flow within him. He was proud of his home and their inn and always appreciated a newcomer's look of appreciation of his family's years of hard work.

"I'd enjoy a cup of coffee very much, but I'm afraid I have to get back. I promised to help out at the services at our church this evening, and as I said, getting here took a little longer than I expected."

"If you wait a moment, I will go get Anna for you. Perhaps you'd rather give her the note yourself, after all."

"There's no need." After a moment's hesitation, she reached out to him. "If you don't mind, though, please pass on a personal message from me."

"Gladly."

"Please tell Anna that I, for one, understand why she did what she did. It took more gumption than I can quite honestly say I ever thought she had in her left pinky to come here. She's done the right thing by my estimation."

He held up his hand and wiggled his fingers. "Left pinky. I will take care to remember that."

"Oh, enough of you," she said with an answering smile. "Just remember to tell her to stay strong and to do the right thing."

The words sounded cryptic. Henry was ready for more details—he needed more information if he was going to be able to help her at all. "Is she still in danger?"

"I don't know if I'd call it that, but I would tell you that her name has passed across a certain elected official's lips more than once, and he's not happy."

"Do you speak of Rob Peterson?"

"I do," Mrs. Lowrey said with a nod. "I've known Rob since

he was in short pants, and I'll tell you that I've never been more proud or flabbergasted by one man in all my days. He's a mass of contradictions, and the power he's obtaining has not served him well."

"What are you saying?"

"I'm saying that I, for one, can see why Anna might be afraid of him. I can understand how many others can be taken in by his easy smiles and effusive charm."

She stepped closer to her car and placed a gloved hand on the roof of it. "There are a lot of people depending on Rob now. He's made promises to important men in the state who are power hungry and ripe for abuses of power. They also believe in his leadership capabilities."

Her excuses sounded far-fetched to Henry. "They'll support such a man, even if they know he means to harm those closest to him?"

Mrs. Lowrey chuckled. "My boy, in my time I've seen men and women do a great many things for what they believe in. Don't get me wrong—some of those things were good, but not all. Like Isaac in the Good Book, men these days don't always do the right thing, and they don't always listen to what they should, either." Lifting her chin, she added, "And, those who follow men like Rob Peterson will believe a lot of lies if it means that they, too, will come out victorious. Sometimes victory is all that matters."

Henry found truth in her words. Even in their community, personalities clashed, and old hurts weren't always immediately forgiven and forgotten.

But that didn't mean he didn't trust Anna, and it didn't mean that she deserved any of what had happened to her.

Yes, the more he'd gotten to know Anna, the more he

was surprised that she'd been so taken in by a man like Rob. Yes, she had a flighty way about her, but she also seemed genuine and true. And gentle with a good heart. Speaking his mind, he said, "Why would a woman like Anna turn to a man like him?"

"I couldn't say, Mr. Brenneman. The same way we all turn to each other, I guess. Sometimes a person just has to trust in the Lord that the people in our paths are meant to be. If we didn't trust anyone, we'd have a very lonely life, now, wouldn't we?"

"I'd say you're right," Henry said quietly. All he had to do was think of Rachel to understand how life was full of surprises. He'd known Rachel all his life, had planned on a future much like his and her parents'. To his way of thinking, she'd wanted no different.

Only afterward had he discovered that she'd wanted far different things in life than he could ever offer, that she'd just kept her dreams hidden, blanketed under an agreeable nature in much the same way as ripe fields lay dormant under a covering of snow.

After another moment, Mrs. Lowery got back in her vehicle and pulled away, the wheels of her car spitting rocks and gravel as she slowly drove down their lane and back onto the highway.

When there was silence again, Henry pocketed the letter and went to the barn. Now would not be the best time to hand Anna the letter. If he pulled her from the chores, it would disrupt her, and the rest of the afternoon.

No, it would be far better to give it to her at a moment when she would have time to quietly read and absorb her parents' note. Nothing done in haste ever came to much, he figured.

After checking on Stanley, Henry flexed his fingers to warm them up a bit, then began the repairs on one of the bedside tables he'd found gathering dust in the attic. With a lot of sanding, polish, and care, Henry felt sure he could restore the table to something of beauty and perhaps even sell it at the next market day.

He decided to pass on the letter to Anna after dinner. "May I have a word with you?" he asked as she helped to clear the table. Katie turned to him curiously, but he determinedly ignored her.

Anna's hands shook. "Um, all right," she said. "Let me just finish up here. Maybe in ten minutes or so?"

Henry nodded, hiding a smile. It was her way—her English way—to constantly refer to the time. So different than the Amish way of thinking, which focused more on chores and work to complete than how long each would take. "It's no hurry," he murmured. "I'll wait for you on the porch."

"On the porch? It's mighty cold out, Henry," Katie said. "Don'tcha think the hearth room would be far better?"

Anna kept her head down. "The porch is fine. I'm, uh, warm right now, and I'll put on a coat, too."

While Henry slipped on his own warm jacket, his father approached. Henry noticed that his father held a fresh branch off one of the oak trees and his whittling knife. Sometimes he carved beautiful canes out of the branches, and Henry sold them at the farmers market every now and then.

"Do I want to know what you are up to?" John asked.

"Probably not."

After checking to see that the swinging door was closed, his daed said, "Are you thinking of courting Anna?"

"No. This is about something far different." He'd wanted to give Anna the letter before sharing the news about the visitor with the rest of the family. It had only seemed right to give her that.

But, because his parents had a right to know what was going on, Henry sought to explain. "A lady came by this afternoon. She brought a letter to Anna from her parents. I want Anna to have some privacy when she reads it."

His father had the same reaction he'd had. "Why do you think her parents didn't come here themselves?"

"I don't know, though I will admit that their absence has brought Anna a fair share of grief. She misses them and needs their support."

"We all need support, I must say." Steepling his hands, his father added, "We all have the Almighty's support always, though. One needs only to ask."

"I hope Anna is doing that. I don't know if she is."

"Trust in the Lord with all thy heart, and lean not unto thine own understanding. In all thy ways acknowledge Him, and He shall direct thy paths."

The quote was a favorite of his father's. He'd quoted it from Proverbs often throughout the years. "Yes, *Daed*. You're right. As always."

That brought forth a fresh taste of laughter. "No, son, I'm not always right at all. But I am of strong enough mind to wish I was! And, to seek comfort and guidance where I might."

"It would serve me well to remember that."

"*Jah*, it would. Of course, you would also need to remember to give thanks for what you have every now and then, as well."

Henry knew where the gentle reminder had come from. Obviously his dissatisfaction with the way his life was had been noticed and discussed. In that, his father was correct, as well. It had been too long since he'd taken the time to give thanks for the things he had—his community, the wonderful world of nature that surrounded them. The opportunity to grow in a loving environment.

One day he would know who the Lord wished him to join with. He knew it as he knew the sun would come up in the morning. The sudden thought of green eyes and blond hair startled him. Was Anna that person? Could she ever be?

Stunned by the thought, he murmured, "*Danke*, Father."

"And thank you, son," his dad said quietly. "Your concern for Anna shows that you've grown up. Your newfound knowledge will serve you well, I am sure of it."

Henry wished he felt half so confident. As it was, his mind was awhirl with doing all he could to try to remember what was the right thing to do.

And since when had he ever struggled with that? He, who'd mistakenly prided himself on always knowing what was right. On knowing better than everyone else. Oh, yes, his pride had surely become his downfall.

Henry had a lot to think about as he put on his black felt hat and thick coat, and walked outside to wait for Anna.

The air was quiet and still. Tonight, it didn't seem as if even the animals felt like making their presence known. Above him, more stars than a man could ever care to count twinkled, offering hope that they'd get a break in the near constant rounds of snow they'd had lately.

Behind him, the door opened.

Like a woodpecker, his heart beat a little faster, calling on the rest of his body to take notice. Anna Metzger affected him like no other.

His father's words still fresh in his mind, Henry battled with his surprise. Was Anna his future?

"Henry? What did you want to discuss? Is anything wrong?"

He wanted to hold her hand and say nothing was wrong. That he had good news for her.

He wanted to take a risk and convey the awkwardness he felt around her. To share his feelings, his questions about her place in his life.

But he didn't dare.

Instead he did as he'd promised. "A woman came by today. Mrs. Beverly Lowery."

Anna swayed on her feet. "I saw you speaking with a woman, but I couldn't see her well from where I was. It was Mrs. Lowery?"

Because she looked to be on the verge of tears, Henry reached out and clasped her shoulders. Finally he escorted her to the pair of chairs in the back corner of the porch. The only spot, really, that wasn't visible from a window in their kitchen or hearth room.

"What did she want?" Anna finally asked. "Where is she?"

"She left soon after she arrived." He could wait no longer. Pulling out the white legal-sized envelope, he handed it to her. "She delivered this."

Anna set it on her lap like its temperature was so hot it

could singe her fingers. "That's my mother's handwriting on the envelope." Eyes wide, she looked at Henry. "What is going on?"

He had no earthly idea. And that, he realized as the verse from Proverbs floated into his mind once again, was exactly the point.

Chapter 12

Anna's hands shook as she held the paper.

Dear Anna,

If you are reading this letter, then Beverly must have made contact with the Brennemans and passed it on to you. For that, I am very grateful.

I can't tell you how relieved we were to hear your message on the machine. Your father and I have been beside ourselves with worry—we've had our doubts from the very beginning that you ever went to Florida. Why did you lie?

Anna cringed. Did they not remember her conversations with them? The way they'd ignored her when she asked for help?

Henry broke his silence. "Anna? You all right?"

"I'm fine." She just needed to remind herself that everyone

hadn't changed. Just because she had over the last month, it didn't mean that they had, too. With that in mind, she continued on.

> *Day after day, we've struggled to figure out what led you to deceive us about your whereabouts. To run, then go into hiding. However, as we've gotten to know Rob Peterson better, we realize there was much about him—and your relationship with him—that we never imagined. Now your father and I feel we understand what led you to run as you did.*

Anna scowled. "If they would have just listened to me before, I would have been so grateful."

"Perhaps you should wait a bit to continue?" Henry stood several feet away, his arms crossed over his chest. But his voice cast a soothing balm over her nerves. Gave her the strength to read more. To read more with an open mind.

"No, this needs to be done."

Perhaps wariness swam in her eyes because Henry, unbidden, stepped closer. "This letter is a *gut* thing, I'm thinkin'."

It was. She was coming to find out truth was always a good thing. Even when it was hard to come to terms with.

"Then what do we do?"

He pointed to the letter that was in danger of being crumpled in her hand. "Finish reading your parents' note."

Eyes burning, she skimmed to where she left off.

> *Anna, your father and I are going to investigate Rob's background more thoroughly. Though we think*

you should stay where you are, we want to continue to correspond. To work together with you to figure how to best free you from him.

We're smarter than we once were, Anna.

"I am too," she murmured.

For reasons we can't understand, Rob is determined to find you. He's searched your room more than once and has taken to following us around. That is why your father and I didn't go to the bed and breakfast to see you. Until we can find someone who is willing to stand up to Rob Peterson and help us, we are afraid to give any hint to where your location is.

Anna, please don't give up on us. Right now your father is meeting with a private investigator who knows everyone in the city. His father is a member of our church, and we feel certain we can trust him.

We will get to you—or send word—as soon as possible.

In the meantime, please know that you are in our thoughts and prayers and that we love you more than you'll ever know. Please continue to be brave, Anna.

Though many miles separate us, you are close in our hearts every waking minute.

Love, Mom

"There's nothing to forgive," she murmured, wishing with all her heart that her parents were there, beside her. "There's nothing to be ashamed of."

Saying those words aloud felt like she'd finally broken free from the last of her guilt. Forgiving her parents—and herself—buoyed her spirits and allowed her to begin to mend some of the many old hurts that had permeated her life of late.

Very slowly, Anna folded the letter back into thirds, then slipped it back into the envelope.

Minutes ran together as they sat on the porch, the cold wind biting their cheeks. She welcomed the sting. It made her feel more alive, stronger. Almost as if she could accomplish anything.

Henry broke the silence. "What did the rest of the letter say?"

"A lot. I'd appreciate it if you would read it, too."

"First, you tell me what you think."

How like Henry to encourage her to once again voice her feelings. "It was full of bad news," she reported, choosing to focus on her mother's words instead of how they made her feel. "Rob's been pestering them. Searching my room. My mother thinks he's been having them followed."

"There has to be some way they can break free of his wrath."

"My dad hired a private investigator. Well, he's talking with one."

She passed on the letter and Henry read it silently. To her surprise, when he finished and placed it back in the envelope, he guided her to one of the rocking chairs. She sat obediently.

Watched as he sat down beside her. And then . . . reached for her hand. To her surprise, she clung to his rough palm like a lifeline. Her pulse raced . . . though was it from the contact or from his empathy?

When their eyes met, he almost smiled. "You neglected to mention all the good parts."

That caught her off guard. "Were there any?"

"I'd say so." Gently, he murmured, "Did you not notice how many times she said she was sorry? Did you not notice how much they care? You haven't lost your parents, Anna." His voice roughened. "I'd venture to say that you've just found them once again. Anna Metzger, you are not alone at all. At the moment, you haven't ever been more surrounded by love and care. Anna, don't you see? You've never been more cared for."

At a loss for words, she focused on his hand in hers. On Henry's body next to hers. On how his strong build and assuring manner calmed her more than she ever thought possible. For whatever reason, she was tempted to lean on him.

With some surprise, she realized maybe she already had. Could that be the reason that she now sat with him so much instead of Katie? Because she needed him?

Or was it because he, too, had known abandonment and rejection? She knew Rachel's departure had hurt him very much. It was easier being open and honest with someone who'd also known heartache—who also knew what it was like to feel betrayed.

Finally she said, "You're right. I should be concentrating on the positives."

"It's difficult, though, isn't it?"

"It is because I don't know what to do. I feel trapped. Like I'm in a hole that's dug too deep to climb out of."

"You're forgetting that there are many ways to get out of such a place. You can build a ladder, ask for a rope, or hope someone will reach down and pull you up."

"I realize now that only with God's help can I get out," she murmured, shocking herself. "But I also know that you've been so helpful to me." She took a risk and met his gaze. "What happened to us, Henry? We used to not like each other."

"We opened our minds, I think."

She swallowed hard. "Sometimes I wish I wasn't going to leave one day."

A new emotion filled his gaze before he replied. "If you want to know the truth, sometimes I wish you wouldn't ever have to leave."

"If I stayed, I'd have to become Amish." To her surprise, the possibility wasn't overwhelming. On the contrary, it only sparked a flicker of curiosity.

What would it be like to become Amish? What would she be giving up?

More to the point, what would she be grabbing hold of?

Henry, as usual, had taken her question and pondered it carefully. "You would need to become Amish. But perhaps . . . it wouldn't be so difficult for you."

"You don't think so?"

He studied her more carefully. "Well, you already look like one of us."

As she spied the humor in his eyes, she laughed. And to her delight, he did, too. "Oh, Henry. I can't believe you're teasing me."

"You shouldn't be surprised. Everything canna be all so serious, Anna."

Their hands separated, and the thick band of tension that had hovered between them dissipated.

Folding her hands in her lap, Anna rocked back as the idea

of becoming Amish settled in. A thousand questions sprang forth. Would she even consider such a thing? She'd heard of people leaving the Amish, but never anyone who joined.

Henry rocked forward. "Anna—"

"Whatever are you two talking about in whispers?" Katie said from around the corner as she joined them on the porch. "It's cold enough out here to wish for an armful of thick goose-down blankets."

"Nothing," Anna lied before thinking.

Henry sprang to his feet. "*Jah*, we were just talking for a bit."

Within seconds, he excused himself, then disappeared into the barn, no doubt eager for the comfort of his work and animals.

For the first time since Anna had known her, Katie wasn't wearing an expression of tenderness and complete acceptance. Instead, she reminded Anna of a mother bear, angry and ready to defend her cub from any nasty intruder. "I've noticed over the last few days that you and my brother have become closer. At first I was mighty happy. The two of you had been at odds with each other since the time you met, and that tension certainly did weigh heavily on my mind."

Katie perched on the chair that Henry had just vacated. "But this . . . sitting in the dark—it is strange." Katie's eyes widened. "Is Henry courting you?"

Anna did her best to keep her expression neutral—not because she was about to laugh, but because she was afraid if she said a word tears would start running down her face.

However, Katie was still waiting for an answer. Anna decided to stick to facts. "You know we couldn't court, even if we wanted to."

"Because you are not Amish."

The earlier conversation with Henry floated closer, imprinted itself. "Exactly."

"But you fit in well now."

"That doesn't matter."

"Doesn't it?" With speculation, Katie eyed Anna with a shrewd expression. "You know much about the outside world, but I know about my brother and I know much about relationships."

Anna seriously doubted that but wisely held her tongue.

Rubbing her arms against the cold, Katie continued. "Perhaps our Lord didn't send you here to merely dress Plain. Maybe you came here in order to live with us and learn. Maybe living here, dressing Plain, adopting our ways . . . maybe it's how you were always intended to live."

Now Anna had no choice but to hold her ground. "Katie, you're making too much of things."

"I think not. Maybe it's time we discussed your future, don'tcha think?"

Unfortunately, Anna had no idea what to say now. So far, she'd had three people deliver far too many surprises. Too many to fully comprehend.

Rob decided to go out to the McClusky General Store himself. William Scott had contacted him again about his displeasure with his bachelor status, and though he'd tried, there was nothing that could ever happen between himself and Tracy. She was too stupid, too yielding, too vain.

The last time he'd taken her out to dinner, she'd worn a gown that had just barely covered her gorgeous figure. When she caused an outburst of attention, he'd caught her preening and enjoying the limelight. Taking the attention away from him.

She would never do.

When his brother-in-law still brought no news about Anna's whereabouts, Rob realized once again he was going to have to do everything himself. Even if he could find a woman to replace her, there was no way he could let her go out of his life without learning exactly how much she knew about his campaign finances. The election board was trying to make a name for itself by combing through each candidate's personal finances. Though he was fairly sure there were no trails showing just where he had spent the money, Rob sure wasn't going to risk the chance that Anna would come out of the woodwork and start talking nonsense about him.

To his left, a herd of cows mooed in a field whose fence was in serious need of repair. In the distance a man rode a horse, the man's hat identifying him as Amish.

Rob gripped the steering wheel of his Mercedes just a little bit harder, the action turning his knuckles white and igniting his temper all over again.

The Amish. Now there was a group of tax-evading backward folk. If he had his way, he'd put every one of them back into society and make them do their part for the economy.

How Anna could even think of associating with such people was beyond him.

After three wrong turns, Rob finally pulled into the lot of McClusky General Store. He parked off to the side, as far as possible from the buggies and horses situated near the entrance. The last thing he needed was a bunch of horse manure dirtying his wheels.

After stepping aside so two overweight women could

clamber down the steps, Rob pasted his "public" smile on his face and did his best to look genial.

The man behind the counter, dressed in an old flannel shirt and worn khakis, looked up when he approached. "May I help you?"

"Maybe." He held out a hand. "Rob Peterson. I'm running for U.S. Representative."

"Sam McClusky." The man shook his hand. "I'd say you're a far sight from home. Too far to be campaigning. And since the Amish don't vote, I'm wondering what your thinking is. What brings you out to these parts?"

Contrary to what the man looked to be, he obviously wasn't a fool. Rob tap-danced a reply. "Not too much. You know how the campaign life can be. So much pressure. Just thought I'd take the time and look around."

The proprietor's shoulders relaxed, though speculation still ran deep in his gaze. "Then this is a very good place to do that. Take your time."

When two men stood behind him, Rob stepped to the side and wondered again how he was going to find out anything.

He wandered the country store, which was an eclectic mix of old and new. Giant canisters of baking mixes and cereal were available for people to buy in bulk. On shelves in the back, kerosene lamps and boxes of candles were available for purchase.

Near the front was a vast selection of homemade canned vegetables and fruit. Apple butter and jars of cider kept company with spicy-looking relishes and pickle spears.

The store wasn't especially crowded. An Amish family was near the baked goods, two daughters who couldn't be much over eight were dressed exactly like their mother. A couple of tourists were talking to the owner now. He was giving them directions to some inn.

When the other man caught his eye, Rob knew he had to either buy something fast or leave. On a whim, he picked up three jars of honey, thinking the jars a fitting purchase since he was about to be sweeter than he'd ever been.

"That all?"

"It is. These are going to make nice gifts."

"They will indeed. Nothing like the taste of homegrown honey."

Rob pulled out a pair of tens and handed them over. "Where might a guy go to relax around here?"

The elder man's mustache twitched. "To relax, hmm? Depends what you want to do, I'd reckon."

"Nothing too out of the ordinary. Sit around, sip a cup of coffee. Learn more about the people out here." Even Rob knew he didn't sound convincing. Passing over a better smile, he added, "I'm really interested in the folks around here. Any chance these Amish will accept strangers in their midst?"

"You interested in becoming Plain?"

Rob was a seasoned politician, and he knew exactly when to tell the truth and when to lie through his teeth. It was the time to tread carefully here. "Not in this lifetime. But I am interested in what might drive a person to leave society to do such a thing. Have you ever heard of anyone doing that? Becoming Amish?"

"No."

"Come on," he prodded, his voice heavy on the Karo syrup. "No one new ever comes and stays awhile?"

"I didn't say that." McClusky eyed him a little more closely, obviously trying to read his mind.

Rob let him look his share. He was used to people trying to figure him out. What they didn't realize was that he could do the same thing a whole lot better. He'd gotten far in life telling people what they wanted to hear. And they all wanted to hear something—every last one.

Carefully putting the honey in a paper sack, McClusky continued. "Well, like anyone else, the Amish have relatives from all over. Some have moved away in order to buy more land. Lots have moved here to Ohio from Pennsylvania way. Land is expensive to purchase."

"Have you seen any new to the area lately?"

"No."

Rob pulled out three hundred-dollar bills. Setting them on the counter in between them, the crisp bills practically begged to be picked up. "Are you sure you haven't seen a woman here, new to the area? She has beautiful green eyes. Very unusual."

The man's expression became a blank mask. "I don't know what you are looking for, but you won't find it here." He pushed the Benjamins back to Rob. "It's time you left."

Recognition had flickered in McClusky's expression when he had mentioned green eyes. He knew something, Rob was sure of it. Fun and games are over. "My fiancée ran away. Her name's Anna Metzger. Her parents are frantic for her. We think she got involved in drugs. She might even have brought her dealer or her supply into this county. She's dangerous. If you see her, contact me. Or better yet, contact Sheriff Grant." Rob passed over another card. "You'd hate a woman like that tainting anything here in God's country. You'd hate to be blamed for a whole community's ruin because you couldn't stand the truth. Because you refused to tell the truth." Lowering his voice to a whisper, Rob said, "I know I'm right."

"Go. Now."

"I will, but I'm coming back." Rob left the bills on the counter and walked off. But inside he felt triumphant. The man had seen Anna.

Finally, finally, he was on the right track. In no time, he'd get Anna, Scott would get off his back, and things would be back to normal.

Chapter 13

Katie had been unnaturally quiet all day. Well, that wasn't exactly true, Anna allowed. Katie had been quiet around her, and her alone.

Anna wondered what she'd done, exactly, that had made her friend so standoffish. The conversation the night before about Henry and adopting the Amish way of life? Perhaps it had more to do with her continued presence at the bed and breakfast, taking up space and getting in the way. Though Katie had been nothing but gracious, she was also human. It was only natural to be tired of a houseguest.

After Anna finished drying the last of the platters from breakfast and put them away, she decided to go find out what she could do to make things better. Anna was well aware of her flaws, and they included being unable to wait for others to come to her. She couldn't handle Katie's cold shoulder.

And, if she'd learned anything over the last month, it was that hiding true, honest feelings was never a good thing.

She found Katie in the hearth room, attaching a collar to a shirt. Beside her was a basket of quilt fabrics for her Center Diamond quilt. The carefully cut pieces of black, cherry red, evergreen, and cobalt blue regally waited to be stitched together. "Hi."

Katie barely looked up. "Hello, Anna."

Though she hadn't been invited, she approached and sat down next to her. "You've been avoiding me all day, Katie. Why?"

Blue eyes widened as she neatly tucked the needle into the fabric. "Why would you ask such a thing?"

"Because you haven't seemed yourself." Anna felt like pointing to the fabric currently getting scrunched under Katie's usually nimble hands. Anyone who knew Katie would realize such behavior was out of character. "I'm worried you're upset with me."

"That's not true." After carefully smoothing out the fabric, Katie pushed the needle through the cloth once again.

"All right." Anna tried to believe Katie, but she didn't at all. Katie's expression and tone screamed uneasiness. "Would you tell me if you were troubled?"

"Of course I would."

"Okay. Well, I'll leave you alone, then," Anna said, afraid to push any harder.

Just as she stood to walk away, Katie tossed the shirt on the table. "I'm mighty *naerfich* nervous about your relationship with my brother Henry," she blurted.

There was only one thing Anna could say. "I know you are."

"You're not going to deny what I've seen?"

"No." Anna owed Katie that much . . . though truthfully, she didn't know what had been going on between the two of them. Not really.

Katie raised her head. "Henry's already had his *rumschpringe*. Did he tell you that? He is not eager to live among the English again."

"I know. Once more, I have no desire to make him leave you or your family. This community is where he belongs— anyone could see that."

"Anyone?"

Katie's posture was like a mother cub defending her own. Anna wondered just how many other people knew that Katie Brenneman was far stronger than most would ever imagine! "Anyone," Anna repeated. "Even me."

"Then you should leave him alone."

"Katie, I'm not a scarlet woman attempting to draw him from all he holds near and dear!"

"I do know that you've been a mite too forward with him. His eyes have strayed."

"I can't help that."

"Of course you can. We all can control our desires for the sake of living peacefully together." Chin up, Katie said, "Surely you wouldn't disagree?"

Quickly, Anna looked to the door, afraid someone would overhear them. Then she attempted to explain herself. "Everything that has happened between Henry and me has been mutual. I think he's enjoyed my company as much as I've enjoyed his. But we're just friends. Don't you see?"

"No. I am sorry, but I do not. I see a light that shines in his eyes when he sees you. Whenever you enter the room. He's hurting from Rachel, don'tcha see?"

"I'm not Rachel, and I'm not responsible for his past hurts. Can't you imagine what I'm going through? I've been hiding out for weeks here. Taking your hospitality. Worried about my parents. Worried that I've brought it all on you."

"But you're still here."

There it was. "Are you asking me to leave?"

A stricken expression entered Katie's face, but she didn't reply. Because in the doorway was Irene Brenneman.

"Whatever is going on here, girls?"

"We're merely having a discussion," Katie mumbled.

Irene raised a brow. "And quite a discussion, too, I'd say. Anna, dear, what's this I heard about you thinking it's time to leave?"

Katie's face went white as Anna hastily sat back down. She didn't know what to say. Already too much had been spoken aloud, perhaps she should now just say nothing.

With a guilty look toward Anna, Katie spoke. "Her leaving would be my doing, *Mamm*. I know she's turned Henry's head and it's not fair."

Irene looked from Anna to Katie, then finally clasped her hands together and nodded slowly. "Yes, I can see how you would worry about our Henry . . . seeing how he has no mind of his own."

If she'd intended for the words to have shock value, Anna thought Irene Brenneman had hit pay dirt. Both her head and Katie's had snapped to attention so hard she was surprised neither of them was complaining of whiplash.

"Anna, I, too, have seen the way Henry has watched you. Have you not?"

"There's a connection between us that is hard to deny," Anna admitted, "But I promise I'm not trying to hurt him.

Or any of you." With all her heart, she wanted to repeat the conversation they'd shared the night before, but she didn't dare. Henry was too private to embarrass him that way. It was also his place to speak to his family, not hers.

"You would hurt us all if he left the order to be with you," Irene agreed. "We'd deeply regret that, though we wouldn't try to stop him."

With a look of wonder at her mother, Katie whispered, "You wouldn't try?"

"You can't force a person to believe something they don't— just like you can't make someone *lieb* you if they don't."

Katie folded her hands across her chest. "I'm learning that myself."

"There's really only one thing to do if you and Henry are really fit for each other," Irene said, her words sounding as if they came from deep within her heart, from a place where only true feelings lay and honest emotions reigned.

And that made Anna nervous. "What is that?"

"You could join us, dear Anna. You . . . could become Amish."

Three conversations in three days. It was time to open her heart and listen to what the Lord was asking her to do. Was it to stay?

Or was it to go back where she came from and try to unravel the relationships with her parents and friends?

Both choices sounded difficult and hard to accomplish.

"I feel ridiculous," Calvin said as they pulled out of the Enterprise Rental Car lot. "Meredith, we have no idea what we're doing."

Meredith privately agreed, but didn't voice her opinions.

"Calvin, all we're doing is taking every necessary precaution."

"Every necessary precaution involves buckling seat belts and making sure we have enough gasoline. What you've reduced us to is mind boggling."

That was true, but it was also true that they were out of options. The initial meeting with a private investigator had been eye-opening. He'd made it clear that it would be virtually impossible to check on Anna unnoticed, and he also detailed the extremely dangerous job it would be to tail someone of Rob Peterson's wealth and influence.

All of it also sounded extremely expensive with few guarantees of learning more than what they already knew.

After much discussion, they decided to go retrieve Anna themselves. They'd waited long enough, and things weren't about to get any easier.

So they rented a car and bought some frumpy-looking clothes. Now they didn't look Plain or even like Mennonites, but Meredith had a feeling that one of their acquaintances might walk past them before taking a closer examination.

She sure didn't recognize herself. For the first time since she'd become a teenager, she wasn't wearing any makeup. Instead of styling her hair and curling it, she'd left it to dry naturally, then tied it into a small ponytail at the nape of her neck.

Instead of her usual bright pinks and reds, she wore a modestly cut chambray blue blouse, neatly tucked into an ankle-length skirt. Loafers and a thick black coat completed her outfit.

As for Calvin, his slacks and shirt looked like any in his closet. But his shoes were sturdy instead of designer and his coat was serviceable and thick.

Gone were the contacts he'd worn for the last fifteen years. In their place were thick glasses. The wire rims changed his appearance more than anything, bringing a casual observer's eye to the lines around his lips and eyes.

"We look older. A lot older." Meredith had to smile—for the first time in her life, she had made getting older sound like a good thing!

Calvin grimaced. "At this moment, I certainly feel older. I feel like we've aged ten years over the last month." As they headed up I-75, he shook his head. "What if we're followed?"

"I think that's a chance we're going to have to take. Anna needs us, and we need her."

"If we bring Rob to the Brennemans, I won't be able to forgive myself."

Meredith frowned. "I already can't forgive myself. This will just add to our list of problems. All I do know is that if Rob finds her before we even take a risk—well, that would be even harder to bear."

The skies turned dark, making the February afternoon seem more gloomy than usual. "Snow's on the way," Henry stated with a frown. "I best go prepare the parking lot and make sure we have plenty of wood for the fireplace."

"I'll see what your mom would like me to do," Anna said through her haze. Sometime during the night before, the cold and stress had compounded and given her a doozy of a head cold. Now it felt like she had weights settling on her sinuses and enough aches and pains to feel like she'd gone five rounds in the boxing ring.

With a wry smile, Henry patted her shoulder. "Perhaps

you should consider resting instead, Anna. You don't look too well."

His criticism stung, though she knew he was absolutely right. She didn't look well. Vanity kicked in for the moment, and she wished she had a bit of makeup to cover the dark circles under her eyes or a bit of powder to hide some of the redness of her nose. "I hate not to do my part."

"You would end up not doing your part if you continue as you are right now. Our guests probably wouldn't fancy their meals served by a sickly Amish lady." A teasing smile lit his eyes. "I don't know why."

Anna refrained from saying another word to that, because she knew he was absolutely right. With a sigh, she sat back down on the rocker in the hearth room. Carefully, she pinned a black rectangle to the main square that would serve as the focal point for the whole quilt. As usual, the painstaking work brought her joy—she truly enjoyed piecing together the bits of cloth, to make a beautiful creation out of scraps of leftover fabric.

Anna also used the time to wonder what the future had in store for her. Around her, she heard the handful of guests talking in the parlor as they prepared to go for a hike in the wooded trails before the snow started falling.

In the kitchen, Mrs. Brenneman had two lady friends over. They were making potato casseroles for the inn and for a family whose daughter was sick and in the hospital. Above her, Katie was bustling as good-naturedly as ever in one of the guest rooms.

And with some surprise, Anna realized that she fit in. Not just because she blended in and no longer looked like a fancy girl. No, she fit in because she appreciated the way of life, and appreciated her role in the household. Before her bout with the flu, she had done her part to help with the inn.

Time and again, Irene had praised her work ethic, which was high praise indeed, for the Amish were notoriously hard workers and not given to handing out compliments for things expected.

What was going to happen with her and Henry? Was he her future? How had their rocky relationship turned into something far different? Something special and fulfilling? Now, she caught herself admiring his capable ways. Admired his blunt way of speaking. Appreciated the way his shoulders were broad and how his gentle ways meshed nicely with his very handsome looks.

She'd felt a tingling of awareness when their eyes caught sight of each other. When they both forgot to look away and allowed a bit of heat and interest to spark.

Was this how it was meant to be?

Not for the first time, Anna wondered if the Lord had guided her to the Brennemans. Oh, she'd gone at first for selfish reasons, to seek refuge in the one place she knew she would be safe. But since then, she'd traded much of her selfish and lazy ways for a more productive and giving nature.

No, it hadn't been easy. But wasn't the Bible full of stories of average men and women who didn't always listen to God the first time? Who needed to be reminded time and again to pay heed to His signs?

Could she leave her old life? Could she leave the modern necessities? The hectic lifestyle she'd thought she'd thrived on, the trips and worldly possessions she'd always thought she needed?

But more important, could she adopt the Amish way

of life, the true way of life, in which religion wasn't just a Sunday activity but something that intertwined through every day, through every waking moment?

She rocked some more. Threaded a needle and began to stitch. Worried about impulsivity. Worried about making a quick decision based on all the wrong things.

Was she suddenly excited about the change in lifestyle because she'd discovered that there'd been a whole other life hidden in her heart, just waiting to be recognized and nurtured?

Or was she still seeking refuge from Rob and from the disappointment in her relationship with her parents and the lack of success in the outside world?

That thought brought her up short. Was she really that shallow?

Days ago, she would have said yes. Of course, days ago—a mere month ago, she wouldn't have taken the time to reflect. No, she would have only concentrated on the things she wanted and the things she couldn't have, never mind the consequences. Yep, she'd been very good at that.

As the flames flickered in the fireplace in front of her, she allowed her eyes to drift shut. At the same time, Anna allowed her mind to relax and feel the guiding hand of the Lord nurture her.

And feel it she did. At once she felt peace and compassion—not just for others, but for herself. Perhaps that was what she'd needed? To accept herself and all her faults . . . but to also accept that she wasn't all bad. That she had a lot of worthwhile qualities?

* * *

"Anna? Anna wake up," Katie said from the doorway.

She struggled to focus her groggy brain. "I'm sorry, I must've fallen asleep. Do you need help? I can go—"

"No, Anna, it's something else." Worriedly, Katie stepped from one foot to the other, as if she wasn't sure whether to join Anna in the hearth room or to encourage her to get up and leave.

Truly curious now, Anna stood up and hastily folded the quilt. "What's wrong?"

Katie's expression turned miserable. "You have visitors, Anna."

The words hit her like a sledgehammer, just as she turned to the doorway and gasped.

Chapter 14

It took a moment, but Anna found her voice. However, what she spoke was far from earth shattering. "You came."

"We did." Flashing a smile, her mother stepped forward. "We couldn't stay away another minute, even if coming here was dangerous."

"We've been so worried about you, Anna," her father added.

"I know." But, really . . . did she?

Anna supposed she should feel compelled to run into their arms. To reclaim everything between she and her parents that she'd thought she lost.

But instead, she stood staring at them . . . just as they did her. They looked nothing like their familiar selves. Her mother was always perfectly coifed and made-up. So much so that Anna had once compared her to a doll to her friend

Julie when they were teenagers. Now, though, her mother's drab, shapeless clothes made her look every bit of her fifty-some-odd years.

Her dad's glasses magnified the wrinkles around his eyes. And, had he always had so much gray hair at his temples?

Or, maybe their awkwardness had very little to do with outfits and everything to do with the circumstances of the situation. Never had Anna imagined that she would be dressed Plain, hiding out from an abusive congressional candidate in an Amish bed and breakfast.

Poor Katie darted worried looks her way and wrung her hands. Henry appeared, guided them all into the room, then offered his hand. "I am Henry Brenneman."

Her dad shook it. "Calvin Metzger. This is my wife, Meredith."

They were all speaking to each other so formally. So businesslike. Not like her parents usually spoke to her. Not like Henry usually did. And she was the worst of all, Anna realized. She knew everyone. Had depended on each person at one time or another. And still, there she stood, as motionless as that hare in the meadow she and Henry had once spied.

Henry continued the social graces as if he was accustomed to doing such things every day. "And this here is my sister, Katie."

Her mother nodded in Katie's direction. "We . . . we know each other. From when Anna took that quilting class." Anna noticed that still her mother hadn't taken her eyes off her.

Of course, Anna hadn't been able to look away, either.

Always proper, Katie cleared her throat. "Anna, are you all right?"

A month ago she would have smiled and said she was. A day ago she would have said everything was not all right, and maybe would never be that way again.

But as of right that minute, Anna couldn't really say how she was feeling. Words garbled in her brain as her two worlds collided—her past, filled with missed opportunities and an aimlessness she couldn't escape. Her life with the Brennemans, filled with hard work, a loving, bustling family, and Henry.

Henry!

She took a deep breath; let His sense of peace flow through her. Suddenly, everything became very clear. It was time to step forward into her new life, and accept all the challenges that came with it. It was time to stop hiding.

Her dad's tone turned stern. "Anna, what is wrong with you? Katie just asked you a question."

"No, I'm not all right."

Her mother swayed and reached out for her father. Katie inhaled quickly.

Only Henry looked her way in understanding. Only Henry wrapped his hand around her shoulder. Touching her in a way that made her realize she wasn't alone. Not here. Not in her heart. She had him, and even more important, she had God's guiding hand.

For a moment, she met his gaze. In his eyes, she saw acceptance and pride. Hope and . . . love?

She tried again. "I mean. I'm not okay but I think I will be." Stepping forward, she reached out for her parents just as Henry's hand fell from her shoulder, leaving a cool imprint of loss.

"Perhaps Katie and I should leave you," he said. "Or would you rather I stay, Anna?"

It wasn't a hard question. As a matter of fact, it really shouldn't matter at all, whether he stay or go. But for the life of her, it felt like a monumental decision was about to take place. "Please stay."

Her father frowned. "Honestly, Anna—"

Henry interrupted. "Mr. and Mrs. Metzger, I think I'll be staying, if you two don't mind."

Her dad looked like he did mind, very much. His eyes narrowed as Henry's hand reached for her hand, showing all of them that there was more to their relationship than any of them might have ever suspected.

As Katie slipped out of the room, Meredith broke into a strained grin. "That's fine. Fine."

Henry took the lead. "Perhaps we should all sit down." Once again, his hand was a guiding force, gently propelling her to a chair. Her parents sat across from them, in the love seat John and Irene Brenneman enjoyed so much. Henry took a seat in an oak ladder-back chair.

For better or worse, Anna needed to hold herself accountable and be ready to face the consequences, even overwhelming ones. Yet, she also couldn't hide or withhold her feelings. She'd spent too many evenings in the quiet of her room, with only her thoughts for company as she worked on her Diamond Square quilt. During those quiet times, she'd dwelled on a lifetime of things she wished she could change. On a lifetime of things she wished were different. Of her faults and her weaknesses.

However, she knew it was a mistake to claim all responsibility. Rob was at fault, too.

But she also harbored resentment toward her parents. And though she could forgive their actions, she also knew she would never forgive herself if she didn't vocalize some of her feelings. "I didn't think you were coming. I didn't think you cared."

"We did." Calvin visibly choked out the words. "You know we care about you, Anna. We always have."

Then why did they try so hard to disguise their feelings all the time? "Your letter said that you couldn't get away."

"Our letter said we didn't dare try and come here," her mother corrected. "However, it didn't change what was in our hearts. And it couldn't change the very fact that we love you and miss you."

Though she didn't contradict their words, Anna knew that her feelings showed through her expression. And no matter how hard she tried to pretend otherwise, she couldn't help herself. In short, she had needed their support and understanding, and the evening before she'd left for the Brennemans', they'd been anything but supportive of her.

By her side, Henry said nothing, but she felt him stiffen. She knew what he thought—that it was time to practice forgiveness. To feel for them and to bear in mind that this whole experience hadn't been easy for anyone involved.

Quietly, her father spoke. "Anna, I know you don't want to believe us because we certainly haven't been there for you in the past. That's something we can't change, no matter how much we would like to do so."

Leaning forward, Meredith said, "I am sorry, Anna. If I could turn back time, I would."

Her mother's words shamed her, and brought her out of her pity party.

Hadn't she planned to show them and herself just how far she'd come from the self-centered person she'd once been?

How easy it would be to let them shoulder all the blame! Let them shoulder everything, and let herself pretend she was completely innocent.

But sometime in between the afternoon she'd knocked on the door and now, Anna knew she'd grown up. She'd matured into the type of woman who put others before herself. Who was able to face the truth even when the truth wasn't good at all. "I'm sorry, too. I know I've worried you," she said quietly.

"Even though it may not seem like it, we've been on your side."

"You've been there for me time and time again."

"Not when you needed us most."

After receiving an encouraging nod from Henry, Anna said, "Living here, living this way, being with the Brennemans— well, it's given me time to think. A lot of time to think."

"Much to all of our dismay," Henry said, surprising them all with a much-needed bit of levity.

Anna smiled. "I think everything happened for a reason. The life I was living wasn't a good one, Mom."

Meredith held up a hand, and Anna waved her off. "Mom, I know you like Rob, but he's dangerous. Yes, his friends are influential and not all of them are bad. But *he* was. He was controlling and wrong." She couldn't bear to say abusive. She didn't want to place that burden on her parents' shoulders.

"We don't think he's the one for you anymore," her dad said.

"Actually, we found out pretty quickly there were a lot of things about him that we didn't want to see. A lot of things hidden under his very handsome face and shiny personality." Meredith fought a shiver. "He came to the house. Several times, actually. When he searched your room, he took a bunch of your photo albums."

Anna could barely get her arms around the idea that Rob had not only been in her room, but had rifled through her belongings. "I wonder why he took the albums. Did he say why?"

"He didn't give us very many explanations, Anna, and the explanations he did give hardly made sense." Scooting to the end of the sofa, Meredith looked first at Henry, then met Anna's gaze. "But one thing I know for certain is that he's determined to find you, Anna. He's so determined that he's stopped over time and again."

"And each time he's spoken to us, he's become more angry and threatening," her father finished. "This is beyond a need to see you . . . he's become a desperate man."

"I knew he was becoming more violent. I just didn't know how to stop him."

"I don't know if you could have. He seems to be on his own path . . . and each time we've talked with him, he's surer than ever that we're hiding you and keeping you from him."

"We had begun to worry that he was just putting on an act, that maybe he'd done something with you, or that you'd injured yourself or come to real harm hiding from him."

Meredith blinked back tears. "Thank goodness Miriam saw you."

"I guess you realized I wasn't in Florida right away?"

"Only after we talked to Rob the first time. That's when I went in your room and did some checking on my own."

"Your mother's been calling old friends, too."

Thinking of the many people she'd pushed away . . . not

wanting to deal with Rob's wrath, Anna swallowed hard. "Did you speak to anyone?"

"We talked to a lot of people. The most illuminating was Julie."

Julie. Her old friend whom Anna had practically abandoned. "I'm surprised she didn't hang up on you when she found out why you called. I haven't been very good to her."

"She was worried about you."

"We think Rob is close to locating you."

Henry leaned forward. "You think he knows Anna's here?"

"I do. Someone told us he went to the McClusky General Store. There is a very good chance someone there might have given your location away."

"That could have happened," Henry said. "This is a close-knit community, for sure."

He had found her. The room began to spin. Once again, Henry came to her rescue, wrapping an arm around her shoulders.

"Anna?" he murmured in her ear, holding her close. "Anna, you okay?"

She reached out for him, she couldn't help it. Henry Brenneman was the antithesis of Rob. In her mind, he'd become a symbol of what was good and decent in the world, and she needed that, and him, desperately.

When she noticed her parents watching her in alarm, Anna attempted to explain. "I'm sorry . . . it's just that I've been in the store."

"Don't you think that was foolish, Anna?" her dad asked. "If you were trying to hide, like you said, you should have stayed hidden."

"Anna going to McClusky's wasna all that unusual, to my thinking," Henry explained. "All of us Amish shop there." Anna liked how he included her in the grouping. Her father must have noticed it, too, because he widened his eyes, though he said nothing more.

"I can't believe I could have run into him." A shudder coursed through her at the thought. "I don't know what I would have done if that had happened."

"But it didn't, did it?" Henry said softly. "Do not be so hard on yourself, Anna. Don't borrow trouble."

His words and his kindness gave her comfort. "I'll try not to."

Hoping to lighten up the conversation, she pointed to the worn chambray shirt and ugly beige skirt her mother was wearing. If she hadn't been so shocked to see her parents, she would have asked her mom right away how she had managed to pick out something that was so very unflattering. "So, Mom, what's with the outfit?"

Meredith chuckled. "Well . . . you know how I usually dress. I thought maybe my usual attire of pants and bright pink sweater might be a little much."

"So you thought to blend in?"

Anna chuckled. Even Henry was getting into the teasing mode. Everything was going to be okay! "Mom, you could blend in with an oak tree . . . that skirt is so big and flowy."

Her dad chuckled. "You'd never believe it, but we did try to be inconspicuous."

"And sneaky," her mother added.

"Well, as sneaky as we could possibly be. We rented a car and tried to disguise ourselves. Mainly, we hoped we just

wouldn't be instantly recognizable. Or instantly remembered for standing out," her mom said.

"We were also afraid Rob would follow us."

Anna was touched and genuinely surprised. "You do care."

"Of course we care. We love you, Anna."

The words felt good. They were so needed. So very needed
and helped fill a gap in her heart that had been forced open.
Standing up, she ran to her mother and knelt in front of her,
wrapping her arms around her mom's waist, just like she
used to do when she was small.

Her mother automatically curved her arms around Anna
and patted her back. "Please don't worry anymore. Please
don't worry, Anna. Everything's going to be okay."

For the first time in a long time, Anna dared to think
that, too.

Nothing was going right. Nothing was going according
to plan. Rob Peterson closed his eyes against the pounding headache, just as Omar the taxi driver took a turn too
quickly and Rob practically slid across the backseat. "Watch
it!" he snapped.

"You said you were in a hurry. I'm getting you to your
place as quickly as possible."

"I want to be in one piece, though." He also didn't want to
attract attention. Though he had no doubt he could talk his
way out of any situation, explaining his presence in the back
of a taxi in the middle of Amish country might be stretching
things a bit far.

Rob held on as the driver flew over a deep ridge in the
road, then braked quickly in order not to charge into a horse

and buggy. The horse neighed and the woman driving stared at them in alarm.

"Hey!" Rob yelled. "You're going to kill somebody if you don't watch out."

Omar met his eyes in the rearview mirror. "Relax, mister. I'm not about to kill anyone today."

Today? A chill rushed down Rob's spine that had nothing to do with the frigid temperatures seeping through the ramshackle vehicle and everything to do with a strong sense of foreboding. Omar seemed unstable. It was a mistake to pay him a thousand dollars to make the trip. He should have found another way to get to Anna. As they zipped past yet another yellow sign emblazoned with a horse and buggy on it, Rob tightened his seat belt and attempted to put his mind on something else. Anything else.

Just as he'd been about to buy a tourist map and start knocking on doors to look for Anna, his worthless brother-in-law had come through. After two weeks of questioning, Grant had found the taxi driver who'd run Anna up to Amish country. And what's more, he'd threatened his green card so well that Omar was willing to do just about anything to make sure he could keep his job. Well, anything that involved being paid a grand or two.

Rob was really grateful for the recent windfall of campaign contributions, otherwise he would have had to dig into his savings account to pay off Omar.

As they practically skidded to a stop at a stop sign next to a plain white clapboard house, Rob snapped, "How much longer?"

"Ten minutes. More or less."

Rob rolled his eyes, then gripped the seat again as Omar

pulled out into the intersection and sped past yet another buggy, this one carrying an Amish lady and three little girls. All three wore violet dresses, black capes, and black bonnets. He might have found the sight touching if not for the fact that each one of them reminded Rob of what he'd lost.

Correction. Almost lost.

He bit back the impulse to ask again how much longer the ride would be, fearing Omar would joke about him sounding like a child on a car trip.

"It's pretty here, don't you think?" Omar murmured.

"If you like snow-covered corn fields."

"Ah, but in the summer, the sights are far different. Knee high by the Fourth of July, right?"

"That's what they say," Rob replied, wondering how on earth the guy knew such a quaint expression.

Then, just when Rob couldn't take another minute of their joyride, Omar slowed. "This is it," he said, slowing the car down.

Rob peered out the window. There, in all its glory, stood a neatly painted oak sign, with the words *Brenneman Bed and Breakfast* carved in block letters. "This has to be it."

Omar swung onto the gray graveled road, taking no heed that rocks flew around them like fireflies in the summer. Stones sprayed the windshield, but Omar didn't seem to mind.

The road leading up to the house seemed about a mile long. In the distance, a large two-story building neatly trimmed in black awaited them. The front porch held four large white rocking chairs.

On a clothesline in the back hung two navy-colored dresses and one bright red, black, and orange quilt.

"This is a nice place," Omar observed. "I remember seeing a pair of black horses last time I was here."

The guy acted like that would be a quite a sight. Hadn't he noticed the horses he'd just about run over? "Whatever," Rob murmured, glancing at his watch. "Park over by the side, in that parking lot, but don't go anywhere."

"Where would I go?" For the first time, Omar's pleasant expression wasn't so pleasant. In fact, it looked almost . . . resentful. Full of animosity.

A prickle of distrust hit Rob hard. Just how desperate was this guy? Desperate enough to go against him even though he'd pocketed half of his money? "Just be ready. I'm going to have a woman with me."

"How long is this going to take?"

With any luck, no time at all. But so far, things hadn't been so lucky at all. "Thirty minutes, tops."

"If it's over an hour, I'm going to charge you double."

The guy was such an idiot. Did he really think Rob was going to give him any more than he already had? "If it's over an hour, you can shoot me," Rob joked. "There's no way I want to be here longer than I have to."

Tires crunched as Omar pulled into the parking lot. On the far side, a black-and-white cow stared at them in interest. Rob hardly spared it a glance. As soon as the car stopped, he opened his door and got out, cold air making his eyes water for the first few seconds.

Right away the smell of manure, cows, and horses surrounded him. A chicken or turkey or something squawked a welcome. Quickly Rob checked his Italian loafers. The last thing he wanted was to step in something and ruin the expensive leather.

Buttoning his overcoat, he was finally about to do what he'd been trying to do for the last month: retrieve Anna.

From behind him, Omar stepped out of the taxi and leaned up against it. A second later, the sweet smell of a cigar floated forward.

As Rob stomped along, taking care to avoid icy slick spots that hadn't been shoveled all that well, it hit him that Omar hadn't laughed at his joke. On the contrary, he acted like he might just have a gun . . . and that he knew how to use it.

Once again, Rob cursed Anna Metzger. She was going to pay for this episode. She was going to pay if it was the last thing he—or Omar—ever did.

Chapter 15

"Excuse me, ma'am. I'm looking for Anna Meztger. Is she here?"

The words carried all the way from the front entryway into the hearth room where Anna, Henry, and her parents sat. Even from that distance, Anna knew the voice.

Rob Peterson had found her.

Across from Anna, her mother stiffened. "Calvin, get up! We've got to do something."

Dutifully, Calvin stood up. Henry did, as well. But Anna knew it was time for her to step forward. "I'll go talk to him," she said, rising from the couch.

Her mother reached for her hand. "Anna, you will do no such thing. Sit back down and stay here."

"No, Mom. He came to see me."

Calvin scowled. "Don't be foolish."

"I'm not being foolish at all," Anna protested mildly. "This is what I need to do." For the first time since she'd gone into hiding, Anna didn't fear Rob or what the future might bring.

Perhaps she'd finally grown up.

But more likely, Anna thought it was that she'd found quite a bit while hiding from Rob. She'd discovered an old friend in Katie. She'd tested and pushed the boundaries of love with her parents and had realized that there was a stronger connection than she'd ever given credence to.

With Henry, she'd discovered love can come slowly, patiently, and not be the by-product of fierce passion and whispered promises, but by the steady security in knowing you are valued as a complete, whole child of God.

Truthfully, that was what Anna discovered the most. During the long days and quiet nights, she'd taken to reading the Bible with the Brennemans. By their example, she'd soon discovered that it was possible to walk daily with the Lord. And in so doing, she'd discovered a great many things she used to take for granted.

Now she found herself recognizing "God moments" in her life. She found herself enjoying nature more. She found herself valuing all things, not just the activities or items that relieved her boredom or gave her a much-needed jolt of energy and excitement.

"I'll be okay," she said softly to Henry. To her pleasure, he nodded and let her pass.

And, as Anna took that long walk toward Rob and her past, she realized she was, indeed, going to be just fine.

Rob smirked when she joined him in the entryway. "Anna, if I didn't recognize those remarkable eyes of yours, I might've walked right by you."

To her surprise, she no longer feared his words or his hand. "Why are you here?"

He looked nervously about, but Anna wasn't sure if his unease came from the arrival of her parents and the whole Brenneman family, or from her new attitude.

She privately hoped it was her. No longer was she submissive. Cowed. No longer was she blinded by his slick good looks or the promise of a diamond ring. Here, surrounded by all the people she loved, Anna felt different in his company, like she could stand up straighter. Speak with a little more force. She now had an inner core of strength that sustained her like nothing she had recognized in her past.

Ignoring everyone surrounding them, Rob said, "I came for you, Anna. We need to talk."

"Go ahead."

Out came the campaign smile. "Not here. Come home with me and we'll get you back where you belong, out of those ridiculous clothes. I've got a taxi outside waiting."

"I'm not going anywhere with you."

"I didn't come for a visit, Anna. I came to retrieve you, and I'm going to do that." His eyes narrowed. Eyes so magnetic and such a dark gray, she'd once thought she could read his mind, just from one of his smoldering looks.

Now she knew she hadn't read anything truthful. "No, Rob, you're not going to 'retrieve' me."

"Don't cross me. It's been a rough month. I've spent more time and money than I care to say looking for you."

"You shouldn't have wasted your time—or the taxpayers' money. Whatever we had was over. Is over, and has been for quite a while."

"I don't know why you're talking that way."

"You hurt me, Rob."

"I barely touched you."

"Barely" didn't quite describe the bruise on her cheek. It certainly didn't describe the all-encompassing fear she'd felt when she'd first fled her home.

Behind her, Anna heard her mother gasp. But to her great relief, everyone else stayed silent. "You won't ever touch me again."

To Anna's dismay he flashed a campaign smile at everyone assembled. "Listen to you—always the drama queen." He chuckled. "Don't you think we can save the dramatics for the high school plays?" Linking his fingers around her elbow, he caught her firmly. "I'm done here. Let's go, Anna. Now."

"Release her. Now." Her father stepped forward. "Never again will you take her anywhere. We're going to press charges against you, Peterson."

Rob's hand fell limply to his side, but his voice was still strong and sure. "For what? Looking for my girlfriend?"

"For following us. Tapping our phones."

"They won't be able to prove a thing." Like a fickle wind, Rob changed course again. His voice turning slow and seductive, he murmured, "Anna, don't make me beg. Come home with me, sweetheart. You know I need you."

As Anna remembered how she'd once believed him when he'd talked like that, she felt sick. "Oh, Rob. You don't need anyone. You're just afraid of what I could tell people about your campaign contributions. About how you've been misappropriating them. I bet some of your large donors would love to have that leaked out to the press."

Turning confident again, he shook his head. "That's not going to happen."

"You forget, Rob, that I've filed hundreds of your receipts and papers. You thought I wasn't paying attention—that I was too dumb to know what you were doing, but I remember everything."

In a split second, he grabbed her. "Stop. Don't say a word."

"Why? What are you going to do, Rob? Shoot me?" She'd said the words with far more sass and assuredness than she felt inside. Inside, she was shaking like a leaf.

To her surprise, Rob very calmly reached into his suit jacket and pulled out a small—but still very lethal-looking— pistol. Very steadily, he cocked it and held it out for her to see. "I don't want to do this here. But if this is what it takes, I will."

Behind her, Anna heard Irene whimper.

"Don't, Rob. You don't know what you're doing."

His eyes, as dark as charcoal, gleamed. "That's where you're wrong. I know exactly what I'm doing." Deliberately, slowly, he leveled the pistol at her heart. "I always know exactly what I'm doing."

Anna was afraid he did. She was afraid he was so intent on claiming her that he was willing to do anything to achieve his goal. Even bringing a weapon in the Brennemans' house.

Even scaring everyone half to death.

Even shooting her in order to get his way, even if killing her would ruin him forever.

Rob Peterson had won.

"I'll go with you," Anna exclaimed. "Put that down."

"It's too late for that."

"It's never too late. It's never too late to change." With slow movements, she opened the front door and led the way to the porch. The bitterly cold wind greeted them, sliding through the gaps in her pinned dress and burning her skin. Anna almost welcomed the sensation. She'd brought all this upon herself. And though she'd naively hoped differently, her worst nightmare had come true—she had endangered everyone in the house. As the wind whipped her skirts, she started toward the front steps leading down to the walkway and parking lot.

Behind her, Henry said, "No, Anna."

"I'll be fine." She was out of choices. As Rob was demonstrating, it was time to stop living in her dream world. In the world she lived, no one was free to do exactly what they wanted.

Everyone has responsibilities. You couldn't neglect them or run from them. They were part of life. And a necessary part of her life was Rob.

Obviously relieved, Rob wiped his brow. In the twilight, she noticed that his skin was sallow and damp. Lines of strain surrounded his lips.

Now that she was used to Henry's wholesome good looks, Anna wondered how she could have ever been drawn to a man like Rob.

"You know we can't work things out, don't you?" she asked as they descended the short expanse of wooden stairs.

"It doesn't matter. People expect you to be with me. They expect *us*."

"But there is no us. Not any longer."

"There can be again."

"Rob, you need to rethink what you're doing."

"I'm in this too deep, and so are you." He grabbed her elbow, his fingers pressing into her skin, bruising her. "Let's go. I'll coach you in the car."

She wanted him away from the Brennemans, but suddenly Anna knew that if she went in that car with him without a fight, she would be putting herself in jeopardy.

Because no one else had followed them outside, she dared to stand up to him again. "Rob, no matter what you do, I won't stay with you."

"Anna, Anna, Anna. I'm through playing games." He jerked her to him roughly. She fended him off with a blow to the face.

Footsteps clattered along the wooden porch behind them.

To her surprise, Henry grabbed Rob by his left arm and pushed him away, easily showing his strength gained from years of toiling out in the fields. Then, before Rob had a chance to recover, her father whacked Rob on the neck with one of John Brenneman's hand-carved wooden canes that always rested next to the front door.

Rob's head ricocheted back, snapping in surprise.

And then he fell. Unconscious.

It was over.

Chapter 16

"Well that's surely the most unusual use I've ever seen for one of my canes," John Brenneman said as he stood over a knocked-out Rob Peterson. "It surely did a good job on that Englisher's neck, I tell you."

Henry burst out laughing. "Next time we sell them at the farmers market, I might be tempted to share that story a time or two. Those canes are a bit sturdier than they look."

"It's our hardy hickory, I'll tell you that," John said with a laugh.

Actually, all of them shared a good chuckle. It felt good to diffuse the riotous emotion that had taken place during the last fifteen minutes.

With a meaningful look toward Anna, Irene said, "Let's hope and pray we never have a need for such a use of a cane again, John. I don't know if my heart will be able to take another episode like this."

"I know mine can't." Meredith half cried and half laughed as she pulled her into a hug. "Oh, Anna. I think I just about had a heart attack, I was so very worried."

"I felt that way, too," Anna admitted, enjoying the feel of her mother's comforting embrace for the first time in what seemed like ages. "I was so scared."

"You surely didn't act that way," Katie commented, grabbing hold of her hand as well. "You looked as cool as a cucumber, I must say."

As she and her mother pulled away, Anna wiped her brow. "Not anymore. I'm shaking like a leaf."

Her dad looked at her with concern. "But you're all right? He didn't hurt you?"

"I'm all right."

"I'm glad of that," Henry said quietly. "There's a length of rope in my workshop. I'll go fetch it and then tie him up."

Mr. Brenneman nodded. Though Rob looked to be unconscious, the older man firmly placed a hand in the middle of Rob's back. "I'll keep him here until you're ready."

Anna's mother pulled out her cell phone and dialed 911.

Her first instinct was to tell her not to contact the police, but Meredith shook her head. "No more secrets. No more promises of lies. It's time to move forward . . . starting now."

Irene wrapped a comforting arm around Anna, smiling softly. "Anna Metzger, I never would have dreamed I'd say this, but I have to admit I've never been so happy to see such English here. Now your problems are over and we can move on. All of us."

Katie smiled brightly. "You are in hiding no longer. Now you can go back to being your regular self."

So many changes, so many close calls, all having taken

place in practically the blink of an eye. Anna felt dizzy. Sitting down on the bottom step of the house, she did her best to take charge of her emotions. But she knew it would take more than just the will to be tough. Tremors flowed through her body. She really had been afraid that she was going to have to go with Rob.

The taxi!

Looking up, she saw a strange man hovering near the vehicle, a look of distrust and . . . distaste? On his face. "Dad, look over there. The taxi driver's still here."

"I'll go talk to him."

Her father met the taxi driver halfway. "We've called the police. I've also written down your license plate number, so don't even think about skipping out of here."

The driver held up his hands as he approached their small group. "I wasn't planning to do any such thing. Instead, I was coming over to offer my assistance." Together, the driver and her father approached the rest of the group. To all of them, the man said, "My name is Omar. This man paid me a thousand dollars to take him here."

Katie's eyes turned into saucers. "A thousand dollars!"

In a burst of recognition, Anna said, "You took me here, too."

"Just yesterday a sheriff approached me and asked me questions. Next thing I knew, this man ordered me to take him here. I couldn't say no."

"I'm surprised you even remembered me," Anna said. "You have to have several dozen clients a day."

"Yes, but none wanting to go way out here. And not too many, I'm sorry to say, with your green eyes."

Her mother shook her head. "My word!"

Omar shrugged. "He paid me a lot of money, yes. But he also threatened my citizenship. He said he was going to pull my green card if I didn't comply with his orders." With a helpless look toward them all, he shrugged. "I am no match against such an influential man, do you see?"

Anna didn't have to be told what it felt like to be under Rob's thumb. "I do see. I've been there myself."

"He's a bad man."

"He is."

Ever the hostess, Irene came out with a Thermos of hot coffee. Katie followed with a tray of mugs. The little group each filled a cup happily, enjoying how the hot liquid warmed them from the insides.

John tilted his head. "I hear sirens. The police are coming."

Sure enough, the screaming sirens, sounding so overly loud and harsh, filled the air. A few cows in the back pasture mooed their dismay.

And then they all turned, watching as one police car after another filed up the long driveway, followed by an ambulance.

As everyone talked and waited for the emergency personnel to arrive, Anna remained apart.

She felt extremely out of sorts, like she was currently standing in two different worlds.

Though the others looked at her curiously, everyone gave her space. Anna knew they thought she was shaken up from the extreme danger she'd been in. And that was true. When Rob had pulled out the gun, she'd only thought of getting him away from everyone she cared for. She hadn't put herself first at all, until she'd seen that taxi and knew that he was desperate enough to be extremely violent.

But that wasn't the complete reason she was upset. Not by a long shot. Selfishly, internally, she knew the real reason she was miserable—and it was plain and simple: now she would have no reason to stay.

She had to go out into the world again, away from the Brennemans' Bed and Breakfast.

Out of the only place she'd ever truly felt accepted. The irony that she could now leave the only place she'd ever felt as if she truly belonged was almost unbearable.

But like the good friend she was, Katie seemed to know more was going on. As the uniformed officers got out of their squad cars and the men rushed forward to recount the events, Anna walked to the step where Katie was perched.

"After everything that happened, I can't believe things are all over."

"I feel the same way."

Quietly Katie watched the officers. "They'll be speaking with you for some time, I suppose."

"I imagine they will. I'm the reason all this happened."

"Haven't you learned anything yet, Anna? This was meant to happen."

"I certainly don't know why."

"You don't need to. But perhaps you need to remember something?"

"What's that?"

"I've liked having you here with me, Anna Metzger. It's been *wunderbaar gut*. Wonderful good."

Linking her arm through Katie's, Anna smiled. "Yes, it has been. Living here with you has been *wunderbaar schee*." When Katie giggled, Anna scowled. "I know that sounded horrible. But I'm learning and trying, aren't I?"

"You are, indeed," Katie said, just as a female police officer and an EMT approached.

Henry spoke with the authorities, and did his best to see to their needs and answer questions quietly and honestly. Sheriff Tucker, though not a friend, was certainly not a stranger.

Over the years, Henry had had time to visit with the sixty-year-old sheriff, either during community fund-raisers or when there'd been some cases of vandalism at the local Amish school. Their paths had crossed again when a buggy had been hit by an English guest at the inn.

Tucker's eyes widened as soon as he saw who was on the Brennemans' front porch. He took frantic notes as one by one, Anna, Meredith, and Calvin Metzger attempted to relay all that had transpired in the last month.

During all of this, Henry took care to check on Anna, who looked painfully unsure and worried. He was torn between wanting to run to her side and ask her if she still yearned to stay with them, or encourage her to go back among the English, where she most certainly would want to be now that everything was much better.

But instead of talking about any of that, Henry stayed away, giving her space to come to grips with all that had happened. Giving himself time to rethink things and to guard his emotions.

Two hours later, Rob was escorted away in handcuffs by Sheriff Tucker's deputies.

"You all did a fine job apprehending him," Tucker said to Henry's father. "Now I know who to call if I'm ever in need of help during a takedown."

John laughed. "Only if canes are needed, I'm thinking." Turning somber, he said, "To tell the truth, I'd be mighty pleased if nothing like this ever passed my way again."

"I hear you. I'll pass the word if we need you to give another statement, John."

"I'll help how I can."

Tucker looked at Anna. "You'll need to be available for more questioning."

"She'll be at home," Mrs. Metzger said, her tone strong and sure.

Henry felt as if his heart had stopped beating when he saw that Anna didn't look surprised to hear her mother's promise.

Well, there it was . . . she was going. Most likely, never to return, just like Rachel.

Standing in the front yard, looking at her parents, Anna felt a jolt of longing for home. A longing to belong, to be content in her surroundings. The thrust of emotion was so strong, it took her by surprise.

Because she wasn't simply looking forward to the life she once knew, she was yearning for the feeling she'd just learned to accept and look forward to.

That caught her off guard. Had she really become homesick for the Brennemans' home, instead of her own? Where was "home" now?

Suddenly, it didn't seem possible to straddle the two worlds any longer. She was going to need to make a choice, and she was going to need to make it very soon.

But once again, her mother was attempting to do it for her.

"How long is it going to take you to get your things together?" Meredith asked. "It's time we got out of the Brennemans' hair."

She wasn't ready! "Mom, maybe we could wait a while."

"For what? The police said they'll contact us later."

Her mother's rush to be on her way caught Anna off guard. Anna wanted nothing more than just to sit for a while, then attend to her chores and spend some quiet time thinking about everything that had just happened.

Helplessly, Anna looked toward Katie, Henry, and their parents. None of them said a word. She couldn't read their posture, either. Were they anxious for her to get on her way? For her to ask to stay?

Finally Anna caught Katie's eye. Instead of a friendly smile, Katie was worrying her lip. Her blue eyes looked troubled and more than a little shocked, making Anna feel guilty about even wanting to delay her departure. This afternoon's excitement had been difficult, to say the least. The Brennemans probably couldn't wait for her to be on her way!

Perhaps it was time to go. "I could be ready in twenty minutes or so."

"That's fine. Dad and I will see how we can help put things to rights around here."

"All right." Fingering her *kapp*, Anna amended her words. "Actually, it might take me a little longer, now that I think of it. I'm going to need to get my things together." And change. It was time to change into her jeans and sweater and uncover her hair. It was time to go back to how things used to be, whether she was ready or not.

A bit of compassion lit Meredith's eyes. "I understand, dear. I do. Take your time."

"We'll see you when you come back down," her dad added.

Suddenly, Anna knew she needed some alone time or else she would scream. "All right, then. I'll hurry." Afraid to look at the Brennemans again, she started up the stairs, head down.

Like a guardian angel, Katie rushed to her side. "Maybe you don't need to hurry so. Perhaps you could stay the night and then leave in the morning?" She looked at Henry. "That sounds *gut*, don'tcha think?"

"I'm not sure." Henry's face was a mask of emotion. "What is it you want, Anna?"

Before Anna could formulate a reply, her mother answered for her. "It's really time she left. Now. We don't want to impose any more on your hospitality. I'm sure all of you are quite ready to have your guest bedroom free again and get your lives back to normal."

John scratched his graying beard. "Normal? I'm in no hurry for that."

But Calvin Metzger didn't even attempt to catch the joke. "It's time we got her home where she belongs, Mr. Brenneman. You've had to take care of Anna long enough."

Irene looked stunned. "She was a *gut* worker. Wonderful *gut*."

"That's good to hear. At home, sometimes she doesn't follow through on everything she says she is going to." Calvin chuckled. "Maybe this is your calling, Anna. To be in the hospitality industry. That's one of the few occupations you haven't attempted yet."

Her mom snapped her fingers. "That's what we could do, Anna. Get on the Internet and research classes in the hotel industry."

Then, to Anna's shame, her dad reached in his pocket and pulled out his wallet. "Seriously, though, we certainly appreciate everything you've done for Anna. Feeding her, clothing her, making her feel so welcome. Let me pay you for your troubles."

Anna put her hand on her father's arm. "Don't."

"Don't what? Thank them?"

"We already have thanked them."

Turning his back on his daughter, Calvin stepped toward Mr. Brenneman. Anna swallowed a lump, seeing that he was now insulting the family even further by ignoring Mrs. Brenneman, who ran the inn so very competently. "So, John, will a thousand dollars be enough to cover her expenses for a month, give or take?" He pulled out his wallet. "Do you take Visa?"

"We don't wish to be paid."

"She used a room. I don't want to think that she's been taking advantage of you."

"She's been like a daughter to us," Mrs. Brenneman said quietly. "You don't ask your daughter to pay rent, now do you?"

"But—"

"Stop, Dad."

Meredith, her expression stricken, finally entered the conversation. "Let's go sit down and wait. Now."

Anna hung her head as she rushed away. At the moment, she couldn't face any of them. Not John and Irene. Not Katie. Not her parents. And certainly not Henry.

She ran to her room and dug out her suitcase. Inside, neatly folded, were the jeans and sweater she'd worn the afternoon over a month ago.

How could she measure all that had happened? It seemed

a lifetime had passed. More experiences than she could put into words or that she had a feeling she would fully realize in the next few days to come.

She'd entered the inn scared and alone. Not trusting anyone. Now she trusted God and His role in her life. She now believed in herself, and valued her worth. She counted Katie as a sister. Irene and John as treasured mentors.

And she trusted and longed for a future with Henry like no other.

Chapter 17

An early spring storm came unexpectedly, bringing with it a batch of brilliant white snow. It continued on for the next twelve hours, keeping everyone in the region indoors. Just when it looked like a break was in sight, the temperature warmed up enough to turn the powdery flakes to sleet. When the temperature dropped again, the results were truly beautiful. Thick sheets of ice coated everything in sight, casting a lovely, shimmery otherworldly glow over Cincinnati.

Anna wished she was in the state of mind to appreciate the wonder of it all. Instead, all she could do was feel trapped.

Two weeks had passed since the afternoon both her parents and Rob had come to the Brennemans' home. In that time, her feelings had run the whole gamut of emotions, from joy to being free from Rob Peterson's abuse to enjoying the many modern conveniences of home to missing Henry.

Things with her parents were rocky. Her mother either

tried to be too friendly or treated her as if she were eight years old.

Anna had had to visibly bite her tongue when her mother had not only asked where she was going, but with whom and when she'd be back. Anna couldn't blame her. She knew her parents had been worried sick when she'd been gone. Therefore, she tried to be patient and give the information that was asked. But still, the heavy-handed guardianship was uncomfortable and confining.

It felt so different than her life at the Brennemans'. Yes, she'd been subjected to the lifestyle of the Amish, and she'd certainly been often surrounded by other people. But she'd also been given responsibilities and the freedom to explain herself.

Now Anna felt lost and unable to completely apologize for her actions. Quite simply, there were no words to say.

"So, that's how I'm feeling, Julie," Anna said after speaking almost nonstop for the last half hour. "I feel torn between two worlds, which seems really ridiculous because I was only pretending to be in one of them."

"Which world were you pretending to be in?"

That took her by surprise, the answer was so obvious. But, because Julie had never been one to be obvious about anything, Anna asked, "What are you talking about? I was only pretending to be Amish, of course."

Julie pushed the bowl of ice cream away, the mound of vanilla having long turned soupy. "Here goes. I'm going to say something that you might find surprising."

Julie had never been one to beat around the bush, either. "Okay."

"I think maybe you were supposed to be at the Brennemans'.

I think you were meant to live with the Amish and adopt their way of life. I think that's maybe where you are supposed to be. That you fit in with the Amish." Slyly, she added, "And with Henry."

"I think you're mistaken. I didn't fit in with them, not really." Anna couldn't even bring herself to talk about Henry, her feelings toward him were too raw and volatile.

"From what you've told me, you were happy at the inn."

Was that the emotion that came to mind? Anna didn't dare risk analyzing that one. She'd been confused at the bed and breakfast. Confused about how she'd come so far as to be the type of person who had to hide in order to save her sanity. Confused about her feelings for Henry. Confused about how she could trust the Brennemans so much when she didn't trust her parents at all. "If you had seen me there, you'd know I wasn't 'happy.'"

"Content?"

Since when did her best friend ever care about things like contentment? "Julie, you've got it all wrong. I did make the best of the situation I was in. And I did enjoy living with the Brennemans. I loved a lot of things about their lifestyle . . . from the satisfying work they did to the way our evenings were spent playing games or quilting or just talking. But, they were merely being kind. I didn't fit in."

"You really didn't? Or have you become so accustomed to not fitting in that you made up your mind that things weren't going to work out? And that you would never be okay there because you weren't willing to work a little harder?"

Now she was psychoanalyzing her! "Julie, what's going on? You of all people—"

This brought a bright smile to Julie's face. "Me, of all

people? I'm no different than I once was. We've known each other forever. We still like the same books, the same television shows. We can still find humor in the strangest places, and even though we sometimes date real jerks—" Julie let her gaze rest on Anna for a moment while that one sunk in—"we're still willing to go to bat for each other, through thick and thin."

"That's true."

"If it's true, then why are you doubting me?"

Julie's words had merit. Her faith in her was also very humbling. But Julie hadn't lived among the Amish. She didn't really know what she was talking about. She couldn't. Could she?

Or had Anna, too, begun to only judge people on appearances instead of what was inside of them? Of what was in their hearts? "I don't want to argue."

"I don't, either. But I also don't want to be ignored. Listen, Anna. Just because I have tattoos and an earring in my eyebrow doesn't mean I care about you—or the things and people around me—any less. You should know that appearances aren't everything."

"I realize that. I just am having a hard time understanding how you would be on the side of the Amish."

"Because your face lights up when you talk about them. I think you have something special there. Especially with Henry."

Just hearing his name made Anna feel warm. His name brought forth images of walks in the fields. Of quiet conversations on his front porch and in his workroom. Of meaningful discussions and jokes and bright light.

But that didn't mean her attraction was right. "The only

way I could have a relationship with Henry Brenneman is if I became Amish. And that decision would be have to be for life. He's been hurt before. The woman he was courting left him for an Englisher. I couldn't bear to hurt him as well."

"Then don't."

"But the only alternative would be to join the order. To become Plain."

"And your problem is—"

Anna stood up in a temper. "Julie, I can't become Amish!"

"Why not? You already were."

"That was just pretend."

"Was it?"

Julie's question, offered so calmly, took the heat from her anger and replaced it with a quiet circumspection. She sat back down. "Truthfully, when I was with the Brennemans, nothing was fake. I felt genuine for the very first time. Honest, stripped of all the layers of coverings I've adopted in order to survive in the 'real' world."

"Would Henry say that he lived in the 'real' world?"

Anna didn't hesitate over her answer. "He'd say that his world was far more real than the outside one."

"I thought you believed in Jesus Christ."

"I do," Anna protested, still thinking it was an odd conversation with Julie. "Do you?"

"I do."

"But the tattoos . . ."

She laughed. "I'm not perfect. I do like to express my personality in the way I see fit. This look of mine fits my lifestyle. But like your friend Henry or Katie, I'm not letting other people's perspectives on my outward appearance affect what is in my soul. Of course, I'm not trying to be Amish, Anna. I'm just trying to be myself."

What Julie said made a lot of sense. And that straight talk also encouraged her to dive into her insecurities. Admitting the one closest to her heart, she said, "I don't know if Henry would even want me."

"Maybe you should ask."

"I can't. They don't have a telephone, and there's no way I'm going to go show up on their doorstep again, uninvited." Just the thought of doing that again scared her half to death. Katie would most likely think she was on the run again!

Still on target, Julie said, "Could you write to him? Tell him how you feel?"

"I could. I mean, I guess I could. But what if he never answers?"

"That would be tough. But would it be any tougher if you never did a thing and your Henry thought you never cared?"

If Henry did feel as invested as she did, Anna was very afraid that her leaving him would hurt him deeply. She couldn't do that.

She knew then that it was time to trust herself and take a step forward in claiming her life. In following God's path and walking toward the life she really felt she was meant to lead.

"All right, I'm scared to death, but I'm going to do it. I'm going to write to Henry. I'm going to be honest and open and tell him how I feel."

"Good girl. And what are you going to do if he feels the same way that you do?"

Anna couldn't help but smile. She loved how Julie wasn't looking for the negatives but the positives. "If he feels the same way, I guess I'll need to go speak with his family. And mine." But in the end, Anna knew, she was going to depend on herself and not on what others expected of her. She was finally ready to be her own person.

Julie grinned, too. "I can't wait to tell people about my Amish friend Anna."

"Henry, this came for you today." Katie handed him a letter gingerly, like it was about to burst into flames. "It's from Anna."

Now it was his turn to handle the envelope with care. "It just arrived?"

"*Jah*. It was in the mailbox with today's bills and reservations."

Katie folded her arms over her chest, obviously waiting for him to open the letter and read it out loud to her. But he wasn't about to. There, on the front of the envelope, clear as day, was his name, neatly printed out. It was to him, and him alone.

That had to be a significant thing, for sure.

He fought off the urge to run his fingers over the ink, just to gain a sense of her. Three weeks had never felt so long. Instead, he carefully set the letter on his workbench. "Thank you for delivering it."

Katie folded her arms across her chest. "Well, aren't ya going to open it this minute and share it with me? I've sorely missed Anna. Even seeing her handwriting brings a smile to my face."

He didn't doubt Katie's words, because he felt the same way. But that didn't change the fact that the letter was addressed for his eyes, not hers. "No, I am not."

"But—"

"I'm going to want some privacy when I read it, I'm thinking." He fought against rolling his eyes at his words. Honestly, if Katie had said such a thing, he'd be teasing her mercilessly.

"Privacy?" Her eyes narrowed. "I know you two had some feelings for each other, but I thought that ended when she left. What could Anna have to say to you that she couldn't tell me? For that matter, why do you think she wrote to you at all?"

Henry didn't dare convey the many private talks he and Anna had had during her time with them. It was too personal, and there was too much doubt in them. After all, what, really, could be shared? It wasn't like they'd had an agreement.

Or could ever have an agreement.

"I don't know why she wrote to me, but I intend to find out. Alone."

Katie folded her arms, obviously ready to stand firm. Anxious to read the note in private, Henry resorted to age-old tactics. "You know, you're acting like you used to when Rebekeh still lived at home. Nosy and too willful."

"That's unfair. I was only a teenager then."

"You see what I mean?"

Outside the room, they heard their mother gathering some jars from the storage room nearby. In a huff, he heard Katie call for their mother. "*Mamm*, what do you think of this? Anna wrote to Henry, and he wants to read her note in private."

Henry glared at his sister.

But then their mother saved the day. "I think you are too interested with Henry's business, Katie. Everyone has a right to a private letter." Handing over several of the jars to Katie, their mother added, "Let Henry have some peace now, and help me with these jars."

"But—"

"Katie, I need your help with dinner, and that's a fact."

Henry caught his mother's understanding smile as she motioned for Katie to join her.

Minutes later the barn was empty, save for the animals and Henry. He picked up the letter once again, afraid yet anxious see what Anna had felt she needed to write. Painstakingly, he broke the seal and carefully pulled out the plain sheet of thick white paper.

As he unfolded the paper, he caught the faint, fresh scent of Anna, teasing his memory and making his hands shake.

Once again, he was mighty happy he was by himself.

With a deep breath, he read her note.

Henry,

Please forgive me if this letter is too forward, but I need to tell you my feelings, and I didn't dare visit you without an invitation.

Henry sat down, shock almost blurring the words on the page. Receiving a letter was a big surprise. To read such a thing almost took the wind out of him.

During these three weeks that have passed, I've tried to get back to my old way of life, but I keep getting distracted by something I hear or see that reminds me of the Brenneman Bed and Breakfast.

I've finally found the strength to be honest with myself and after many attempts, have finally decided to share with you my feelings, for better or worse.

See, the thing is . . . I miss you and your family. But even more important, I miss belonging. And I felt I belonged with you and the Amish.

Is that wrong? Have I just completely messed everything up by being so honest?

Henry shook his head. No, her feelings weren't wrong, because he'd missed her just as badly.

Henry, I know we became friends, but I need to know if you think there's ever a chance that we could become more. That is, if I became Amish. I mean, if the bishop and ministers and elders in your order would let me. If your parents would ever be able to find it in their hearts to accept me as a suitable wife for you.

Had Anna Metzger just asked him to marry her?
Henry was so stunned, he now wished he had his whole family around him. In his memory, he'd never heard of anyone wanting to join the order. Their way of life was a hard one to adopt. It would be necessary to learn Pennsylvania Dutch, as well. Did she realize that? Was she ready?

And—what about all her conveniences? She'd have to give up her car. That cell phone. Her job.

*I know this is forward. And I know I may be set-
ting myself up to be hurt. Or worse, hurt you by embarrassing you. And, I don't mean to do that.*

*But Henry, if you think there is even a possibility
that we could have a future, would you please write
me back?*

She signed it simply. Before he even realized what he was
doing, Henry traced her name with his finger. *Anna.*

In a daze, Henry stood up. After walking back to the stalls
and checking on the horses, he made his way back to the
house. Still clutching the letter, he walked into the kitchen.
There, his parents and a morose-looking Katie sat.

All three looked at him expectantly when he joined them
at the table.

"I need all of you," he said without preamble. Pushing forward the letter, he murmured, "As you know, I received a
letter from Anna today."

Katie glared. "Oh, Henry. Tell us something we don't
know, why don'tcha?"

"All right then. Either I have just received the best news of
my life, or the worst." He sat down across from his father and
ever so slowly, pushed Anna's letter forward. "I need your
advice, *Daed.*"

Katie attempted to read the note over her father's shoulder. When he moved it so she couldn't see, she said, "Would
you read it out loud? I'm dying to know what it says!"

"Patience, daughter."

"But if it's good news, I want to know now."

His mother clucked. "Isn't that how things always are with

you, my *liewe* Katie? Be patient. Good or bad, we'll all know soon enough."

The room was silent for a moment as Henry's father carefully read the letter, then without a word, passed the letter onto Irene.

Finally, his mother folded the note and looked at the three of them. "What do you think, Henry?"

"I'm not sure."

Katie glared. "What is going on?"

"Anna wants to become Amish and marry me," Henry finally snapped, his patience at the end.

"Oh!"

His father nodded, though his eyes twinkled with a hint of merriment. "*Jah*, this is mighty important news, Henry. I'd say something this important calls for prayer before discussion."

Henry bent his head and did pray. *Help me, God. Help me know what Your will is. Help me not walk alone.*

Almost instantaneously, Henry realized something he hadn't appreciated for a very long time . . . he never had been alone. The Lord had been guiding him all along.

He had just finally listened.

Chapter 18

Anna didn't have to wait a week to hear back from Henry. In fact, it took only two days.

Anna,

I think we need to talk. Would you meet me at the Horse and Plow on Wednesday at suppertime? I'll be there waiting. If you don't come, I'll know you have changed your mind.

Henry

Suppertime. That would be roughly around five o'clock, when the sun went down and his work in the barn would be over.

Since it was already Monday, she felt a burst of pleasure to know that she'd be seeing him in just two more days.

"Anna? Was that a note from Henry?"

Anna tried not to feel irritated that her mother was in her business once again. After everything that had happened, Anna supposed that her mom had every right to want to cling to her personal life just a little more than she used to.

And because of that, Anna decided to be more forthcoming than she used to, as well. It was time for their relationship to change again . . . this time growing stronger. More real. "Yes." She swallowed. "Henry asked me to meet him for supper on Wednesday."

Slowly Meredith sat down on the corner of Anna's bed. "Why?"

"It's probably because I asked him to consider deepening our relationship." Well, that was putting it mildly!

"I don't understand. Does he want to leave the Amish?"

A second flew by. Two. It was time to tell her the truth, even if it was going to make her mother upset. Even if Henry didn't want her.

Surprisingly, it felt easy. "No, Mom. I am thinking about becoming Amish."

"What?" She shook her head in dismay. "Anna, what in the world am I going to do with you? Just when I think you've grown up, you take on yet another crazy-haired scheme."

Anna struggled to not let her mother see just how badly those words hurt. "This isn't crazy."

"It certainly sounds crazy! Once again, you aren't thinking through things. Haven't you learned anything?"

"Mom, let me explain."

"There's nothing to explain. Now, I held my tongue about Rob, but I'm not going to let you go chase some random Amish boy."

Held her tongue? She'd practically pushed Anna into marriage with Rob! "Henry is not a boy, Mother."

"Well, he's not for you, either. Once you get a job and get back into the swing of things, I know you're going to realize that your time with the Brennemans was just a pleasant experience. But not your real life."

As Anna looked around her room, so full of childish things and past amusements, she knew that she wasn't where she needed to be, either.

Instead of correcting her mother about the "pleasant experience" of hiding from Rob, she concentrated on the future she knew she wanted. "I have done some thinking. And I've been praying for guidance. I've fallen in love with Henry, Mom."

"You were just in love with Rob a few months ago."

The criticism stung, but Anna knew it was no less than she deserved. "Although I wasn't in love with him, I hear what you're saying. But this is different."

"You can't become Amish. We'll never be allowed to see you!"

"The Amish are very family oriented. They would never not let me see you. We'll still be family; I'll just have chosen a different lifestyle."

Meredith picked up Anna's jewelry box, which had been their sixteenth-birthday present to Anna. "You're just going to abandon everything?"

"Mom, I'm not trying to abandon you, I'm trying to finally uncover what has been inside of me all along." Carefully, she pulled the box out of her mother's hand and set it on the dresser. Then she deliberately grasped her mother's hands and spoke slowly.

"Ever since I graduated high school, I've been unsettled and unhappy. For the last six years, I've been trying to fill that void with things and boyfriends and high excitement. But nothing ever felt right. And I tried, Momma. I tried to enjoy college. Tried to think of an occupation that would excite me."

"Life doesn't need to be exciting. One day you'll realize that."

"But life needs to matter, don't you think? Mom, all this time, I couldn't concentrate. And I've been fighting with myself, hoping to make things right. Hoping to fit in."

"You've just dated the wrong men."

"No."

"Your dad and I shouldn't have spoiled you so much. If you weren't running around, expecting the world, you would have had a better time of it."

Anna was disappointed at their conversation. It felt like they were speaking in two different languages. "It's not a man's fault. It's not your fault. I agree that I was spoiled, but I don't think my searching was for selfish, silly reasons."

"Anna, if you could only hear yourself!"

"Mom, I could say the same thing to you. Yes, I chose wrong with Rob. But a lot of other people were also wrong about him! Now that federal charges have been made against him and his campaign is dead, all the truth about him is coming out. He is a very bad and manipulative person. I didn't know who the real Rob Peterson was until it was almost too late."

"So you're refusing to take the blame?"

Anna stood up. Maybe one day they'd be able to be close again, but it obviously wasn't going to happen right away. "Yes. I'm refusing to take *all* the blame for Rob's abuse and stalking of me."

Her mother's face crumbled. "Anna, please listen to me. Maybe you should go on a vacation. Dad and I will pay for you and Julie to take a trip to Florida. A real trip—"

"Stop. Julie's working, Mom. And I can't go to Florida because I'm going to see Henry in two days and plan a future with him."

Tears fell, one after the other. "You're making a mistake."

"I don't think so."

"What am I going to tell your father?"

"Nothing, because I'm going to tell him the same thing I've told you." Softly, she added, "I've been through so much. Enough to know when it's time to follow my heart. Please try and understand."

"I can't."

"Then I'll only ask for your prayers for me."

"You won't like my prayers, because I'm going to pray that you finally come to your senses."

Anna nodded. "May I still stay here until I know what to do?"

"You can. I'd never ask you to leave."

"Thank you."

When her mother stood up and left her bedroom, Anna sat in silence. Looked at the stereo. The closet full of clothes; the vast number of purses and shoes and knickknacks.

Would she miss all of this?

Honestly, yes.

Would giving it all up in order to be with Henry and to feel like she fit in be worth it?

Without a doubt.

The Horse and Plow wasn't very busy. Anna arrived before Henry. After debating whether to wait for him out front or at a booth, she finally decided to go sit down. The temperature was in the low thirties—too cold to sit outside in her SUV.

After much debate, she'd decided to just wear a calf-length denim skirt and a long sleeved top. It wasn't close to looking Plain, but it wasn't overly fancy, either. And the violet color of her shirt made her eyes seem greener, she'd been told.

And though she shouldn't care about such things, Anna knew that she hadn't changed completely. She was still a woman who cared about her looks and wanted the man she loved to think she was pretty.

Then, she forgot all about herself when Henry walked through the door. Once again, she was struck by just how solid he was. Thick muscles and years of healthy food and hard work were evident under his plain white shirt. His cheeks were freshly shaved and the dark hair that skimmed his collar looked damp.

But when his gaze met hers, he looked the same as always—serious and concerned. Honest and fresh. After nodding his hello to the proprietor, he took the chair across from her.

Anna was glad she knew his ways, and the ways of the Amish. Public affection was frowned upon. Actually, drawing any notice was frowned upon. But his lack of exuberance didn't dim her feelings in the slightest.

Actually, his lack of emotion was reassuring, and made her feel like they had something very important and special between them. Secret and meaningful.

"I'm really glad you came," Henry said.

"I am, too. You are looking well."

His cheeks stained red. Anna knew she'd embarrassed him. But when he met her gaze once again, she knew everything was going to be okay. "I'm glad you are pleased to see me. I feel the same way as you. Tell me what's been going on."

His lips curved. "I imagine quite a bit, but I wouldn't know of it. You see . . . I've been focused on a letter I received from a certain lady I know."

There it was: no pussyfooting around. "And?"

"It's concerned me greatly."

Well, that didn't sound good at all. "I see."

The server came and took their order. Anna chose chicken and dumplings with vegetables and a glass of tea. She'd already seen the array of pies on the back counter and was looking forward to a slice of coconut cream pie.

Henry ordered beef stew and hot rolls.

Then, when they were alone again, Anna knew they would once again get to the subject at hand. "I meant what I said in my letter, Henry. I have feelings for you."

"Truly? I'm not just a passing fancy?"

His words stung. Not because he didn't have the right to ask such things, but because they were so close to her mother's harsh questions.

But that's where the differences presented themselves. Henry was obviously laying his feelings out. He was as much at risk to be hurt as she was. With a thoughtfulness she didn't used to possess, she chose her words carefully. "I knew when

I was at your home that there was something between us that was special. I feel a connection toward you that has nothing to do with childish whims or silly crushes. But I don't know if you feel the same toward me. I mean, I wasn't sure of the extent of your feelings."

Their server delivered their food. Both she and Henry bowed their heads to give thanks in silent prayer. Then Henry eagerly dove into his meal. As she saw him eat heartily, she looked at her own bowl. Suddenly, the chicken and dumplings didn't look very appetizing at all.

In fact, at that moment, she was wondering why she'd ever thought she could eat, her stomach was in such knots. Obviously, she'd been too optimistic. Too sure that Henry would still care for her. Too sure that he would want to wait for her to learn the *Ordnung*, the rules of the Amish, and Pennsylvania Dutch.

"Anna, I, too, think we could have a future."

"Really?"

Now he wasn't even trying to hide his amusement. "Yes, *liewi* Anna, dear Anna. I've prayed over our future, and I've spoken to my family about it."

"What did they say? What did Katie say?"

"They were not surprised."

"Really?"

"Really," he said, obviously amused that she kept saying such inane words.

Henry bit into a roll and chewed with relish. Anna, noticing that her stomach was turning hungry again, scooped up a few bites of her chicken dinner and savored how the thick broth warmed her insides.

"They were only hoping you would recognize the differences between pretending to be one of us, and actually—"

"Becoming Amish?" she interjected. "I do. I mean, I think I do."

"We could never marry," he paused as his cheeks colored again. "We could never marry until you adopted our ways."

"I know that."

"Anna, I would do a lot for you, but I cannot change hundreds of years of customs in order to make your life easier. You'd have to learn our language. You'd have to abide by the *Ordnung.* Our way of life is not always easy. The restrictions can be difficult, even for someone who grows up Amish."

"I know that. I didn't come to this decision lightly."

"Then you know that communication with the outside world would be far limited?"

"I know."

"And . . . children?" He swallowed hard. "We Amish have large families. Would you want children?"

"I would want children with you."

"Running an inn can be difficult, and at first we would have to live there with my family, until there was time to build us a home."

"Henry, I know all those things. Why do you insist on reminding me?"

"Because I want you to be sure."

"I am sure." She said the words with as much certainty and power as she possibly could. There were no doubts in her mind, now that she'd seen Henry again, she felt no doubts at all.

"Then what do you see when you look at me and our way of life?"

"I see a future that's secure. I see living with the Lord on a daily basis, not just on Sundays or just when I'm in need. I see being a helpmate to you, Henry."

Inside, Anna yearned to say far more. She wanted to hold him as her husband. To wake each morning by his side, to grow old together.

A spark entered his eyes, but he said nothing, only leaned toward his bowl and ate a few more bites.

Anna contented herself with doing the same. Now that they were speaking of all the things she'd only imagined in the privacy of her room, Anna, too, found the need to have time for reflection.

In short order, their plates were picked up, and Anna ordered a piece of coconut cream pie and a cup of coffee. Henry picked cherry cobbler.

When they finished, Henry carefully paid the check then turned to her. "I know it is mighty cold out, but would you care to go for a short ride? I put extra blankets in the buggy."

Nothing sounded more romantic. She walked by his side to the parking lot, past her own SUV, to where his buggy and Stanley were hitched. Like an old friend, Anna greeted the horse. "Stanley, you look fetching in your winter coat."

Henry's lips twitched as he helped her in, then he even took care to tenderly wrap a thick quilt around her lap.

After settling in next to her, he motioned the horse forward, and down the gravel path, the one that veered from the main road. "I didn't even know this was here."

"It's right lucky it is. It makes traveling at night far better than risking spooking the horses with the passing automobiles."

As minute after minute passed, all the lights from the town faded away until it only seemed like the two of them existed.

The gray skies had cleared, uncovering a twinkling kaleidoscope of stars. The moon had risen and lit their journey. Around them, wind brushed the tall grasses. But inside, Anna had never felt so comforted.

Henry was sitting closer to her than ever before. Their legs brushed against each other's, her shoulder rested against his muscular arm. Though layers of cotton and wool separated them, their chaste contact felt more intimate than anything she had done with former boyfriends in the past.

"Anna, if you would have me, I would like to court you. When you become Amish."

Never had words been so easy to say. "Henry, if you would have me, I would like for you to court me," she replied slowly. Then, with a smile, she added, "When I become Amish."

With an easy motion, Henry directed Stanley to a smooth patch of land off the main road. When they were stopped and no sound could be heard except for Stanley's jangling bridle, Henry tenderly took Anna's hands. "So, your answer is yes?"

She nodded excitedly. "Yes."

Such a look of pure relief and joy entered his expression that Anna felt a jolt race through her. Finally she had a future, a future that felt right and real.

"I'm pleased. My parents would like you to come back to live with us. Katie is eager to help you learn our ways."

"They're not worried about the two of us under the same roof?"

"I'm going to live down the road a-ways, with my aunt and uncle and their family."

She sure didn't want to kick him out of his own home! "Henry—"

He placed one finger to her lips. So gently. "Hush, now. It's what I want, Anna. If you are willing to do so much for me, I can do this, yes?"

"Yes. When . . . when would you like me to move to the inn?"

Slowly he turned to her. "In four days' time? Now that we're together again, I find I don't want days to go by without being able to see you."

She laughed. She'd fallen in love, finally, after all this time. By his actions, she knew Henry felt the same. "I'll be ready. I'll have my dad drop me off."

Henry glanced around them. No one was around for miles. Only the wind and the stars. Very slowly, very deliberately, Henry curved an arm around her and pulled her close.

He smelled like soap and soup. Like horses and cold, crisp snow. Like her future and her present.

Like nothing in her past.

She rested her head against his chest and gazed out into the distance. There, in the reflection of the snow, sat a wild hare. Its body was covered in a speckled fur, but it was out for anyone to see.

"Look," she whispered to Henry, to the man who now meant everything to her . . . who would one day be her husband. "Another rabbit."

He gently rubbed her back. "And this one isn't hiding. He

must have found all he was looking for and is daring to come out into the open."

As the hare ventured out, Anna knew the feeling. There in the winter's night, she was hidden no more. She felt free. Alive. She belonged.

And the moment was so perfect, so right, it was almost overwhelming.

WANTED

Sisters *of the* Heart

BOOK TWO

This is the day which the Lord has made. Let us rejoice and be glad in it.

Psalm 118:24

We did not inherit this land from our fathers. We are borrowing it from our children.

Amish Proverb

Chapter 1

Katie Brenneman noticed that Jonathan Lundy was crushing the brim of his hat. Round and round he turned it, fingering the black felt as he spoke. Every few moments, without warning, his fingers would clench and the rim would succumb to his grip.

If he continued the process much longer, Jonathan was going to be in dire need of a new hat.

"Katie, are you listening, Daughter?"

She started, daring to glance at her mother, who was sitting across from her on the love seat, her current sewing project forgotten in the basket next to her. "Yes, *Mamm.* I'm listening."

"You have hardly looked at our guest once since he's arrived. You haven't spoken more than a few words." Her mother treated Katie to a look she knew well. It said she had better shape up and soon. "Is everything all right?"

Irene Brenneman was a lot of things, but a fool certainly wasn't one of them. Katie swallowed. "Of course."

"Then you are interested in what Jonathan has to say?"

Katie had been fond of Jonathan Lundy for years. She'd always been mighty interested in what he had to say. Not that he seemed to notice. "Yes."

The hat took another beating as Jonathan spoke. "I have something to ask of Katie. Something that I am hoping she would think was a mighty *gut* idea."

Now Katie was all ears. Had Jonathan finally seen her as she wished? As a woman available for courting? Stilling herself, she inhaled.

Her mother's cheeks pinkened. "What was your idea, Jonathan?"

He swallowed uncomfortably. "I'm . . . I'm hopin' Katie—that Katie . . ."

Her mother leaned forward. "Yes?"

"Well, I'm in need of Katie here to help with my daughters."

Her *daed* coughed. "With your daughters?"

Crunch! went the brim again. "*Jah*. Just while my sister Winnie goes to Indiana for a bit."

Katie exhaled swiftly. Well, she'd certainly been mistaken! Jonathan had been thinking of her, but not as a future bride. Oh no. As a nursemaid for his five- and seven-year-old daughters.

"For how long?" her father asked. Usually, he joked around, or whittled on one of the many canes he was famous for creating. Now, though, he only sat solemnly, his expression grave.

"Two months."

Two months of living at Jonathan Lundy's home? Of caring for his daughters like their mother. Of seeing to his household, making his meals, cleaning his home. As a wife would do.

After a long moment of thoughtful silence, her father said, "Two months is a long time, I'm thinkin'."

"I know it."

Oh! Jonathan Lundy still hadn't looked her way! Katie bristled. She hated being talked over like she had nothing to say for herself.

Though she surely didn't like the sound of this conversation, either. She was about to speak her mind when her mother spoke.

"Mary and Hannah are nice girls, to be sure. And they are a pleasure to be around."

Jonathan nodded. His expression relaxed. For the first time since he'd arrived, the hat hung limply in his hand. "Thank you. Ever since my Sarah died, I've had a time of it."

My Sarah. Those words told Katie everything she needed to know. Jonathan might never think of anyone other than Sarah. Ever.

Her mother winced. "Sarah's accident was a tragedy, we all know that. But you and your sister, Winnie, are raisin' the girls just fine. I know Mary has missed her mother something awful, and it wasn't easy when young Hannah was still little more than a babe."

Jonathan's face became expressionless. "Neither Mary nor Hannah understood death at first. Hannah woke up crying for her mother more often than not, and Mary . . ." His voice lowered. "Well, Mary refused to ride in a buggy for months after the accident. But they're better now."

"Yes, indeed. I know they are better." Her mother paused, as if measuring her words. "But, you see, I don't think it would be right for our Katie to take on such a job."

Her father slapped his hands on his thighs. "Not at all. This job you speak of is not the one for Katie."

"If you're worried I would take advantage of her, I promise I will do no such thing. I'll move to the *daadi haus* and be always respectful."

"We are sure you will."

"And I will pay her, too. Please don't think I wanted Katie to work for nothing."

This conversation was getting worse and worse. It was so uncomfortable that Katie no longer minded that they were speaking about her as if she wasn't there. She didn't want to be there.

"Money is not the problem, Jonathan," her mother said sternly.

The decision had clearly been made. Katie didn't know whether to be thankful or disappointed. Here was her opportunity to show Jonathan just what kind of mother and wife she could be. Here was her chance! But it was also a risk that Jonathan would only see her as a caregiver for his girls.

And though she'd always wanted to be a wonderful *gut* mother and housewife, she wanted to be valued as *Katie*. As someone special. Perhaps that would never happen in Jonathan's home.

Jonathan looked surprised. "Oh. I see. I was just thinking that you might have an extra hand, now that Anna Metzger is living here."

Katie smiled at the mention of her best friend's name. Anna had been living at their inn for seven months now, and quite an adjustment it had been! Her dear friend was determined to learn the ways of the Amish, join the church, and eventually exchange vows with Henry, Katie's brother.

Katie's father spoke. "Anna is a great help, to be sure. But that isn't the problem."

"What is?"

With a tender look her way, her mother spoke. "It would be improper for Katie to live with you, that way."

"In what way? She'd only be caring for the girls."

With a hint of censure in her tone, her mother said, "She is a young woman of marriageable age, Jonathan. Certainly you agree?"

For the first time since he'd arrived, Jonathan looked at her hard. From top to bottom. Katie did her best to sit still, chin up, as if she didn't mind being stared at like a horse at market.

Jonathan's hat fell, whether the brim gave out or he was startled, Katie didn't know. But, he did look mighty flustered. His brow was damp as he reached down to pick the hat up.

The tension in the room increased. Helplessly, Katie turned to her mother. *Say something!* she ordered silently. *Say something to make things better!*

But her mother remained silent. Her father shot her

a troubled glance but merely waited for Jonathan to respond.

He finally did . . . very slowly. "Th- . . . though Katie seems . . . Is. Mighty nice . . ." He shifted. Pulled at his shirt. "I'm not in the market for a new wife, you see."

Her *mamm* raised a brow. "Ever? All girls need a mother." Gently, she added, "Perhaps one day you might even find yourself eager for a wife."

Jonathan looked awkwardly at the floor.

Katie felt stung. Had Jonathan become so terribly entrenched in his world of loneliness that he didn't even see that chance of future happiness?

"I've heard enough. I'm sorry, but we canna allow Katie to live there, with you." Her father stood up with a groan. "Now, I best get to work, there's a lot of things that need doing."

"I wish you would reconsider," Jonathan interrupted quickly. "There's really no one else to turn to."

"That may be the case, but honestly, Jonathan, we have Katie to look after. Don'tcha see?"

Jonathan stood up, his expression grim. "I see. I see that I shouldn't have asked for so much."

To Katie's surprise, neither parent refuted Jonathan's words. Instead, her father merely walked him to the door, then followed him outside.

A feeling of loss flowed through her. Well, there was her chance, and it had come and gone in mere minutes. As they heard Jonathan's buggy roll down their gravel drive, Katie turned to her mother. "I feel sorry for him. Jonathan is a proud man. It had to be difficult to ask for help."

Her mother picked up her sewing again. "We both know pride is a sin, Katie. He will be fine. It is far better if you stay here at home. Where we can keep a close eye on you."

Katie felt her insides come apart. All at once, the true reason for her parents' reluctance for her to be at the Lundys' began to dawn on her. Her parents were not concerned with Jonathan's behavior.

They were far more worried about her own. Perhaps her past mistakes were not as swept aside as she'd thought. "I'm twenty years old, you know."

"Just twenty. Your birthday was only two weeks ago."

"I'm just sayin' that twenty is much older than sixteen."

Her mother jabbed her needle through the fabric. "That is true."

"What do you think Jonathan will do now?"

"It is not our concern."

"But Winnie really wants to go to Indiana. She told me she can't wait to go. And, well, she doesn't get to take time for herself very often. The only instance I recall her asking for a break was last spring, when Anna had first come to live with us."

"Winnie's caring for her brother's children. She shouldn't need breaks from that. It's best that she concentrate on her duties, Katie. We both know what can happen when duty is forgotten."

Katie glanced at her mother again. Her mother's shoulders were stiff, her posture rigid. With great effort, Katie tried to stop her hands from shaking. What could her mother know?

"I'm going to go check on Anna," she said, abruptly scurrying from the room.

Miraculously, her mother let her go without a word.

But as Katie rounded the corner and faced the beautiful front staircase, she knew she couldn't visit her best friend just then. She didn't want to burden Anna with her troubles, or be surrounded by her joyful nature. Yes, lately, Anna had been very joyful.

She'd had every reason to be. Anna was unofficially courting Katie's brother, Henry. She was also in the process of learning everything she could about the Amish and practicing her Pennsylvania Dutch, all in preparation to join the church.

Bypassing the stairs, Katie threw open the door and strode outside, just as quickly as her feet could take her.

The mid-October sunshine brought welcome rays of warmth to the blustery air. As the multitude of crisp yellow, orange, and red leaves crunched underfoot, Katie took a moment to quiet down. To remind herself that she was safe.

Just as she closed her eyes to pray for guidance, a fierce yip of a small black-and-white pup caught her attention.

There, at front of the whitewashed two-story barn sat her brother, a wiggly puppy in his arms.

Katie hurried closer. "Henry, whatever are you doing with that dog?"

His smile was broad and transformed his usual solemn expression. "Caleb Miller's Daisy had a litter. He gave me a pup in exchange for the work I did in his shop last Friday and Saturday."

Unable to help herself, Katie reached out for the pup, then carefully cradled him in her arms. After a bit of squirming, the puppy leaned closer and licked her face. "Oh, he's *wunderbaar schee*—wonderful nice, that's for sure. What are you going to do with him? Is he for Anna?"

"No. She's got enough to do, with the inn and her lessons," he said easily.

Her brother used to take everything seriously and saw little humor in even the silliest of things. His relationship with Anna changed all that. Now the two of them were entering into a bond that went beyond all their cultural differences. Each was becoming a stronger person because of it.

"This puppy is for you."

"Truly? Why?"

Looking suddenly bashful, Henry shrugged. "I don't know. Maybe because you love puppies so?"

She was prevented from replying when the puppy wriggled some more and yipped out his own reply. "Oh, he's a dear. Look how he has three black paws and one white one." The puppy yipped again and stretched two paws, just like he was showing them off. Katie couldn't keep the smile from her face.

Henry laughed. "I think the two of you will get along just fine."

"Do *Mamm* and *Daed* know?"

"*Jah*, they know." Scratching the pup on its head, he said, "Don't worry so, Katie." Motioning to the open windows of their house, he murmured, "I overheard some of Jonathan's visit."

Katie avoided his eyes. "I don't know what I'm supposed to do with my life."

Henry clicked his tongue. "You will. What's meant to be will happen. It always does."

"I hope so." Even though she knew she'd regret scrubbing the stains out later, Katie sat down on the dusty ground to let the pup scamper. He leaped from her lap, sniffed impatiently around the area, then eagerly ran to her again, his tail wagging like they hadn't seen each other in days.

He'd come back to her. He hadn't chased after Henry. Though she knew it was a silly thing to be happy about, Katie was pleased. Perhaps everything did work out the way it was supposed to. Perhaps everything with Jonathan Lundy would work out one way or another, as well.

Perhaps one day, her past would finally stay in the past.

Finding comfort in prayer, she whispered, "Dear Lord, my gracious God, please help me remember how far I've come from my past. Please help me remember to enjoy the present. And please help me see where my future lies. I do so want to follow your will."

With all her heart, Katie did want to follow where the Lord intended to lead her. She knew she did.

So why was she always wishing and hoping for things that could never be?

"Anna, you must be careful filling the jars," Katie cautioned four days later, as she carefully lifted the jar out of the boiling water then poured exactly one cup of preserves into the glass container. "If you are not careful, you're going to fill them too much and then they won't seal properly."

Anna pursed her lips. "I thought this was supposed to be an easy job."

"It is." Katie had been helping can since she was old enough to scrub vegetables. She found it awfully strange that Anna had reached adulthood hardly knowing how to take care of a house and home. "Canning is a most agreeable chore, to be sure."

Anna held up a finger. "Not for me. Look at my fingers." She held a finger up for inspection while blowing on it so hard the paper behind her fluttered on the counter. "Do you see the blisters? They really hurt. I got burned when the boiling jam got the best of me."

Katie had nothing to say to that. The blisters would teach her to be more careful in the future. But she didn't have to say a single word because Henry entered the roomy kitchen and made a beeline for Anna.

He frowned as soon as he noticed her pained expression. "Anna, you hurt yourself?"

Just like a child, she held up a finger. "It's nothing. Merely a blister."

"It looks terribly painful, though."

Anna nodded. "It is."

To Katie's chagrin, her older brother carefully pressed Anna's fingers to his lips before leading her to the sink. And Anna, why she was letting him lead her around! As Katie watched her brother coddle her best friend, she could barely hold her patience. Anna had suffered a tiny burn, not a disastrous accident! Oh, she had much to learn. No self-respecting Amish woman would fuss over a burn so much.

She was just about to mention that when she realized neither Henry nor Anna would notice if she spoke at all. They were standing in front of the sink, cool water running, lost in each other's eyes.

Suddenly, it was too warm to be there with them. Too confining. Too much.

"I'm going to check on Roman," she said, anxious to see the new puppy.

Neither looked her way.

Frustrated, Katie ran out to the pen that Henry had made for the puppy. He wiggled with delight when he saw her and yipped. She opened the gate, freed him, then sat on the ground as he jumped and played all around her. But to her surprise, even the bundle of black-and-white fur didn't lift her spirits.

No, he only reminded her that she had no special person of her own. And, unfortunately, that she had once had someone who had cared for her very much. He'd cared for her and she'd pushed him away.

Her mother, who'd been out feeding the goats, slowly approached. "I do believe this is the first time I've not seen you laugh and giggle at this puppy's antics."

Her mother made her sound awfully young. "I need more than just puppies, *Mamm*. I am older now, remember?"

"*Ach*, Katie, you are surely havin' a time of it, aren't you now?"

Katie scrambled to her feet and followed her mother back to the goats' pen. "I'm all right."

"Come now, I saw you running out here. What is wrong?"

"I don't know." How could she ever put into words everything she was thinking? She could never admit to her mother all the selfish and confusing thoughts that were brewing inside of her.

Her mother nodded to Katie's hand. "Come now, something's wrong. Look what you are doing! We both know you would never pet Gertie without a reason."

That was unfortunately true. Oh, how she'd always hated those ornery goats. She had ever since they'd gotten loose one fine spring day and found her first Log Cabin quilt on the line. In a matter of minutes, Billie and Gertie had chewed on that quilt, making a mess of years of careful hard work.

Because her mother was patiently waiting for an answer, Katie gave her one. "It's nothing. Anna and Henry looked like they needed a moment or two of privacy."

"I suppose a courting couple needs a moment or two from time to time." Looking toward the house, she wrinkled her brow. "I thought you were working on jam this morning. Did you already fill the jars?"

"No. We had to take a break when Anna burned her fingers." Unable to stop the flow of words any longer, Katie blurted, "The way she carried on, you would think her finger was on fire. And of course, it happened just when Henry was coming in for some lemonade. The moment he saw her he rushed over and put her fingers under the water." Katie didn't even feel like mentioning how Henry had kissed Anna's fingers, too.

"That was good thinkin'."

"But that isn't the point! Anna could've tended to a blister by herself. She didn't need to act so helpless around my brother."

"*Ah.*"

Katie ignored her mother's smile and continued. "As a matter of fact, she wouldn't even have been burned if she would have listened to me and been more careful." Thinking again to how long it was taking to can preserves, Katie felt her temper explode. "Anna doesn't listen, *Mamm*! I've told her time and again to only fill the jars two-thirds of the way full, but she always ignores my suggestions."

"I doubt she ignores you on purpose. This is all new for her."

"Everything is new, even after being here seven months. She is helpless."

"She's accomplished in other ways."

"But that hardly matters now. Amish women need to know how to can."

"And she will learn," her mother soothed. "We all learn what we need to learn in our own time, don'tcha think?"

Now that her temper had calmed, Katie felt embarrassed for her behavior and cross words. Her mother was exactly right. Anna was doing the best that she could. "I'm sorry."

"I'm not sorry that you're sharing your thoughts with me. Come now, what is really bothering you?"

Katie knew she couldn't keep all her mixed up feelings inside any longer. And, because she trusted her mother's advice more than anyone else's, she whispered, "Anna is getting everything I've wanted."

Her mother's lips twitched. "You've wanted to burn yourself canning?"

"No, of course not." Reluctantly, she mumbled, "Soon Anna will have a husband."

"*Ah.* You are still thinking of Jonathan Lundy and his offer."

She couldn't help herself. For the last few days, it was all she ever thought about. "I want to go to Jonathan's house, *Mamm.*"

"Staying in his home and watching over his girls does not seem like a terribly wise decision, especially if you have a fondness for Jonathan."

"You knew I cared for him?"

"I would have had to be blind and dumb not to know that, Katie." Leading the way out of the goats' pen, she turned to her. "I'm sorry to say this, but the fact is that he does not feel the same way. He might never feel that way. Everyone knows he misses Sarah. You'll be setting yourself up for heartache."

"Then let me have heartache while I'm at least trying. My heart already hurts now and I've done nothing." All she'd been doing for months was helping her friend learn the Amish ways.

"I see." After looking at Katie once again, her mother picked up her skirts and shook them. "I'll do some more thinking about this. In the meantime, go see to Anna." With a bit of a smile she said, "I do believe Henry left her, so she's all alone in the kitchen once again."

Katie could only imagine what Anna was doing if she

still wasn't nursing a hurt finger. "No telling what mess she's made now."

"Thank goodness she has you to show her the best way to clean things up, yes?"

Katie couldn't think of a suitable reply.

Chapter 2

Some days, Jonathan missed Sarah so much he thought his insides would break. Sometimes, he longed for his wife so much, he'd be willing to do just about anything to see her again.

It was one of those days.

Outside the kitchen, the air was crisp and the sky a beautiful robin's-egg blue. The maple near the house was intent to fill the area with its glory . . . the leaves seemed to change to burnt red right before his eyes. Yes, the Lord had blessed them with a perfect late fall day. Within days, the air would become colder and the fields would be covered with a pristine white blanket of snow.

But not quite yet.

When Sarah was alive, she would have been singing a happy tune and would have had every window in their house open to greet the day, regardless of how sharp the wind was. Now he only opened one.

Oh, how he used to grumble about the frostiness of the kitchen. Now, a far different chill permeated the room. One of silence and emptiness. No matter how many people might take up the space, things weren't changing. His wife was gone and in her place was a giant gap of a hole that couldn't seem to be filled.

And he'd tried.

But it was no use. Like a doughnut, there was no center to their lives. The imagery almost made him smile. When Sarah had been alive, he'd taken it for granted that he was the center of the family.

He'd been much mistaken.

Winnie's presence was helping, though lately he'd seen a shadow in her expression. Jonathan knew what the shadow was for. At twenty-two, his sister was yearning for a future of her own. A family and home of her own.

Being his lifeline wasn't giving her the satisfaction he'd hoped it would. If he were honest with himself, he knew he should be happy for his sister. The Lord asked everyone to find a life partner and raise a family. It would be a terrible shame if Winnie did not yearn for those things, too. But oh, he wished she would have chosen to wait a bit longer for his sake.

Outside the window, a pair of cardinals flew by, the male so proud and bright, his mate's colors far more subdued. Yet together they made a mighty fine pair. Could he fault his sister for wanting what all creatures had?

He could not. But what still remained was his needs. He

needed someone to watch his girls while Winnie went to meet her beau.

"I still canna believe that the Brennemans refused you," Winnie stated over her half-drunk tea. "Your idea was most reasonable."

He'd thought so, too. Carefully, he flipped the eggs in the pan, grimacing as yet again one of the yolks broke and ran across the griddle's surface, hardening in seconds. "Not everyone wants to care for another person's children, I suppose."

"No, that's not it." She drummed her fingers on the oak table he'd inherited from their parents. "What did they say again?"

Even though they'd discussed the conversation over and over during the past week, Jonathan dutifully recounted the encounter again. "John and Irene said they did not want their daughter living with me. Alone."

"But you would be with the girls, and in the *daadi haus*, too." Winnie frowned. "And what is with that nonsense, anyway? Don't they realize that your heart has already been taken?"

It had been, indeed. He had loved. Once. And then, to his shame, he'd felt that love fade into something far different. Something that only in the privacy of his thoughts could he admit was disappointment.

Now he only felt guilt for how Sarah died. That guilt weighed heavy on him. Now that it was almost two years since the accident, Jonathan figured he'd be carrying that burden for the rest of his life.

Yes, his heart was locked up somewhere else and wasn't

going to escape any time in the near future. Most likely, ever. Katie Brenneman had nothing to be afraid of.

"Between work and the girls I am busy indeed, but I've a feeling that they don't see it that way."

Winnie joined him at the counter. With easy movements, she wiped off the crumbs of her toast as he pulled his own bread from the confines of the oven. "I should go talk to Katie. I'm sure she could talk her parents into changing their decision if she just put her mind to it."

"Winnie, you mustn't. John and Irene have already made their decision." After shaking a healthy amount of pepper on his eggs and placing the toast on top, Jonathan carried his plate to the table. "Maybe, you could put off your trip for a while."

Her hand tightened on the rag. "Don't ask me to do that. I must go to Indiana. I need to go. Malcolm has been so wonderful *gut* in his letters, there might be something between us." More quietly, she added, "I hope there might be."

He said the obvious. "Indiana is far away." And because he wasn't as good a brother as he wished he were, he added quite peevishly, "They may be quite different there, too."

"Like how?"

"I don't know. But different is different."

She shook her head slightly. "Oh, *bruder.* Sometimes different is good. Sometimes change is what the Lord wants."

"Sometimes not."

"Jonathan, once you followed your heart. Now it is time for me to do the same."

He knew she was right. Winnie was a pretty girl, to

be sure. Thin as a reed, she used to look somewhat like a beanpole. Now, though, she merely looked slender and feminine. Her light blue eyes emphasized her ivory skin and dark, almost black, hair.

Yes, it was time for Winnie to be thinking of courtship and love. "I hear you."

Looking satisfied that she won, she plopped his hot pan in water. "I'll figure something out for you, I promise. I will not go at the expense of Mary and Hannah. I'd never leave if I didn't feel they were in good hands."

"What are you talking about?" Mary asked, popping her head into the kitchen.

Winnie blushed. "Nothing, child."

"It is something," Mary said in that forthright way of hers. The way that had been Sarah's. Sure, confident. At times too much so. "I heard my name."

"You shouldn't be eavesdropping, Daughter."

Mary crossed her arms over her chest, yet another true imitation of her mother. "I didn't listen on purpose. But I did hear my name."

Slyly, Winnie raised an eyebrow Jonathan's way. Yes, Mary was a handful.

"Your aunt and I were discussing the particulars about Katie coming to live with us," Jonathan finally said.

"Why?"

"Because I am going to go to Indiana for a spell and Katie and I have been friends for a long time." She touched Mary's nose gently. "Since we were your age."

"Why do you want to go away?"

"I'm not going for certain. I just might." Winnie picked up Jonathan's plate and rinsed it off. "Would you like an egg this morning, Mary?"

"No. I just want toast."

"Daughter, you should eat more."

As expected, Mary ignored her father. "Katie hasn't come over lately."

"That's because she's been busy. As have I."

"Well, I don't know her. Not too good."

It didn't escape Jonathan's notice that his daughter wrinkled her nose when she spoke their neighbor's name. "You certainly do too know her."

"Not well. I don't see why we want her here. I don't."

All brusque and business, Winnie shooed Mary and little Hannah, who'd just appeared, toward the table. "Sit down, now. It is time to eat."

But the ever-curious Hannah stopped in her tracks. "*Who* do we not want here?"

"No one," Winnie said as she shuffled Hannah to the broad oak bench. "I'm making you an egg. Eat some toast while you're waiting."

Obediently, she picked up a piece of toast. But to Jonathan's dismay, Hannah was not to be put off, either. "Who, who, who?"

Just as Jonathan was about to tell the youngest to be quiet, Mary answered. "Katie Brenneman."

Suspiciously quiet, Winnie slipped an egg onto a plate and placed it in front of Hannah.

Hannah looked at them all with wide eyes. "Why don't we want Katie here?"

"I want her here," Winnie said.

"I don't. And you don't either, Hannah," Mary proclaimed.

"Yes, I do. I like Katie." Smiling sweetly, Hannah speared the egg with her fork. "Katie gives me cookies at gatherings. And she always has a friendly smile."

Sounding far older than her years, Mary said, "Cookies do not make for a nice person."

"Why not?"

Jonathan could not take any more. "Katie is indeed a nice person, and that is all we will say about that. It is sinful the way you two are gossiping."

"I'm not gossiping and telling tales," Mary retorted, obviously offended. "I'm only telling you my feelings. Can't I even do that?"

"Of course you can. But you mustn't say those things about Katie."

"Why not? Why must we not have feelings about Katie Brenneman?"

"Daughters, eat your breakfast and get ready for school. We've had enough talk for now, I think."

While Hannah busied herself with butter and jam, Mary narrowed her eyes. "But—"

Winnie turned away from the sink. "Listen to your father, Mary."

As silence filled the room again, Jonathan stood up. "I'm going outside," he murmured as he walked to the hooks by the door. Before any of the girls could ask another question, he slipped on his coat and walked out into the crisp, cool air. Into the type of day that Sarah had always enjoyed.

He'd never told her how much he far preferred the hot, long days of summer.

In fact, he'd never told her much about his tastes and wants. Instead, each had ventured into married life determined to be as busy as possible. Sarah had been terribly independent, always going wherever she needed to go. He'd never thought much about the dangers of her driving the buggy so much.

Maybe if he had, she'd still be with him. Maybe if he'd tried harder to tell her how much he liked her being at home, she'd still be there. But now, of course, it was far too late.

With a sigh, Holly Norris signed the letter with "Your friend, Holly," then slipped the piece of stationery into the envelope and addressed it to the McClusky General Store.

"Well, Brandon, I don't know if Katie will ever see this, but at least I'll know I tried." She looked fondly at her older brother. "Right?"

If Brandon heard, he gave no notice. Today was one of his bad days. Four months ago, he'd been diagnosed with cancer of the liver. Since then, his health had been steadily declining. At first, the doctors had talked about chemotherapy and radiation treatments. But after several scans and exhaustive tests, it was obvious that he was never going to get better. Actually, it was becoming obvious that Holly was about to lose him very soon.

Every time she thought about Brandon dying, Holly choked up. He was the only family she had left. Their mother died of breast cancer four years ago. And their dad—well, neither of them had heard from Graham Norris in almost a decade.

For most of her life, it had only just been she and Brandon.

And lately, it had just been her. She'd never felt so alone.

For a few hours each day, Brandon would regain consciousness. Luckily, she was always there to witness it.

Holly mentally thanked her boss, Dr. Kinter, for allowing her to take a leave of absence from her job as a veterinary assistant. What would she do if Brandon woke up, only to find no one was sitting by his side?

During those moments of consciousness, Holly would try and sound chipper and chatty. For her sake, he would attempt to smile, but they both knew even that effort cost him. Brandon was slipping away. He was losing interest in almost everything in their world, talking more about the past and their mother than Holly could ever remember.

There was only one subject that ever drew a familiar spark into his beautiful hazel eyes—Katie Brenneman.

Almost three years ago, he'd fallen hard for Katie. In return, she'd led him on, then broke his heart. Katie had broken Holly's heart as well. She'd thought they'd been good friends. Best friends.

Then she'd found out that Katie had just been pretending to care about them. She'd never intended to go to trade school with Holly. She'd never intended to one day be roommates like she'd promised. She'd never intended to ever fall in love with Brandon.

No, she was Amish.

To Holly's dismay, Brandon still carried a torch for Katie. And now she was the only person he wanted to see. So Holly was swallowing her pride and doing everything she could to contact Katie.

Even though, really, Holly couldn't care less whether she ever saw Katie again. She didn't appreciate being used.

As the machines clicked and sighed around her brother, Holly nodded to the nurse on duty, then walked to the hospital's front lobby and posted the letter.

The irony of the address didn't escape her. The truth was, even though she'd felt she had become best friends with Katie, the fact remained that really, she hadn't known her very well at all. She didn't know where she lived, only that she shopped at the McClusky General Store.

Oh, and that Katie had lied to them all. About who she was and what her dreams were. About who she loved and what she wanted to be.

As Holly watched the envelope slide down the glass mail slot, she wondered what Katie would do when she saw it. Not wanting to put Brandon's news in the letter, Holly had asked Katie to meet her at the Brown Dog Café. Part of her hoped Katie would ignore the note.

But even though Holly wished that, she hoped and prayed that Katie would rush to Brandon's side. He wanted to see her. He needed to see Katie.

And so, Holly knew she would do whatever it took to give him what he wanted. Even reaching out to the girl she'd hoped to never see again.

Chapter 3

"I know my brother Jonathan's intentions are true. They are without reproach, and without any ulterior motives. Katie's presence is surely needed."

With a sense of alarm, Katie looked at her mother, who was busy frying chicken. Beside her Anna was peeling potatoes. She, herself, was rolling out pie crust. Winnie was pressing some napkins for the evening's meal at the inn.

Though the tasks were mundane and their hands busy and useful, the conversation certainly was not. It seemed to bump along and halt like a wheel stuck in a rut, stopping and starting in rough movements.

Anna looked so ill at ease that she'd most likely peeled more potatoes than they would need over the coming week.

Katie felt her own nerves being pulled as the silence stretched on. *"Mamm?"* she said. "Did you hear?"

"*Ach.* Yes." With a frown, her mother glanced up from the frying pan. "Things are not as simple as you make them seem, Winnie."

"Sometimes they are," Winnie fired back. She placed the hot iron she'd been using back in its holder. Chin up, she looked at them all, her light blue eyes shining, the perfect contrast to her dark-as-night brows and hair. "I think you may be making things too difficult. Jonathan and I need help. That is all. We need another pair of hands."

"You are not asking for only our hands, Winnie. You are asking Katie to live with you."

Katie's cheeks heated. She knew that tone in her mother's voice. It plainly said her patience was wearing thin and to tread lightly.

It was obvious Winnie heard no such warning. Still ignoring her pile of ironing, she crossed her arms over her chest. "I thought your offers of assistance were genuine when Sarah passed on."

Anna groaned and grabbed another potato.

Katie sucked in a breath. Winnie's words were mighty harsh. Of course all of the Brennemans had offered to help back at Sarah's funeral. But helping when they were able and her living with Jonathan were two different things.

"My offer was indeed genuine, Winnie," *Mamm* said quietly. "I have helped your family out time and again over the last year and a half."

Katie kept her head down, concentrating on fluting the pie crust's edges. Oh, her mother was in a fine state. Winnie shouldn't push so.

But still, she did. "It would just be for two months. Let's see, it's the first of November now. In two months, it will be the beginning of January." She pointed to the frosty windowpane, evidence that the weather outside was finally getting colder. "What's two months, after all? The spring crocuses won't even have started to bloom."

"Two months can be a long time if it's the wrong situation."

"I've waited a long time to meet the right man," Winnie said.

Katie's mother clucked. "You will find the right man sooner or later."

Winnie nibbled on a bottom lip. "None of the boys I talked to at singings interested me. No one since, either. Before long, I'm going to be *en altmaedel*."

Katie chuckled in spite of the serious conversation. "You are not an old maid, Winnie. You are hardly more than two years older than me."

"You can't deny it has been a long time since we used to look forward to our Sunday singings. We are not so young anymore."

Katie did remember how much fun she and Winnie used to have together. They'd go to the singings on Sunday evenings, eager to meet other teenagers. Eager to find a special boy.

Unfortunately, neither ever had found anyone special. As the years passed and they attended other friends' weddings, they'd begun to drift apart.

"I feel like an old maid, and that is the truth," Winnie

proclaimed. Turning to Katie's mother again, she said, "Are you worried about the girls? Mary can be a handful, but she's a sweet girl at heart."

"It's not the children that concern me, Winnie."

"Then what?" Winnie turned to Anna. "What do you think? This is my time to actually meet Malcolm. I figured you, if no one else, would understand the obstacles I am facing. It is hard to learn about someone from mere letters."

Anna blushed but said nothing. Only the potato peels flying onto the counter at a frantic pace gave notice to her discomfort.

Words warred inside of Katie. She yearned to push her mother to give in. To let her live with the Lundys. But, she didn't like how Winnie was pressing them, either. Guilt and obligation didn't make a fitting pair.

Once all the chicken was drying on a copy of the *Budget*, her mother sighed. "Tell me about this young man you are writing to."

"He's a Troyer. Malcolm's great-grandmother was Ruth Troyer. Do you know of the family?"

Grudgingly, her mother nodded. "I do. They're good stock."

"I knew it." Winnie's smile, with those perfect dimples, lit up the room. "I could tell from the way he described his family that they were people I would like to know and would get along with."

"Now, I didn't say that, Winnie."

Winnie waved a hand dismissively. "You've said enough.

Besides, I know Malcolm quite well now. We've been cor-responding for some time."

"Letters don't always tell what matters about a person," Anna interrupted. "It's hard to get a real sense of what a person is like from just a few words, or even a few meet-ings."

"Malcolm's letters are more than brief messages," Winnie replied. "They're truly thoughtful notes revealing his heart and soul."

Katie bit her lip as she noticed Anna and her mother exchange amused glances.

Seemingly encouraged, Winnie continued. "Our notes to each other are personal and heartfelt. Like there's something between us that's special." She glanced toward Anna, and then finally to Katie. "You both know what that's like, don'tcha?"

"I do," Anna answered as a faint blush stained her cheeks. "Henry and I have written a few notes to each other."

This was news to Katie. "When did my brother write to you?"

"When we were apart." Turning to Winnie, Anna said, "But, Winnie, I must say that nothing takes the place of conversations face-to-face. Whenever Henry is pleased, he gets this crease in between his brows. Now I know when he's tired because he will favor his right leg a bit."

"It never did heal up right after that horse kicked him," Katie's mother commented.

Anna's expression became tender. "Now that Henry and I have gotten to know each other better, I know he and I will make each other happy when we are married. Because we've taken the time to get to know each other better. I . . . I've never felt this way before."

Winnie flicked a snowy white cloth in the air to snap it open. "See, Mrs. Brenneman? I need to be near Malcolm. I need the time with him, face-to-face."

"I hear what you are saying."

Winnie turned to Katie. "What about you? Have you ever been in love?"

Katie jabbed another pie crust with a fork. "You know I'm not courtin' anyone." Her words exposed everything she'd always wanted to hide deep inside of her. Frustration, wistfulness. Regret.

But Winnie, too intent on her own problems, didn't take notice. "Not even during the singings? Or afterward? I seem to remember you spent quite a bit of time out and about during your *rum*—"

"No," Katie said quickly, cutting Winnie off before she could say a thing about Katie's running-around years. Of her *rumspringa*.

Katie hated to be reminded of that time. Of the things she'd done. Primly, she put a stop to Winnie's sly insinuations. "Everyone experiments a bit during their running-around years. I did nothing out of the ordinary. *Nothing.*"

Winnie looked at her in surprise. "I didn't say you did."

"I was baptized and joined the church in June, you know."

"I know." With a half smile, Winnie said, "I was there, remember?"

Just as Katie began to think that perhaps all talk of her

past was behind her, Winnie pressed again. "But what about your time among the English?" she pressed, her voice light and full of mirth. "Tell us the truth. Didn't you ever find an English boy attractive?"

Katie felt all three pairs of eyes turn her way, capturing her with direct stares. Her mother's regard felt hot, like Winnie's forgotten iron, searing the layers of lies she'd cloaked over herself. Anna merely looked curious.

She shifted uncomfortably and stayed focused on the poor pie shell, which had done nothing to deserve her harsh treatment with the fork.

"Do you intend to answer, Katie?" Winnie asked.

"There was no one special."

Winnie raised a brow. "Indeed? I could have sworn I heard you keeping company with a certain *Englischer* with raven black hair. A terribly handsome English boy."

"That is just gossip, of course," Katie said quickly. Afraid to lie and bring her past sins into the present, she added, "I'm happy to be among the Amish. This is where I belong."

"We all realize that, Katie." With a snap of a freshly starched napkin, Winnie closed her trap. "Since there's no one keeping you, and you're so happy and all, won't you please consider helping Jonathan and me, then? I've never had my chance for love, what with Sarah passing on at such a young age."

"The decision was never mine, it was my parents'."

Unperturbed, Winnie turned to her mother. "Okay, then. Mrs. Brenneman, will you and John please reconsider? The girls would be truly happy to have Katie's company, and her presence would solve a fair amount of problems for both Jonathan and me." She paused. "He has been working very hard at the lumber factory. It is a good job. He can't afford to miss any time off work."

"I am glad he is doing so well at the lumberyard. And I do understand that he can not take days off to tend to the girls."

Anna bit her lip and looked down when Katie tried to catch her eye.

Winnie seemed to take the moment as a good sign. "Please?"

"I'll talk to John," her mother finally said, breaking the silence. "Perhaps we can come to some agreement, after all."

Cheeks as rosy as a spring day, Winnie beamed. "*Danke.*" She turned to Katie. "And, thank you, too, Katie. There's no one else I would trust to care for the girls." Setting down the iron again, she said, "I'll write to Malcolm today and tell them that there is still hope."

"Nothing is decided, Winnie."

"But nothing is *not* decided, either." Moments later, Winnie Lundy left them, twenty napkins neatly pressed, but at least half that many more left to do.

Irritation sliced through Katie as she glared at the chore. Surely the least she could have done was finish what she started! Oh, that was so like Winnie—determined and scatterbrained. More than one teacher had said it was a regrettable combination. "Well, now I must finish Winnie's chore."

"That girl doesn't give up, does she?" Anna said with a laugh. "I thought she was going to start digging her heels right through the wood floor."

Her mother chuckled. "She never was one to give up. Not even in a blue moon." Crossing the kitchen, her mother sneaked up behind Katie and gave her a squeeze. "I'll make everything all right, dear Daughter. Don't fret."

As always, her mother's touch made her feel better. "I won't."

"*Gut*. Now you two finish dinner preparations. I'm going to go check on things in the front parlor. This latest batch of visitors is a handful, I'll tell you that." She bustled out of the kitchen.

When they were alone, Anna looked at Katie with concern in her eyes. "Katie, are you okay?"

She did not feel okay at all. Instead she felt dizzy and flushed, like she'd been bent over too long picking beans from the garden. "*Jah*. Sure. Why?"

"Oh, I don't know. It just seems that you're not as happy as I thought you'd be." Softly, she said, "I thought you liked Jonathan."

"I do."

"Then why aren't you happier? You heard your mother. You're about to get what you want."

She was happy. But how could she admit all her insecurities to someone like Anna, who had experienced so much and now was just months away from marriage? "It's . . . it's just that Winnie and her bossy nature is vexing. We used to be such good friends." Picking up a dishcloth, she bent and swiped up a bit of flour that had fallen to the wooden floor. "I don't remember her always being so pushy. It's like she doesn't even want to listen to anyone but herself."

"She does sound desperate," Anna agreed. "But maybe it's just because she finally feels like it's her time for love and she's afraid to let the moment slip by." Moving across the kitchen to Katie's side, Anna picked up Katie's finished pie shell and carried it to the oven. "I bet she's still the same person you always knew underneath. Sometimes circumstances can change a person, you know?"

"I know."

Taking two bowls to the sink, Anna said, "Actually you are the one who sounds strange. Ever since I've known you, you've had an eye on Jonathan Lundy. Now, though, you seem far more wary of him. Did something happen between the two of you?"

"No. Nothing has ever happened." Or was ever likely to.

Of course, that was the problem. Longingly, Katie looked toward the door. Oh, how she wanted to get away from everyone, for just a little while.

"Well, then, are you embarrassed around Winnie? Do you think she knows about your feelings for her brother?"

"No," Katie said. She wished that Anna would just stop. *Stop.* Her feelings for Jonathan were too mixed up. Especially now.

"If you were embarrassed, I'd understand. It's hard admitting to having a fancy for someone's brother."

"I don't fancy him, Anna." The words came out harsher

than she intended, but for the life of her, Katie wouldn't take them back. She was tired of being seen as only a silly girl. She was more than that. Why, if everyone only knew the things she'd done. . .

They would be mighty surprised, for sure.

Eyes wide, Anna stepped back. "Sorry. I didn't mean to press."

Katie was sorry for her words, too. But she didn't feel like apologizing. Yet, she knew she must. "I'm the one who is sorry, Anna. Please forgive my sharp words."

Green eyes blinked. "Is there anything that I can help you with?"

"No."

"Is it me? Does my being here bother you?"

Finally she could speak the truth about something. "No, Anna. Your being here is wonderful *gut*. Truly. Now let's do what we're supposed to do, *jah*? We have to finish preparing dinner, cleaning the kitchen, and ironing napkins, just like *Maam* said."

Anna chuckled. "I'll finish up those napkins, Katie."

Later that day, after they'd served dinner, the kitchen had been cleaned and the animals tended to, after her father had read from the Bible and they all said good night, Katie was alone with only little Roman for company, snug in his basket with his favorite blanket that he liked to chew.

Carefully she opened the chest of drawers and pulled out a box from her past. A fancy papered box left from her time with the English. Like a fugitive, she'd smuggled it into the house, deathly afraid her mother would find it. Would ask why such a gaudy piece of work was in her possession.

Katie couldn't rightly say. All she did know was that she couldn't bear to part with the memories.

Not even the bad ones.

With a furtive glance toward the door, Katie carried the box to her bed and settled in. And then she lifted the lid. The heady fragrance of her secret life roared out of the enclosure like the spirit of Christmas past.

She blinked away the memories each scent envisioned.

Mint. A crushed rose. A tiny stuffed bear. Several fancy store-bought cards. With a sigh, Katie picked up the little brown bear and rubbed it against her cheek. If she closed her eyes, she could remember receiving it. Remember the joy she'd felt. The longing for things that couldn't be.

Of things she shouldn't want.

As if burned, Katie hastily tucked it back into the box and closed it. But still the scent lingered. Remnants of another time. A time that unfortunately wasn't so long ago.

In her stark room, the memories seemed out of place. Foreign. As if they belonged to someone else. Someone reckless and wild. They belonged to the person she'd been for fifteen months.

It had all started out simply enough. She'd gone with two other teens to the back of Jonathan's land, where a duffel bag was hidden. Inside were jeans and sweaters and T-shirts. Donning them felt exciting and terribly scary.

She'd felt far more wicked when she took off her *kapp* and loosened her hair. Laura gave her an elastic to put it in a ponytail. Then she, Laura, and Laura's neighbor James walked to town.

Looking back, Katie knew they'd looked nothing like regular *Englischers*. She had the wide-eyed expression of a deer in the glade.

But when they'd gone into a coffee shop called the Brown Dog, Laura introduced Katie to Holly and her brother, Brandon. The moment Brandon had looked her way and suddenly smiled, Katie had been smitten.

Oh, he'd been so handsome. He'd looked just like a man in one of Anna's fashion magazines that she'd shared with her back when she used to visit for quilting classes.

And Holly, well, she'd liked Holly so much, too. Though Holly was a few years older, she liked many of the things that Katie did. And she'd been so nice. So friendly. She introduced Katie, Laura, and James to a number of her friends. And because Holly had accepted her, the other teenagers had, too. One hour passed, then two. The next thing she knew, Laura was telling Katie that they needed to leave as soon as possible.

To her delight, Brandon had looked disappointed. "Can I have your phone number? I'll give you a call later."

Since of course the only phone they had was for business at the inn, she put him off. "My folks don't like me to receive phone calls."

"Oh. Well, how about I stop by?"

"No, that's probably not a good idea, either."

Puzzled, he raised his eyebrows. "Well, will you at least come back here soon?"

His eagerness to see her again brought forth a rush of

pleasure. Had she ever felt so wanted before? "Sure. I can do that."

"Tomorrow? We'll be hanging out here again tomorrow."

Holly had grabbed her hand. "Please say you'll come back."

Though Laura and James were tapping their feet impatiently at the front door, Katie nodded. "I will. I'll see you both tomorrow."

"Promise? We still have so much to talk about. You haven't even told me about your school or your friends."

"I will come back. I promise."

Moments later, Laura called out her name. "Katie, we must go *now*."

Holly chuckled as Katie practically ran out the door. "See you!"

The whole way home, Laura and James had talked about how strange the *Englischers* were. Laura in particular was uncomfortable. "If that is what we've been missing, I have to say I am glad," she'd stated. "Katie, did you see the way that one boy was looking at you? I think he liked you."

She had noticed. "I did."

"He talked to you a lot, too. What was he talkin' about?"

"Nothing special." The lie felt horrible sliding off her tongue, but Katie did her best to look innocent.

"He was fairly handsome, I mean for an English boy." With a sweet look toward James, Laura added, "I much prefer the Amish men I know."

Katie had said nothing, mainly because she'd known that Laura really only wanted James to notice her.

So, she never told a soul she had plans. Secret plans. The first of many.

Katie's hands shook as she stared at that box. Quickly, she put it away, hoping its removal would banish the memories.

Still they remained, stark and vivid. Not the least bit faded.

Quickly she put on a thick nightgown, hoping the soft flannel would chase away the chill that was surrounding her.

After checking on Roman, who was still happily curled in a little ball, Katie crawled under the thick layers of blankets and quilts. But sleep wouldn't come. Why was she thinking about Holly and Brandon after all this time?

Could it be because of the things that Brandon had said? Because lately she was realizing that maybe no one would ever say words like that to her again?

Katie closed her eyes to ward off the memory. To ward off the wishes.

When no relief came, she did the only thing she could— she prayed to the only one who could give her peace. "God, please help me. I've been so good lately. I'm doing everything I can to make amends. Is that what is important? Is that enough?"

Only silence met her words. Swallowing hard, she spoke a little louder. "Lord, I can't go back to the way I was. I need the protection of my family, of my Order. I need Your healing grace. Please stay with me and hold me. Walk by my side. Show me the way." She closed her eyes and prayed one of her favorite verses. "Blessed is everyone who fears the Lord, who walks in his ways." But even the quote from Psalm 128 did little to ease her burdens.

In fact, all Katie noticed was that the lingering scent of roses and mint still hung thick in the air.

Katie was playing with Roman, enjoying the rare afternoon sun when Henry approached, his expression as serious as if he was going to a burial.

"Someone left this for you at McClusky General Store," Henry said as he handed her a white business-sized envelope.

As she turned it over in her hands, worry gripped her. "Did *Daed* see it?"

"No." He looked at her curiously. "The person said it was for an Amish girl named Katie. Ron said he didna know of anyone else by that name. Is it yours?"

"Maybe. Probably." As she looked at the writing on the envelope, Katie fought to keep her expression innocent.

It was mighty hard to do, because from the moment she'd spied the writing on the envelope, she'd known immediately that the letter was for her and her alone. More important, she also knew who the author was. Holly's handwriting had had those distinctive curves. No one else had ever written her name so fancy.

It seemed a strange coincidence that Holly had written her so soon after she'd just been thinking about her.

Unfortunately, Henry was not as easy to fool as she might have hoped. "Katie, who would be writing you in care of the general store? What is the note about?"

"Nothing. I . . . made some friends among the English. You know that. This must be from one of them."

"But you aren't looking at the note like it's from a dear friend. You are looking at it like it might bite you."

She gripped it harder. Wished she could just wish it away. Wish that neither Henry nor she had ever seen it. With even greater effort, Katie fought to keep her voice calm and neutral. "Don't be silly."

Still playing detective, Henry said, "If this person is such a good friend, why didn't she have your address? Why all the secrecy?"

"I don't know the answer. I haven't opened the letter yet, have I?"

"Well, then, open it up." He crossed his arms over his chest and waited, just like he'd used to do when they'd walk to school and she hadn't been able to keep up with his long stride.

There was no way she wanted him to spy the contents. She slipped it in the pocket of her apron. "I will, later."

"But—"

"It's private, Henry."

"Private?" A pair of lines formed between his brows.

In her pocket, the letter's weight burned. "I'm allowed privacy too, aren't I?" Remembering how she'd interrupted him and Anna kissing just two days ago, she said, "Or is privacy only for courting couples?"

Henry bowed his head in embarrassment. "Of course you may have your privacy. You are as prickly as a cactus lately. I don't know what's wrong with you."

"Nothing is wrong, Henry."

"You canna fool me, Sister. I've known you too long for that."

After securing Roman in one of the stalls in the barn, Katie scrambled to her room, letter safely hidden in her apron, Henry's words echoing in her heart.

Yes, she had changed. And it didn't matter how sweet and kind she tried to be now. Inside, where it counted, she'd always be the girl who made a very big mistake . . . and had run from it.

As she stared at the letter she only knew one thing for certain: she was wanted again.

Chapter 4

Winnie was in good spirits. "Malcolm's letter was a full three pages. He gave me news about his family and their neighbors. He sends his good wishes to you, Jonathan."

"I appreciate that," Jonathan mumbled. When Winnie looked up, he turned back to his task of loading the wagon so she wouldn't see his expression. It was getting harder and harder to keep his personal feelings about Winnie's pen pal to himself. It was even more difficult to refrain from sharing his thoughts about her infatuation.

"Do you appreciate his wishes? You don't sound like you do." She walked by his side as he continued to load the wagon. Halfheartedly, she shoved in a pail of nails next to a pile of wood. "You don't sound interested in my letter at all."

The moment she turned, Jonathan rearranged things so the nails wouldn't fall over.

"This letter, it is your business, not mine." When he noticed her shoulders slump, he wished he could take back his words. But really, at the moment, he begrudged his sister's interest in Malcolm Troyer. He was an interloper in their life.

"Well, he extended an invitation again."

"*Uh-huh.*" *Jah*, this Malcolm was an inconvenience, that's what he was. He needed Winnie's attention here in Ohio. Jonathan needed her help with the girls.

Plus, he had no desire to stand around and discuss every written word in Winnie's letters yet again. His sister could wrestle with each sentence's meaning for an hour at a time.

He had no desire to do that. Besides, he'd been meaning to work the back fences today. There was much to do, since he only had Saturdays to get anything done. Over the last few years, he'd gradually worked more at the lumberyard with Brent and farmed less. The money was better, and far more stable. That was a good thing, since so much in his personal life felt unsteady.

Still holding the letter, Winnie said, "It's time I went to visit him. Past time."

"It's a shame he can't travel here. That's the way of things, don't you agree?"

"I already told you that his father is sick, and that Malcolm must run their hardware store. Honestly, Jonathan, didn't you hear me?"

"I heard you." Yes, he heard her, but other things weighed on his mind, most especially Mary and Hannah. Once again, they'd seemed whiny and angry the evening before. Mary had gone about her chores so slowly that they took double the time that they should. Hannah just frowned and clutched the doll Sarah had made for her even tighter.

It's been almost two years now, Lord. When are You going to make things better?

"Jonathan?"

"I'm sorry. I am, *uh*, interested, just busy, you know."

She took his apology without much thought. "I worry about planning ahead, but I feel that something is mighty special between me and Malcolm." Dimples showing, she blurted, "For the first time in my life, I have hope for a family of my own. Perhaps I'll be planning a wedding soon."

Jonathan bent down to pick up a shovel in order to hide his scowl. Winnie sounded so happy and optimistic. However, at the moment, he couldn't think of a worse thing than Winnie courting and marrying. What would he do with the girls then?

"Jonathan?" She picked up the leather glove he dropped. "What do you think?"

With a nod of thanks, he took the glove and paired it with the other. "I think you're counting chickens," he mumbled, though even to his own ears he knew he sounded grumpy and terribly old. When had he forgotten what it was like to be in love? To want to be in love?

"Not necessarily."

"Winnie, you've never even met this man, face-to-face."

"But I will soon."

"Well, I just don't want you to go getting your hopes up." Now that was a foolish thing to say, indeed! Her hopes were already up so high, a kite could be attached to them.

"Did you and Sarah always know you were going to be married?"

The question brought to mind images of Sarah. Of her ruddy face and matter-of-fact ways. Of her easy laugh. Of the first time he'd kissed her. "No. Not always."

"When, then?"

"I couldn't say." When had he first thought about a life with Sarah? When he'd first spied her at a neighbor's wedding? When he'd known she'd return his feelings?

Winnie leaned against the wagon. "Come now, Brother. Tell me something worth remembering."

"There isn't much to tell." And there really wasn't. If a person was looking for a story about flowers and romance, their engagement was surely not it.

But because Winnie still waited for a reply, and she did so much for him, and because she was asking and she didn't ask for much, he tried to remember. Slowly Jonathan said, "As you know, Sarah and I met when we were young. Courting and marriage seemed like a *gut* idea."

"You were anxious, right? You married young."

Had he been anxious? All he remembered was that it had been expected and he had no reason not to marry Sarah. But that sounded so harsh. Clearing his throat, he murmured, "We were ready. *Mamm* and *Daed* helped us, remember? We lived at home for quite a time."

All moony eyed, Winnie nodded. "I remember that. You and Sarah, down the hall."

Yes. To his shame, Jonathan had been terribly happy with the arrangement. His mother had been a good buffer between him and his demanding, outspoken bride who always had something to say about everyone and everything. At least once a day he would wish she'd hold her tongue more. But she never did.

No, Sarah was a gregarious sort. That was for sure. She'd always eagerly invited scores of people over to their home, creating extra work for everyone. She had often complained about how much he worked and finally asked him to spend most of Saturdays with her. She'd never understood his need to work.

She'd never understood his reluctance to be around people. No, Sarah had not been a wallflower. Not even a little bit of one.

Winnie cleared her throat. "Jonathan? Well? What happened then?"

"You know what happened. We moved here. Then . . . well, you know . . ."

"Everything's so different now." A cloud fell over his sister's face.

That much was true. Not two years after he and Sarah had taken their vows, their father was diagnosed with cancer and died. Then Sarah's accident . . . What would have happened if Sarah had not been so intent to return from her outing at twilight, on such a foggy night? The dim light, combined with the fog, had made it near impossible for the approaching car to see either the reflective tape on the side or the slow-moving vehicle sign on the back of the buggy. Within seconds, Sarah was severely injured, the buggy mere toothpicks, and the horse dead. Sarah had died before the ambulance reached the hospital.

After the accident, when he and his girls were still numb, his mother had lived with him. Last year, when it became obvious her health was failing, too, she announced that she would go live with her sister, his aunt up near Lancaster, Pennsylvania. It was decided that Winnie would be a better helpmate to Jonathan and the girls.

"Our family has had its share of sadness," he said, though that statement didn't near describe all the topsy-turvy turns his life had taken.

Winnie pushed away from the side of the wagon and practically skipped by his side. "I'm fair to bursting about going to Indiana. I hope Katie comes to her senses soon."

Oh, how uncomfortable that visit to the Brennemans had been. He'd near ripped his hat in two, he'd been gripping it so hard. "I hope so, too."

"I have a feeling that something else is going on besides Irene and John not wanting her near you. Did you get that feeling, too?"

"It doesna matter what I think."

"Now Katie is someone who I'm surprised didn't marry right away. She's so pretty. When we were best friends, all she ever talked about was wanting to be in love. I tell you, I always saw her making little things for her hope chest and planning her marriage. What do you think happened? Why do you think she hasn't met her match?"

He walked to the barn to get Blacky, their horse. "Don't ask me about such things."

"Don't be such a stick in the mud. Come now, you must have had some thoughts on her."

Katie Brenneman was a fair sight, for sure. Blue eyes as fresh as spring. A slim, becoming figure. Light brown hair always plaited neatly under her *kapp*. A pleasant disposition. A pretty smile and an adorable way about her that had always drawn him close. "Her married state is none of our business."

"I know, but—"

"I best get going, Winnie. You know I canna stop and chat all day. Work has to get done."

"Oh, all right. Jonathan, you are far too serious sometimes."

"I know." He kept walking in silence, but privately argued fiercely over that. When he was younger, he'd been always up for fun and mischief. He loved a good joke, either of the practical nature or a simple story.

Time and again, their father had encouraged him to mind his manners a bit more. Sarah, on the other hand, had wanted him to be more lighthearted all the time.

Yes, Sarah had never had a problem with telling him what she thought.

Jonathan had a feeling life with Katie would be different. She had a sweet way about her and an easy laugh. Yes, he did, indeed, find her very pleasing. He'd also been aware that she'd fancied him. And though he shouldn't feel flattered and full of himself, he did, indeed.

We need to talk about Brandon. Can you meet me on Sunday at noon? I'll be at the Brown Dog Café, just like old times.

Katie's hands shook as she stared at the note again. What would it be like, going back to the Brown Dog? She hadn't been there since she'd confessed everything to Brandon and Holly. She'd certainly never stepped inside the coffeehouse dressed Amish.

Church services at neighbors' homes only took place every other Sunday. This Sunday was an off week, so she'd be able to go, if she really wanted to.

The Brown Dog was in walking distance, if a person didn't mind the windy roads to get there. Situated in Peebles, it sat on the outskirts of a small town and attracted a variety of people. Mostly teenagers and college students hung out in the booths and old tables. Mixed in with the teenagers were a few young adults eager to take a break. Katie had liked the place from the moment she'd followed James and Laura inside.

The walls were exposed red brick. Black-and-white photos in silver frames hung scattered all over the walls. The scenes were of places in Europe. Exotic places Katie had never dreamed of seeing.

Places Katie knew she'd most likely never visit.

And that had bothered her mightily when she was seventeen. She'd opened her eyes to music and art and fashion and had been inundated with sites and smells and images so completely unfamiliar and strange that she'd been drawn to them.

Not so her other Amish friends. No, Laura and James had first taken her there one evening, but then had found nothing in the Brown Dog that was worthy of note. After that, Katie had gone by herself.

Events had spiraled at a breakneck speed, then fell apart, shattered as a finely made glass. The shards had pricked her, too. Some still lay embedded in her skin, pushing to get out, making her wince if she moved suddenly. If she forgot they were there.

When she'd left Brandon and Holly for the very last time, Katie had felt terribly embarrassed and ashamed. It had been difficult to admit to being a liar for almost two years. And that was what she had been.

Their questions and confusion had echoed in Katie's mind long after she'd torn out the front door, grabbed her bicycle, and pedaled as quickly as she dared back to everything that was familiar. Right then and there, she'd promised herself to never stray again from the Amish way of life. To never pretend to be someone she wasn't.

An hour later, in the woods bordering the Lundy's farm, Katie hopped off the bicycle, removed the jeans and sweater, and slipped back on her dress. The air had been chilly—she'd welcomed the sting on her skin. With easy, comforting movements, she'd braided her hair and positioned her *kapp*. By dipping a cloth into the edge of the river, she'd removed the last sheen of pink lip gloss.

Finally, she gathered up all her "English" clothes into a pillowcase and tossed them into the river. After valiantly attempting to float, the items sunk.

Very slowly, she walked the rest of the way home. Head down. Proper. Circumspect. But she couldn't forget who she'd pretended to be.

We need to talk.

Stunned into the present again, Katie stared at the

words. The note sounded so desperate and sure. What in the world could Holly want? What could she possibly want to speak to Katie about after all this time?

More important, what had happened in Holly's life to prod her to even want to contact Katie? Holly had been so mad when Katie had confessed everything. Katie would've thought nothing would ever have encouraged Holly to seek her out. The note sounded urgent and determined, which made Katie feel even more on edge.

Closing her eyes, Katie remembered so many good times she'd shared with Holly and Brandon. They'd gone to the mall, hung out in front of the TV, all things that Katie knew weren't wrong. But the web of lies she'd told about her life at home had been.

She'd made up stories about super-strict parents and baby sisters so Holly and Brandon would stop asking to visit her house. She'd held Brandon's hand and let him speak to her about proms and dances and college visits— just as if she would one day do all those things.

With a rush of heat, she remembered the feel of Brandon's arms around her, the way his lips had felt against her own when they'd kissed for the first time. The way he'd looked at her, like he really liked her. Like she was special.

Her parents thought they knew most of what she'd done. That was why they'd been so confused about her decision to join the church as quickly as possible. But they didn't know everything.

They couldn't.

If they did, they'd never look at her the same, and Katie

wouldn't be able to hold her head up in their community. Good people didn't do the things she'd done. Most important, good Christians didn't tell lie after lie to people who cared about them.

Did they?

Despair filtered through her once again. How could this all have happened, anyway? She'd prayed to God to help her move on with her life. Why hadn't He listened? Why had He encouraged Holly to contact her?

Katie wanted to tear up the paper. She wanted to burn it and turn it to ashes. To pretend it had never arrived.

That is what she would do. It was her only option. She couldn't visit the Brown Dog now, even if she'd been inclined. She was no longer a dreamy girl who was a tad bit rebellious. She was a responsible woman now. Moreover, there was a chance she was finally about to get to know Jonathan better. That couldn't be ignored.

But what would happen if she didn't go? Most likely nothing. Holly might be angry, but she surely wouldn't care if she never saw Katie again. Yes, that was the right thing to do. Keep the past in the past, where it belonged. Where she wouldn't have to think about it.

Where she could pretend it had never really happened.

"Katie, there you are, Daughter."

With a start, Katie noticed her mother standing in her doorway. She scrambled to a sitting position. "*Mamm.*"

"Haven't you heard me? I've been calling for you time and again."

"I'm sorry." After stuffing the letter and envelope under a pillow behind her, Katie stood up. "What do you need?"

"Your time, of course." After treating Katie to a particularly pointed glare, her mother turned on her heel and headed downstairs.

Katie had no choice but to follow. Her steps sounded louder than usual as they clopped on the wooden stairs, the noise jarring the relative peace of the inn.

After a burst of guests, their inn was remarkably quiet. Just the other day, Henry had announced that there'd been a curious drop in reservations for the next two weeks. The news was unusual, but not unwelcome, at least to her brother.

Katie knew Henry would rather work on projects in the workshop or fuss over Anna. He might call it "tutoring," but he was as besotted as any man in love and didn't try hard to hide it.

After entering the hearth room in silence, Irene Brenneman sat on the couch next to her husband. Roman had followed. Now he was there, too, sprawled out on the braided rug and chewing on a knotted piece of rope Henry had fashioned for him.

After gently scratching Roman's ears, Katie moved to sit across from her parents. Her heart was beating so loud, Katie was sure her parents could hear it.

Without fanfare, her mother said, "Your father and I've been talking about Jonathan and his offer for you."

"Oh." Katie swallowed with relief. Oh, for a moment she'd been sure they were going to question her about the letter.

Her father's lips twitched. "That is not the response I had imagined you would have."

Katie thought quickly. "I don't have any response prepared. I assumed a decision had been made."

"It had not." After glancing her father's way, her mother replied. "After Winnie came by and we had that discussion, your father and I did some more thinking. In a nutshell, Katie, we have reconsidered."

Their decision caught her off guard. "I'm surprised. I didn't think you wanted me to be at the Lundy home."

"In truth, we do not."

"Then why are you allowing me to go? What has changed your mind?"

With a weary expression, her father pulled out his knife and picked up the latest cane he was working on, obviously needing something to occupy his hands. After carefully lifting off a layer of birch, he met her eyes. "While it is true we did not want you to live at the Lundys', we decided that perhaps we were not right in withholding this opportunity because of our reasons."

"I'm not sure what reasons you mean."

Her mother sighed. "Daughter, simply put, we know you have particular feelings for Jonathan. We do not want to see you get hurt." Her mother's eyes turned worried as she continued. "Jonathan may not ever care about you the way you might wish. He might not ever want to marry again."

It was mortifying to know that her feelings for Jonathan were so obvious. "I know that."

"And you are fine with that? In two months' time, you could return here without a hint of a future with Jonathan."

That was most likely true. But no matter what, Katie couldn't deny that she wanted to be near him. She also wanted him to get a chance to see her in a whole new way: as Katie; as a capable, considerate woman, not just as Henry's little sister. "I'm fine with the risk. No matter what, I think it will be an adventure for me."

Her father scowled. "A mighty strange adventure, I think."

"In many ways, you are still an impulsive girl, Katie," her mother said slowly. "I had hoped that in time you would have learned to curb it."

"I have."

"Have you? Truly?" Her father glided the knife over the wood with ease. Under his hand, a smooth sphere was taking shape. "We know you did some things of which you might not feel proud. Back when you were younger."

The world felt like it was spinning too fast. Was this about the letter, after all?

Had Henry already somehow read her letter? Had he also blabbed to Anna and her parents about the contents? "Those times are behind me."

"Time can not always be forgotten, Katie. It passes, but our deeds stay with us. Mark us. For good or bad, our past transgressions and deeds make us who we are—even when we do things just to see what they are like. Even when we do things without meaning to hurt ourselves or other people."

Her father's words were true. She did feel marked and jaded. "I have tried to continue on the best that I could. I think I have been successful."

"We know that."

"Do you?" Thinking about how time and again she'd been asked to tutor Anna, Katie blurted, "You have asked my help for Anna. I have tried my best to teach her much about our life. You seem to trust me to teach her well. But when it comes to trusting me to make good decisions, you act as if I am too young. I am not too young."

"That is true. And it is also true that you have been a fine teacher for Anna, and an able helper at the inn," her mother said. "Your actions have shown us your sincerity time and again."

Her father smiled gently. "It is with that in mind that we've been reluctant to see you go from us. But that is not the right thing, I don't believe. Everyone needs to follow their own path, even if it isn't quite what parents always want."

"Yes, my Katie. It is time we let you go."

Her mother sounded resigned. With some surprise, Katie realized this time was as difficult for her parents as it was for her. They loved her.

Katie realized one day she, too, would marry, have children, and then eventually let them go. For the first time, she was able to acknowledge her parents' struggle—of letting her make decisions, even when they might be different from the ones they would have chosen. "Following God's path is not always an easy one to take," Katie murmured. "Sometimes I don't always know what He wants me to do."

"That is why there are rules to our society, the Ordnung. That is why He gave you family and friends, to lovingly guide you. Remember, Katie, no matter what, you are never alone."

Katie blinked. While her father's words now felt comforting, there'd also been a time when they'd sounded mighty confining, as well. "Yes, *Daed*. I . . . I don't want to be alone."

More gently, her mother murmured, "Of course not. Take care now, Katie. No one asks for perfection. We are all flawed."

"Sometimes, it is hard to see everyone else's flaws. I only seem to see my own."

"Then look around you more carefully. Look at Anna and her struggles."

Katie couldn't help but chuckle. Anna's attempts to become one of them had not been without amusements. Anna's canning mishaps were becoming legendary. When she wasn't burning her fingers on hot jam, she was struggling over the water baths for the jars. But still, she'd overcome many things. "I would never have guessed Henry would be so patient with her."

Her mother wasn't laughing. Instead, she pushed the conversation deeper once again. "Henry, he cares for Anna. He knows she has made mistakes, but he also has forgiven her, and seen that those mistakes made her stronger."

Katie had never heard her mother speak that way. In the past, it had always seemed that her parents had expected only obedience and perfection. Anything less was treated as a disappointment. That had been hard when she'd been following Rebekeh's footsteps. Her older sister—a full six years older than herself—had made everyone so proud, so seemingly effortlessly, Katie had always known that she'd never measure up.

When Katie's silence continued, her mother leaned forward. "Anna feels the same way."

"I know."

"She's made a fair amount of sacrifices for her love. She's given up so much."

Katie looked at her mother in surprise. "I never think of you ever seeing the outside world as something to give up."

"Why is that? Katie, though you seem hard-pressed to forget such things, I, too, was once much younger. I know of the distractions and the temptations that can entice us all. Yet you and I only had a few years of the outside world. Until Anna came here, it was truly all she'd ever known. That is a very big sacrifice, I think."

To her shame, Katie realized she had begun to take Anna's efforts for granted.

"But are you sure you want to help at the Lundys'?" her *mamm* asked. "I fear it will be a thankless task."

At least Katie knew she was not hoping for heaps of praise at the Lundys'. "I am not looking for thanks." Steadfastly, she told herself that she was not looking for affection from Jonathan, either.

"Mary is a difficult child."

Mary was still hurting from the loss of her mother. "I think I may be able to help. And I do want to help them. Even Winnie." Winnie, who also was searching for the right helpmate in life.

"Yes, I can see that." But still *Mamm*'s voice sounded doubtful.

Wondering the cause, Katie said, "Do you think Winnie has found her true love? Or do you think she's just following a flight of fancy?"

Her mother's eyes opened wide. "I don't know. Dreams are all fair and good, and have their place in our lives. And as for true love—why, it's a fanciful thing, I think. Love comes after a time of working side by side and believing in each other. But I do have to admit that I think it is not unreasonable for her to want to follow her own heart for a change. She should not be expected to always feel content to raise her brother's children. Winnie has always wanted a family of her own."

"Love, side by side. Was that how love was with you and *Daed*?"

To Katie's amazement, her parents shared a warm smile. "I don't know how our hearts became joined. Your father and I felt love and companionship. He made me feel peaceful and whole."

Katie thought of Jonathan. Thought of how her heart jumped whenever he was near. Truly, she never felt "peace" in his presence. No, it was more like a jumpy, nervous pounding in her heart, where every sense was on alert. Was that how she was supposed to feel? Or was there something different between them? Something more fanciful and dreamy? Fake.

Patting Katie's hand, her mother murmured, "Please pray on this, Katie. Take out what everyone else wants, and pray on the Lord's guidance. Then you'll know."

"I'll know." Her smile was brave. Inside, though, she was breaking.

Katie feared she'd never know what God wished her to do. Would never know what the Lord wanted.

Or worse, Katie feared that she would be unable to do what He asked. Deep dread filled her once again. If she couldn't carry out the Lord's will, what would she do then?

More important, what kind of person would she be then?

Chapter 5

"Henry, I just don't know if I'll ever be as good an Amish wife as you deserve," Anna Metzger said as she entered his workshop in the barn.

He chuckled but didn't look up from the bridle he was oiling. "Anna, the things you say. What brought this on?"

"Oh, I don't know." It had been a particularly trying day. It was bitterly cold, she was tired, and in a burst of selfish temper, she had told Katie that she wished she were back home, tucked in an electric blanket, watching TV.

Needless to say, that remark hadn't gone over very well.

But she couldn't share that with Henry, so she just shrugged, her eyes still on him, willing him to look up and say something to make her feel better.

Instead of talking, he held out a hand. The gesture was perfect, so Henrylike. Eager for a reassuring hug, she approached, but somehow managed to trip over one of Roman's toys. Henry reached for her just as she'd held out her hands to stop her fall. "Anna, are you all right?"

Her ankle did throb, but not enough to complain about. Unfortunately, though, tears still threatened to spill. It had been that kind of day. "I'm fine. Just embarrassed."

After settling her in his seat, Henry stood up and rubbed her shoulders. For a second, Anna thought he was going to cuddle her close. But, like always, his inner resolve and obedience shone through. Instead, he leaned forward, looked into her eyes, and gently smoothed back a lock of her blond hair into the confines of her *kapp*. When he spied her tears, he murmured, "Do you have a headache, *liewe* Anna?"

Liewe Anna. Dear Anna. A little flutter raced across her heart at the sweet words. Since he knew about her occasional migraines, she sought to put him at ease. "No. It's just been a long day."

Stepping a few inches away, he took her hands. "What happened?"

"Everything and nothing. I messed up a few things and spoke harshly to Katie. And, well, I hadn't seen you in hours."

Dawning understanding lit his eyes, along with a fair amount of humor. "I see."

Oops. Henry really did see. She'd come in for his attention, which she missed very much. It was hard to find time alone with him, even though they were almost a courting couple.

And though Katie warned her that it was not the Amish

way to speak of such things, Anna knew that she longed to be in Henry's arms and perhaps steal a kiss or two. Before she could stop herself, she laid her head on his shoulder. Instead of moving away, Henry curved his arms around her back. "I've missed you too, Anna," he murmured, pressing his lips to her temple.

If Anna didn't know better, she would have guessed that Henry was very wise in the ways of the world. Very wise in relationships and the silliness and insecurities of women. That was disconcerting. But at the moment, it was comforting, too. After hugging him tightly, she pulled away. It wouldn't do for his father to come in and see them hugging. "I guess I should go now."

"Because?"

"I don't want to disturb you."

"You are not disturbing me." *Ah*, but a shadow fell away from his eyes. Something bright and playful took its place. Perhaps he wasn't immune to her, either? "Did you have another bout with the laundry?"

Anna was sure she would never like doing laundry. She hadn't even liked washing clothes when she'd had every modern convenience at her disposal. Now doing much of it by hand was particularly difficult. She'd found pinning garments to clotheslines especially challenging—at least once a week a pair of pants, a dress, or a quilt would fly off the line, get soiled, and need to be washed again. "No. I just seem to do something wrong every day." She pointed to her ankle. "I mean, come on, who else trips over dog toys and stumbles in her skirts?

Eyes sparkling, he murmured, "You are not the first person to trip." With an amused expression, he glanced down at Roman, who was inspecting a spider in the corner of the room. "And puppies do have a lot of toys."

"I know, but it's just so silly."

"No one is judging you, Anna. Truth be told, everyone is in awe of your efforts."

"Even you?" She didn't want him to regret choosing her.

Heat replaced mischief in his expression. "Especially me," he murmured.

To her delight, he reached for both of her hands once again and linked his fingers through hers. "Most especially me."

"I just hope you know what you are getting. I'm not perfect. And what's more, I don't think I ever will be perfect."

Gently, surprisingly, he rubbed the tops of her knuckles with his thumb. Though slightly calloused, it felt warm and sent yet another spark of awareness through her. And another jolt of longing for him. "Hush, now. I don't want perfection, I want you. What's more, I never forget the sacrifices you are making for me. It is not an easy way of life, ours."

"I don't mind. This is the place for me."

"I am grateful for that. But, what about you?"

"What do you mean?"

A knowing look entered his eyes. "You're getting the same old Henry. Perhaps you are disappointed?"

"Never. I could never be disappointed with you."

Anna glimpsed a hint of satisfaction, completely male

and especially tender, enter his eyes before she closed her own, just as he kissed her.

When they parted, Anna couldn't resist pressing her fingers to her lips. "Oh."

"You are not alone, Anna. I promise, you are not alone."

She didn't know if his words or his actions flustered her more. "I . . . I better go work on the laundry again. The clothespins don't always stay . . ."

"I'll see you at supper."

"Yes." And then she ran. Maybe everything was going to be just fine, after all.

"And, Katie, this is where you will sleep," Winnie finished, pointing to a bare guest room. Only a twin bed with a dark pair of quilts, a forlorn bedside table with an ancient-looking kerosene lamp, and a thick shade decorated the room. Though the November sun was shining merrily outside, no one inside of this guest room would ever guess that such a thing was happening. It was as dark and gloomy as if the sun never peeked out among the clouds.

"I don't see hooks for clothes. Are there any?"

"Oh yes, I forgot. Jonathan said he would bring in a chest of drawers from the *daadi haus* and nail up some hooks soon."

It was a most unpleasant, bare, and cold space, devoid of even a bright quilt to warm things. Everything looked cold and stark—so different from the guest rooms at the inn.

At their inn, each room had been given particular care and attention. Framed quilts adorned the walls, while a pleasing mix of traditional quilts and thick goose-down comforters covered the beds. Fluffy feather pillows and thick, crisp sheets made each bed a welcoming sight after a day of sightseeing or hard work. And the rooms smelled different—like lemon oil and sunshine.

This room smelled musty and worn, as if it hadn't been opened or aired out in years. Surely that couldn't be the truth? "Did you empty it for me and my things?"

Winnie blinked. "No, it's never been used all that much. It's just an extra place to sleep, after all."

"Back at the inn—"

"Neither Jonathan nor I have had the time or intention to worry about decorating a bedroom." Softening, she added, "I'm sorry, Katie. I know it's not what you're used to."

Now Katie felt ashamed, indeed, of worrying about such vanities. "It's fine."

As Winnie scanned the room again, she frowned, regret in her gaze. "I suppose things do look a bit gloomy. You are more than welcome to spruce things up to suit you."

"You wouldn't mind?"

"Not at all. Jonathan and I want you to be happy here."

But Katie heard every word that was unspoken, clear as day. Winnie was saying if Katie thought a cozy, pretty bedroom was important, then she was spending her time focusing on the wrong things.

"This room is . . . fine."

As if looking at the room for the first time, Winnie scrunched up her brow. "Your inn is a beautiful place, to be sure."

"It's fine," she said again. Yes, the inn was beautiful, but

Katie was very aware of the amount of time she'd spent polishing spindles, starching and ironing curtains, washing walls, and waxing floors. "I didn't come here to have fancy knickknacks."

"Oh. Yes." Winnie swallowed. "I know you came to help us out. To help me, most especially. I am grateful."

"You are most welcome. I had a need to come here, as well."

As if reading Katie's mind, Winnie murmured, "I'm sorry Jonathan wasn't here. His boss couldn't let him off today. He mentioned something about a big order for a builder in Michigan. "

Obviously, everyone knew about her infatuation with Jonathan! "There's no need to apologize. I didn't expect him to be here, waiting for me."

"But I am sure it would have been nice. After all, this is his home."

"Don't worry so, Winnie. You've got a suitcase to pack and a trip to get ready for."

Winnie's cheeks bloomed bright. "I can't believe that tomorrow I'll be boarding a bus to Indianapolis! I'm *naerfich*—as nervous as a young schoolgirl."

Katie could scarce believe it, either. From the moment she'd made her decision, with God's help, to go live at the Lundy home, things had moved with lightning speed. Now, here it was, the second week in November, and she was moving into her new room.

Yes, she'd been as busy as a bee during the last two days. At the inn, Anna helped her pack and asked a dozen questions about completing some of the chores Katie usually did. Her *mamm* and *daed* had each pulled her aside and offered bits of encouragement and advice.

Even Henry had offered her a hand and had promised to take care of the pup in her absence. Katie had been grateful for her family's support, realizing once again how strong their love was. They were willing to support her and help even when they didn't completely agree with her actions.

Thinking again of Holly's letter, Katie wondered what everyone would say if they met Holly or Brandon. Most likely, everyone would like them a lot. It would only be when people realized how close Katie had been to loving Brandon and to leaving the community that eyebrows would be raised.

Of course, she wouldn't have to guess what her sister, Rebekeh, would have to say about lying to them. Rebekeh would be critical, indeed. "It's a shame you haven't yet put into practice the teachings of the Bible, Katie," she would say. "Perhaps you should do some more thinking and praying about treating others with care and concern."

Then Katie would feel exactly how she always did around her sister—childish and inept. Because it had been Katie in the wrong.

Not Holly. Certainly not Brandon.

After closing her new bedroom door behind them, Katie and Winnie walked down the scuffed oak planks that lined the hall. The walls were painted a glossy white but were as bare and plain as most of the other walls in the home. As Winnie pointed out a few drawings that Mary did, and they joked about the art projects they'd once done side by side, Katie felt herself warming to Winnie once again. Eager to return to their former easy camaraderie. "I would also be terribly nervous about going all the way to Indiana, Winnie. It is hard to travel by oneself."

"I've scarcely thought about the travel. I can only think about meeting Malcolm for the first time." Picking up an envelope from the kitchen table, Winnie murmured, "I just know he's going to be as perfect as I've dreamed him to be."

"But what if he is not? Win, what if you find you don't like Malcolm? Then what will you do?"

"I . . . I don't know. I've never considered such a thing, to be honest. The letters we've shared are wonderful. No man who writes such words could be much different in person."

Katie knew better. She knew firsthand how people could look one way but be far different inside. She'd been that way for a time.

She and Winnie spent the majority of the day working side by side. Winnie had carefully written out the girls' usual routine and had shown Katie where to find everything necessary for cleaning and cooking. They walked the large cellar where only a few fruits and vegetables had been canned.

Katie bit her tongue rather than ask what in the world Winnie had been doing. Amish women were proud of their home and took great pains to see that it was pleasing to the eye and a comfortable haven for all. After all, the home was the heart of the family.

In addition, most women busily canned from sunup to sunset several times a week at harvest time, carefully storing food for the winter and spring. If the job was too big for a woman to do on her own, neighbors and relatives were only too happy to help. Katie had accompanied her mother on many an occasion to help can or freeze necessities for the coming year.

But, now that she thought of it, Katie couldn't think of a time during their long friendship when Winnie had ever asked for help. She'd always tried to be self-sufficient as possible.

Maybe she should have offered to help Winnie more?

Katie noticed that there was little mention of Jonathan in Winnie's notes. Because she wanted to please him, she said, "What about Jonathan? You've got nothing written about his needs. What time does he leave for work? When does he return? What do you make for his lunch?"

Winnie frowned. "He's a grown man, Katie. He can take care of himself."

That sounded surprising to Katie. All Amish women took pride in taking care of their families. Did Winnie never attempt to help Jonathan with his meals?

She was prevented from saying anything more by the arrival of Mary and Hannah. "Hello, girls," she said with a smile as she hurriedly tried to help them off with their cloaks and hang them on the hooks by the back door. "I've been eager all day to see you both."

Seven-year-old Mary stopped in her tracks. "Katie, you're here already?"

Winnie clucked. "Remember how I told you this morning that Katie would be comin' to stay today?"

Wordlessly, Mary grasped Hannah's hand. They both nodded.

Katie looked to Winnie with a smile. "I'll be here for two months. Are you two ready to help me?"

Mary looked at Hannah, then at Katie with a reproachful glare. "No." She then walked away, leaving her lunch pail and satchel on the table.

Katie waited for Winnie to chastise the girl. But instead of correcting the girl's behavior, Winnie merely picked up Mary's abandoned items and put them to rights.

Yet more strange behavior followed. Dinner was a haphazard affair. No one waited for Jonathan. Instead, Winnie just put some food on a plate for him.

After dinner, the girls went up to their room instead of gathering around the hearth like Katie's family always did. Soon after, Winnie went to her room to finish packing.

Finally, at almost seven o'clock, Jonathan entered. As soon as he noticed her presence, his steps slowed. "Katie. You came."

"Of course I did. I said I would." When she smiled his way, Jonathan blinked and he dipped his chin, as if embarrassed.

"Well, I'm . . . glad. The girls need you here." He looked at her again, then turned away.

"I had a busy day. Winnie showed me around your home."

"I hope you found everything to your liking."

Suddenly, she couldn't have cared less about her bare

room or the unfamiliar surroundings. "Everything is most pleasing."

After removing his black coat and hanging his hat on a peg by the door, he walked quickly to the sink, washed his hands, then picked up the plate she'd set out for him. "Is this for me?"

"Of course." Taking a chance, she dared to tease him a bit. "Who else would it be for? I hope you like meat loaf."

"I like it fine." Once again those pale blue eyes seemed to seek hers for a moment, then drop in embarrassment. Somewhat stiltedly, he went to his meal. After taking it to the table, he offered a quick silent prayer of thanks, then he proceeded to eat without so much as warming it up for a bit in the oven.

Katie joined him. "So, how was your work at the lumberyard?"

"It was good."

She tried again. "Did you do anything interesting? What, exactly, do you make there, anyway?"

Wearily, he wiped his mouth. "We make shells. You know, lumber frames for homes. We have a large contract for a builder out near Toledo. We build furniture, too, sometimes."

"That sounds interesting," she murmured, though it didn't, not really. "Do you like it?"

"I like it well enough. My boss, Brent, is a good man." Jonathan turned his plate a quarter turn so he could continue to shovel in his meal. In sync with his fork hitting the plate, he shrugged. "There isn't much to say. The work is hard, but plenty. And the pay is *gut*, too. That's a blessing."

For a moment, Katie found herself noticing everything about Jonathan, all over again. The way he held his fork. The scar along the base of his thumb. The way his cool blue eyes seemed to always find hers. "Indeed. Well, I spent the day getting organized."

"Did you have any problems?"

"No. Not at all." She swallowed hard as once again his hand stilled and he looked long at her. "*Um*, please don't worry about the girls. I will care for them just fine."

"I assumed you would."

"Oh. Well, then . . ." Her voice drifted off. When she noticed him shifting, about to leave the room, about to stand up, she blurted, "How did you get that scar?"

He stilled. "Which one?"

Before she could stop herself, she reached out and touched his thumb. His skin felt so different than hers, rough. Cool. He started from her touch. "That one."

"Oh. I cut it years ago when I was mending some fencing." He ran his other thumb across his hand, just like she had done.

"It must have been some cut." Feeling terribly girlish, she amended her words. "I mean, it's almost an inch long."

He looked at his hand as if he was looking at that scar for the first time. "I guess it was. It healed, though, and I'm right as rain." For a moment, their eyes met, and his expression gentled—almost like he cared about her. Then, just as suddenly, he stood up. "I . . . I am going to wash up now."

Stunned, Katie watched him pick up his plate, set it near the counter, then walk away. Leaving her alone.

As she looked around the suddenly silent kitchen, Katie thought that perhaps her parents had been right. Perhaps her stay here would be a thankless one, indeed. The girls were not eager to get to know her. The house was empty and far too quiet. Winnie would be gone soon.

And Jonathan . . . Jonathan seemed wary around her. Watchful. Almost bashful?

Chapter 6

Brandon was sitting up in bed half watching television when Holly arrived at the hospital that afternoon. Pausing at the door, tears pricked her eyes. For once, Brandon looked almost like his usual self. It had been a rough week—there'd been a few times when neither the doctors nor the nurses thought he would last to the next day.

There were times when she wasn't sure she'd be able to make it, especially since all the news was now increasingly dire. Holly was finding it hard to stay positive.

But of course, that was what he needed. "Hey, you," she said when she finally walked through the doorway. "How does it feel to sit up in bed for a change?"

With effort, he turned her way. "Pretty good. So, are you ever going to actually come in? I've been watching you stand there for five minutes."

"Sorry. My mind was wandering, I guess," she murmured, walking toward him. After squeezing his shoulder, she pulled up her usual chair and sat down next to him. "So . . . are you feeling a little better?"

"Yeah. I think those new drugs are helping with the pain."

His words told her everything she needed to know. He wasn't healing. A miracle wasn't about to take place. His prognosis wasn't going to change. He just wasn't feeling as bad as he usually did. "Oh. Good."

Brandon motioned to the remote control on the bedside table. "Turn off the TV, would you? I want to ask you about something."

"Anything," she said as soon as the screen went black.

"Did . . . did you ever get ahold of Katie? Did you find her?"

"No." Regret consumed her as she watched his expression fall. Oh, she'd give just about anything to have different news for him. "I wrote Katie a note and asked her to meet me on Sunday but she didn't show up." She'd waited three hours. As each minute passed, Holly's anger had intensi-fied. It was just so unfair. Here Brandon was hoping to see Katie one last time before he died—and Katie couldn't even trouble herself to give Holly a few minutes of her time.

"Oh." With a sigh, his eyes drifted shut.

If Katie was standing in front of her at that minute, Holly knew she would have reached out and shaken her, hard. "I'll try again, Brandon."

For a long moment, the only sounds in the room were the plethora of machines that monitored his vital signs. At last, he spoke. "Why do you think she didn't show?"

"I don't know." When he tried to grip the electronic control to lower the head of the bed, she stood up and pushed the button herself, helping to adjust the pillows under his head as he shifted. "Maybe she didn't get the note. I had to leave it at the general store, you know. I'll go over there this afternoon and check."

"You don't have time. You've got work. I know you've got your job, Holl . . ." His words were slurring. Either the pain medicine was really kicking in or his body couldn't wait to rest.

"Sure I do." Reaching out, she clasped his hand. "I'll find her, Brandon. I'm going to find her and bring her to you. I promise."

His eyes still closed, he almost smiled. Almost.

Holly sat back down and watched her brother sleep. It was time to face the painful truth. They were almost out of time. No matter what—no matter what it cost to her pride or her feelings—she had to get hold of Katie.

Life was very different at Jonathan's home, Katie realized as she walked down the hall to the girls' bedroom one morning just days after Winnie had left with a smile and a wave before boarding her bus.

She missed the hustle and bustle of the inn as much as she missed her parents. At home, it was rare to find a moment's peace, never mind an hour of it.

"Girls, it's time to wake up," she said after poking her head in the door.

The two bundles under matching blue and yellow quilts hardly moved. Katie couldn't help but smile at how cute they looked. Their small sleeping forms brought back memories of her own childhood. Although, back when she was small, it had been Rebekeh's job to wake her up. Only Rebekeh's promise of hot chocolate would rouse her from slumber.

Softly venturing in, she gently shook each of them awake. "Mary, Hannah? It's morning."

Hannah rubbed her eyes as she sleepily sat up. "Katie?"

"Yes, dear. Time to get up."

Obediently Hannah sat up. "You look pretty today."

"*Danke.*" Brushing a silky strand of hair away from Hannah's sweet face, Katie smiled. "You look *schlafrig*. Sleepy."

Just like she had the morning before, Hannah giggled, pushed back the covers, then scrambled out of bed. "Not any more! Good morning!"

"Good morning to you." Turning to Mary, Katie shook her shoulder gently. "Now, Mary, you must get up, too. The sun is waiting for you."

"I will." But still, she didn't move.

"Now, please."

Sullenly, Mary groaned. "I'm getting up. Where's *Daed*? Is he still here?"

"No, he left for work early today."

Actually, he'd left almost three hours earlier. She'd had to scramble to get downstairs and help him make his breakfast and lunch before he hitched up his wagon.

"Tell me when you want to eat breakfast in the morning and I'll have it ready for you," she'd said, once again trying so hard to be near him.

But instead of looking grateful, Jonathan had looked disconcerted in her presence. "You don't need to go to so much trouble. As a matter of fact, there's no need for you to be even getting up with me."

She'd chuckled. "You obviously have forgotten that I'm used to living at an inn. I've made breakfast for dozens of folks. You will not be much trouble at all." She'd opened the refrigerator. "How about some eggs and toast?"

"That . . . that would be fine."

"And lunch? Would you care for some soup and sandwich?"

"Anything would be fine, Ka-tie."

She'd busied herself at the stove so he wouldn't see her blush. But she couldn't seem to stop her reaction every time he said her name, so slowly, with a slight lilt. Like he was drawing out every sound.

Clearing her throat, she fussed around the girls' room for another moment or so. "I'll see you when you get to the kitchen. Don't tarry too long."

"I'll hurry, Katie!" little Hannah said.

As expected, Mary said nothing.

Once again, Katie cooked a large breakfast. But just like the day before, the hearty meal of eggs and bacon, toast and fresh jam was a battle to get through. "These eggs aren't like Winnie makes them. Yours are too runny."

Katie knew she made a fine fried egg—there were dozens of guests at the inn who could testify to that. But she tried to look remorseful. "*Hmm*. I'll try to do better tomorrow."

"I don't like this bacon, neither."

"You'll be hungry then, won't you?"

After a moment, Mary obstinately began eating, leaving Katie ready to go back to bed. With neither Winnie nor Jonathan there to run interference, Mary's jibes felt especially hard to take. She hoped Mary would back down from her one-girl war against her soon, because Katie knew her patience was near its end. One day soon she was going to retaliate with something mean right back.

Katie did her best, but the good Lord knew she was most certainly not perfect.

After breakfast was the usual running around, packing lunches and double-checking for all the homework supplies. Katie waved them off as they walked hand in hand to the Amish school, which was less than a mile away.

After the house was empty, Katie took the time to sip another morning cup of tea, then, without much more dillydallying, began her chores with a sigh.

This was when her day seemed the hardest.

She was used to the companionship of her mother, and the constant comings and goings of guests at the inn. Most recently, she'd had Anna—dear, talkative Anna. To Katie's pleasure, Anna had become her best friend in the world despite her few frustrations. Not only did they laugh and enjoy each other's company, making the tasks go by more quickly, but Anna also helped shoulder a lot of Katie's chores and work. Now, though, it was just her by herself. Katie found it lonely.

* * *

On her third day, just as she'd put on a kettle for tea, her mother came to visit. As soon as she opened the door and saw her, holding a large basket full of supplies, she burst into tears. "Oh, *Mamm*. I'm so glad to see you."

"*Ach*. Are things that bad?" she asked, curving a reassuring arm around Katie.

"Yes. No. Oh, I don't know." She stepped aside so her mother could enter, then followed her to the kitchen, where only half the dishes were cleaned.

Her mother looked at her in surprise. "Katie?"

"Things are so different here. Even though I'm by myself, I'm having a heap of trouble keeping up with everything." She pointed to the barn. "The animals. The chickens. That goat."

Her mother chuckled. "That goat always was a nuisance. No one could ever get it to mind, even before we sold it to the Lundys. It gives good milk, though."

Katie shook her head in wonder. Obviously some things never changed. Leave it to her mother to mention that fact. "It's not just that. I can't seem to get everything done."

"You never had any problems at home."

"At home I always had you and Rebekeh."

Her mother almost smiled. "Careful, Katie, or you are going to sound as if you almost miss Rebekeh's bossy ways."

"I almost do." She held up a hand when her mother threatened to give into laughter. "Almost. Anyway, I guess I'm having trouble getting used to doing everything myself. Even working with Anna was a blessing."

"Many hands make quick work. But even the most industrious can not be expected to do the work of many, Katie. Perhaps you are being too hard on yourself."

"It's not the work. Well, not everything. *Mamm*, the hours drag by."

Understanding dawned. "You are lonely."

"I am. I'm sorry. I know that's not something I should complain about."

"I would find this solitude difficult, too, Katie."

"Really? You would?"

"Indeed I would." With a thoughtful smile, her mother murmured, "My goodness, the Lord knew what He was doing when he guided your father and me to open our house as an inn. I have a lot of joy in our constant stream of guests."

Katie's shoulders slumped. "I think I had joy there, too."

"Well, no matter. Soon enough you will be back."

"I suppose."

"You suppose? What does that mean?"

"I don't know. Maybe I'm destined to be a single woman, helping out at the inn. But what if that's not my future? What if things improve between Jonathan and me? What if one day he is interested in having another wife . . . and I find that I've fallen in love with him? What would I do then?"

"*Ah*. Those are tough questions." To Katie's surprise, her mother calmly considered the questions instead of just offering quick advice. "Katie, have you been praying?"

"I don't have time."

"That, my daughter, is the problem, don'tcha think?"

Katie didn't think so at all. At the moment, taking time out to say a prayer merely felt like one more thing to do. But she couldn't admit that. "*Mamm*—"

Her *mamm* hushed her, then took her hand and walked her to the only clean room in the house. The *sitzschtupp*, the living room, the good room that so far no one ever used. After sitting down beside her, her mother gently said, "Let us give thanks to the Lord our God."

They fell into silence, each praying with the Lord in her own way. A sense of peace filled Katie as she took time to give thanks for family and good health, for good neighbors and sunny fall days. As she relaxed and reminded herself that her life was in the Lord's hands, not her own, she felt all the stress from the past few days fall from her shoulders.

Her mother saw the difference instantly. "See now, dear? Nothing is so hard that it can not be shouldered with God's help."

"I do see. Will you stay for a while?"

"For a little bit. I brought you some things for the girls."

Katie was interested. "Such as?"

"I brought you your sewing and some new fabric. I thought you could help them work on a quilt."

Katie struggled to conceal her dismay. "*Mamm*, I just don't know—they haven't shown much interest in sewing."

"They will if you encourage it. Those girls will look to you for guidance, Katie."

"But what if they don't?"

"You won't know unless you try. And it will do all

three of you some good, to keep those little girls busy. They'll see your love for quilting and want to give it a try. I promise."

"But if they don't—"

"Then they won't. But in the meantime it might help all of you out." She looked at Katie carefully. "Don't you agree that busy hands help an eager mind?"

But what of sour dispositions? Yet, her mother did know so much. It was worth a try. "*Danke,* though I don't quite know how to get them started."

Her mother chuckled. "It is easy, dear. Simply pull out the fabric and tell them it is time to begin." Tenderly, she cupped her cheek. Her mother's hand was rough and strong, reminding Katie of just how much she'd done all her life to make their family life good and comfortable.

Had she ever truly appreciated her mother's sacrifices?

Leaving the basket in the living room, Katie followed her mother into the kitchen, where she efficiently put on an apron, then pushed up her sleeves and got to work on the dishes.

"Don't do those, *Mamm.* You have more dishes than you can count at home."

"Anna did them today. Together we will clean, Daughter, then we'll cook, *jah?*"

For the first time in years, Katie was grateful to get to work and be told what to do.

Chapter 7

That evening after the girls had their supper and they were waiting for Jonathan to return, Katie led the way into the living room. "Look what my mother brought over today—fabric." After sitting down on the couch, she spread a few of the especially beautiful pieces of cloth on her lap. The rich colors of butter yellow, dark red, and bright, vivid blue made Katie feel like she'd just brought the best of God's bounty into the room. "Aren't these fabrics pretty? Which one is your favorite?"

Hannah shyly pointed to the yellow.

Katie moved to place it on top of the others. "*Jah*, that is a wondrous color. It shines as pretty as the daffodils in May." Turning to Mary, she said, "Which one do you like?"

"None of them." Instead of sitting, Mary remained where she was, militantly glaring at the fabric like the swatches were terrible intruders infringing on her routine. "We're not supposed to be here in this room."

"Why ever not? It is a pretty room, to be sure."

"It is the *sitzschtupp*, our special living room. It is only for visitors."

It was on the tip of Katie's tongue to remind Mary that that was exactly what she was. She sure hadn't been treated like part of the family.

However, her mother's good example was fresh in her mind, and that gave Katie the courage to push a little harder to make inroads. Sooner or later, Mary was going to have to bend a little, surely! "There's a mighty nice fireplace, we could ask your *daed* if we could make a cozy fire and begin work on a quilt tonight."

Though Hannah carefully nodded, Mary scowled. "He's going to say no."

"He might surprise you. All men enjoy a new quilt."

"I don't want to make a quilt. You're not going to make me do this, are you?"

"No, of course not," Katie said, but had a difficult time hiding her surprise and disappointment. Quilting had always brought her a great amount of joy. It was also something she felt proud about and comfortable teaching others to do. She'd been hoping to use quilting to forge a bond with Mary.

Meekly, little Hannah tugged on Katie's sleeve. "I do. Am I too small?"

"Not at all!" Opening her arm, she moved to one side as Hannah scooted closer. "I was younger than you when

I pieced my first quilt. Mary, by the time I was your age, almost seven—why I was anxious to begin all kinds of projects."

Mary backed away, literally pulling away from her in both spirit and space.

However, Katie couldn't let Mary do that. If she didn't make the girl do anything she didn't want, they'd never make progress. And Katie really wanted to become friends with the little girl. "Come here, Mary, and give me your time, please. This task is important to me."

"No, I—"

"Please Mary. Sit down. I think you should try, yes? If not for my sake, then try working on this for my mother's. She was so hoping you would enjoy quilting."

Little by little, Mary unbent enough to come forward and join her sister.

With a glad heart, Katie watched Mary try her best to join in the activity. For an instant, Mary's behavior reminded Katie of her own. She remembered more than one occasion when her attitude had not always been pleasing or kind. Mary might be going through some of the same growing pains. In a worthy imitation of her mother, Katie stated, "We're going to start on this quilt. I've decided."

Mary's eyes narrowed. "*Daed*'s still going to be upset we're using this room."

"I will ask your father about it when he gets home."

At that moment, the back door opened wide. "Here he is," Hannah announced. "*Daed*'s home!"

Katie heard Jonathan carefully remove his coat and hang

it up. "*Daed*, we're in the *sitzschtupp*," Mary called out.

Slowly, he walked to them. "Hi, Jonathan," Katie said, greeted him with a sunny smile.

Once again, he met her gaze, then cleared his throat. Somewhat gruffly, he said, "What are you all doing?"

"I was showing the girls some fabric. I'm going to teach them to quilt." Katie grinned again, hoping her enthusiasm would catch on.

To her dismay, Jonathan didn't look encouraged. "They already have school, homework, and chores. Isn't that enough?"

Before Katie could explain how quilting gave her joy, not the burden of work, Mary snidely interrupted. "She wants to take over this room."

A muscle in his cheek jumped. "There is no reason for that."

Katie made a decision. "Girls, please go put your things away."

However, Mary and Hannah did not instantly obey. Instead they looked to their father for guidance. It was only after he nodded that they stood up and walked out of the room.

When they were alone, Katie motioned for Jonathan to sit. Like the girls, he seemed terribly reluctant to do so. Instead of leaning back in the chair, he perched on it, looking eager to rise and leave at a moment's notice.

"What is it about this room that makes you uncomfortable?"

"It doesna make me uncomfortable. It's rather that it is

a special place. You see, it was Sarah's pride and joy." His words sounded bitter. Resigned.

To her eye, the room looked as plain and unwelcoming as the rest of the house. "It is a pleasing room, to be sure."

"I would rather you not dirty it."

"Since I am the one cleaning, I think that option should be up to me."

"The girls—"

"Need something to do at night," she interrupted crisply. "You read *The Budget*."

"Even Winnie—"

Katie was tired of being compared to his sister. "I'm sure Winnie had other things to do. Jonathan, when you asked for my help, you didn't say I had to follow your directions like a child." She stood up and stepped toward him, consciously pulling her shoulders back and lifting her chin. "I am not a child."

Something flashed in his eyes that she couldn't quite recognize. Embarrassment? Awareness? "I know you aren't, Katie."

Something about the way he said her name—the way he looked at her so directly—made her heart beat a little faster. She felt flustered and at a loss of words. Suddenly she wasn't all that sure what had upset her so much. "I . . . I had hoped we would be getting to know each other better, Jonathan."

As the air surrounding them thickened, he murmured, "We are."

A second passed. Two. Katie could hardly look away.

He spoke again. "I'm . . . sorry if I haven't seemed appreciative of your efforts. I . . . I am, Katie."

She wasn't sure what to say to that. So many feelings were brewing inside her, she felt disjointed, confused. Finally, she settled on claiming practicality. "Then, would you please help me build a fire in here? It would make this room cozy and welcoming. I'd like to instruct the girls on quilting this evening."

After a long moment where he seemed to be at war with himself, he finally nodded. Rubbing the scar on his thumb, he said quietly, "Katie, I did not plan for this."

She hadn't planned on many of the things that had happened at the Lundys'. She hadn't planned on feeling so alone, or having to constantly prove herself to the girls. She hadn't planned on being so aware of Jonathan's moods. Of being so excited to see him at the end of each day. Of the keen sense of disappointment when a meal passed and he'd hardly dared to look her way.

But things seemed to be changing. "I know you didn't," she murmured, wondering if he, too, might be feeling the pull between them.

"When I asked you here, I was only thinking of my daughters. I had only wanted you to watch over them."

"There's more involved with girls than simply making sure they are fed and clothed. I want to get to know them, and have them know me. Jonathan, I can't help being myself. I can't merely sit meekly for two months. That is not who I am."

"No, it's not." His eyes lit up. "I . . . I am starting to see that I hadn't known you before."

"I'm tired of being kept at an arm's length as if I'm hired help. It isn't fair. I came here as a friend."

Pain entered his eyes, like he'd known he'd been hurting her feelings but hadn't known what else to do. "I realize that."

"I've been terribly lonely. Won't you consider letting me in your life . . . if only as much as a little bit?"

Obviously at a loss for words, Jonathan swallowed hard, blushed mightily, then abruptly stood up, turned on his heel and left.

Feeling bemused, Katie watched him leave. Had she made any headway . . . or merely made things worse?

"Katie?"

Thank the Lord for Hannah! The little girl was peeking around the corner, her eyes wide and her mouth shaped in a little "o." "Come in, Hannah," she said with a smile. "We have much to do." Pointing to the fabric, she said, "We need to think about what size squares to make for our quilt."

Thumb hovering near her mouth, the five-year-old tiptoed in. "I havena seen my *daed* talk like that before."

"I did not mean to upset him."

Blue eyes blinked. "You just wanted your way?"

In spite of her jangling nerves, Katie laughed. "I suppose so. I guess I'm not quite as easygoing as everyone thought I was, *hmm?*"

Hannah sidled closer, her dark indigo dress brightening

up the vacant room as much as her cheery personality. "You're different than Aunt Winnie."

"I know. She'll be back soon."

Hannah nodded, then picked up her favorite piece of fabric. In her arms, the buttery yellow stood in vivid contrast against the dark blue. "Winnie doesn't know how to sew."

"She can sew well enough, I imagine."

"No, she can't. She sends out for the sewing. She bought my *daed* a suit from Mrs. Yoder for his birthday."

Katie struggled to hide her surprise. No Amish woman was expected to be an expert at everything. Sure enough, there were many who bartered or traded goods to get unpleasant projects done. But sewing was as much a part of her family as baking shoofly pie for guests. It was hard to imagine Winnie not sewing at all. In fact, Katie distinctly remembered working on a quilt with Winnie when they were just girls.

But perhaps Winnie had never really enjoyed such activities? "Mrs. Yoder does fine work."

"Does Mrs. Brenneman do that, too?"

"No. My mother is a very fine seamstress."

After a moment's reflection, Hannah confided, "Mary said my *mamm* didn't like to sew, neither."

"I can teach you if you'd like to learn."

"We'll use this yellow?"

"Definitely. I think we'll make a quilt called Sunshine and Shadow. It's made up of light and dark squares. It's a very lovely pattern."

"What if you leave before it's done?"

Unexpectedly, the thought of leaving caused Katie's

heart to tighten. Hannah's smiles and sweet nature had claimed her heart. Katie looked forward to more days of holding Hannah's hand when they went to inspect the goat after school. Of baking buttermilk cookies with her, of showing Hannah how to measure ingredients just right. "I'm close by," she murmured, realizing her voice sounded husky. "Even if I'm living at the inn, we'll still have sewing lessons then."

Finally satisfied, Hannah crossed the two feet that had separated them and scrambled up on the seat next to Katie. "I'm ready."

"Then I'm ready, too."

Together they looked at a pattern book her mother brought, so intent that Katie hardly noticed Jonathan had come back in and was building up a fire.

And she was not aware of the pure relief that crossed his features as he saw how Hannah had taken to her. Katie only concentrated on the girl next to her.

As Anna stood next to Henry at the counter of Mr. Mc-Clusky's store a week before Thanksgiving, she could hardly believe the differences in her life. Mere months ago, she had accompanied Henry there for the first time. But unlike now, she'd tried to stay in the shadows. Lurking. Afraid of being found. She'd also been fiercely doing her best to deny her feelings for Henry Brenneman.

No, that wasn't quite right, she decided. For the first two weeks or so, there wasn't much to deny. She'd made up her mind to not like him. And the feeling had been mutual.

But now, dressed Plain and very close to taking her vows to the church . . . and later to Henry, Anna felt at peace. Henry was a good man, good in his heart and strong and stalwart. Sometimes she didn't know what she had done to deserve this new life of hers.

The door opened, bringing in a trio of women, dressed in harvest-colored sweaters and wool slacks. One of the ladies had a turkey pin on her jacket. Another wore a diamond cross around her neck. Each was holding Amish-made crafts and candles.

They were tourists, obviously. And they were staring at Anna and Henry as if they were the major specimens of their science project. Their interest made Anna want to check for crumbs on her cheeks, but Henry merely nodded in their direction.

Mr. McClusky acknowledged the tourists with a gracious smile. "Ladies. Good afternoon."

"Afternoon," they chorused, all eyes still pinned on Anna and Henry.

"May I help you with anything?" Mr. McClusky tried to engage the ladies.

The tallest woman, the one with the turkey pin, shook her head. "No, thanks. We're just here to sightsee." She turned back to stare at Anna like she'd just discovered a great wonder of the world.

Anna felt the blood drain away from her cheeks. "Come," Henry said in German, pulling her away from the curious stares.

Anna wasn't aware she was holding her breath until they disappeared down the aisle.

Once in relative privacy, he stopped her. "Are you all right?"

"*Jah. Danke*," she murmured, only realizing after the fact that he'd spoken to her in Pennsylvania Dutch and she'd replied in the same fashion. "I *um*, didn't realize I'd be so uncomfortable being stared at."

"It is different outside of the inn, isn't it?"

"Yes. At the inn, it's your parents' home, so it feels like we're the hosts. Here, I feel so exposed and at their mercy."

"They mean no harm."

"I suppose. It's just that it's different at the inn."

He gently clucked his tongue. "Anna, the inn is your home now, too, yes?"

His sweet words made everything feel right again. No matter what, she was happy with Henry, and happy with how things were going with their life. She needed to remember that. "Yes."

"Let's pay for our things and go home." His voice seemed to linger on the word.

Contentment settled over Anna as she followed him to the counter and stood by while he paid for the pasta and flour that their kitchen had run out of. Taking his bags from Mr. McClusky, Henry said, "Good-bye, then."

"Bye, Henry, Anna," the older man said with a knowing smile, making Anna wonder if he, too, was thinking of not so long ago when she didn't quite fit into this world. Much like the "sightseeing" ladies in the store. "Oh, I almost forgot." Sam McClusky's forehead creased. "Katie got another letter."

"Another?" Anna's hand shot out before Henry could claim it. She looked to Henry in alarm. *What was going on?*

Sam nodded. "Yeah. The first one came about ten days ago, right, Henry?"

"More or less."

As Anna looked at Henry curiously, Sam continued. "I have to tell you both, the girl who's been dropping these letters off looks pretty desperate. It ain't my business, but if I were you, Henry, I might talk to Katie. I wouldn't want to have some stranger looking for my sister the way she is."

Henry looked genuinely alarmed. "Thank you for the note, and for your concern." He frowned at the envelope in Anna's hand before facing the proprietor again. "When did you say the girl dropped this off?"

"Three or four days ago. She was asking all kinds of questions about Katie, about where she lives, what she does, but I put her off." With a self-satisfied smile, he waggled his white bushy eyebrows. "You know me, I'm not about to divulge anything to outsiders."

Anna knew she would be forever grateful for that character trait. "I know that for a fact, Mr. McClusky. You certainly kept your silence when Rob was after me."

"He was no good, Anna." Shaking his head in dismay, he added, "I still can't believe he tried to bribe me in order to find you."

"If he had known what kind of person you are, Rob Peterson would have never tried such a thing," Anna said. "I can't imagine you ever accepting a bribe. You are a *gut* friend, indeed."

"I appreciate your help," Henry said before ushering Anna out into the brisk wind. As they walked across the busy parking lot toward their buggy, he murmured, "Something isn't right."

Anna had a sudden desire to toss the envelope in the trash and never tell Katie of its existence. Turning to Henry, she asked, "Did she let you read the first note?"

"Nope. She got right angry when I tried to learn about the contents, too. Anna, Katie had quite a rebellious time during her running-around years. I'm wondering if her past has come back to haunt her."

Anna knew all about running from her mistakes, but yet, Katie was the sweetest girl she knew. "I doubt that. What did Katie do during her *rumspringa*, stay out late one or two nights?"

To her surprise, he shook his head. "Oh no. It was more than that. She'd go out almost every night. She wore makeup, too."

Anna couldn't help but chuckle. "Oh, Henry. That doesn't sound too strange. If you could have seen some of the girls in my ninth grade class—why the makeup they were trying out was crazy!"

"No, it wasna like that." He narrowed his eyes as he remembered. "It wasn't the makeup she wore, it was more the way she seemed to embrace everything about the English. And . . . her running around lasted a long time. My sister, Rebekeh, and I were sorely worried that we were going to lose her."

"Lose her? To what?"

"To the outside world." He held up his hand when it was obvious she was about to find offense. "Her leaving was a real matter of concern. She wouldn't talk to us about her new friends, wouldn't let even Rebekeh counsel her. She kept saying that we wouldn't understand."

"If it's her past that is bothering her, I know she won't get very far. I'm proof the past always comes back. You can't hide from it for long."

"That's what makes me *naerflich*. I think my sister is truly worried about being reminded of her past, but she won't let me help."

"I can understand you being nervous. Well, I'll go to the Lundy farm tomorrow and deliver the letter. While I'm there, I'll try to get Katie to tell me what all this means."

He glanced at her in gratitude. "You'd do that?"

She reached out to him, clasping his hand. "Of course I would. I care about Katie. She's like a sister to me."

But as she said those words, a deep sense of foreboding nagged at her. From the day they'd first met, Katie had felt like a sister. Last year, she'd spent hours confiding to Katie about Rob, about his abuse. All along, Katie had just been supportive and caring.

Why hadn't Katie ever given her even a hint that she knew what the outside world was like? That at times, she, too, had made mistakes and felt regret for her actions?

More important, why wasn't she trusting Anna now?

Chapter 8

"You are truly my best friend, Anna," Katie said as she led the way into the *sitzschtupp*, which she'd stubbornly taken over. She'd become tired of Jonathan's rules and hearing about how Winnie and Sarah had always done things. Though she might only be in the Lundy house for a short time, she was determined to at least try and fit in—walking around like an unwelcome guest had become mighty trying.

Because of that, she had made the front parlor a cozy area. After a few begrudging remarks, even Mary now seemed to look forward to their nightly lessons in measuring, cutting, and piecing together fabric. The result was cheery mix of three-inch squares waiting to be added to their Sunshine and Shadow quilt.

Anna patted the bright yellow, blue, red, and cream colored fabrics lovingly. "These are beautiful. I like the size of the squares, too. The last Sunshine and Shadow quilt I made, the squares were cut so small, it made my eyes dizzy just to look at it."

"The larger pieces are easier for the girls to manage. We're going to add wide borders, too."

"I think it's going to be pretty." With a winsome look, Anna sighed. "I've been hoping to do some quilting myself, but I haven't had much time."

"You've been busy with other things, things far more important than piecing together a new quilt, I'm thinkin'."

"I wish I had more to show for all the time I've spent studying." Anna grimaced. "Katie, I'm afraid my Pennsylvania Dutch isn't getting much better. What am I gonna do if I never learn that language? I promised Henry I'd do my best."

"And, you are doing your best, *jah*? Don't be hard on yourself, dear Anna. You forget that most of us learned Pennsylvania Dutch before English. And never at such an old age." As she heard herself, Katie felt her cheeks heat. "Oh! I mean old . . . I just meant that most Amish learn to speak Pennsylvania Dutch first."

To Katie's relief, Anna didn't take offense to the "old" remark. Instead, she looked relieved. "You're right. I forget how much of what I'm learning you practically take for granted."

"You shouldn't. I know neither Henry nor our parents ever forget your sacrifices. You've changed so much for Henry."

"I have changed, but not just for Henry. I've changed the way I look at things, and I have to admit that I do like this 'new' me. Well, most of the time. Other times, I feel so awkward, I'm sure that I'll never be comfortable."

"Don't fret so. At the end of the day, Henry wants you to be in his life, not a master of two languages."

"I don't seem to be mastering much. I ruined one of your mother's tablecloths yesterday. I scorched it."

"There's ways to fix scorches. I'm sure my mother told you."

"Not that mess. I ruined it something awful, Katie."

Katie did her best to keep a straight face. "It's just fabric. We all make mistakes."

Anna rolled her eyes. "Those horrible hens hate me. They peck my fingers something awful."

"That's because they know you fear them."

"Of course I do! Their jabs hurt! I don't know what to do about that. I think your *daed* has just about had enough of me and my accidents."

"I know that's not true." Reaching out, Katie clasped Anna's hand. "Hush, now. One day I'll tell you about all the things I've done wrong at the inn. And there's a great many things I've done wrong."

"Promise?"

Katie hid a smile. Anna's look of hope was almost comical. "I promise. Well, I will if you vow never to mention bread baking around Henry. He loves to recount my first attempts making cloverleaf rolls."

"I'll give you my word. Though I have to tell you that I'm very curious about what happened."

"I can only tell you that it involved too much yeast, too much salt, and a dining room full of paying guests." Katie shuddered at the memory. "We went through a record amount of water that evening."

"Oh, Katie. You do make me laugh! I knew I was right to pay you a visit."

"Your timing couldn't have been better."

Immediately concern filled Anna's green eyes. "Why? Are you having a difficult time?"

Though Katie would have loved to cry on her friend's shoulder and tell all, she knew better than to give into such foolishness. She'd wanted to be at Jonathan's home. She'd fought and cajoled her way to be here. She certainly didn't want to seem ungrateful or flighty—or inept. Especially not after she'd been giving Anna so much advice about managing an Amish household.

However, there was one matter that she was justifiably nervous about. Something that made even the most exacting housekeeper shudder and fret about. "I just heard today that we will be hosting church services here in two weeks' time."

Anna's eyes widened. "Are you sure? I was sure Irene told me it was the Barr's turn to host."

"The Barr's youngest has been sick with tonsillitis. Now the doctor says the tonsils need to come out. In light of that, Jonathan volunteered his home."

"Oh, Katie. We have a lot to do."

That was somewhat of an understatement. Holding church services was a big undertaking. The whole house would need to be cleaned top to bottom, food prepared, and room made for the benches and tables. "Thank you for saying 'we.'"

Anna laughed. "Of course I'll help you. Why, we all will!" Looking around, she asked, "I haven't been here for church before. Where does Jonathan usually hold the services?"

Katie pointed to the door that led to the bottom floor. "In the basement. There's lots of room."

"Enough to seat two hundred people on benches?"

"Jonathan says so. Luckily, the area shouldn't need too much work to be ready to host. It's fairly clean and tidy and is sparsely furnished. There is also a door that leads outside so everyone won't track mud and dirt through the house. It's everything else that makes my stomach turn in knots."

"What do you plan to serve?"

"The usual fare. Coffee and tea to drink. Trail bologna sandwiches, with fresh bread and relishes. And of course, peanut butter and jelly for the kinner." Katie thought some more. "Oh, and cookies. I thought we'd have cowboy bars, oatmeal cookies, and snowballs."

"Your *mamm* and I can do the baking. We'll bake the bread and cookies."

"*Danke*. Some other ladies will come over next week to help me clean."

Anna reached out and clasped her hand. "Everything will work out just fine. I feel certain."

Katie smiled. "That's what I told Jonathan. However, I have to warn you he didn't look as confident as you sound."

"He doesn't know you like I do. Remember, you are the woman who taught me to cook for a crowd. If you can do that, you can handle this."

"I'm glad you have so much faith in me." Turning back to the beautiful quilt fabric in front of her, Katie said, "But for now I want to spend some time on this quilt. That is important, too."

They both started organizing the fabric. It was almost impossible to sit still when there was quilting to do. Anna eyed Katie a little more closely. "So are you going to tell me how things are going?"

"You heard what I said."

"And, I also heard what you did not say. Come on Katie, this is me."

Anna was right. Maybe her ear really was what Katie needed. A friendly person to listen objectively. "All right," she said haltingly. "Things have been . . . more difficult than I had imagined."

"How so?"

"I don't rightly know. Things have been awkward in so many ways. I'm having trouble finding my place here. I had hoped that Jonathan and I might have some time together, but that seems like it will never happen."

"It's only been a few weeks."

But what an isolated time it had been! "That is true."

"How are the girls?"

"Confused. Hannah is a dear, but Mary harbors a lot of anger, I tell you. She doesn't trust me."

"It must be hard, losing her mother."

"I'm sure it is. There's been lots of other changes, too. Jonathan's working at the lumberyard has been a hard adjustment, I'm thinkin'. The girls were used to knowing he was close by even if they didn't see him."

After hesitating about whether to divulge more information, Katie decided to add some more. "And, then there's everything going on with Winnie."

Anna leaned forward. "I've been thinking a bit about her trip and that first meeting with Malcolm. Have you heard from her? Was Malcolm everything she'd thought he was going to be? Is she happy?"

"Anna! You sure you've only been thinking about her trip a 'bit'?"

"Okay. Maybe more than a little bit. Though we don't know each other too well, I do hope the best for her. I know how hard it is to jump into a new situation. So, what have you heard?"

Thinking back to the sound of Winnie's voice, Katie hedged. "Well, she called Jonathan at the lumberyard to let us know she arrived safe and sound. The Troyers have a phone booth at the end of their road to use for emergencies and such."

"I'm pleased to hear that, but I'm more curious as to how she's finding Malcolm. Did she say? How are they getting along, face to face?"

Katie looked at her friend with a new awareness. "I'm now realizing that you are not terribly hopeful about Winnie's trip."

This time it was obvious that Anna was the one who was choosing her words carefully. "I'm hopeful that she finds happiness."

"But you don't think Winnie will?"

"I didn't say that."

"It's what you are not saying that interests me. Truly,

Anna, you don't sound as if you hold out much hope for a happy ending for Malcolm and Winnie."

"I don't, not exactly. Before she left, Winnie seemed so eager to find Malcolm as everything she wanted. I'm afraid that she will either not see his faults or not take the time to really get to know him," Anna said, not looking away. "This sounds obvious, but people are hard to really know. Sometimes it takes weeks or months to see who the real person is. Sometimes first impressions can be so misleading."

"You are speaking of Rob, aren't you?"

Anna looked away. "It's hard for me not to think of Rob when I hear about Winnie's excitement to meet the man behind his letters. I mean, on the surface Rob looked polished and handsome and successful. He was running for a seat in the House of Representatives. It was only after we'd become serious that I realized how controlling and abusive he was. It's easy to only look at the surface of people. Far harder when you dig deeper. We all have so many layers on for reasons."

"Even Henry?"

Anna grinned. "Most especially Henry. He'd been hurt when Rachel left him for the *Englischer*. When we first started talking, I was sure he was just a sour, glum man."

"And he thought you were simply a spoiled, flighty fancy girl."

Anna looked serious again. "We were lucky, because we found out that our hearts matched and complimented each other. That isn't always the case, though."

"No, I imagine not."

Rubbing a worn spot on the wooden table, Anna added, "You might not know about this, but there's lots of stories in the news about men and women who pretend to be something they aren't on the Internet. That makes me wonder about this man's letters. Malcolm may have good intentions, but he may not be everything he says he is. It's only natural to want to downplay a person's flaws."

"I don't believe Winnie is finding that to be true. While she hasn't sounded over the moon about Malcolm, she sounds happy enough in the letters we've received so far."

"I hope she will be."

"I do, too. Maybe we shouldn't worry so much, Anna. I've learned that Winnie is a woman of strong will and character. She might want to be in love, but she is no *dummkopp*, no dunce. If this man has shortcomings, she'll discover them." Katie shrugged. "In any case, because of Winnie's trip, I think the girls are even more unsettled. I think they've overheard Winnie talk about her wish to one day be with Malcolm. To them, it's one more person stepping out of their lives."

"You'll win them over."

"With the Lord's help I might." Katie did not say that lightly. She was finding so many stumbling blocks, it would be a miracle if the girls and she reached common ground any time soon. Pushing the quilt project to one side, she stood up and smoothed her skirt. "I suppose I'd better get started on supper."

As they entered the kitchen, Katie motioned to a plate in the sink, where she'd set out pork chops to thaw. "I thought I'd season these for a bit before I bake them."

Suddenly she doubted everything about herself. "Does . . . does that sound like a *gut* idea?"

Anna squeezed her hand. "You are a wonderful good cook. I imagine anything you make will be tasty."

Katie couldn't believe how much she needed to continually hear the praise. She'd always thought of herself as a strong woman, but at the moment, she'd never felt more alone and weak. "I thought we'd have applesauce, too. I made some yesterday."

"All *kinner* like applesauce."

The Amish way of speaking of children perked Katie right up. "You sound mighty *gut*, Anna. I bet your guests at the inn think you are Amish, born and raised."

Anna giggled. "As long as I can tell them about where to shop, they are happy."

"And answer all their questions."

"Oh, all those questions! Someone asked me the other day if I had an alarm clock in my room. She had supposed a rooster woke me up every morning."

Katie laughed merrily. "Oh, can't you see my *daed*, having to fuss with a noisy rooster every morning? We'd be having it for supper after a week."

"I'd eat it, too. Well, as long as I didn't have to cook it."

"Don't worry, Anna. No one would ask you to."

They laughed again, barely catching their breath before Anna would mention another funny story about one of the guests.

Impulsively, Katie reached out and hugged her hard. "I'm so glad you came."

"Me, too." As the sense of true warmth and friendship

flowed through them, Anna's eyes widened in alarm. "Oh my goodness, we got so busy talking about things, I almost forgot to give you this." She pulled a white envelope out of her patchwork tote bag.

From the moment she recognized the handwriting, Katie felt dizzy. "Where did you get this? Did it come to the house? To the inn?"

"No. It was left at McClusky's store. Sam handed it to Henry and me the other day."

Obviously Holly was still determined to talk to her. Why? It just didn't make sense. When she noticed Anna studying her carefully, Katie did her best to act nonchalant. "Well, thank you for delivering this. I'll *uh*, read it later."

"Huh?"

Katie felt her cheeks heat. Even to her own ears her words sounded stilted and awkward. "I'm sure it's nothing important. Thank you—"

Before Katie could reach for the envelope, Anna set it on the counter. "Enough with games. Henry said this was the second envelope you've received. What is going on?"

Struggling to keep her voice even and true, Katie said, "Nothing. I received a letter, Anna, not a bomb."

"I know something's going on. No one receives letters at a store."

"The Amish—"

"Don't 'Amish' me," Anna retorted crisply. "I may struggle with a lot of things, but like Winnie, I am no dunce. You have a mailbox. There's got to be a reason you're not receiving letters here at home. Tell me what is going on. Let me help you."

Shame, and the pure petrifying worry of what was in the letter, kept Katie from divulging all. Her past troubles were her own problems to bear—no one else's. "I am having some . . . difficulty, but it's nothing you can help me with."

"What kind of difficulty? And why wouldn't I be able to help you?"

"You wouldn't understand."

"Of course I would. Katie, I lived most of my life in the outside world and seen some shady sides of it." With a look of amusement, she added, "I've seen more hours of daytime television that you can imagine. Believe me, there's nothing you could say that would shock me."

Perhaps that was right. But Anna had one thing Katie never had—an openness about her. Katie always preferred to look as perfect as possible to the people in her community. By doing that, she was able to keep her private struggles to herself. And the plain truth was that there was nothing Anna could do to help her, anyway. She had made the mistakes. She was the one who had hurt people. Therefore, it was up to her to solve the problem. "I'm not ready to discuss it."

Anna stepped right through her fragile barrier and pushed some more. "Won't you at least tell me who is writing you?"

"It doesn't matter. You wouldn't know her."

Anna grabbed hold of the clue. "Why wouldn't I? Sam said she looks desperate. Why do you think that is? What does she want? How did you meet her?"

The panic was back. Engulfing. "I meant . . . I meant . . .

oh, stop, Anna! There's no reason for you to be involved."

"I care about you. I see how worried you are. That's reason enough for me to be involved." Reaching out for Katie, she gripped her arm. "So it's an English girl writing you?"

"Anna, I would rather not discuss it."

"Where did you meet her? At the general store? At Mr. McClusky's?"

"No."

"Where then? At the inn?"

"Let's not speak of it, please."

"But I'm confused. Katie, we used to write to each other all the time. I've also seen you chat with any number of *Englischers* at the inn. It seems strange that these letters you are receiving are bothering you so much. Who do you not want to speak to? Why does this woman not even know where you live?"

"I'd rather not say."

"Katie, I promise that you'll feel better if you let someone else share your burden."

"Anna—"

But still Anna fired off another question. "Are you worried someone wants to do you harm? Is it safe for you to be alone?"

As much as she hated to shoo away her visitor, Katie resolutely walked to the kitchen door and lifted Anna's coat off the peg. Having Anna involved would not solve Katie's problems and only bring a lot of new ones to Anna.

And no matter what she had done so far, at least she hadn't brought trouble into her friend's life. Anna didn't deserve that. No one did. Taking care to keep her expression blank, she said, "Thank you for stopping by and for delivering the letter. Thank you, also, for offering to help so much with the services."

"You're welcome. And, I'll share the news about you hosting with your mother, though I imagine she's most likely heard about it by now. Irene seems to know everyone and everything around here."

Katie knew that was almost true. "When Jonathan brings the wagon with the benches, dishes, tablecloths, and such, I'll look forward to your help."

"You can count on it." Reluctantly, Anna stood up. "Pushing your problems away doesn't solve anything, you know. They'll still be there until you face them. I know that more than anyone."

Anna shook her head. "I tell you, no one would ever guess how stubborn you really are, Katie. You look so sweet and innocent." With a small smile, she said, "Promise me you'll let me help you the moment you are ready to talk."

Katie liked how Anna phrased her offer. It reminded Katie that Anna knew about keeping secrets and not always feeling able to share them. "I'll see you soon."

"Hold on. I could visit you tomorrow?"

"We both have work to do, Anna. I'll see you soon."

"But—"

Katie practically shut the door on her friend. "I'm sorry," she whispered to the thick wooden frame. "I'm sorry but I just couldn't take another question."

But more than that, she just couldn't make herself lie anymore.

Her body shuddered. She felt out of breath, like she'd just run a long distance in the cold. Yes, that was what her body felt like—frozen.

Outside the door, Katie heard Anna talk to Stanley, her buggy horse. She couldn't help but smile at her friend's chatter. Anna was truly determined to treat her buggy horse like a pet.

Still the letter waited.

Time had proven that pushing things off to the side didn't make things go away. No, it just delayed what was bound to happen. With thick fingers, she tore open the letter.

This time only a few hastily written words greeted her. *WHY DIDN'T YOU MEET ME? Katie, this is important. I won't go away. Meet me at the Brown Dog on Sunday. Please.*

I won't go away.

That was a threat, indeed. It also sounded much like a fact. For whatever reason Holly had, she was not going to give up or give in. And unfortunately, she felt very sure that Holly did intend to find her. After all, what did Holly have to lose?

Katie had so much to lose. After she'd spent one agonizing night thinking about how her life would be if she never joined the order, Katie had made the decision to tell everything to Holly and Brandon and never see them again.

After Holly had gone between tears and anger, and Brandon had simply stared at her in shock, Katie had gone home and tried to be the person her mother had raised her to be. If all the truth came out—about how close she'd come to giving everything up for Brandon—Katie felt like she'd lose everything she was and everything she'd tried so hard to be.

And what about Jonathan? Would he not want a woman like that raising his girls? Perhaps every hope she'd had for a life with Jonathan would vanish into thin air.

It was impossible to think of. It was all she could think about.

Feeling dizzy and sick, Katie rushed to the door and scrambled outside. Ready to share the awful note with Anna after all.

Ready to accept help.

To seek advice. To tell someone—anyone—all about everything she'd done and every horrible choice she'd made.

How she'd taken advantage of Holly's friendship. How she'd let Brandon imagine she returned his feelings. How she'd lied to her family because she enjoyed Brandon's admiration. But as she looked for Anna's buggy and prepared to call out to her to stop, her heart lodged in her throat.

Anna had already left. Once again, Katie knew she was all alone.

Chapter 9

All day Jonathan had looked forward to the moment he could come home from work and relax in the comfort of his own home. But as he entered the living room and eyed Katie's gently curving shoulders and pale neck bent over a bit of sewing, he felt his face heat up.

Oh, Katie affected him so.

In fact, every time he heard her voice or spied a bit of her pretty form, he could feel himself becoming tongue-tied and the muscles in his shoulders starting to bunch. No matter how hard he tried to not be different around Katie, things were out of his hands. The plain truth was that he fancied her. He couldn't help himself.

And that wasn't right. He had no need to marry again, well, beyond his girls needing a new mother. But that didn't seem like a sound reason in the long run. Jonathan didn't plan on being married to a woman he wasn't sure he could love.

And fact was, he wasn't sure if he was capable of loving again. Did the Lord desire a man to do such things? His will was a mystery to Jonathan.

Yes, his feelings about Katie most certainly did not make sense. Surely if he was meant to marry again, it would be to a woman not so different from his first wife.

Someone not so terribly young and fresh and merry.

Though, perhaps he didn't need a copy of Sarah, after all.

Things with Sarah had been rocky at times, that was the truth. Her sharp tongue had cut his feelings more than a time or two. Their union hadn't been all that he had hoped it to be. His efforts to hide their strained relationship had been a surprise, as well. Jonathan had always prided his honesty and forthrightness. He'd thought those two qualities were integral to the type of man he was. But during those last months with Sarah, he'd been a master of doublespeak and avoidance.

Even his *gut* friend Eli had commented on it one evening when they'd been raking gravel for the church services. "What is going on with you, Jonathan?" he'd ask time and again. "You seem so quiet and blue. How can I help?"

But instead of seeking Eli's advice and assistance, Jonathan had brushed him off. He'd been too embarrassed about the state of his marriage. Too ashamed that he wasn't happier.

Now, though, Jonathan realized that in spite of his intentions, his heart and head were thinking about companionship again with a certain blue-eyed woman. Every time she smiled, he imagined a life with her. Every time she laughed, he'd find himself dreaming about the possibility of not being alone night after night, with only his shadow for company.

But was Katie Brenneman the answer? Part of him thought she could be. Katie had a sunny nature which encouraged him to smile. He liked the way she treated others and how she was just bossy enough so as he wouldn't be tempted to run roughshod over her.

She also had a winsome way he found as beguiling as anything he'd ever come in contact with. It made him want to protect her and keep her safe.

Though he was not anxious to admit it, he liked how she did not always bend to his will. She stood up to him, but not in that brash way Sarah used to. No, it was more Katie's way to listen to him, then state her reasons for wanting things differently.

She was a surprisingly good negotiator, that Katie.

In spite of himself, he smiled. As every day passed, Jonathan found himself becoming more eager to see her. Every morning when she made him breakfast, it was becoming harder and harder not to admire the way she moved about the kitchen so competently.

Not to notice how pretty her skin was when the morning light shined on her just so. How her clothes smelled of lemons and her eyes were bluer than a fresh spring iris.

But in spite of his awareness of her, he still found himself to be at a loss for words around her. Part of him wanted to encourage her attentions, to show her that he welcomed them. But old hurts from his past would curb his tongue.

Now he worried that his distant manner had wiped out any feelings she'd previously had for him. Would she now even want such a man as himself? Someone so much older than she? Katie was twenty, while he was twenty-eight. Eight years was a fair difference. Perhaps she would notice his age over time.

He'd also noticed how she had tried to please him. She'd taken to making applesauce bread when he'd commented how much he liked it. But, had he even attempted to praise her cooking skills? He doubted he had—sometimes when he looked at her, all thoughts would run from his head and it would take all he had just to remain in the same room with her.

Fact was, from the time he could remember, people had commented on Katie's fair beauty, both in looks and in spirit. While it was true rumors had circulated about her running-around years and how she'd been a bit too wild, Jonathan had long since pushed those stories off. Gossip seemed to be inevitable in their small community. No, Katie Brenneman was a fair faultless woman, and therefore, most certainly not the type of woman for him.

The only remedy he could think of for his preoccupation was to keep away from her. He decided to do just that, and began edging backward out the doorway. Perhaps he could read through *The Budget* again. There might be some article or bit of news he'd overlooked the first time he'd read it through.

Or he could work some in the barn. He'd neglected the

tack room something awful lately. Blacky's bridles could use a good oiling.

"Jonathan, please don't go."

Caught, he froze. "Hello, Katie. *Gut-n-owed*."

"Good evening to you, too."

Something in her voice was different. High strung. Concerned, he stepped forward in spite of himself. "Are you needing something?"

"No, it's not that." She treated him to a ghost of a smile. "I just—well, I was alone all day and now the girls are asleep. Want to come in here and sit for a bit?"

He did not. What would he have to say to her that she would find interesting? What would she do if she caught him staring at her, like a young boy?

She nibbled on her lower lip. "I won't keep you too long. I promise."

He couldn't refuse such an offer. "All right."

Katie was a near wonder—he'd feel bad if he didn't try to nod to her wishes at least a little bit. He moved forward and hesitantly sat in the large rocking chair across from her. "Are you warm enough?"

The fire was roaring, and she'd even thoughtfully laid a crocheted afghan along the back of his chair. "I'm comfortable. This room has become mighty cozy, don'tcha think?"

The room had never looked so inviting. But if he admitted that, it would shame Sarah's memory. Wouldn't it? "The fire is warm."

Something faded in her expression. Raising her chin,

she tried again. "That rocking chair there is a fine piece of furniture. Have you had it long?"

He paused to rub the soft, buttery wood under his arm. "*Jah.* My *daadi*—*my grandfather*—made this chair soon after he and my *mammi* Leonna married."

"What kind of wood is it? Oak?"

"Oak, *jah.* But it's stained a fair shade." Remembering Sarah's criticisms of it, he mumbled, "Some think it's a bit too dark."

"It's beautiful. I've taken to rocking in it when the girls come home and want to read with me."

The homey bit of information brought forth inviting visions of the way he'd always envisioned his life being. Of security and comfort at home. Of his house being more than it was now—a shell of a place. "Mary and Hannah enjoy sitting with you, Katie. You've done much to help them."

"I like being with them."

"They can tell. You are so . . . so chatty." Jonathan closed his eyes as he felt his cheeks burn yet again. *Chatty?* For goodness' sake!

But to his great surprise, Katie acted as if he'd just given her the greatest of compliments. She laughed. "I know I'm too chatty! Henry has told me more than once that I am too talkative by half. It's a failing of mine, to be sure."

"We don't think so." Jonathan felt the blood rush to his face once more. Would she notice that he'd included himself in the compliment?

Hesitantly, Katie ventured, "To be honest, I miss my family."

Like glass breaking, the tender moment was shattered.

"I'm sorry—but it's only for a short time that you will be here." Somehow he knew the place was going to seem even emptier than it had felt before Katie, with her bright blue eyes and winsome demeanor claiming every corner.

She blinked. "No, that isn't what I meant at all. I was going to say that I miss the way my family gathers together in the evenings. We read or quilt or knit. It's a very pleasant time."

Jonathan didn't know if he could sit with her in the same room for hours on end. With nothing to occupy himself except for the distraction of her smile and the girls. "I've never been much for reading anything besides *The Budget*."

"We could do other things." Eagerly she looked around. "We have puzzles at the inn. I could bring over one of those. Once Henry and I completed a two-thousand-piece jigsaw. It took us weeks!"

Just the image of sitting next to her, putting pieces together side by side made his throat feel dry. "I don't have—"

"Or any kind of game?"

He could see he was not about to get out of her suggestion so easily. "I'll do some thinking about that."

To his surprise, Katie chuckled. Intrigued, he asked, "What is so funny?"

"You are! *Of course* you are going to have to think about things, Jonathan. You do everything slow. As slow as molasses."

That sounded mighty critical. Stung, he said, "There's nothing wrong with takin' my time."

"There's nothing wrong with walking backward, either," she said with another chuckle. "I'm just surprised that you never want to shake things up a bit."

"My life has been shook enough, Katie."

All merriment fled from her face. "Oh! Jonathan, wait! I'm sorry! I didn't mean to hurt your feelings. Surely you know I was only joking?"

Embarrassment made his tone sharp. "My feelings are not hurt." And how could he even imagine telling her if they were? She'd probably laugh even more!

"So, please stay for a bit. We have much to discuss . . . to plan for the service."

"We've already planned most everything, *jah*? Eli and Henry will help me prepare the outside so there will be plenty of room for all the buggies and horses. They're also going to help with a path to the basement door. You said you had the menu in hand."

"I do, but I'm still worried."

"Many hands will make quick work of it all." To his surprise, he found himself speaking gently with her, like he would to Mary.

Like Mary, she responded to his encouragement. Sitting up a little straighter, she nodded. "You're right, Jonathan. Many hands will help. Yesterday afternoon the girls and I swept the basement well and washed the walls. Things already look better."

"The wagon with the oak benches will come tomorrow. Several men are going to help me unload them and carry them inside. Then, together, we'll wipe down everything until it shines."

She frowned. "It's too bad it's winter. I always enjoy the services when they are in a barn and we get to eat outside."

Almost naturally, he sought to calm her fears. "This will be nice, as well, Katie. Don't worry so. Plus, everyone knows our circumstances and will not judge too harshly if everything is not as perfect as it could be. You can't help that Winnie is gone and the Barrs had to cancel."

Her blue eyes sparkled. "I'll try to remember that. *Um*, how is Ruth, by the way? Did she recover from surgery all right?"

"I stopped at McClusky's for some supplies and heard the latest. Ruth did fine and now she is hoping for a lot of ice cream."

"I do love ice cream. It almost makes me wish I had a reason to enjoy a steady supply of it."

She liked ice cream? That was an easy enough way to make her smile. And, well, she was doing so much for him—it was the least he could do in return, right? "I'll bring you home some tomorrow, if you'd like."

To his pleasure, Katie blushed. "Oh. Well, thank you."

"Any special flavor you like?"

"Strawberry?"

"I like strawberry, too." Just as he was about to close his eyes in frustration—he sounded terribly young and foolish—Katie smiled. He felt her regard to his toes. Perhaps Katie and he might one day have a future, after all.

Reaching into a large basket, she pulled out the latest edition of *The Budget*. "Would you like to read for a bit? We don't have to talk anymore if you'd rather not."

At that moment, Jonathan trusted his eyes to focus on the paper instead of his tongue to say the right words. "I . . . yes. I'd like to sit here and read with you. If only for a bit."

"Only for a bit is fine with me."

As the glow from the kerosene lamps mixed with the glow from the fire, the room became illuminated in warmth. A sense of calmness filtered through the air, mixing with the apple-scented candle and igniting his senses.

Finally Jonathan was able to admit to himself that this was the scene he'd always pictured in his mind, the type of moment he'd always wished he and Sarah had had more of.

After years of wishing for companionship, years of resigning himself to a lifetime of being alone, Katie Brenneman was showing him that there was still time to find love again.

She was someone he could trust his heart to. And that knowledge was incredible, indeed.

Chapter 10

I won't go away.

Katie bolted upright in bed and scanned the room, searching in the dim light for Holly. She'd heard the words so clearly, for a moment she'd been sure Holly was in the room with her. Her pulse beat rapidly, every muscle felt on alert. Taking deep breaths, Katie willed herself to settle down.

She also realized she'd come to the inevitable truth. It was time to meet Holly. Avoiding her wasn't working— all avoidance did was foster feelings of guilt and sleepless nights.

Surely, anything was better than receiving her notes from Henry and Anna and being faced with their questions.

But of course, she was alone. Katie shivered. In spite of the cold weather, her body was covered in sweat. With a grimace, she pulled at the neckline of her nightgown. It felt too snug and confining. Damp.

Little by little, as the chilly air met her skin, the dampness dissipated. She looked at the clock near her bed, its plain white face illuminated by the moonlight. Barely could she make out the numbers. Two a.m., or near that. Too early to get up. Four a.m. would arrive soon enough.

With a force of will, Katie lay back down again. But though she closed her eyes and breathed deeply, sleep was far away.

All that seemed to enter her mind were the awful words. Holly's sentences were as completely puzzling as they were frightening. "I won't go away"?

Why would Holly write such a thing? They'd hadn't seen each other in almost a year. What could be so important now? The only thing Holly could be speaking of was Brandon, and Katie knew it would be terribly foolish to ever see him again.

Sleep was surely never to come. After lighting a candle, she pulled out her memory box. The little teddy bear with the golden eyes stared back at her when she lifted the lid.

Gingerly, she held it in her hands, stroking the soft fur. Remembering how she'd felt when Brandon had placed it in her hands. Even now, she was reluctant to part with it. Such sweet moments were rarities.

"It's for you," Brandon had whispered. "It's just a silly toy, but it reminded me of you."

She'd sat there, mesmerized. "How did such a thing make you think of me?"

His expression teasing, Brandon had tapped the bear's

head. "First, it's very cute. Like you." He'd leaned closer. "There there's its eyes."

She'd been completely confused. So terribly naive. "Mine are blue, Brandon. This bear's eyes are brown."

He'd laughed. "But they're almost as pretty. And they have a look of wonder in them. Just like you do, Kate. I love your sweetness. I like you so much. "

She'd closed her eyes then. Every sense had been aware of him. He always smelled like cologne. His feelings had always been so open toward her. So caring, as if she was special.

"Oh." She'd looked around the room for something to comment on, for something to say so she wouldn't sound so tongue-tied, but nothing else held her attention. Holly had left them to talk on the phone to one of her friends. That meant the two of them had been alone, with only the television to act as a chaperone.

Very gently, he placed the bear into her hands, like she mattered the world to him. "No matter what happens, take it, Kate. I bought it for you. Whenever you look at it, you can think of me."

"I won't need the bear to recall you."

Her frank words had made him chuckle. Oh, she'd always taken his words so literally! "You might."

And so, she had held that bear in her arms. She'd kept it even after he'd told her he loved her. Even after she'd told them the truth about who she was.

Even after she told them that she didn't love him. Not enough, anyway.

To her shame, Katie had encouraged his attentions.

She'd smiled and flirted and hinted that she wanted everything he did.

Yes, she had disregarded everything she'd known to be morally right. She'd lied to her new friend, and instead of feeling vaguely guilty about hurting Holly's brother, Katie had felt triumphant. Important. Oh, so very full of herself.

Looking back, Katie wondered how she could have gone so far astray.

"Thank you," she'd said, giving the bear a little hug.

"Thank me with a kiss, Kate."

Kate. Brandon had called her Kate only a few times. But each time had felt special. Like she was part of his group, and had a nickname like all the others.

Like she belonged with him. And because she wanted it, too, she'd leaned closer and kissed him. His arms had curved around her. His hands had rubbed her back, then skimmed her body, his touch heavy and sure. Within moments, that kiss had become heated and out of control.

Almost.

In the flickering candlelight of her temporary bedroom, Katie flinched. What had possessed her to encourage him so?

Because it had been exciting? Because it had felt wonderful to be wanted?

Because no matter how much she'd smiled Jonathan Lundy's way, he'd only looked blankly back at her in return, his grief too overpowering to notice anything else?

And, yes, she had started to think about Jonathan a fair bit. After Sarah had died when Katie was almost nineteen, she'd seen him at community functions after a few weeks of isolation. He'd looked so stalwart. So alone. She'd begun to dream about helping him. Imagine being the one to make him smile again.

And though she'd thought she'd been rather secretive, it had been fairly obvious to everyone around.

Especially to her sister, Rebekeh, who was always so practical and always so blunt. After spying Katie's infatuated gaze for a good long minute, she'd nipped those dreams of infatuation. "Jonathan is not yours, and never will be," she'd said after Katie had almost embarrassed herself by eyeing Jonathan from across the way one Sunday after church.

"I know that." But, in truth, she had hoped that one day he would look over and notice her, too. Especially since no one at the gatherings had ever stirred her interest before.

No one had except Brandon, and she'd always known he wouldn't be an acceptable beau.

"Do you? You don't look that way. You look like you're imagining a life with Jonathan." In her usual, no-nonsense way, Rebekeh made a proclamation. "Mark my words, that's not going to happen."

"It might. One day I bet he's going to want another wife. One day he's going to want someone to help raise his daughters."

"He has Winnie to help."

"Winnie isn't going to want to live with them forever."

In reply, Rebekeh had merely handed Katie a casserole dish to carry to the picnic table. "You don't know that.

What you are thinking is mighty wrong, Katie Brenneman. You'd do best to put it out of your pretty head."

Katie had tucked her head in shame but couldn't seem to help her wayward thoughts.

When Sarah died, Katie had already been enjoying her *rumspringa* for a year. She'd been enjoying Brandon's attention, though she'd also had begun to feel wary around him. It was becoming obvious that Brandon felt far more serious about her than she did about him.

Then, she'd started imagining a future with Jonathan, Mary, and Hannah. And those daydreams had been hard to shake.

Especially the dreams about being his wife.

She'd imagine saving him, removing his worried frown, taking her place in the community as a married woman. She'd think about raising his daughters, and to have more kinner of her own. She'd picture what it would be like to look across the dinner table and feel his approval. To receive warm, sweet glances from him, the way Brandon looked at her. To be loved. For him to want her as his wife.

Outside a wind blew through the trees, brushing two stray branches against the windowpane. Reminding her of the bitter truth. As one month passed into two, then three, Katie had begun to respond to Brandon.

He'd made her feel special and pretty. Though she'd never intended to have a serious relationship with him, never had seriously doubted joining the church one day, she'd enjoyed pretending that she was emotionally involved.

And then late that night when she'd received that bear, after Brandon had told her how he loved her, everything had fallen to pieces. She'd confessed who she was. She revealed how she never intended for their friendship to be anything but a fleeting experiment of sorts. And when Holly had looked at her, so hurt and upset, when Brandon stared at her in shock, why, Katie felt the truth fall over her, plain as day.

She'd intentionally set out to deceive them and had succeeded.

However, the fact that she'd finally acknowledged the truth didn't justify her actions or make them easier to accept.

Suddenly, all she'd wanted to do was run. Katie had grabbed that bear, run to the front door, thrown it open, and burst out into the night. As she made her way home, she'd vowed to start over again. She almost had.

In the dark chilliness of the terribly bare guest room, her head began to pound. That had been months ago. She'd moved on with her life. It was time the doubts and self-recriminations moved on, too.

But still she felt restless and unsettled. Thinking herbal tea might be the answer, Katie hastily wrapped herself in a thick robe and slippers and padded to the kitchen. She'd just filled the kettle with water and set it to heat on the stove when Mary came in.

"What are you doing?"

For once, Mary didn't sound accusing. Instead, her voice merely sounded sleepy and young and curious. "Heating water for tea. I couldn't sleep. What about you?"

The little girl moved closer, her thick rag-wool socks muffling her steps. "I couldn't sleep, neither."

Katie noticed Mary's eyes were suspiciously bright, as if she was on the verge of tears. If it had been Anna, she would have hugged her friend and demanded to know the problem.

But things weren't quite that easy with Mary. The girl was as prickly as a porcupine and sent barbs her way just as frequently. Gently she stated the obvious. "You've got school tomorrow. You need your rest."

Mary merely shrugged. "I know." To Katie's surprise, the girl pulled out a chair and sat down. "Can I have some tea, too?"

"Sure." When the water boiled, Katie strained some chamomile, then carefully carried two mugs to the table. "Here we are. Be careful now, it's hot."

Almost in unison, the two of them blew on the hot brew, then sipped. The feel of the hot water sliding down her throat felt good and immediately calmed her insides.

Mary looked to be enjoying the brew as well. Tentatively, Katie asked, "Are you excited about hosting church on Sunday?"

"*Jah*. We are all going to play hide-and-seek after we eat."

"Henry and Rebekeh and I used to do the same thing. I really looked forward to hosting church, though it is a very big job."

Mary took another sip, then a third. "We worked hard in the basement."

"We certainly did. You and Hannah were mighty *gut* helpers. The floor is bright and shiny clean."

Solemnly, Mary said, "We might have to sweep again after the benches are put in."

"I imagine so. Well, we'll have to hope that the weather stays cold. If it warms up, we're going to have mud to pick up!"

Mary's eyes widened. "Katie, we'd be cleaning all week."

"Yes, indeed we would. But I have a feeling you and Hannah would make even that messy job a joy."

"Maybe," Mary agreed, then sipped again on her tea. After she set her mug down, she looked at Katie with eyes that showed she'd experienced quite a bit during her seven years. "You know, things are different with you here."

"Are they?" Used to Mary's stinging criticism, Katie braced herself to hear what awful thing she had done now.

"Even getting ready for church feels different."

Since Mary didn't sound critical, Katie sought her advice. "Am I forgetting to do something with the house? What does Winnie usually do to get ready? Does she do more in the basement than we've done?"

"I don't think so." Mary shrugged. "No, I'm not thinking about church." Mary sipped again before expounding. "See, when Winnie is here, it was more like when my *mamm* was alive."

"I know you miss your *mamm*. She was a wonderful woman."

Mary's cheeked pinked as she looked away. "I miss her. But, it's not that."

"I see." Tentatively, Katie tried again. "Your mother and Winnie were *gut* friends, weren't they?"

Mary nodded. "They were."

"That is a fine thing. It is a blessing when family gets along well. I like my sister's husband, Olan, very much."

Still struggling with her attempt to say what was on her mind, Mary pursed her lips. "That's not what I meant." She waved a hand, obviously trying to search for words not on the tip of her tongue. "You . . . you've shaken everything up."

Katie felt shaken up at the moment. "I'm sorry you feel that way. I've been doing the best I can for you, but I can't be someone I am not. I can only be myself."

"Daed said that, too."

That was news. Katie hadn't realized Jonathan had spoken to the girls about her. "Does he think that is bad?"

Mary shook her head.

When the silence stretched, Katie said, "Well, soon things will be back to how they used to be. Soon I will be gone and Winnie will return." Katie tried to keep her voice upbeat, but it was hard.

"Katie, I . . ." Mary sipped again, almost hiding her brown eyes as she did so. Mumbling around the rim of the ivory mug, she said, "I like you here. That's what I'm tryin' to say."

"You do?" To her great surprise, Katie's eyes filled with tears. Lately, she'd been so worried about her past and her future, and so torn with insecurities about how she was managing everything day to day, she hadn't even hoped to hear good news from Mary. "I can't tell you how happy I am to hear that."

"You don't look happy, you look sad."

"I'm happy. I promise."

Reassured, Mary said, "You know so much and are so pretty, I like being around you. I like learning to quilt." She rushed on. "You cook a lot of good food, too. I know my *daed* likes it."

Katie felt a rush of pleasure. "How do you know?"

"Sometimes he comes home early to eat dinner with us. He used to never do that. Now, though, he acts like he's waiting on you." Mary raised a brow. "Did you make him do that? Make him join us for dinner?"

"No. But I am glad he comes in. My family eats together every evening."

"Even with all those people there?"

"Especially with all those people there. Like the Lord, our loved ones need some special time carved out."

Mary sipped her tea as she continued to stare at Katie thoughtfully. "Hannah seems happier, too. She used to cry a whole lot more."

Katie almost asked what was the source of Hannah's tears, but for the first time in a long while, she bit back her impulse and sought patience instead. "I'm glad Hannah is not crying so much."

"Me, too. There was no way I could make things better. My mother is gone to the angels."

"Yes, she is."

Eyes wide, Mary whispered, "Why do you think God took her from us so early? We all ride in buggies. Why did she get hurt and no one else?"

"I don't know."

Mary slumped. "I guess I'll have to ask when I get to heaven."

That made Katie smile. "I don't know if our eternity goes that way. I would think it would be mighty time-consuming for our Lord to sit and answer questions."

"I'm not going to take up too much time. I just want to know why."

"Put that way, I suppose it's a reasonable request."

Their tea was almost done. Staring at the scant bits of tea that had seeped through the wire mesh and sunk to the bottom of her mug, Katie said, "We should probably be getting to bed now. It's near three in the morning. Are you more tired?"

As if on cue, Mary stifled a yawn. "No."

"Something tells me that might not quite be true."

In a rush, Mary blurted, "What if you wanted to stay longer? What if we wanted you to? If we were to ask you to? Would you do that?"

To her surprise, Katie didn't know the answer to that. Would she want to stay with Mary and Hannah out of duty? To stay only as someone who could look after the house? "The answer to that would depend on your aunt and father. Remember, we don't know what is going to happen with Winnie."

"She might move to Indiana."

"But she might not. She went out there to get to know Malcolm, and to get to know his family. Not to make plans."

"But what about you? If my father said you could stay here with us, what would you say?"

There was the question. A few months ago, Katie would have thought she'd do anything to attract Jonathan's regard. During her first few days at the Lundys', when she was so sad and lonely, she would have said she couldn't wait to return home. Now, though, she wasn't sure what the future had in store for her.

"I don't know," Katie finally murmured. "But I will tell you this: it is better to not always think about the what-ifs in life. If you give yourself to the Lord, then He will make clear all the hard decisions, and we won't have to worry about so much. Remember, the future is in God's hands, not ours."

Mary scowled as they set their mugs in the sink and started up the stairs. "When do you get to be old enough to have your future in your own hands?"

Instead of reminding her again of the Lord's will, Katie chuckled. "You, Mary, remind me of myself. So impatient."

"Really?"

"Really." Cupping Mary's shoulder as she paused, Katie added, "I have always been in a hurry. I used to shame my mother with my impulsiveness. I got into trouble a time or two at school as well."

"I didn't know that."

"That's because we don't know each other well. Maybe soon we will."

There'd been a time when Katie had felt that she was in control of everything. Now she was smarter and stronger. Now she realized that she wasn't in control of anything. Her future felt as slippery as ever. "But, to answer your question, I don't know if we ever get old enough. Our future is in the Lord's hands. It's best to remember that, don'tcha think?"

"Maybe."

Katie reached the landing and turned to Mary. "It's time we slept. Morning will come even if we're not quite ready to greet it."

Mary nodded solemnly, then to Katie's surprise, reached out and wrapped her arms around her.

Automatically, Katie hugged her back. The little girl's arms felt wonderful wrapped around her waist. Bending down, she pressed a kiss on her head. Yes, the Lord did work in mysterious ways.

"Ready for the weekend, Jonathan?" Brent called out at five o'clock on Friday, just as Jonathan was slipping on his coat and gloves. "I feel like it's been the longest week imaginable."

"It has been tiring, for sure," Jonathan said as he waited for his boss to approach. "But we did get all the frames made for the builder's contract. That is something to be praised."

Brent chuckled. "For a while there, I didn't think it was going to get done. I sure appreciate your team staying late on Wednesday night."

"I always appreciate the overtime. Plus, things are crazy at my house. I didn't mind escaping things for a bit."

"Why are things crazy? Because Winnie's gone?"

"Yes, but that's not all. We are hosting church this weekend."

"Already?"

Jonathan appreciated how Brent took the time to get to know their ways. "*Jah*, it's been a year since we hosted last. It just feels like it happens more quickly."

Brent slapped Jonathan's shoulder. "Best of luck with that. I have some time tomorrow, do you need help unloading the benches?"

"Eli and Henry are coming to help. But I thank you just the same."

"Well, good luck. I'm going home with my fingers crossed. What do you think my chances are that Tricia has dinner ready?"

Jonathan chuckled. "Slim to none." Brent's wife was a teacher. It was standard practice for Brent to take her out on Friday nights. "You best plan to get gussied up and take her out. She'll be mighty pleased with that suggestion."

"Spoken like a man who's been married before," Brent said with a grin. "I'll definitely take her out. See you Monday, Jon."

Jonathan waved him off. As he watched Brent practically scamper to his car, he tried to recall the last time he'd eagerly run home. He couldn't remember.

Oh, he loved his girls, and he was always eager to spend time with them, but that wasn't the feeling he longed to experience.

But moments later, as he and Blacky were making their way home, Jonathan found himself thinking of Katie once again. Perhaps she'd made pork chops or a roast. Katie was a mighty fine cook.

But her skills in the kitchen were not what he kept thinking about. No, it was her sunny nature. The way she smiled tenderly at Hannah.

The way she greeted him when he walked in the door— just like he was worth waiting for. With that in mind, he found himself spurring Blacky on. He'd been waiting all day to see her, as well.

Chapter 11

"I don't know if I'll ever be able to move again," Katie moaned as she finally sat down at the kitchen table after a number of the folks had left Jonathan's home from the church service. "Every bone in my body aches. Jonathan, try not to trip over me tomorrow morning when you wake up."

"I canna promise you that. The way you are sprawled out, why it would make a man have a difficult time getting around you."

With effort, Katie pulled a foot in so it rested under the table. "Better?"

Jonathan pretended to have a difficult time squeezing through the opening. "Only a bit," he said, sucking in his stomach comically.

Katie couldn't help but notice that he didn't have much of a stomach to tuck in. No, Jonathan Lundy was all solid muscle, and that was the truth. But no matter how attractive she found him, there was certainly no way she could let him—or anyone else in the room—see that. "How's this?" she asked, pulling in her chair a bit more. But in her soreness, the feet of the chair only moved an inch or so in.

He took things into his own hands and merely pushed the chair forward, then walked around her easily. "This is much better, now."

As everyone around her chuckled, Katie did her best to not let everyone see how drawn to Jonathan she was.

When she'd first arrived, he'd seemed terribly aware of her, yet emotionally distant. But things had changed during the last two weeks. Little by little, he'd unbent enough for Katie to see glimpses of the warm person underneath the distant manner. This playful attitude drew her to him even more than his handsome looks.

Blissfully unaware of her feelings, Jonathan walked passed her and joked some more. "If I would've known a simple church service was going to wear you out, I would've asked for more help."

"I did just fine."

The laughter in the room rose again. "He has you there, Katie," her mother said, her voice merry. "If you complain much more, we'll all think preparing for services was too big a job for you. You might have to get up, after all."

"*Jah*. Otherwise, you will be covered in footprints." With a wink toward Anna, *Daed* said, "And you would dirty your new dress."

Katie sat up and smiled at her father. "Well, I certainly don't want that to happen." With only a bit of a wince, she stood up and faced her family. "I can't believe how worried I was about today. *Mamm*, even though I helped you prepare the house for church many a time, I never fully understood why you would get so short-tempered with us just hours before everyone was due to arrive. Now I know."

"I was never short-tempered."

Henry folded his arms across his chest. "No, *Daed* always spent most of his time in the barn during preparations for no reason at all."

"Well, maybe I was a bit cross."

"Only a bit, Irene," Katie's father said with a smile.

Jonathan perked up. "I think Katie did a fine job. We had a lot of people here, and everyone enjoyed both the worship and the luncheon. Our house looked neat and shiny clean, as well. You did all of us proud, Katie."

Katie beamed at the praise. Though she felt as if she could sleep for a week, she also was terribly pleased with how well everything turned out. Of course, none of it could have gone so well if not for the many hands that worked together. Over the last three days, the Lundy home had been full of women helping to clean the kitchen, prepare the meal, and help tend to the walkway. Cabinets shone and the oak floor gleamed.

"*Danke*, Jonathan, but we know it took many people to make today a success." Looking around the room, she added, "I know I would have burst into tears yesterday if not for knowing that all of you were working by my side."

"Hosting one hundred fifty people is a lot, no matter how prepared you are. I, for one, am glad that we will not be hosting next," her mother said.

"Me, too. I was so nervous about making sure everything was perfect that I thought I was going to get sick," blurted Anna. Then, as she realized how she sounded, she looked around the room. "I hope that's okay to admit?"

"Only among family and friends," Eli teased. He rocked back on his heels. "And speaking of family, I think I'd best get going. I promised my nephews I'd play basketball with them later."

As he walked to the door, Eli scanned the group of them again. "It's just a shame that Winnie wasn't here, you know? It didn't feel the same."

As the door shut behind his friend, Jonathan nodded, his features far more reflective. "I have to admit to feelin' the same way. I want Winnie to be happy, but it is difficult to imagine her not being here in the future. I hate the thought of her always living in Indiana."

"If it's any consolation, I can tell you that I've found that worrying and second-guessing makes no difference," Katie said softly. "People will do what they will. All we can do is hope their decisions are good and that they made their choices with both their head and heart."

"That is good thinkin'. I'll pray that Winnie is thinking that way."

As was the norm, the adults took time to relax and enjoy each other's company while the *kinner* bundled up, played outside, then ran into the kitchen and asked for snacks. As the hours grew late, toddlers found places to nap in back bedrooms and older members found themselves nodding off.

As the sun set, families hitched up their buggies and began to leave. More friends waved good-bye, promising to stop by later in the week to help load pews into the wagon.

At last only Katie's family remained. Happy for Anna's and her mother's company, she used the opportunity to show off the progress Mary and Hannah were making with the quilt. Attentively, she listened as her mother offered additional suggestions for more simple projects.

However, no matter who was at the house, Katie was constantly aware of Jonathan. His soft, distinctive voice echoed to her whenever he spoke. Every so often, she'd find her eyes straying to him, noticing how handsome he looked in his cornflower blue shirt. She smiled when he laughed with the other men in front of the fire.

She couldn't help but notice that Jonathan also seemed to be looking her way more than once or twice. He'd hurried to help her when she'd carried a load of quilts to spread out for the children. He clasped her elbow when she almost stumbled on a step.

Most of all, he seemed to be enjoying himself. That had to mean things were getting better between them. Perhaps they'd set the groundwork for a future together.

Perhaps her dreams of sharing a life with him weren't so far-fetched, after all?

* * *

"I can't help but feel sorry for Winnie," Jonathan said to Katie two days later as he folded up his sister's latest letter. He'd brought it inside with him when he came home from work, but had waited until after their dinner of pork roast and stuffing to read it.

Katie and he were now enjoying carrot cake and coffee and discussing the letter. "Though I tried to warn Winnie about the dangers of getting her hopes up, I feel bad that things aren't turning out like she'd hoped."

Katie felt the same way, as well as a little bit dismayed. The practical part of her had always assumed Winnie would be returning with wedding plans. After all, such a forthcoming agreement must had been understood between Winnie and her Malcolm, otherwise, why would Winnie have been so all fired up to go?

Now, though, Katie realized that she'd been just as swept away in Winnie's flights of fancy. "Perhaps she needs to be a bit more patient. It takes time to plan a future. Winnie must know that."

"She might. This Malcolm may not be so sure." He speared another chunk of cake. "And if he's not sure about Winnie, then it is best she finds out now. He'd have to go a fair distance to be good enough for my sister." Warming up to the subject, he added, "Winnie's got a lot to offer, don't you think?"

"Indeed," she said, smiling as Jonathan scooped up another bite of cake. Oh that man did enjoy his sweets!

"I think she's mighty pretty. Don't you think so?"

"I do." Winnie was tall and slim and willowy. She handled herself well, too, walking proudly, never timidly among their people. Katie had a feeling that if Winnie were dressed like an *Englischer*, she'd catch the attention of quite a few people.

"*Jah*? That's it?"

"I don't know what else to say. Yes, she's pretty." Sometimes Jonathan's manner was so like Henry's that they could be twins. Henry, too, had always been protective of her and her feelings. Feeling sorry for him, she finally added, "Brothers always feel protective of their sisters though. I'm not sure if you would see her flaws, if she had any."

After scraping the last of the plate for a smidgen of frosting, he chuckled. "Your words are fair." Pushing back his chair, he stood up. "Well, anyway, perhaps it is just as well, then. He doesn't seem to understand how much she would be giving up to be his wife. And, if he's not aware of that, then he surely doesn't sound like the man for her."

"Who knows who that will be?"

"Well, not someone like Malcolm sounds to be. We've now received ten letters from Winnie. She doesn't mention Malcolm doing much other than working at the hardware store."

Katie found she had to agree. "I'm sure Winnie is wondering why he invited her out to see him, if he isn't making any time for her. When I wrote to her last week, I encouraged her to hint to him that she'd enjoy going for walks or visiting the shops around his home."

Tapping on the latest letter, Jonathan frowned. "If he's done any of that, we haven't heard about it. Yes, this Malcolm is definitely not the right man for Winnie. I do not think they would make a good match of it. Poor Winnie. I wonder what she'll do now. Maybe she should just hurry home."

Though Jonathan seemed to be talking to himself, not her, Katie wondered the same thing. Winnie wasn't afraid to speak her mind, even to the men and elders of their order.

And though she was loyal to a fault and a hard worker, Katie had always sensed a slight dissatisfaction in her, as if she wasn't quite sure what she was unhappy about, but it was there all the same. Though no one in their circle of friends had ever openly commented on it, Katie had spied knowing looks between other girls when Winnie blurted out something that was slightly too brash.

She didn't look much like the rest of them, either. Her hair was a dark, dark brown. Almost black. The opposite of Jonathan and his light, almost golden head of hair. Her light blue eyes warred for attention with her dimples. More than one man had commented on them.

But underneath her striking looks and strong personality was a warm heart just begging to be loved and nurtured.

Katie was sure that with the right love and affection, some of Winnie's armor would melt away, leaving just a gentle heart and sweet nature for all to see.

Eli had been right when he'd stated that it had been strange not to have Winnie around. She added a lot to every conversation and her fun laugh was infectious.

But by the sound of Winnie's letters, Malcolm didn't see any of that. Or if he did, he wasn't sharing his thoughts with Winnie.

Tracing one calloused finger along the crease in the letter, Jonathan frowned. "Katie, I feel mighty responsible for her plight. I should have known better than to let her go off to Indiana like she did."

"You had no choice." Giving into impulse, Katie reached out and patted his arm. "Malcolm couldn't come here, not with his father doing poorly and the hardware store his sole responsibility. You had to let her meet him. She is old enough, too. Old enough to know her own mind."

"*Jah*, but perhaps I should have asked her not to stay for so long."

"Everyone thought his family sounded amiable and kind. We all assumed she'd be happy."

"But I could've said no."

"If you'd done that, there would have been trouble, too. After all, she's your sister, not your daughter."

"It is still my duty to protect her."

"But isn't it also your duty to be there for her even during difficult times?"

"But this was of her own making. Now she's hurting. I could have prevented this."

"I disagree. She did not bring this disappointment on herself, it was just how things worked out."

He pushed his dessert plate to one side. "But I should have known."

"How could you?" Because she felt she had some knowledge on the subject, Katie said, "Winnie had to take a risk in order to be happy. She had to do something for herself, just to see if she could. She had no choice, don't you see?"

"Not at all. There's plenty of men here for her."

"Then why hasn't one taken her fancy?"

Jonathan shook his head. Katie knew even if he did have some ideas, he would never say anything. His loyalty to his sister would never permit that. More softly, Katie said, "Jonathan, Winnie has only done what she intended. She wanted to get to know Malcolm and his family better. She's gotten to do that."

"But it hasn't worked out well."

"Jonathan, you're going to have to come to terms with the fact that Winnie wants to have her own life—not just help you with yours."

Like the flip of a page, his expression shuttered. "You make it sound as if I've made her stay here. That is untrue."

He might never have said the words, but Katie knew the Lundy family well enough to know that it had been expected. She would have expected as much out of her family. But she could also see that she'd just inadvertently hurt his feelings. "I'm sorry I spoke out of turn."

But if Jonathan heard, he didn't give notice. "Winnie has never said I asked too much of her."

His sharp tone made her retreat further. "Yes, I . . ."

"You have no idea what it has been like," he added quickly. "Losing Sarah. Trying to raise two girls. Realizing that my days of farming are over, at least for a while. Learning a new trade at the lumberyard."

She felt terrible. "You're right. Sometimes I talk without thinking."

He stood up. "I'd say you do that a fair amount. I mean, you really have no idea about what it is like, to have to worry about other people, do you?"

"That's hardly fair, Jonathan. I may not have children, but I am part of a family. I worry about them."

"It is not the same."

"All right." She felt his hostility like it was a tangible thing, especially since it brought forth all those guilty feelings about Brandon that she'd done her best to keep hidden. Maybe Jonathan was right. This was *Jonathan*. The man she'd secretly yearned for ever since she saw him standing alone during church.

This was the man she'd fought her parents to see, the man she was finally getting to see on a regular basis.

But no longer was she willing to simply just have him. No, she wanted him on an equal basis. She wanted him to desire her in his life not because she so obviously wanted to be there, or because his girls were taken care of, but because of who she was. Inside.

"I wasna trying to make you upset. I was only speaking my mind. There's nothing wrong with that."

"You speak it mighty freely in my home."

Now her ire was up. "When you arrived at my home, hat in hand, you neglected to tell my parents that in addition to care for your daughters, you also desired someone to always agree with you."

"You are deliberately twisting my words."

"Then that makes two of us." Katie stood up. "I'm going to go be with Mary and Hannah."

"I'm going to the *daadi haus*," he said, turning away.

To his back, she muttered, "I didn't doubt you would, Jonathan. Why don't you go on and be by yourself? Again."

His footsteps slowed. "Perhaps I should arrange to have Winnie return early."

Oh, he was so obstinate, once again trying to think for everyone! "If that is what you want."

Without another word, he stormed off. With a scrape of her chair, she left the kitchen, too.

But the greeting of resentful silence in the living room told Katie no comfort was going to be found there, either.

Hannah greeted her with wide eyes. "What did you say to Daed?"

"Just something that was needed. . . ."

"You made him mad."

"I know. He made me mad, too."

Just then, Mary appeared from around the corner, a scowl on her face. "Katie, you said you were gonna make things better here."

Katie had wanted to. She'd wanted to befriend the girls and build a relationship with Jonathan. However, every time they took a step forward, two steps back seemed to follow soon after. "I can only be myself, Mary. Your father is a capable man. He doesn't need a woman like me to fix things; he only wanted me to be here for a spell."

"Maybe you should have listened to him."

Katie sighed. As always, she should have done a lot of things. But that didn't excuse his rudeness. And truly, she wasn't about to change her words. She'd meant what she said, and that was the truth. "I'm trying to listen to him. But sometimes, he has to listen to me as well. I can't always keep my opinions to myself. That's not who I am. If you learn nothing else from me, please try and remember that. At the end of the day, we can only find solace in our hearts." Thinking of her running-around time, she slowly added, "Pretending to be something we are not is a thankless task."

Mary folded her arms over her chest for a good long moment. "I brought out the fabric," she finally said.

"*Ach*, good. Perhaps we can pin a few pieces together. Soon, I'll take you to the inn and show you how to work my sewing machine. What do you think about that?"

Their tentative smiles were all she needed to wave them closer.

Chapter 12

"Hello, Mr. McClusky," Katie said when she and the girls entered the general store a week later. "How are you today?"

The proprietor laid his elbows on the counter. "Not as well as you, Miss Lundy. I see you have some great helpers with you today."

"I do at that," Katie agreed, looking fondly at the girls, who'd just stood up a little straighter. "Mary and Hannah are *wunderbaar schee*—wonderful nice helpers."

"We've got some peppermint sticks in for the holidays. Would you two girls like some?"

After hesitantly looking toward Katie, they nodded, then trotted after Sam McClusky. As she watched them walk together, Katie felt an unexpected burst of motherly pride. After witnessing her argument with Jonathan, things were getting better between her and the girls.

They'd come to an understanding that she could only be who she was. And, once they realized she didn't intend to replace either their mother or their aunt, they embraced her wholeheartedly.

Their companionship more than made up for all the tension between her and Jonathan.

She was now far less homesick for Anna and the bustling schedule at the inn. Instead, she'd begun to feel pleasure in the many tasks of keeping a good home. Jonathan's home began to feel like her own. Just as important, as she'd gotten braver, she'd uncovered a lot of things about his home that she liked very much.

It was obvious that Sarah had been a good housekeeper. It was just as obvious that Winnie's interests didn't lie in that area. Linens and tablecloths were neatly organized and folded, as were the children's old clothes. Newer items were more haphazardly packed away or pushed into cabinets. Over the last few days, Katie had decided to wash and dust the inside of most cupboards and to sort the contents. She felt that Sarah would be pleased with her diligence.

Katie didn't bother to tell Jonathan about her work; it was obvious that he would neither be interested in her progress nor appreciate the efforts it took.

Of course, they didn't talk much at all now. He was still stewing over her comments about his and Winnie's relationship.

But that was all right with Katie. She felt she was growing and changing at the Lundy home. And in all ways, for the better. Now that Christmas was mere weeks away, she wanted to make the girls a surprise, new dresses for the season. There was to be a gathering in a few weeks and she wanted the girls to have something new and pretty to wear.

She'd just pulled out a bolt of evergreen-colored fabric when she felt the unfamiliar sensation of being watched. Slowly she looked up. There was no one directly in front of her. Yet, a shiver ran through her. What was going on?

Quickly, she glanced toward the girls. Peppermint sticks in their mouths, they were chatting with another pair of girls—Corrine Miller and her two daughters—over by the baked goods. Katie knew it would be just a matter of moments before Hannah's sweet tooth got the best of her and she came running over to ask for a cookie.

She pulled out the evergreen fabric again and tried to guess how many yards would be needed for two dresses. She was going to need to ask Mr. McClusky to wrap the fabric so Mary and Hannah wouldn't ask what such beautiful fabric was for.

But oh, what a wonderful surprise those dresses would be on Christmas morning! And, she'd noticed that their robes were a little short and that Hannah's looked particularly worn. Perhaps she could buy them new robes, too? She picked up a pretty lavender robe, made of the softest material Katie had ever felt. Already she could imagine Hannah's look of delight when she wrapped it around herself Christmas morning.

"I hardly recognized you."

Katie almost jumped out of her skin. With a gasp, the robe fell from her hands onto the floor. "Holly."

"Yep. That's me." An unfamiliar bitterness swept over

her features. "I'm surprised you even remember who I am. I wasn't sure if you even remembered my name."

"Of course I remember you." Katie fought the urge to hug her. Oh, but Holly looked exactly like her memories. She was still as tall as ever—almost Jonathan's height. Her blond straight hair played off her dark brown eyes. She looked so like the friend she'd had in her faded blue jeans, blue sweater with an embroidered moose on the chest, and boots.

So much like everything Katie had wanted to imitate.

Yet, there was a difference about her, too. Her expression was pinched. Her eyes guarded. A sense of desperation surrounded her like a luminous cloak.

What had happened?

Wondering if her actions were all to blame, Katie bent to pick up the robe, using the moment to settle herself. Around them, shoppers continued to chat and converse. Finally settling into the inevitability of it all, Katie faced the girl she'd hoped to never come in contact with again. She should have known sooner or later they'd meet. "I'm surprised to see you here. Few *Englischers* other than tourists come here to shop."

"You know, it would have been a lot easier for both of us if you would have met me at the Brown Dog. Why didn't you? Are you really that busy?"

"It wasn't that. I . . . I just didn't know what we would have to talk about."

"You have a lot of nerve. We were good friends, Katie." Impatiently, she thrust a clump of blond hair away from her forehead. "I thought we were *best* friends."

"We were good friends, that is true. But, things have changed." Behind her, Katie could hear Sam talking with another customer and the girls and their friends eagerly trying out one rocking chair after another. "Things are different now. I . . . can't pretend I'm not Amish anymore."

Holly shook her head in dismay. "Is that all our friendship was? Just an experiment to see what it was like to be someone else?" Her voice cracked. With effort, she breathed deep. "Is that all Brandon was to you?"

Embarrassed, Katie shook her head. "Of course not."

"Then why did you just take off like you did?"

"Don't act like we only had a simple disagreement. Holly, that last time I saw you, why, we argued something fierce. Don't you remember?" Katie knew she'd never forget the looks of scorn Holly had sent her way. How Holly had told her that she'd never forgive Katie for using her like she did.

The quiet, crushed acceptance of Brandon's face when he had realized that his feelings were far stronger than hers had ever been for him. "I didn't think you would want to ever speak with me again."

"I hadn't planned to . . ."

"I really am sorry for my lies." Katie knew she could never forget their last, tumultuous conversation. They'd been at Brandon and Holly's house. They'd been sitting around, watching TV, doing nothing.

Then Brandon had told her he'd loved her.

And Katie had known that she hadn't loved him. Worse, she realized she'd encouraged his feelings because she'd enjoyed the attention. She'd loved the freedom of pretending to be something she wasn't.

But at that very moment, Katie had known one simple truth—she would never leave her faith.

Holly shook her head. " I probably said a lot of things I should never have uttered aloud. But, I was angry, Katie."

"You had a right to be."

Just as if Katie hadn't spoken, Holly continued. "You lied to me. You lied about everything about yourself. But after all this time, don't you think I had a reason for contacting you?" Folding her arms over her chest protectively, she lifted her chin. "This was the only place I could figure out to find you. I've been having to stand around here, waiting . . . hoping that sooner or later you'd show up. I don't have the time for this. Things would have been a whole lot easier if you'd just met me at the Brown Dog."

"I couldn't. I . . . just couldn't face you. You might not believe me, but I do feel awful about my lies. Holly, what do you want from me?"

"I need you to go see Brandon."

Katie felt the wind being knocked out of her. "You don't understand." In spite of all attempts for control, her voice started to raise. "I can't see him. I'm *Amish*."

"You were Amish when we were friends, too."

"That's not quite true. We Amish do not join the church until we are adults, or close to it. When I met you and Brandon, I hadn't joined yet." Even to her own ears, Katie knew she was splitting hairs. In a quieter tone, she added, "Now that I've joined, I adhere to our customs. I would not feel right courting an *Englischer*."

"I'm not asking for that."

"Then why—" She cut herself off, feeling uneasy. Just

a few feet away, Sam was watching them with intense interest. If he got wind of their conversation, it could be common knowledge in no time. Nervously, she cleared her throat. "Perhaps you should leave. I mean, I think it would be best now if I . . ."

Holly gripped her elbow. "Walk with me outside."

"I can't—"

"Yes, you can. I'm not going to wait any longer. Come out, or I swear I won't even try to keep our conversation private. In no time everyone in here will know all about your lies. They'll know for sure you aren't near as sweet as you look. I mean it, Katie."

Holly leaned closer, the look of fierce desperation in her eyes more powerful than any words could be. "I'm not the one at fault here. You have to listen to me. And you have to listen right now. You know I'll do it. After all, I've got nothing to lose."

"I've got to check on the girls first."

Just as Holly walked out, Katie quickly approached Hannah and Mary. "I'm just going outside to speak to an English woman for a moment. I'll be right back."

"All right." Mary was obviously having too good a time to worry about Katie's conversations.

Katie found Holly sitting in one of the rocking chairs that dotted the wide front porch. "So . . . what is it about Brandon that you needed to talk to me about?"

"Brandon was diagnosed with cancer."

Glad for the thick wooden railing behind her, Katie gripped it hard. "What?"

Her expression crushed, Holly said, "He's really sick. It

had already spread to his liver by the time they discovered it. He's . . . he's not going to last much longer."

"But surely the doctors can do something? I know of a woman who had cancer two years ago but she's doing fine now."

"This isn't the same, Katie. It's bad." Her voice cracked as she strived for control. "The medication he's on isn't to cure him . . . it's to help with the pain. Some days he doesn't seem to even want to wake up."

Raising her head, Holly looked Katie straight in the eye. "But he wants to see you, Katie."

"Why me?"

"He loved you once. I think he still does."

Katie shook her head. Wanting—needing—to deny Holly's words. "I am not the person he thought I was. He knows that, yes? He remembers?"

"He doesn't care. Don't you see? Brandon just wants to see you again. To make sure you're okay. He's worried about you. Wondered what happened to your life."

"I . . . I don't deserve his worry. I treated him terribly."

"Don't you get it? He doesn't care." Slowly, Holly added, "See, that's the thing about my brother. He doesn't care if I'm not perfect, if you aren't, either. He just doesn't want to be forgotten."

"I never forgot him, or you."

"Then don't let him think you did." Holly opened her purse and pulled out a slip of paper. "Here's the name of the hospital. My phone number's on there, too. Go see him before it's too late. I'm begging . . . I'm begging you," she said, obviously choking on the words. "Even if you don't care about me, please go. Please just care about Brandon."

"I *do* care." Yet, even as she said the words, she felt ashamed. Caring people didn't ignore friends. Not even former ones.

"For what it's worth . . . I'm glad I found you. You look . . . happy."

"I am. I mean, I was." Swallowing hard, Katie held out her hand. "Thank you for finding me. I *will* go see Brandon. I promise I will, as soon as I can find a driver to take me to the hospital."

"Try and hurry." Holly clasped her hand with a hint of a smile, then walked away.

Behind her, the door opened again. "Katie? Katie can we get some pecans?"

Blinking away her tears, Katie nodded. "Sure. *Um*, Mary how about you ask Mr. McClusky if we might have a pound. I've a notion to make pecan tarts with you today."

"All right." Mary looked at Katie curiously before pointing to Holly's retreating form. "Who was that?"

"Her name is Holly. She is a friend of mine."

"But she's English."

"I know." As Mary sidled closer, Katie wrapped an arm around her slim shoulders. "She is."

Just as they watched Holly get into her car, Hannah looked up at her. "She sure is tall. She's as tall as a horse."

Katie chuckled at the comparison. "She's tall, but maybe not like a horse." Though it felt as if her throat was closing from so much suppressed emotion, Katie did her best to smile comfortingly. "She's nice, too."

"She looked sad."

"She was tired I think." After smoothing back a nonexistent strand of hair back into her *kapp*, she added, "She . . . she has a lot on her mind."

"Oh." Turning away from Holly's retreating form, Hannah said importantly, "I'm gonna go ask for pecans so we can bake today."

Later, as she walked the girls to the buggy, Katie realized that Holly had finally accomplished what she'd set out to do . . . she'd found Katie and brought up the past.

Now it was Katie who had to figure out what to do with her future.

Chapter 13

"I saw Katie, Brandon," Holly blurted the moment Brandon woke up from his nap. "She finally went to that general store I told you about."

It took her brother a few moments to focus on her. More time passed before he spoke. "What happened?"

"I talked to her."

"A-a . . . and?"

He looked worse. As she pressed the remote control button so he could sit up, Holly used the time to school her features. The nurses had warned her he was having a bad day. His sluggish words and dark marks around his eyes showed they hadn't exaggerated.

"Hol?"

Taking a deep breath, she mentally attempted to moderate her feelings. The last thing Brandon needed was to see her stress. "Oh, well, at first I couldn't believe that it was actually Katie. She was standing with two little girls and all dressed in Amish clothes."

"Two girls? Is she married?"

"No, I later found out that she's just watching them."

"How did she look?"

"Different. Her dress was a violet-blue. It was pretty, but hung loose. Some kind of black apron was pinned over that. Her hair was all twisted and pinned up under a sheer white little hat."

Brandon shook his head. "No. How did she *look*, Holly?"

He still cared so much. "She looked different. But, pretty, too. She looked happy. Well, she did until she saw me." In a cross between a chuckle from the memory and a sob that threatened to erupt from seeing the condition her brother was in, Holly tried to find the words to describe Katie's face when she saw her.

Maybe a cross between utter dread and complete surprise? "Anyway, we talked. She . . . apologized, Brandon."

"She feels guilty."

"I imagine she does. And she's got a ton to feel guilty about, too. I know you really liked her, Brandon."

"I loved her." Closing his eyes for a moment, he added, "Maybe I still do, in a way."

"I told her you wanted to see her."

He stared at her again. "What did she say?"

"She said she would visit you." She clasped his hand when hope entered his expression. "She promised."

"When?"

"I don't know. I guess when she can get a driver."

"Why a driver?"

Showcasing her knowledge, Holly explained. "The Amish don't drive, Brandon. Most don't even own cars. But they're not against using vehicles as transportation—just as having them as conveniences. So they hire people to take them places."

"You . . . you should have," he said weakly.

"I know I should've." A better person would have thought to offer. But she hadn't. In truth, she'd been so overwhelmed with emotion that she hadn't even given it a thought. All she could think of was that she'd missed Katie, and that she could have used her friendship and support over the last year. Clearing her throat, "Anyway, I'm thinking maybe she'll be here on Monday or Tuesday."

"Maybe." As if the conversation was too much, he closed his eyes again.

"She'll show up," she said with more confidence than she felt. But Katie had to show up. It was Brandon's dying wish.

She'd promised. Holly hoped Katie had finally started keeping some promises.

Late that night, long after the girls were fast asleep and Jonathan had gone back to the *daadi haus*, Katie pulled out her memory box again from under the bed.

After carefully setting the container on top of the pale lavender quilt, she gingerly opened the cardboard top. Oh, it wasn't a fragile thing. One the contrary, it only contained fragile memories. Ones she was both afraid to abandon completely and wary about confronting again.

As she set the lid to the box on the floor, once again the scent of another life burst into the air.

But this time, instead of only recalling the things she'd done wrong, Katie started recalling the good times she'd had. Remembering the laughter she'd shared with Holly. Her first impression of a shopping mall. The sense of freedom she'd felt, just by spending a Saturday doing nothing except watching episodes of *The Brady Bunch* on Holly's television.

Oh, how she'd enjoyed that show.

Finally, she recalled how torn up she'd been inside, wondering what God planned for her future. Wondering what the right path was to take. She'd been so confused, she'd sought out Henry, though he hadn't been in the best spirits, either. Rachel had left him for an *Englischer* just weeks before.

She'd found him in his workroom, supposedly sanding an old trunk they'd found in the attic. In actuality, all he'd been doing was sitting with his dog, Jess.

"Henry, are you ever going to smile again?"

He'd looked at her and scowled. "Leave me alone, Katie."

"I truly am sorry about Rachel."

He shrugged. "It's not your worry."

"But it is. Don't you know how I worry about you?" She'd swallowed hard. What she'd really wanted was for him to see how she still needed him. She still needed him to worry about her, to offer her guidance.

But Henry was so good. He would never understand her willfulness. Her dreamy nature. Her impulsiveness. He'd never understand her ever even thinking about living among the English.

Absently, Henry rubbed Jess's side. "I'm glad you care. If I was to admit the truth, I'd guess I'd tell you that I'm sorry Rachel wanted someone else. Wanted a different way of life."

"Did she ever tell you why?"

"*Why?*" He paused to consider her question. "I don't rightly know. I don't think Rachel was running from me in particular, though maybe she was. Maybe she wasn't even running from anything." Picking up his sandpaper, he rubbed it against the side of the trunk once. Twice. "More likely, I think Rachel was running to something else. To another man."

Reaching down, he rubbed Jess's neck. The dog thumped his tail in bliss. "Rachel was in love. I can't fault that, you know? When a person is in love, there isn't much choice. If you don't follow your heart, then the rest of the world isn't as right. It's like everything is off-kilter."

Katie had been mesmerized by his words. Henry had sounded so wise. And he'd spoken directly to her heart.

And that's when she'd known the truth—she didn't love Brandon.

That conversation had spurred her decision, but had also fueled her regrets. Katie imagined anyone would feel as she did—it was hard to not love someone when they wanted you to. Sometimes, no matter how much you wanted to love someone, those feelings just never surfaced.

Now that time had gone by, Katie knew she'd made the right decision. Yes, she could have handled things far better. But if she had to go back and live her life again, she knew she wouldn't choose Brandon over Jonathan. She wouldn't choose to live a different way.

She had the Lord and His watchful ways to thank for that.

He certainly had guided her through many rough patches. Now she needed His guidance once again. She needed to make things right with Holly. To ask for Brandon's forgiveness. To move forward. To run to something. To run to the path that was meant just for her.

Closing her eyes, Katie said a prayer from Psalm 105 that had always brought her comfort. *Seek the Lord, and his strength; seek his face evermore.* "Help me, Jesus. Help me know what to do, help me know what the right thing to do would be."

With bated breath, she waited for a sign that He heard her words. Waited to feel a new sense of peace. But nothing came.

The wind picked up, blowing branches, which in turn scraped against the outside walls of her bedroom. Quickly, Katie closed the box again and pushed it back under her bed. After blowing out the candle, she burrowed down into the covers and listened to the wind, closed her eyes, and prayed with all her heart. In the dark room, she finally confessed to all of her sins. Confessed to all of her transgressions, asked for forgiveness and guidance. Holly's reappearance in her life had made one thing painfully clear.

She couldn't make decisions alone anymore. She would

ask God's help and finally do what He wanted her to. Only then would she ever find peace.

The following morning, Katie knew what she had to do. She had to go see Brandon. There really was no other decision to make. He was sick, he had asked for her, and poor Holly had gone out of her way to find her.

The moment Mary and Hannah left for school, Katie donned her favorite blue dress, then quickly slipped on her black cape, hitched up Blacky, and rode to the Dutchman Inn. There were phones there as well as a place to board Blacky for a few hours. Once she arrived at the inn, she could either ask if there was a driver available, or she could contact one of the people she knew who made a living out of doing such work.

Luckily, Katie didn't come in contact with much traffic on the small, winding roads that led to the inn. The few cars that did pass her waved before slowly making their way around her buggy. She waved back and used the time on her hands to think about Brandon. It was hard to think of him being in so much pain and facing the end of his life.

She shouldn't have pretended she'd never known him. She should have been mature enough to at least try to remain friends instead of blocking all memories of their relationship away, hoping they'd never surface again.

All too soon, she pulled up to the side entrance to the Dutchman Inn, settled Blacky, then approached the manager.

"I'm needing a driver today, Mr. Pruitt," she said as soon

as she saw the forty-year-old manager working at one of the back tables. Terry was the original owner's son, and he had taken over the management of the popular restaurant when his parents were tired of the day-to-day grind. "Any chance you know of someone here who could help me?"

"Where you going, Katie?"

She pulled out the sheet of paper that Holly had given her. "Adams Community Hospital. Do you know of it?"

"I do. Amy delivered all four of our kids there." He looked at her over a pair of half-moon reading glasses. "Everything okay?"

"Yes. I'm just paying a call on an old friend of mine." Thinking that he might be wondering why Henry or her parents weren't accompanying her, she added, "It's kind of a sudden visit."

"How long do you need to go for?"

"Not long. Maybe an hour or two?"

Terry nodded. "I can take you. Give me five minutes and then we'll be on our way, okay?"

Thirty minutes later, she walked into the main reception area. Terry had dropped her off, promising to return in one hour.

Now she was on her own.

"Excuse me, I am looking for Brandon Norris. May I pay him a visit?"

The dark-haired lady looked on her computer then directed her to the fifth floor. When Katie arrived at the nurses' station, she was met with a trio of interested stares. "Brandon Norris, please?"

"You Amish?"

"I am." When they all kept staring, she cleared her throat. "I came to pay him a visit?"

"Oh. Sure." A nurse came around the bright turquoise desk, motioning down the hall. "He's in room 505. Have you been to see him before?"

"No."

"Oh. Well, some days are better than others. His sister, Holly, is sure he can hear everything you say, so if he doesn't open his eyes, don't be shy about talking." She stopped at the door. "We've been keeping visits to about twenty minutes. All right?"

She left before Katie could reply. But Katie was glad. She felt so nervous and worried; she didn't want another person there to witness her struggles. Slowly, she turned the doorknob and stepped inside.

And then quickly wiped tears as she saw him.

Oh, Brandon.

When she'd first met him, he'd always seemed so infallible. So bright and strong. The complete opposite of the man in the bed in the dim room. The Brandon she'd remembered had an easy smile, sparkling hazel eyes. An infectious laugh.

The man in the hospital bed looked at least thirty pounds lighter. His skin was sallow and pale. An IV tube was attached to his left arm. The brown hair she'd admired so much was cut short.

His eyes were closed.

She stepped closer. Recalling how the nurse had said she

should talk, she did her best. Surely an apology was the right way to start? "Brandon? It's me. Katie. Katie Brenneman. I . . ." She swallowed. "I heard you had wanted to see me." Only the machines clicked in reply.

Steeling her nerves, she continued. "Listen. I'm . . . I'm sorry. I'm very sorry about what I did. I'm sorry for lying to you."

He didn't move.

She approached and sat down in the cushioned vinyl chair next to him. What to say next? "I . . . I saw Holly yesterday. She told me you were under the weather. I . . . I didn't know."

Slowly his eyes flickered open. Katie inhaled sharply. Now those were the eyes she remembered. Lovely, multicolored, perceptive. When they focused on her, she tried to smile. "Hi, Brandon."

"You came."

Oh, there was such pleasure in his voice, Katie was sure she was about to burst into tears. "I . . . did. *Jah.*"

"*Jah?*"

"I'm sorry. When I get nervous, I start thinkin' in *Deutsche.*" She shook her head. "Oops. I mean, I think in Pennsylvania Dutch."

"Are you nervous?"

"Yes." Steeling herself, she leaned forward. "Brandon, I'm verra glad you wanted to see me. This gives me a chance to say that I'm sorry. You know, for causing you pain. For lying about who I was."

"Why did you?"

"I don't know." With a shake of her head, she forced herself to speak more slowly. To choose her words with more care. Brandon deserved that much. "That's not true. I . . . I think it was because I wasn't sure what I wanted. Back when we first met, I was feeling trapped. Restless. I wanted something new. Wanted a chance to be someone else." She chewed on her bottom lip for a moment, then confessed the rest. "But . . . only for a little while."

"And then you went back."

"*Jah.*"

Brandon stared at her for a long moment. "I guess I can understand that." Swallowing hard, he never took his eyes off of her. "You look so different, Katie. My memories of you are so different."

"I know." Self-consciously, she patted her dress. "I think I only wore jeans when we were together. Not anything like this."

"It suits you, though."

Looking at her dress, at her trusty thick-soled black shoes, she smiled. "I suppose it does." She pushed herself to speak some more, to say what needed to be said. "For what it is worth, my feelings for you were genuine."

"Did you ever love me?"

She knew the hope she spied in his eyes. She'd felt it many a time. And though she realized now that she'd loved the *dreams* he represented, not him—she could have never left if she'd truly loved Brandon—she said the words he needed to hear. "I did. Well, I loved how you made me feel. I loved spending time with you and Holly and laughing. I loved the chance you gave me—to just be Katie."

And just like that, he knew the truth. Stark reality filled his expression as the ray of hope faded. And it was as clear in his gaze as if he and Katie had talked for three hours.

He knew.

She hadn't loved him the way he'd loved her. She hadn't loved him enough to risk everything she was, everything she believed in.

With a sigh, he shifted. "Thank you for coming to visit, Katie."

She stood up. "Can I get you anything? Is . . . is there anything you need?"

She felt her cheeks heat as the irony of the situation became apparent. It was obvious he needed a lot of things. But Brandon only nodded. "Maybe some water?"

"Oh. Sure." She poured him a cupful. Standing up, she held it for him as he slowly sipped through the white straw. Then, as if that effort had exhausted him, he leaned back again. When his eyes started to close, she impulsively reached for his hand and held it between her own. "You . . . you are a right *gut* man, Brandon," she whispered. "I . . . I am lucky to have known you."

After another minute, when it was obvious he slept again, she slipped through the door. Quietly, she entered the elevator, felt so in a fog that she was barely aware of the curious looks in her direction.

Terry was waiting for her when she arrived back at the reception area. "Are you ready, Katie?"

"*Jah.*"

"All right then." She followed and got into his car without a word.

The drive back to the restaurant passed in a blur as she thought of Brandon. Thought about how glad she was to have seen him.

And what a shame it was that the Lord would be calling him to heaven far too soon.

Chapter 14

Katie almost cut her finger to the bone when the back door opened without warning at one in the afternoon a few days later. Then, as she saw who entered, her hands got shaky for a whole other set of reasons. "Jonathan."

"Hi there, Katie."

He stood there silently, almost motionless. It gave her a moment to collect her thoughts. "Is everything all right with you? You're home mighty early."

He pulled on the neck of his shirt. "I am fine. I was, *um* wonderin' if you would like to accompany me to the woods today. I thought I might gather some wood and such for a project I'm working on."

Since she'd been at his house, Jonathan rarely spoke of anything other than the great amount of work he needed to accomplish. However, at the moment, he seemed mighty different than the usual man she thought she knew. Jonathan had a glow about him, and that glow caused all kinds of things to churn deep inside her. "A project for Christmas?"

"Actually . . . yes." His lips twitched. "It's a project for Christmas, to be sure."

"What are you going to make?"

"It's a secret." Walking across the kitchen floor, his dusty boots making a mess on the planks that she'd just swept, he almost smiled. "Can you keep a secret, Katie?"

"Indeed I can." Unable to help herself, Katie blinked once, twice more. Whatever had come over him? Ever since they'd argued about Winnie, things had been strained between them. Mealtimes had been near silent. Could he have finally decided to make amends? "I do enjoy a secret now and then."

"I was hopin' you'd say that. So, will you come even though snow still covers a lot of the land? Can you spare me the time?"

"Why, *uh*, *jah*." Once again, his teasing manner caught her off guard. He was such a complicated man. True and loyal. Hardworking. At times, terribly brusque. But then, just like a shooting star in the dark night sky, he would tease and joke. Those comments would lighten his temperament just like a flash of light in the night sky.

To her pleasure, Jonathan continued to grin while the cat held her tongue. "It's a pretty day. *Gut* day for a walk, even through the last of the snow."

"Indeed. It is." It would be wonderful to take a walk outside in the unexpected sunny day. Though it was terribly cold, she'd felt rejuvenated by the brilliant sunshine when she'd gone to gather eggs that morning.

And, of course, she was always hungry for companionship. No matter how she tried, Katie couldn't help but miss the bustling activity of the inn. The constant comings and goings of the guests, the chatter from them and her family as well, the never-ending chores that took up much of her time and left little room for moments of loneliness.

But now . . . suddenly, he was offering—asking, actually—to spend time with her. That was something she couldn't disregard and didn't intend to ignore.

She'd come to realize that no matter what had come between them, the infatuation she'd once felt for him had grown to something deeper and stronger. "I'd like to help you with your project. I'll get my cloak."

When she returned from her room, after slipping on her black bonnet and claiming her thick wool cape, Katie found yet another surprise waiting for her. Jonathan was pouring hot chocolate into a sturdy crock and fastening the lid on. "I thought we might enjoy this after our ride," he mumbled somewhat clumsily.

He was trying so hard, trying so hard to make their trip special, that once again Katie felt flustered. "I'll wrap the crock in towels to help ward out the cold. And maybe some cookies, too? We have jam thumbprint cookies left over from Sunday."

He pulled out a basket. "I could never refuse those."

"And maybe a sandwich and apples?" Katie couldn't forget that he'd been up and out the door many hours before the sun.

"Anything is fine."

After he left to hook up the wagon, Katie put together a haphazard picnic for two, gathered up her mittens, then picked up an extra scarf, just in case Jonathan hadn't thought about keeping his neck warm.

When she finally joined Jonathan outside, she saw he already had the wagon prepared. Blacky was hitched up, thick blankets were already spread out on the seat, and the bed of the wagon was already organized. An ax with a thick oak handle lay on the floor as well.

"You sure got all of this together fast."

Jonathan tucked his head. "I had hoped you would accompany me."

In order not to embarrass him, she said the obvious. "Preparing for a project—any project—is a big job."

"It is at that."

After settling in, Jonathan clicked for Blacky to go forward. They were off, the wheels crunching over the ruts in the ground, then later crunching leaves, twigs, and fallen pine boughs. Around them, clumps of snow dotted rocks and shady areas, making all the colors of the woods seem brighter. A crisp pine scent filled the air, causing Katie to breathe in deeply. A cold breeze stung their cheeks as the horse gained speed. Katie did her best to burrow under the blankets. Jonathan scooted nearer, sharing his body's warmth.

She looked his way shyly. He looked straight ahead, but she sensed he, also, was noticing the way their bodies brushed against each other as the wagon shifted and swayed. The way everything felt so right, to be sharing a blanket.

It was no exaggeration to say that this was the closest she'd ever been to Jonathan. Though inches of space and blankets did, indeed, separate the two of them, in her mind's eye, they were practically pinned together. Katie couldn't help but cast interested looks his way.

He had always been handsome to her eyes. His face was angular and solid looking. His beard was so light and soft that it always took her by surprise in the summer, when it seemed to fade against his golden tan. As always, his clear blue eyes made her think of a winter sky. He seemed terribly strong and stalwart and solemn, sitting next to her.

Of course, he'd always seemed that way. If Katie was honest—and she was trying hard to be, that was for sure— she could admit that never had Jonathan encouraged her. Never had he given her special smiles or an extra bit of attention.

He'd been polite and respectful. Whenever he came over to the inn, he'd spend most of his time talking with her parents or with Henry. If their paths did cross, he'd usually only nod to her.

A horrible, dark thought entered her head. Though they'd come far in their relationship, there was a chance it would never be the romantic, close one she'd longed for. What would she do, then?

She'd always wanted to be a wife and a mother. Would she be brave enough to set her sights on another man in the future? Would she ever be able to only think of Jonathan Lundy as a nice, pleasant neighbor who she'd helped for a time?

"Katie, I've never heard you so silent. Are you all right?"

"Of course I'm fine."

"Not too cold?"

"No."

"I can get you another blanket. Or we can turn back, if you'd like."

"I can be quiet sometimes, just like you, Jonathan. I'm not always a chatterbox." She hoped she sounded mature and upright. Maybe he would soon see her in a new light, too. "I'm happy to sit silently and admire the beauty that surrounds us."

He glanced her way before replying. "Yes, God has given us beauty everywhere."

Her pulse jumped. Just like that, all thoughts of being forever his friend vanished. Awareness filled the gap. "*Um*, what project are you thinking of? Can you tell me a bit about it?"

"I can. I need wood, you see. I intend to make Mary a keeping chest for Christmas. She's a little young for it, but she's been through so much, I think she will like it fine."

The news made her smile. "That is a special gift, to be sure. Every girl, no matter what her age, likes having her own keeping chest." Katie remembered when she'd received her own trunk. Her *daed* and Henry had worked on it for months, smoothing and sanding and staining the oak until it was a rich, burnished coppery-brown. She'd been so surprised and touched to see it on her fourteenth birthday.

Over the years, she'd put all kinds of things inside. Quilts, candle holders, a particularly fine basket. A recipe box. All of those treasures were currently waiting for the day when she would become a bride.

"I hope Mary will like it. As I said, she's a bit young for such a thing, but I've been thinking she needs something of her own right now. Something that will be lasting and solid."

"I agree. She will love the chest. But just as important, she will love it because you made it for her."

His lips turned up. "I'm glad you came with me, Katie. Ever since we argued, I've felt bad about things."

"I have, too. I can be too outspoken and insensitive to other people's feelings."

"I have not noticed that. As for me, I need to remember to ask your opinions. I've become too used to only taking my own advice. It has not always served me well. We live in a community for a reason. I need to learn to grasp the hands that reach out toward me."

Katie thought that was a fine way of putting it. All obstacles in life would be easier to manage if help was accepted. "Jonathan, if it is okay with you, I'd like to treat today as a new beginning. We have much in common and much to be thankful for. Too much to be constantly bickering."

To her great relief, Jonathan nodded. "I would like that." Shyly, he glanced in her direction. "I would enjoy a new . . . a new beginning for us, Katie. Back when I came to your home, to ask you to help with the girls, I said that I had no need to think about a future, about a wife. Now

I realize how wrong that was. Your presence has encouraged me to see the world and all of its glories again. I feel like our Heavenly Father has given me a second chance."

Once again, Katie's heart fluttered. What was he saying? That he wanted a future with her? Or that he wanted another woman as a bride one day?

She gripped the side of the wagon as they traveled across the snow, their path leaving a thick trail behind them. After a few more moments Jonathan halted Blacky and assisted her out of the wagon. Then side by side they tromped through the thicket of trees, stopping and staring at each one and giving it either a yes or no.

Playfully Katie stood in front of an especially tall tree . . . its height was far over ten feet and its branches looked wide enough to fill a whole room. "What do you think about this one, Jonathan?" she asked, all innocence. "Do you think there might be enough wood here for Mary's trunk?"

"Why . . . well, *hum*."

"It's a nice, sturdy tree, yes?"

"Yes." It was hard for Katie to keep her expression neutral as Jonathan obviously struggled to give the tree a close inspection. "It's tall, that's for sure."

"And very full."

After a pause, he knelt on one knee and patted the trunk. "You chose well, but I had in mind something a fair bit smaller."

"I'm only teasing you, Jonathan," she said, unable to keep from laughing. "I know it's far too big."

To her pleasure, he laughed, too. "I was getting worried.

And poor Blacky—he would have had a time pulling it."

"We would have had to rig you up to pull, too!"

"I'm glad you don't really want this tree, then."

Her mirth vanished in an instant. "You would have chopped it down if I'd asked you to?"

"Yes. I wouldn't have wanted to hurt your feelings."

Now she felt bad. "Oh."

Almost tenderly, he gazed at her. "I didn't ask you to accompany me just to ignore your opinions."

Her pulse quickened. "You didn't?"

"No." He bent down, brushed some snow off a boot, then quick as a cricket, flicked a bit of snow from a nearby pine her way. "I took you out here to get the best of you, too!"

When the cold, wet snow hit her right on her nose, she gasped. To her surprise, he had the nerve to sound dismayed. "Oh, I am sorry, Katie. I didn't realize a little bit of snow would bother you so much. Henry told me you have had your share of snowball fights."

"Oh! I'll show you! Henry taught me well." Her first throw caught him off guard when it landed right in the middle of his chest.

"How well?" With lightning speed, he threw a ball at the branch above Katie and laughed heartily when a clump of snow landed on her black bonnet.

"Mighty well," she exclaimed. Well, attempted to, around a mouth of frozen slush.

It was every man for himself. Katie formed snowballs as quickly as she could and threw them at her attacker. Jonathan proved to be a very able fighter himself. His aim was true and his laugh merry.

After a few minutes, they both were slumped against trees and laughing loud and heartily. "You surely managed to surprise me, Jonathan. I didn't know you could be so lighthearted."

"I didn't know you could throw so hard," he teased. "I thought you'd throw like a girl."

"Henry taught me many things. You'd be surprised at what I can do." Lifting her chin, she said, "He even taught me to play basketball."

"I guess we each still have much to learn about the other." Brushing a stray clump of snow from her nose, he added, "I welcome that, Katie."

His declaration left her as breathless as the snowball fight had. "I . . . I do, too." Yes, their connection felt even stronger now. Katie knew something subtle had changed between them. Tension filled the air as they stared at each other. For a moment, Jonathan looked about to speak, then, shaking his head, he slowly stood up. "I suppose we better find a suitable tree."

"Yes. We had better." She scrambled to her feet as well. When a clump of snow clung to the hem of her dress, she shook the fabric harder than she intended. "If we don't hurry, we'll run out of time."

The silence shifted again, filling the distance between them with a sweet expectation.

Slowly, they continued to walk through the trees. After a few moments, over a ridge in the distance, Katie saw a buck, its grand rack of antlers proudly displayed. She pointed.

"*Ah*, yes. He is a beauty, for sure." Together they smiled when two other deer carefully moved out of the cover of evergreens and stepped into the clearing. Then, as one caught sight or smell of them, they darted away as one.

"Did you have your rifle?" Katie knew deer meat would last a good long time.

"I didn't need it today. I shot a deer at the beginning of hunting season. Eli and I divided it up—he's making sausage for me. So, I don't need any more."

"I'm mighty glad. I do love to look at their graceful presence."

"I do, too."

Finally they came to the perfect oak tree. It was a homely, rather short and stunted thing, but the trunk was good and solid, and the lines were lovely. With little effort, Jonathan chopped it down. Birds and squirrels around them squawked in annoyance as the branches cracked and fell to the ground with a hefty thump.

Holding the sturdy ax in his right hand as if it was no heavier than a fork, he glanced her way. "Could you hold this for me?"

"Surely." She tried not to show her surprise when she realized just how strong Jonathan was. The ax had to weigh over ten pounds, at least.

Katie then stood to one side as Jonathan wrapped a rope around the bottom branches and began to pull.

By the time they got back to the wagon, Katie felt glorious. Her cheeks burned from the cold, but her body was warm, thanks to the added weight of the ax and the brisk pace in which they returned to the wagon. After securing the tree onto the open back, Jonathan pulled out the basket. "Do you think we could have our snacks now?"

"Of course." Feeling like a child playing house, Katie scrambled back to the bench seat and poured two cups of cocoa into thick ceramic mugs.

Jonathan sipped gratefully. "It's still warm."

Wrapping her mittened hands around her mug, Katie nodded. "I'm glad." She opened a tin. "Cookie?"

"You like to bake very much, don't you?"

She was surprised he'd noticed. "Yes."

"It shows. You are a mighty good cook."

"Thank you. I . . . enjoy cooking." Handing him the tin, she hastened to come up with something else to say. "Hannah was in charge of making the thumbprints in each one of these."

He bit into his with obvious pleasure. "It's been nice to see the kitchen so busy. You have a great way with Mary and Hannah. The girls' moods have brightened considerably since you came."

"I'm glad. I like being with them."

"I know they like you, too. The girls enjoy your company, Katie."

She bit into a cookie to refrain from answering.

But that seemed to be just fine for Jonathan. To her surprise, he even seemed to be in the mood to chat. "Katie, when I first came to your home, when I first came to speak with you, I was only thinking of needin' someone till Winnie came back."

"I know."

"When your father mentioned how they were worried about the two of us being alone, I have to tell you, it took me by surprise. I had always assumed things would stay the way they were. I hadn't counted on things changing."

"Have they?"

"I think so. Yes. Especially after our talk the other night."

"How do you feel now?"

He hung his head. "Well, it's like this. After I went back to my room, I did a lot of thinking. I thought about the past, and what I hope to find in the future. I did some thinking about Winnie, too."

"What did you discover?"

"It occurred to me that your advice made a lot of sense. I can't be responsible for everything that's happened in my life. That's God's job. It is mine to accept and to prayerfully let the events guide me." He paused, as if carefully weighing each word. "I also realized that I can't blame myself for Sarah's death anymore."

His words shocked her. Everyone had known that Sarah's buggy accident was just that—an accident. "I never knew you felt you were to blame. Why do you?"

"She was my wife. I let her go where she wanted to go. I let her drive that buggy whenever and wherever she wanted to. Maybe if I had told her no, it wouldn't have happened."

In spite of the gravity of the conversation, Jonathan's words made her smile. "I knew Sarah. She was a good woman. But she wasn't the type of person to be told what to do, Jonathan. Even I know that. I don't think she would have listened to you if you had told her no."

"I think I finally have come to believe that, too." After sipping the last of his drink, he set the mug down. "Yes, it is definitely time for me to move forward. And that is why I think it is time that we came to an agreement."

With shaking hands, Katie set her mug down as well. Was this what she thought it was? "An agreement?"

Jonathan's face couldn't have been more beet red. "I've seen how wonderful good you would be for our family. I see that there is much I've been missing. You are perfect for the girls. Mary and Hannah need a woman like you—a person of honor and goodness to look up to."

That was all fine and good. Katie did, indeed, want to be a good mother to the girls. But love from two little girls wasn't all she needed. She needed love from their father, as well. "And you?" she whispered. "What . . . what do you need?"

"I need a wife."

"I see."

"Any man would be happy to have a wife like you, Katie."

His words weren't enough. She wanted them to be. She wanted to be excited about a life with him. But in her heart, Katie knew she had to have love. Otherwise, how could she ever live with her regrets about Brandon? She could have had a life with Brandon, but she'd refused to marry someone she didn't love with all of her heart.

Now, here, the opposite was happening. She could have the man she loved, but she wouldn't have his heart.

The irony of it all—the frustration of it all—made her want to burst into tears. When was it ever going to be her time? When would she ever find a relationship that was equal and meant to be?

Of course, she could never bring up all of that to him.

Neither could she tell Jonathan about Brandon. After all, what would he say if he ever learned just how close she'd been to leaving their order? What would Jonathan say if he knew that she'd made many mistakes? That she'd taken advantage of Holly's friendship because she wanted freedom. Because she'd wanted to know how it felt to have an English boy like her.

What would Jonathan say if he found out she was not as near as complacent as she'd led him to believe? Would he still want her?

Of course he wouldn't.

Just as important, what would happen if he never found out about her *rumspringa*? Could Katie face a future filled with secrets?

She quickly sipped her hot chocolate to keep from answering.

Yet, he noticed her dillydallying. "Katie, do you have an answer for me?" Scanning her face, he added quickly, "I intend to speak with your father, of course, but I was eager to speak with you first."

She couldn't give him an answer. Not yet. It was hard to wrap her mind around his proposal. The moment felt so different than how she'd always imagined it would be.

Did she even love him? Or was Jonathan Lundy yet another "goal" she'd tried to attain?

To even think such a thing felt wrong.

Against her will, she thought of Brandon. He'd freely confessed his feelings for her. She'd known in an instant that she needed to get away from him. It wasn't right to use his feelings.

But . . . Jonathan hadn't mentioned love.

"Katie, must you make me wait so long? The question wasn't a hard one."

But that was the problem, wasn't it? It was a terribly hard question for her to answer. "Jonathan . . . I am not without faults," she said slowly.

"I know that. I have my faults, too. None of us is without sin."

She shook her head. "No, that is not what I'm trying to say."

Cool blue eyes met hers. "What are you trying to say?"

Here was her chance. She could tell him everything. Then she would know if he loved her enough to overlook her past and her faults. Her burdens would be gone and she could start anew.

But just as she opened her mouth to do that, all the words stuck in her throat. With some bit of disappointment, she realized she couldn't do it.

She wasn't as strong and stalwart as she'd always hoped to be. She was too afraid of rejection. Too afraid to make a lifelong mistake. "I . . . I mean . . . I need to think about this. Is that all right?"

"Oh. Well, *um, jah*, sure. If that is what you want."

Katie could tell he was disappointed. She was saddened, too. She was disappointed in herself, and, to a certain extent let down by his proposal. She'd hoped for more words of love and caring. Less about duty and her ability to care for his daughters.

She felt choked by the many complicated feelings rolling inside her, and the many harsh truths she had learned about herself.

Slowly, they put away the picnic supplies and settled in for the long ride home. As the breeze picked up, Katie looked around at her surroundings. No longer did the snow-covered ground look magical. No longer did the air feel invigorating and crisp against her skin.

Now she just felt cold.

Jonathan motioned Blacky forward. Without complaint, the sturdy workhorse plodded forward, the weight of the heavy tree not seeming to be a burden. They were on their way home. But this time, instead of moving closer for warmth, they spread farther apart, in accordance with the emotional distance each was feeling.

The cold wind no longer felt fresh and bracing. Instead it burned her cheeks and stung. Her clothes suddenly felt damp and frozen from their snowball fight.

Inside, she felt empty and hollow. She breathed deep and hoped tears wouldn't fall; she wouldn't know how to explain them.

Chapter 15

Two days had passed since Jonathan almost proposed. During those forty-eight hours, Katie's feelings had run a gamut of emotions. At times she felt as elated and buoyant as a new day. Other times she felt sure her life had come full circle and she was in a mighty dark place, indeed.

Had Jonathan's offer really been a proposal? Or had it been merely an offer to form an agreement of some sorts, in order to keep things the same? Jonathan didn't seem to make any spur of the moment decisions. Katie doubted he offered marriage without careful consideration of what it would mean to his future.

What would it mean for her future? She was capable of taking care of Mary and Hannah. She could cook and sew, and Jonathan had thought she was companionable. Once again, she remembered watching him just weeks after Sarah's funeral and wishing she could do something—

anything—to bring him comfort. She'd felt so sorry for him. So sorry for his loss.

Back then, when she closed her eyes after her evening's prayers, she'd think about Jonathan. She'd wonder if Rebekeh had been right, that Jonathan would never wish to marry again. But then, she'd also dare to dream that maybe he would. That maybe he would one day look at her differently. With wonder and yearning. Of course time spent getting to know Jonathan had changed some things. Now she no longer thought of him as just a man who needed help and a partner. She no longer just hoped for his attention. She no longer imagined him without flaws, and therefore above her reach.

Instead, she knew him for everything he was, both good and bad. Jonathan kept to himself, while she reached out for people. He still had many feelings for Sarah, while she only had feelings for him.

And, of course, he only saw the best parts of her. He never guessed of the many mistakes she'd made over the years.

If she continued to try to be perfect, she would win him, and win the life she'd always wanted. But then, of course, it would come with a mighty heavy price.

It was all terribly confusing. All she knew was that the thought of what she might be settling for brought tears to her eyes. Though Katie had never been especially close to Rebekeh, her older sister had always been far too practical to pay any mind to dreamy Katie, she tried to recall Rebekeh's feelings about love and marriage.

But all she could remember was inevitability. Rebekeh

had always known she'd marry as soon as she could. Her lovely, practical sister had been courted, engaged, and finally prepared for the wedding with the businesslike manner of a banker. She'd never given a single sign of ever having second thoughts or of looking back and feeling regret.

As far as Katie could tell, Rebekeh was still living that same way. Marriage agreed with her. Duty and faith and family sustained her. To Katie's knowledge, her older sister had never thought about any other path for herself.

Maybe that's where Katie had gone wrong. She was too dreamy and had her head in the clouds too much. Her people wanted structure and predictability in their lives. They wanted faith and function and steadfastness.

Yes, Rebekeh would say Katie thought too much. Heaven knows, her mother had said that time and again. Always her father was more direct. "You are not in charge, Katie," he liked to say. "God is, and it is His will you should be following. Trust Him, and all will be well."

Katie, indeed, did trust the Lord's presence in her life. Trusted His hand in all things. But she also felt He was probably too busy with life and death situations to worry about her mixed-up feelings concerning Jonathan Lundy.

Now, though, Katie would give anything for time to re-think the last two days. Though Jonathan hadn't pressed her for an answer, Katie felt the burden of waiting just as strongly as if he was over her shoulder and watching her every move.

With Christmas just one week away, she kept herself busy with Mary and Hannah and did her best not to think about what could be or what might never be at all. Two days after the girls got out of school for break, Katie bundled them up and took them in the buggy to her parents' home.

Funny how it no longer seemed like it was *her* place. Instead, it was her parents' now. Yet, when she walked in the kitchen and smelled the wonderful scents of almond and vanilla and the sharp tang of peppermint, and oranges, Katie knew she was once again in her family's tender care. Nothing smelled like her mother's kitchen in December.

Anna greeted her with a floury smile. "*Gude mariye,*" she said cheerily. "Good morning."

Hannah giggled at the awkward pronunciation, but for once, Mary wasn't a picture of disproval. No, her lips twitched, too, finally bursting into an encouraging smile. "You learning more *Deutsche*, Anna?"

"I am. Well, I am, slowly. I want to surprise Henry tonight and only speak in Pennsylvania Dutch. What do you think?" Again, the words were awkward sounding and slow.

Little Hannah wrinkled her nose. "I think he will be eager for you to speak in your own English."

Katie would have laughed more if her friend's expression didn't look so crestfallen. "You are certainly sounding much more like us, that is for sure. I, for one, am sorely impressed."

"*Jah?* But what will Henry say?"

Katie knew she'd do her best to find Henry before she left and remind him to compliment Anna, no matter what she sounded like. "We won't worry about what Henry says," she said confidently. "I have a feeling he will tell you soon enough."

Katie spied Anna looking longingly at her mother. "I hope he won't be disappointed. I so want to be a good Amish *fraa*."

Her mother reached out and hugged Anna with a chuckle. "Oh, Anna, what did we ever do without you? You make me smile so much. Dear, don't you understand? Henry wants you, not an ideal woman. And, well, even we Amish women have our faults."

With a wink in Mary's direction, her mother added, "We Amish are not perfect, though sometimes we'd like to think so."

Looking pleased to be included in such a grown-up conversation, Mary lifted her little chin. "We can only do our best," she said solemnly.

"I supposed you're right," Anna replied. As if to give evidence to that, one fierce blond curl escaped from her *kapp*. Hastily, Anna tried to secure it but instead caused two other curls to break free and sprinkle flour over her cheeks and forehead in the process. "I don't want to be perfect. But I do want Henry to feel proud of me."

"He already does, child. We all do."

For the first time, Katie realized she didn't feel a bit of jealousy about Anna's courtship. Instead, she found herself agreeing wholeheartedly with her mother. "Henry's said more than once that he's amazed at the amount of information you've learned. Our way of doing things can be quite daunting. I, for one, know you will make a fine Amish wife." She'd chosen her words carefully, wanting Anna to be reassured.

"Thanks for saying that," Anna said softly and with a grateful expression. "It means a lot."

"We came to make cookies," Hannah proclaimed importantly. "Can we help?"

Mamm nodded. "Yes, indeed." Wiping her hands on a towel, she said, "If you've a mind to work in the kitchen, you've most certainly come to the right place. Grab an apron, wash your hands, and I'll put you to work. We need to make cookies for us, our friends, and for our guests here."

"We give little cookie boxes to our guests when they stay here during the holidays," Katie explained to the girls. "It's a popular tradition."

Again, Mary seemed to enjoy the grown-up job. "Something *I* make might go to a guest?"

"Yes, indeed," Katie replied. "It is a very important task, this cookie making is."

With ease of one who knew exactly what to do with little girls, her mother gave both girls jobs. Hannah's was to crush pecans with a rolling pin. Mary was put to work rolling out another batch of dough and cutting out stars.

Katie and Anna worked on thumbprint cookies and peanut butter squares, while *Mamm* supervised them all with the ease of many years' experience.

All the while, Katie was caught up on the latest happenings with the guests. It seemed the inn had been even busier than usual, with most guest rooms constantly filled. And, to everyone's pleasure, many of the guests were repeat ones. They greeted the Brennemans like old friends, which, of course, they were.

Katie enjoyed hearing who had gotten married, had more children, or had other special news to share.

"You're going to have a lot of cookies to box and eat," Hannah said much later, after Katie's mother took yet another batch of cookies from the oven and set it on a rack to cool. "More cookies than even all your busy guests could *ever* eat, I think." Still staring at the rows and rows of tantalizing baked goods with wide eyes, she said worriedly, "I don't think everyone at the inn will be able to eat so many."

Katie grinned. Indeed, cookies of all types decorated every counter both in the kitchen and on the makeshift card table they'd set up in the hearth room. Soon it would be time to begin boxing up the treats or there would be hardly any room to walk around, much less prepare the evening meal.

"You'd be surprised," *Mamm* replied. "Many a couple come just to be a part of our Christmas traditions. They know we put our best into those cookie boxes."

Katie laughed. "Girls, one year, we had a couple who only came for dinner and a cookie box. They didn't even stay the night!"

"I would never do that," Hannah exclaimed. "Well, I don't think I would."

By now, Katie knew what Hannah was hoping for. "We might need to help out the guests and take some cookies home for us, Hannah."

"We can do that?"

"Oh, I hope you will," her *Mamm* said merrily.

"These cookies are *wunderbaar*." Hannah sidled up to Katie and exuberantly gave her a hug. Touched, Katie hugged her back.

"*Maam* made cookies sometimes, but not like this," Mary said thoughtfully. "And Winnie isn't too good in the kitchen."

"Oh, I almost forgot to ask you about Winnie. How is her visit going? Has she written you any more letters?" Anna asked.

Katie shook her head slightly, giving her mother and friend a silent warning. Aloud, she said differently. "I think she is glad to have gotten to spend so much time with Malcolm and his family. She is learning a lot about them, I think."

Just as she was learning a lot about Jonathan and his girls.

Though she hadn't realized it before, now Katie recognized that both she and Winnie had been working on fulfilling the same girlish dreams. And, just so, they'd each realized that their dreams were only that—dreams. Paper-thin replicas of what living was really like.

Anna stretched, breaking the momentary silence. "Mary and Hannah, I don't know about you, but I am more than ready to get out of this kitchen. What do you two say we take a break for a bit?"

Hannah's full cheeks puffed out as she peeked into the dining room. "What should we do? Do you have more chores to do?"

"Oh, there are many chores we could do, but I have something much better in mind."

After exchanging a look with Mary, Hannah said, "What?"

"Go check on Katie's puppy, Roman, of course," Anna said. "He's out in the barn keeping Henry company."

Her mother rolled her eyes. "More likely causing mischief. He chewed up one of my shoes last week."

Katie grinned. "He would probably love to play ball with some little girls. Would you like to do that?"

The girls needed no more encouragement than that. Hastily they tore off their aprons and ran to the door. After Anna helped them into their black cloaks, they scampered outside. In a flash they were racing each other down the familiar path.

Katie leaned against the counter as she watched the girls through the window. Then she turned to her mother. "I'd say we have quite a task before us. We have cookies to box and dishes to wash. What would you like me to do?"

Her mother surprised her by taking a chair instead. "Neither. I'm more interested in sitting for a spell. So tell me, *Totchter*, are you ready to come back home?"

Katie didn't know the answer to that. "Why do you ask?" she hedged.

"There's something a little different about you today. I see an anxious look in your eyes that wasn't there before. Did you and Jonathan argue?"

"No, not exactly. *Mamm* . . . Jonathan Lundy wants to court me."

Her mother blinked. "Are you sure?"

"I am. He . . . he more or less asked me to be his wife."

"Well, that is wonderful-*gut*!" Just as she was leaning forward to hug Katie, her mother paused. "More or less? That doesna make much sense. And, I must say, neither does your disposition. I would've thought such news would make you happy, Katie."

"I would've thought so, too." Nothing was making sense. Not Jonathan's transformation into a reluctant beau, not Winnie's dissatisfaction with Malcolm and his family.

"What is wrong? I thought you had a special place in your heart for Jonathan."

"I did."

"Have you now decided he isn't what you want, after all?"

"No, he is still who I want. I think so, that is." Briefly Katie told her mother about their walk in the woods, and how they'd shared the hot chocolate. That story flowed into others. Before she knew it, Katie was relaying stories about making Jonathan dinner, and how she'd claimed the *sitzschtupp* and was teaching the girls to quilt.

She told her mother about how it had felt to work with Jonathan to prepare for the church services. How Jonathan seemed to be impressed with her industriousness. How she'd spied him staring at her more than once, and how sometimes, in the midst of things, they'd meet each other's gaze and share a smile. Actually, there had been many times that were memorable.

When she was done, her mother crossed her hands over her chest and beamed. "These stories you shared tell me everything I need to know. I'm happy for you, Katie."

But Katie couldn't let her mother think everything was fine. There was a darkness looming over her. Katie was sure things couldn't stay this way. Something was going to happen. Her past was going to be discovered and Jonathan wouldn't want her anymore. "*Jah,* I've had some special times with Jonathan, that is true."

"So why do you hesitate?"

"He didn't tell me he loved me. I'm afraid he doesn't really know me, Maam. I'm afraid he thinks I'm better than I am."

Instead of looking shocked her mother merely nodded. "*Ah.* You are thinking about your actions during your *rumspringa?*"

She couldn't lie. "I am."

"I thought you'd worked those things out."

"I had thought I had, too, but maybe not. I made mistakes, *Maam.*"

"I know."

"And . . . I thought just being with Jonathan was enough. But now I realize that I want his love, too."

"I've seen him gaze at you when he thought no one was looking. There's feelings there, I think."

Still ignoring the many bowls and measuring cups, her mother stood up and put the kettle on. As Katie watched her efficiently make two cups of tea, she marveled at her mother's self-assured manner. Was she ever going to become so confident?

Returning to the table, her mother set the two cups down. "Marriage to Jonathan is something that you've always wanted. Love is, too. In my heart I think you may find both with him. Give it time, Katie. In time you and Jonathan will find your way." With a tender smile, she said, "Katie, you know, I just realized that you never told me what you said."

"I told him I needed some time to think."

Chuckling, her mother reached out and gave her a hug. "I do believe you have finally learned some patience, Daughter. Praise be to God."

Katie swallowed hard. That, actually, was true. Maybe she had grown up more than she'd realized.

Chapter 16

Contrary to what most thought, Jonathan found he did not mind working in the lumber factory among the English. Perhaps it was because his boss, Brent Harvey, was a decent sort of man who valued much the same things as Jonathan.

Every day at lunch, Jonathan would pull out his basket and eat his sandwiches that Katie packed for him, sitting beside a number of other men who ate sandwiches, too. Manly conversation would flow around them all, which he thoroughly enjoyed. After years of farming, spending most days by himself, he enjoyed the fellowship of other men, the rough and tumble conversations. The laughter.

"Got another trail bologna sandwich today, Jonathan?" Brent asked in what had become an almost daily ritual.

"I do. Three, in fact. Would you like one?"

Like boys in a schoolyard, Brent sat next to him as he

pulled out a bag of chocolate chip cookies. "Only if you'll have these in exchange."

"Deal." After a few bites, Jonathan said, "The work is going well today, I think."

"I agree. Productivity is up this year. I hope you'll consider staying with us when spring comes."

"That will be a hard decision. Spring planting is a busy time. And then there's the girls, they'll need watching."

"Winnie will be back then, right? Surely she'll be able to watch Mary and Hannah."

It pleased Jonathan that Brent cared enough about their friendship to remember his sister's and daughters' names. "I don't know about that. Winnie, she's in Indiana now. She might be planning a marriage."

Brent's eyes crinkled merrily. "Congratulations."

Jonathan tried to smile, but failed. "I don't know if a marriage is in the future. But her leaving has made me realize that she needs time and opportunity to follow her dreams." With some surprise, he realized that he wasn't just saying those things. He meant them. When had all of that happened? When had he started living again, and realizing other people had to move forward, too?

Keeping things the same was not the way to go through life. And though he'd attempted to cling to the notion that tradition and consistency was part of who he was—as integral to being Amish as forgoing much of the technology of the outside world—it was likely he'd forgotten that people's needs did grow and change. And once more, it was acceptable.

"Jon, you don't sound very excited about the man Winnie

is seeing." After pulling out a bag of chips, Brent popped two in his mouth. "Do you not like the guy?"

"I've never met him. Actually, Winnie hadn't met him face-to-face until she arrived there in mid-November. She'd only been writing to him for several months. But I've been getting the feeling that maybe he is not everything she'd expected."

Brent laughed. "Nothing ever is." After sipping from his can of soda, he added more soberly, "But if Winnie's man is far different than what she imagined him to be, that will be hard to swallow."

"Jah."

"Of course, different isn't always bad, you know?"

"You've got a point, there." Jonathan took another bite and chewed slowly, once again thinking about his life with Sarah. The way he'd struggled to raise the girls on his own, and how he'd come to terms with always being alone for the rest of his life.

It had taken Winnie's insistence to reach her dreams to shake him up.

Because Winnie had wanted to grow, he had sought Katie's assistance. And her role in his life had brought about a whole new barrage of feelings. Now he found himself rushing home to Katie. He found himself thinking how her eyes had sparkled when she'd tossed snow his way. He realized how often her laugh and her smiles were the focus of his thoughts when he drove his buggy home each evening. Her presence had awakened him to the world again.

Katie Brenneman had caused him to dream again.

Maybe Winnie needed that surge of expectancy just as much. "Maybe Winnie is just having a time figuring out what she wants. Different may be all right, after all."

Brent chuckled. "Love. You know as well as I do that it isn't as smooth as some would like it to be."

The bologna suddenly felt dry in his mouth. "I would tend to agree about that." After marriage to Sarah, having two children, and then, ultimately, losing her and finally grieving her loss, Jonathan had been sure he'd never think about marriage again. He hadn't thought another woman would ever occupy his thoughts again, the way Sarah once had. Boy had he been wrong! All it took was one blue-eyed woman with a resolve of steel hidden behind a sweet disposition to turn him inside out. Taking a chance, Jonathan admitted, "I'm learning time and again that love and marriage isna' ever an easy thing."

"Time and again?" Brent peeked at him under the brim of his ball cap. "What's going on? Have you found someone new?"

"I don't know. Maybe." Jonathan was thankful Brent didn't say "already" or "again," though part of him sorely felt that way. Things were happening to his heart that made him feel like a young boy again, unsure and scared of saying the wrong things.

"Is she Amish?"

"Oh, yes. Of course."

"What's she like?"

There was the rub. "Confusing."

Brent roared with laughter, loud enough that the other

men turned their way. "They're *all* confusing. Some days I never know where I stand with Tricia."

Jonathan was becoming mighty glad to have a friend in Brent. He had never realized that all men had trouble figuring out their wives' likes and dislikes. "Yes, but I thought after Sarah . . ." His words drifted off. It sounded uncaring and petty to bring Sarah into the conversation.

"I've only been married once, but I tell you, my Tricia keeps me on my toes. I never know what I'm doing right or wrong. Just yesterday she yelled at me because I was helping the kids with their homework."

"Whatever for?"

"She said I was doing it wrong. But last week she got mad at me because I never offered to help. Women."

"*Jah. Women.* I fear I'm mainly doin' everything wrong."

Instead of offering advice, Brent chuckled, then patted Jonathan on the shoulder. "Good luck with that," he said before getting up to go to his office.

"*Danke.*"

He used the momentary patch of silence to do some thinking. What had happened, anyway? He'd been so sure he had done the right thing when he'd asked Katie to be his wife.

He was not so blind as to see that she had had special feelings for him for quite a while. But instead of acting all overjoyed, she'd just looked worried and spooked.

Yes, spooked was the word. She acted like he had just found out something about her that was horrible.

It had not been the reaction he'd hoped for.

This was when he missed his father something awful. He wished there was someone who he could reveal all of his hurts and frustrations to. Who would listen to him without rancor and give him direction.

As Jonathan ate the last of the chocolate chip cookie, he suddenly smiled.

Well, of course. Someone *had* always been there for him—Jesus, his Lord and Savior. He'd given Jonathan Winnie when he'd needed help the most. He'd given Jonathan good friends like Brent. Now, He'd brought Katie into his life.

Dear Lord, he silently prayed, *thank you for all the blessings you have given me. Thank you for providing me with a great many people and friends. Please help me continue to follow Your will—and to remember to spend quiet moments to give thanks to your guidance and patience. Amen.*

Feeling lighter in step than he had in years, Jonathan stood up and went back to work. Perhaps things were going to work out, after all.

Chapter 17

Feeling restless in the quiet of Jonathan's home, Katie hitched up her buggy and drove to the inn. The quiet rolling hills and pristine countryside were a sight to behold. The crisp, fresh air invigorated her senses and stung her cheeks.

But not even the terribly beautiful surroundings could stop her from thinking about Brandon.

For so long, she'd blocked out all thoughts of him. She'd also pushed aside all memories of her time with him, sure that her behavior had been so wrong, it was wrong to even recall any of the good times she'd shared with her English friends.

Her recent visit to Brandon had changed all that. His need to see her again, his obvious pleasure to renew their friendship encouraged Katie to recall many moments they'd spent together. It hadn't been all bad, after all. In fact, when she'd looked into his eyes, she recalled the many good times she'd shared with Holly and Brandon.

She remembered the many reasons they'd become friends. It hadn't been all false on her part. On the contrary, most of what they'd shared had been real and genuine, indeed. It had been a mistake to push them away—to not even give Holly or Brandon a chance to make their own opinions about her lifestyle. She should have stayed after telling them about herself. She shouldn't have just expected scorn and anger.

Because she loved her brother, Henry, so much, Katie knew just how much Holly loved Brandon. And because she now understood just how sick Brandon was, Katie knew it was time to reach out to Holly. Holly was going to need all of the friends she could get in the coming weeks. No longer would Katie push someone away because she wished she'd behaved better toward them.

After parking her buggy and playing with Roman for a bit, she said hello to her mother and Anna. But then, still feeling restless, Katie knew what she had to do. With purpose, she walked to the reception desk, pulled out the note Holly had given her, then, before she lost her nerve, Katie picked up the phone and dialed. The phone rang two times before Holly's familiar voice answered. "Hello?"

Katie took a deep breath. "Holly? This is Katie Brenneman."

"Oh. Hi."

Katie frowned. Holly sounded hoarse. "I just called to let you know that I visited Brandon last week."

"I know. He told me."

"You were right to encourage me to see him, Holly. I'm glad I visited him. It was the right thing to do."

After a few seconds passed and Holly didn't offer any more information, Katie cleared her throat. "So, *uh*, how is he?"

After a lengthy pause, Holly whispered, "I'm sorry . . . I thought you knew, though now I don't know why you would have. He passed away the day after you came."

Gripping the phone harder, Katie felt her world shift and sway. "What?"

After a ragged sigh, Holly said, "I'm sorry to tell you like this. *Um*, it was sudden, though the doctors said not completely unexpected. And, well, he'd been in a lot of pain."

Katie had seen the pain in his eyes. "I'm sorry. He . . . he was such a special person."

"He was. I'm just glad he got a chance to see you. It meant a lot."

"It meant a lot to me, too. When I saw him, I realized how special he was to me. How special you both are."

"I . . . I had thought so, too."

"Is there anything I can do for you?"

"No. You already did what I asked of you. That was enough."

"Would you mind if I called you again?"

"Why?"

Because she didn't want to abandon her again. But because that sounded a bit too much, Katie simply said, "Because I care."

"Oh. Well, then. Sure. Call again if you want."

Gingerly, Katie replaced the receiver. Once again, it felt as if her world had shifted. Closing her eyes against the flood of tears that threatened, she prayed. *Dear Lord, please be with Holly as she grieves. And help me know how to move beyond the past and into my future . . . whatever it may hold.*

Slowly, Katie began to see that He had always been beside her. Guiding her. It had only been her insecurities and fears that had held those things at bay. It was time to tell the truth and face whatever consequences came. Even if she failed.

Even if people were disappointed in her.

Even if Jonathan didn't want her any longer.

Decision made, Katie picked up the phone and dialed Holly's number again.

"Katie? What's going on?" Holly asked.

Before she lost her nerve, she said, "I know it is short notice, but . . . perhaps if you are not doing anything . . . perhaps you'd care to come over this afternoon?"

"What? You want me to come over? To your home?"

"Yes. Well, to my parents' inn."

"Why?"

Holly deserved honesty, even if they never spoke again. Even if friendship now meant that she had to do a very tough thing. "I'd like us to be friends again. I thought . . . I thought you might need me." She swallowed. Oh, this was so hard to say. "I thought you might need a friend, since Brandon is gone."

A moment paused. Two. "You've already apologized. That was enough. I really can't think of anything else for us to say to each other."

"I believe there is more than you might think. Please, Holly? I'd love to introduce you to my family." *Finally*.

After what seemed like forever, Holly spoke. "When, this afternoon?"

"Whenever you want." She felt so relieved, a half chuckle, half sob escaped from her. "What are you doing now? Can you just come on over?"

"Yeah. I've just been sitting here, trying to sort out some of Brandon's things, but I just couldn't do it. Your call came at just the perfect time."

It did feel perfect. It felt like it truly was time for her past to meet the present. "Do you have a pencil? Let me give you directions," Katie said. After Holly's promise to come out shortly, Katie hung up the phone with a huge sense of relief.

"Katie? What are you doing? Why were you on the phone?" Her mother approached, her expression one of concern and irritation. The phone was only used for guests' emergencies and to make reservations. Katie could hardly remember ever using it for herself.

It was time to face the truth. Slowly, she said, "I had an important phone call to make. To Holly Norris. I invited her to come over. She's on her way now."

"Who is Holly Norris?"

"She's an English girl I met during my *rumspringa*. I was once good friends with her. With her and her brother, Brandon."

Her *mamm* put her dusting rag down. "Yes?"

Taking a deep breath, Katie said, "*Mamm*, I have a story to tell you and Daed, if you'll let me."

For the first time, Katie saw that her mother was visibly flustered. "This sounds serious. Perhaps we should wait until after dinner to discuss things."

"This is serious. And, *Mamm*, it can't wait. What I have to say can not wait a moment longer. I've waited long enough."

After studying her carefully for a long moment, she nodded. "I see. Well, then, Katie, now is just fine. I'll go and fetch your father."

The hearth room had never felt so cold, even though a fire was blazing in the hearth. When the three of them were seated, Katie gripped a portion of her dress and stood up.

"Like I said to you earlier, *Mamm*, Holly is on her way here."

Her father looked confused. "Who is that?" her father asked.

"She is an English girl I met during my . . . my *rumspringa*." She told her parents about how they first met, Katie in her borrowed clothes. That first visit to the Brown Dog.

"Come now, Katie. There must be more to this story,"

her mother said. "Why is she coming here now? Why have you never mentioned her before? Is there more you aren't telling us?"

"Yes. During that time, when Holly and I were such good friends, I . . . I saw much of her brother."

"Saw much?" After her parents exchanged glances, her mother spoke. "You'd best tell us the full story, dear."

"When I met Holly and Brandon at the Brown Dog, I . . . I wasn't sure how I felt in my life. Rebekeh was always so perfect. So much more perfect than I could ever be. "

Her father sighed. "None of us are perfect, Daughter. And, I never wanted you to be just like Rebekeh."

"I understand that now. But back then, well, I wasn't so sure about everything. I was mixed up. Emotional. I suppose I was feeling somewhat sorry for myself." She glanced at her mother then. "I know that is shameful."

"But honest. Nothing wrong with that."

"Anyway, out of all the kids I met, two people made me feel like I was a part of their group, Holly and Brandon. I liked being with them. They were fun. They took me to the mall. They introduced me to silly TV shows. I liked Holly a lot . . ." Her voice drifted off. How could she fully put into words her feelings for Brandon?

"What happened, Katie?" *Daed* asked.

"After meeting them at the coffee shop, I went to the Norris house for a time or two. Over time, I grew to like Brandon. Though, not as much as he liked me, I am ashamed to say. He began to talk about future plans. He talked like we would do many things together. That I would always be there for him. And, well, I let him think that." Feeling her cheeks heat, Katie tried to convey why she had let things go on for far too long. "See, it felt good to be wanted. I liked feeling pretty and special."

Her mother smoothed her hands over her skirt. "That is only natural, I suppose."

"It would have been natural, I think, if I had been honest about who I was. But I wasn't."

Katie continued, determined to tell everything about that confusing time. Only by completely divulging her past sins was she going to be able to find forgiveness. "About this time, too, Sarah Lundy passed away. Soon after her funeral, I saw Jonathan and his girls." Remembering that moment, she shrugged helplessly. "Something happened."

To Katie's surprise, her father looked like he completely understood. "You looked at him in a new way?" he murmured.

Katie nodded. "I started thinking about his family. My heart went out to him . . . I felt sorry for him, but I also started imagining a place for me in his life."

Her mother nodded knowingly. "John, I told you she'd been taken with Jonathan for quite some time."

"Poor Sarah's death meant two things—it shook me out of what I thought was important with what actually was. And it, I'm ashamed to say—gave me hope." Katie hung her head. It was terribly difficult to admit to wanting Jonathan, even back when he was still grieving for his wife.

"One night, I told Holly and Brandon the truth about

who I was. And then I left them and never looked back, though what I had done and said weighed on me. Then, just after I went to go help with Mary and Hannah, Holly contacted me again. She sent me letters. I didn't know what to do."

"You should have told us about your worries, Katie," her mother chided. "I could have helped. I could have least listened and prayed with you."

"I think I had to face these fears on my own." Taking a deep breath, she finished her story. "The last time I was at Mr. McClusky's store, Holly found me." Ignoring her mother's gasp of surprise, Katie continued quickly. "She wanted me to go see her brother. He was dying of cancer and had never forgotten me. I went to see him last week." Swallowing hard, she added, "He died soon after my visit."

Her *daed* frowned. "That is a terribly sad story."

"It is. I know Brandon's life was in the Lord's hands, but I do feel guilty for never reaching out to him before. Anyway, now poor Holly is all alone, and I can't let her be. I want to be her friend again, if it's not too late."

"It's never too late, I don't think," her *daed* said. "What you are doing takes courage."

"I don't feel brave, but I do feel better now that I am not hiding secrets any longer." Looking around the room, she felt the soothing comfort of her Savior. "I don't want to be a shell of a person anymore. I don't want to be just the happy Katie who tries hard. I want to be seen as whole . . . even if everything I am isn't so good."

Hesitantly, she looked to her mother. Her mother was the best person she knew. Back when she was sixteen, when she'd thought she couldn't ever measure up, she hadn't even tried. But she'd always wanted her approval. Now she just asked for understanding. "I'm sorry I wasn't what you wanted me to be."

"You are exactly what I hoped you would one day be, child. A woman stepping forward. Reaching out. I like this Katie, I think."

Suddenly, admitting her past didn't feel so terrible. It wasn't shameful anymore. Katie realized those past hurts were about a different person. A person other than herself.

That person had shame and self-doubts and fears about her future. The person she'd become felt different. Oh, she had the same wants, but they were deeper and more meaningful than a mere desire to seek belonging. Now she had a sense of peace within her soul, and the knowledge that no matter what happened, she already had obtained the forgiveness of her Father. And He still wanted her. "Let that therefore abide in you, which ye have heard from the beginning," she murmured, quoting 1 John.

Reaching out for her hand, her mother finished the verse. "That which ye have heard in the beginning shall remain in you. You shall continue in the Son and in the Father."

It was very true. No matter what had happened in their past, everything was going to be all right. The doorbell rang. "That will be Holly."

Her father stood up. "I'm looking forward to meeting her."

As the doorbell rang again, she left the hearth room and quickly stepped across the foyer. As soon as she opened the door, Katie said, "Hi, Holly. Please come in."

Hesitantly, her friend stepped through the threshold. "Are you sure it's okay that I'm here?"

Katie reached out and clasped her hand. "I can honestly tell you that there's never been a better time for you to visit. Please come meet my parents. And then we'll have some tea in front of the fire."

As they crossed the foyer, Katie knew everything was going to be all right.

Chapter 18

"So, you'll forgive me?" Katie asked Jonathan later that evening. After they'd eaten dinner and got the girls settled, she'd asked him to listen while she told him a story.

Oh, it had taken some time. They'd sat in the cozy *sitzschtupp* with mugs of hot tea, and with little fanfare, Katie recounted her story one more time.

Through it all, Jonathan had been silent, only asking questions to clarify information, not to judge her. Katie was mighty grateful for that. But when she thought of how different things could have been if her parents hadn't been so supportive, if she hadn't had Anna, who had already been through so many trials of her own . . . Katie couldn't help but feel blessed.

But so far, this telling had been the hardest, even harder than facing her parents or even Holly. Perhaps it was because she had so much to lose. Katie knew that she wanted a future with Jonathan, but only a marriage and union based on realities, not his imagined ideas about her.

Her worries made her emotions run high. Tears streamed unchecked down her cheeks, though she'd tried her best to keep them at bay.

Tenderly, Jonathan wiped a stray teardrop away with the side of a thumb, then rested his palm against her face, cradling her cheek. "I've told you, there's nothing to forgive."

"Are you sure? I had assumed you would be terribly mad at me."

"Why?"

"Because I've kept so much from you. Jonathan, I know you never dreamed I would've been involved in such things."

Jonathan smiled wryly. "Well, that is true."

Had she lost him?

Tears rushed forth again as she remembered their afternoon in the woods when time had seemed to stand still and so much of their animosity had fallen away, leaving only true, tender feelings. She wished she had thought to keep a reminder of the day for her memory box. That, indeed, would bring her much happiness months and years from now. "I know you wanted someone far more perfect."

But his expression didn't waver. Almost regretfully, he lowered his hand from her cheek and clasped her hands, his two work-roughened thumbs gently stroking her knuckles. "Come, now. We both know that was never true. In God's eyes, we are all worthy of His grace. Do not be so hard on yourself."

"I'm merely being *ehrlich*, being honest."

"I will admit that I had wanted a wife who would make me happy, and who would make my daughters happy. In my rush to do that, I built expectations that could never be met. None of us is faultless, Katie, and, I don't want anyone who pretends to be."

She couldn't keep the surprise from her voice. "Truly?"

"Truly." A bit uncomfortably, he looked at her.

"I don't know what to say."

"There is nothing to say, not really," he said with a smile. He looked away. "I don't want to blemish Sarah's name. She was a *gut fraa*, a good wife. She tried her best and so did I. I just want you to know that I do understand what it is like . . . to keep so much inside."

"Thank you. Your words mean a lot."

"As do yours." Tugging on her hand, he pulled her toward him, so close that their thighs and shoulders touched. "I would be lying now if I did not say that you are perfect for me."

"Still?"

He squeezed her hands. "Especially still."

Katie's heart seemed to stop beating. Never in a million years had she expected to find forgiveness so easily. As their eyes met, a thousand words passed between them, unspoken.

When she remained silent, his lips curved. "You don't have anything to say?"

"I can't seem to think." Truly, she couldn't. What was happening was far more special than any of her dreams or imaginings.

"That's all right, I think. I seem to have enough words for both of us. See, the thing is, Katie, when I look at you, I see everything I ever wanted. I see everything I once dreamed of having but had given up hoping of receiving."

"I feel the same way."

"Are you sure?" His eyes betrayed his doubts. "I know I've been difficult to live with. I canna promise you a future without problems."

"I never asked for a future like that. I only want a future that is real. That I can count on. And Jonathan, you are not so difficult."

Jonathan leaned close and clasped her hands. "Katie, I have fallen in love with your bright blue eyes and your sweet disposition. I've fallen in love with the way you point out my faults and encourage me to be a better man. I like how you make me smile, and I love how my girls adore you."

At last Jonathan looked into her eyes the way she'd always dreamed he would. "Katie, I want you to be my wife. I can't promise I will be the easiest man to live with, but I can promise I will treasure you always. Please . . . please say you'll be mine. Please say you will marry me."

Katie bit her lip. Maybe—just maybe—dreams could come true, after all. "Yes, Jonathan, I will marry you," she whispered.

And when he leaned his head down to kiss her, and

carefully held her close, Katie knew she had just gotten everything she'd always thought she had wanted. Everything she always hoped to have.

And so very much more.

Epilogue

"I canna eat another bite of this wonderful Christmas dinner," Jonathan said to the large gathering surrounding the oak table in the Brennemans' dining room. "You *damen* prepared a mighty fine table, that is for sure."

Katie's mother smiled. "I have to admit to being pleased with how everything turned out. What do you think, girls?"

Katie turned to Anna and Winnie, her two best friends, and in so many ways, the sisters of her heart. One day soon Anna would marry Henry and she would marry Jonathan. Eventually Winnie, too, would find love. All of them could look forward to many years of meals prepared and enjoyed together. "I think it was a fine meal, indeed." More hesitantly, she looked to her sister. "Rebekeh, what did you think?"

"The same as you," she said, smiling in just the way their mother did. "It was mighty fine. Especially since I only brought a pie."

"That was enough this year," their mother said, as Rebekeh awkwardly stood up. "You should be off of your feet as much as possible."

Chuckling, Rebekeh's husband, Olan, said, "I wish you could pay a call on us every day and tell her that. My Rebekeh never seems to want to sit and rest."

"She never did," Henry said with a wink toward Katie. "Though, I have to admit to wishing she would have relaxed more when she was younger."

"Then we could've relaxed, too!" Katie said with a laugh.

Primly, her older sister clucked her tongue. "You two needed me to watch over you. At least *Mamm* did."

As their mother looked at all three of them, she shook her head. "Come, Rebekeh, come sit with me for a bit in the front room. If you stay here much longer, Katie and Henry will tease you even more."

Henry whistled low. "Katie, should we tell everyone about the time Rebekeh made us set the table twice?"

Katie laughed at Rebekeh's expression. "We'd better not. Go sit down, Rebekeh. We'll take care of things here."

Laughter echoed through the inn as Rebekeh followed Katie's directions and followed their mother to the front room. As the men moved to the couches near the fire, Katie motioned to Mary and Hannah to help her carry dishes to the kitchen. "We best get these dishes cleared and washed. They won't get finished without our hands."

"I've got the carrots!" Mary proclaimed.

Hannah rushed to keep up. "I'll carry the basket of rolls."

"Do be careful, girls," Katie called out.

Beside her, Winnie picked up an almost empty dish of potatoes. Katie thought she'd been especially quiet all evening. As they walked far more circumspectly to the kitchen, Katie murmured, "Are you all right?"

"Oh, *jah*," Winnie replied, though Katie noticed that her smile didn't quite reach her eyes. "I am just glad to be home, and am excited about my new job in town."

"I'm sorry things didn't work out with you and Malcolm."

"I am, too." Winnie shook her head. "Oh, Katie, that Malcolm was nothing like his letters. I guess Anna really was right when she said that nothing takes the place of conversations face-to-face. In person, I found him to be difficult and inattentive. I'm verra glad to have my new job."

Almost the moment Winnie returned from Indiana, she'd informed Jonathan that she was going to take a position at the Crazy Quilt. Jonathan, knowing that she was hurting and needed to move on, understood.

Katie had moved back home, but now went to Jonathan's the few afternoons that Winnie worked late. During those visits, she spent time with the girls, fostering their relationship and working on the quilt together. Sometimes she stayed and visited with Jonathan for an hour or two before returning to the inn.

After four more trips to the kitchen, Winnie, Anna, and Katie were put in charge of sorting leftovers while Irene, Mary, and Hannah carried cakes, pies, and dessert plates to the dining room.

When they were once more alone in the kitchen, Anna

said, "Katie, Henry told me you received another letter from Holly. What did this one say?"

"All kinds of good things. Holly has met someone, and even went on a second date."

"I hope she'll bring him over soon," Anna said. "We're going to need to approve."

"Something tells me she'll wait to bring over any of her dates, though she did tell me she wants to come over soon and spend the weekend with me." When Winnie and Anna looked at her in surprise, Katie announced her news. "She wants to make a quilt!"

Winnie burst out laughing. "You'll have everyone you know quilting soon, Katie."

"Maybe I will! All I know is that Holly's letter and good news was a wonderful Christmas present." So was her friendship. That, truly, was what made her heart sing the most.

Jonathan peeked his head in. "Katie, are you almost done? I thought we could maybe take a walk outside for a bit."

His gaze was so warm and loving, Katie felt her cheeks heat. "Yes. I . . . I'm almost done, Jonathan. I would most certainly enjoy a walk with you," she replied quickly, ignoring the giggles of her girlfriends.

Anna playfully bumped Katie with her shoulder. "While Holly's news is wonderful good, I'd say you received a far better Christmas gift, Katie. Jonathan Lundy is mighty attentive these days."

Even Winnie chuckled. "He acts like it's not blustery

and cold outside, he's so anxious to be alone with you. We better hurry with the dishes."

Katie hastily rolled up her sleeves with a smile. Yes, Jonathan's love was a wonderful present. He'd given her joy and his family, and a reason to be herself. Most of all, he'd reminded her that by the grace of God, every one of them was blessed and special in the eyes of the Lord.

And that was, indeed, a most wonderful present to receive. . . . especially on Christmas Day.

FORGIVEN

Sisters *of the* Heart

BOOK THREE

To Arthur and Lesley,
for more reasons than I could ever list.

Judge not, and ye shall not be judged. Condemn not, and ye shall not be condemned. Forgive, and ye shall be forgiven.

Matthew 6:14

Friendship is a lighted candle
Which shines most brightly
When all else is dark.

A bit of wisdom from
The Wooden Spoon Cookbook

Chapter 1

Crack.

Jerking awake, Winnie opened her eyes. What was that? It was most unusual to hear anything in the middle of the night. Their farm was miles away from the city. By and large, the only noise to echo around their home was the impatient bleating of Nellie the goat or one of the horses.

Her eyes slowly focusing, she turned to look at the clock on her bedside table. Two A.M. Maybe she had imagined it.

Winnie lay back down. Well, perhaps the good Lord had summoned her awake for no reason at all. Slowly, she closed her eyes and tried to relax and remember her prayers.

But then it came again.

From the cozy comfort of her bed, Winnie turned toward the window, the cotton sheets tangling around her legs as she shifted. Beyond the window, a fierce wind blew, creating an unfamiliar howl in the darkness.

Ah, a storm was coming in. Well, the horses wouldn't care for that much.

Just as she closed her eyes, another snap rang out. A sharp pop followed seconds later. Sharp and loud, like the clap of a rifle. Winnie bolted upright.

Something was terribly wrong.

Outside, a low roar floated upward from the ground, mixing with the high, panicked scream of a horse.

Winnie ran to the window and pulled back the thick plain curtain. Shooting flames and clouds of smoke greeted her.

Oh, sweet heaven! The barn was on fire!

She clasped a fist to her mouth as she watched Jonathan frantically run to the barn. Flames ate the opposite side.

She grabbed her thick robe, then flew down the stairs. She opened the front door just in time to see her brother throw a blanket over the top of Blacky's head and lead him out. "Jonathan!" she called out.

He didn't so much as look her way—the rage of the fire had swallowed her words.

Smoke choked the sweet spring air. A chalky black haze blurred everything around her . . . mixing with the cool gray fog of the early March night. Winnie stood motionless, stunned, feeling like she'd stepped into a dream.

Another crack screamed through the near dawn, drawing her attention to the pens next to the barn, where the goat and chickens slept. She'd just lifted the lever to free the squawking hens when the sky was suddenly alight with flames. The force of the explosion threw her to the ground. Sparks and ash fell through the air as she pulled herself to her feet to run toward cover.

Winnie couldn't seem to move. The soles of her bare feet burned, were blistered and hot. Smoke ran thick. Her chest tightened. She coughed, the sound of it echoing in her ears as her vision blurred. Blazing pieces of hot, burning wood nicked her back and shoulders, bringing her down—just as if the devil himself was behind her. The pain was fierce. Crippling.

Terrifying.

She was barely aware of Jonathan yanking her by her shoulders and pulling her to safety.

Jonathan watched his friend Eli Miller arrive at the farm just as an ambulance skidded to a stop in front of their farmhouse. After Jonathan motioned him forward, Eli hurried over. "Jonathan, I'm glad to see you whole and unharmed. I came as soon as I could. The flames of your barn lit up the night sky."

Jonathan knew there were a great many things he should say to ease his friend's worries. But his heart seemed to have no room left in it for others. He was too stunned about the barn. And too worried about Winnie.

But if Eli was bothered by his quiet, he didn't act like it. Looking around, he frowned. "Where're Winnie and Katie and the girls?"

"Katie took the girls to her parents' inn for the night, so they're safe, thank Jesus. But Winnie . . ." Jonathan pointed to the inside of the ambulance. "She is in there."

"In the ambulance?" Eli's normally assured manner faltered. "Is she hurt bad?"

"*Jah*. She's in . . . She's in poor shape."

"That's terrible news."

"It is." Jonathan wasn't surprised by his friend's reaction. For as long as he could remember, he and his family had known the Millers. Eli's brother Samuel and his sisters had played with Winnie when they were small, and Jonathan had helped their family with spring planting more than a time or two. Winnie was like another sister to Eli, just as Jonathan felt like an older brother to Eli's youngest brother, Caleb.

Eli attempted to control his voice. "What's wrong?" Staring at the last of the flames, he murmured, "Is she badly burned?"

"I think I got her out before she was too injured, but I'm not certain." Jonathan tried to school his features, but it was difficult. "Some boards must have hit her . . . she fell . . . her feet are in a bad way, too. One might be broken. I . . . I had to carry her away from the area." Pain-filled eyes teared up before he wiped them impatiently with a hastily bandaged fist. "She's a fair sight."

Around them, the barn was still smoking and animals were howling their displeasure. Eli grasped his arm. "What can I do?"

"Well, now, I . . ." The question seemed to push away

a portion of Jonathan's shock. After looking at the charred remains surrounding them, he reached out to touch the shiny red side of the ambulance. "Would you go with her to the hospital? Would you mind leaving your brother Caleb alone?"—Jonathan stepped toward the barn, toward the crowd of firemen talking to a man dressed in a coat and tie—"I canna leave. I have to speak with these men. And Katie and the girls will likely return soon. I'll need to be here for them."

"Of course you need to be here for your daughters. And your wife."

"Danke." Even though there was so much trouble, Jonathan felt a rush of warmth at the thought of his new wife. Barely two months had gone by since he and Katie had exchanged their vows in front of the whole community.

"I'll be happy to travel with Winnie. Caleb's almost seventeen. He'll be fine on his own." I'll contact Samuel, too."

Jonathan nodded. *"Danke.* It will set my mind at ease, knowing that she's not alone. If Samuel could help, I'd be mighty grateful. I heard he helped out Ingrid and Ben when they were at the hospital, tending to Ben's heart problems."

"He'll want to help. He and Winnie have always been good friends, plus he lives not two blocks from the hospital."

Pure relief washed over Jonathan. "I never thought I'd say this, but right now I'm glad Samuel's been living with the English. It will be nice to have someone there for Winnie."

"I think so, too." Though it had been hard to see him go, Eli had never faulted his brother. Surprisingly, no one in their family had been terribly shocked when he'd announced that he wasn't ready to join the church. Sam had always been a bright and inquisitive man. He'd ached for knowledge and the university like most Amish men ached for the land.

"Between Samuel and me, we'll make sure Winnie is taken care of. Don't worry. Winnie's like my sister. I won't let anything happen to her."

Clasping Eli's hand, Jonathan nodded. "I'm grateful."

As the flashing lights of the ambulance switched on again, one of the workers reached out to pull the door shut.

"Wait." Jonathan stopped him. "This man is coming with you."

The attendant nodded. "Hop in."

"I'll call the Brenneman's Bed and Breakfast with updates as soon as I know something," Eli said as he scrambled in. "That's the closest phone, right?"

"*Jah.*"

"Sam and I will watch over her," Eli called out as he obediently sat where the attendant motioned him to go. Jonathan hardly had time to nod before the doors slammed shut and the ambulance set into motion.

The crowd of people surrounding what was left of the barn got bigger and bigger. Not twenty minutes after the ambulance left, Katie and his daughters, Mary and

Hannah, arrived in their black buggy. "Oh, Jonathan," Katie cried, the moment she helped the girls down. "I'm so sorry I wasn't here."

"I'm not. I'm glad your mother needed an extra pair of hands at the inn. I would have been terribly worried about you and the girls."

"One of the men called the inn. I heard about Winnie!"

"Eli is with her in the ambulance." He started to brush back a stray lock of her hair but stopped when he caught sight of his sooty hands. "I was afraid to leave here."

"Eli will look after her."

Leaning down, he gave both Mary and Hannah fierce hugs.

"You smell like smoke!" Hannah cried.

"Everything does, but we'll be okay."

After another round of tearful hugs, Katie's mother, Irene, arrived. With easy efficiency, she led the girls into the house to prepare coffee and muffins for everyone. Jonathan knew before long, the yard would be filled with horses and buggies. Friends and neighbors would come from miles around to lend their support.

But no one helped ease his tension like his wife. "Katie, I hardly know what to do," he murmured after he'd told her about Winnie and her possible injuries.

"You don't need to know," she said without a pinch of doubt in her words. "The Lord will watch over Winnie, and He will take care of us, too." With a faint smile, she waved a hand around them. "He already has, wouldn't you say?"

Jonathan believed in the Lord with everything inside of himself. But that didn't stop his feeling completely lost. Gathering up his courage, he admitted, "I'm not sure what to do next."

"He'll let us know. You just have to believe and be patient."

After another hug, Katie left to go help her mother.

Jonathan watched her go, then looked at the crowd gathered. In spite of his fellow community members, he felt oddly alone. As the whole situation sunk in, Jonathan realized he had no words to describe his pain.

The fire marshal said he could wait inside if he wanted. But Jonathan didn't want that. He had to keep watching as the firemen battled the blaze.

After a bit, Katie's brother, Henry, stood by him, holding a mug. "Katie sent this out to you. A few sips might do you good."

Experimentally, Jonathan sipped. Henry was right. The steaming beverage did taste good. The hot liquid warmed his insides and the strong brew provided him with a much-needed jolt. *"Danke."*

As they stood together, staring at the smoldering ashes, Henry spoke again. "What happened?"

"I'm not altogether sure. I heard a loud pop. Once, years ago, my grandfather told me about the fire that struck their farmhouse. The noises I heard were ones he'd described. As fast as I was able, I got up and went to fetch Blacky."

"My *daed*'s over with the animals now, checking

them out," Henry said. "Others are coming to help, I'm sure."

Jonathan expected nothing less. "I'll be grateful for the help." Thinking back to the fire, he said, "It spread something fierce. I could hardly believe it. A large explosion burst the side of the barn, whether it was from the hay or a container of kerosene, I don't know."

Henry was prevented from saying any more when the fire marshal returned, his expression grim. "Mr. Lundy, we'll do some more checking as soon as things have cooled down and the sky lightens up, but I'm afraid things don't look good."

"I don't imagine it would—my barn's gone," Jonathan said dryly.

"No, that's not what I mean." The tall thin man tugged at his necktie. "Mr. Lundy—"

"Jonathan, please."

"Jonathan, I hate to be the one to tell you this, but I'm afraid a cigarette caused this." After he said the words, he looked Henry's way, as if for help.

Jonathan didn't understand. Maybe the smoke was finally gettin' to him? "I don't smoke. No one here smokes cigarettes."

"All the same, it looks to be what happened."

Beside him, Henry cleared his throat. "Say again?"

If anything, the marshal looked even more uncomfortable. "What I'm trying to say . . . is that we found traces of a lighter and cigarettes near the back of the barn. We'll know more information in the morning, but it looks as if someone ran away in the back field as soon

as the fire started. This fire might have been an accident, but it was definitely started from someone's carelessness, not by a force of nature."

"Cigarettes?" Henry repeated.

Behind them, Katie dropped the mug of coffee she'd
been bringing out to her brother. Her gasp, along with
the clang of broken pottery, brought Jonathan Lundy
out of his trance.

His barn was gone. His sister was badly burned. Someone had been on his property without his knowledge.

Meeting the fire marshal's gaze, Jonathan looked him
square in the eye. "You are right. This is a mighty bad
happening. A mighty bad happening, to be sure."

Chapter 2

Sam Miller rushed down the third-floor hallway of Adams Community Hospital, to the obvious irritation of the nurses on duty.

"Sir!" one called out. "Sir, this is a *hospital*."

"I know." He raised a hand in apology, but kept on going. He'd finally spotted Eli.

His brother was sitting ramrod straight in the miniscule waiting area near a narrow window, a fuzzy television screen, and a waxy-looking potted plant. Sam exhaled. "Eli."

Eli jerked toward him, relief replacing the lines of weariness around his mouth when he saw his brother. "Sam."

His brother could ride rings around him on a horse, outwork him in the fields, and was one of the most upstanding, direct-talking men he knew. However, among the English, Eli was a babe in the woods.

Eli stood up and hugged Sam close for a moment, just like he used to do when they were small. "It's good to see ya. I'm glad you could come so quickly."

"I got here as fast as I could."

"You came. That's what counts."

As orderlies pushed carts and nurses and doctors strode by, their expressions filled with determination, Sam concentrated on his brother. "How are you doing? How's Winnie? Is Caleb here, too?"

"No. I let him stay home. As for me, I'm all right—it's Winnie that I'm wondering about. Samuel, I can't get any information. I tell you, finding out the truth here is near impossible." Directing a scowl down the hall, Eli added, "Every time I get up and ask a question, those nurses act like I'm bothering them."

Clasping Eli's arm, Sam took the seat next to him. "How long have you been here?"

"Hours. Since daybreak."

"Would you like me to speak to the nurses now? Or just wait with you?" The last thing Sam wanted to do was offend his older brother.

"Find out what you can, wouldja?"

"I'll be right back," he promised, already standing.

"I don't understand why they won't allow me to see Winnie."

"Maybe there's a good reason. I'll see what I can do."

Backtracking to the nurses' station he'd hurriedly passed just minutes before, Sam directed his attention to the most friendly-looking of the nurses. "Excuse me.

My brother and I are concerned about a patient. Winnie Lundy?"

The nurse stepped close enough for him to read her name badge. Rebecca. "What do you need to know?"

"More than we know now, which is nothing." Smiling slightly, he leaned forward a bit. "Rebecca, can you tell me how she's doing?"

"Not yet." Little by little, her frosty demeanor thawed. "We're waiting for the doctor's report."

"How long might that be? My brother's been here for hours."

"I'm sorry, sir—"

"He's worried. Certainly you understand that."

After pausing for a moment, she picked up the phone. "I'll do some checking and get back to you."

Sam hated the runaround. But worse, he hated his brother getting the runaround. "When might that be?" he pressed.

She looked put out. "Within the hour."

"I don't know if I did much better, Eli," Sam said when he made his way back to the set of orange vinyl chairs. "However, I did get one of the nurses to promise she'd fill us in as soon as she could. She promised we'd hear something within an hour."

Eli slumped. "That's something, I suppose. I hate the idea of poor Winnie sitting somewhere by herself."

"She might not be. She's probably getting seen by a number of doctors and nurses and that's why we can't disturb them."

"Perhaps."

Hoping to take Eli's mind off the terrible wait, Sam said, "Tell me again what happened. Jonathan's barn caught fire?"

"*Jah*. It was a terrible thing. Flames shot up something fierce, and then all the hay in the loft ignited. I overheard some of the English say it looked like a bomb. All the commotion woke me up."

"Is the whole barn gone?"

"Oh, *jah*. Well, enough that it can't be saved." Eli shook his head sadly. "A lifetime of work, gone in an instant."

"That's terrible."

"It is. A shame."

Sam reckoned his brother was right. It was a shame. While it had been a good three years since he'd been to the Lundys', he knew the farm well. Lush, green, and well kept, it was a showcase for the area. The barn, with its green metal roof, was especially eye-catching.

For a fire to have burnt the whole thing down, it was almost as if part of history had been wiped away. He remembered their father talking about the barn raising as if it had been yesterday.

Eli leaned back in his chair. "It was a fair sight, to be sure. The flames lit up the sky. When I arrived, Jonathan had already gotten the animals out, but Winnie was in the ambulance. She's been burned, and I think maybe her foot is broken. I don't know what else." He turned to him. "You remember Winnie, don't you? Black hair, dimples in her cheeks?"

Sam recalled a skinny girl with too much on her mind. But it had been years since he'd seen her. "Of course. She was a few years behind me at school."

"I had forgotten that. Don't know why." Circling back to the original problem, Eli muttered, "I wish someone would come out and tell us what is going on. I'm not used to sittin' around."

"I know you're not."

Sam, however, was far more used to waiting on other people. Government lines, post office lines, shoot, even the lines at the grocery store. He was used to either texting people on his cell phone or making do. Eli, so used to the insular life in their community, was not.

Eli worried his black felt hat. "I promised Jonathan I'd look out for her, and I know he's waiting for some answers. I feel bad I haven't called him." Frustration tinged his words as he gave up trying to make sense of it all.

"Waiting seems to be the norm for everything nowadays."

"Maybe so. I'm fortunate to have a brother who will still drop everything to help him at a moment's notice."

The praise embarrassed Sam. Instinctively, he half waited for Eli to point out the obvious. Yes, he'd come today to help. But what about all the other times Eli had needed him but he hadn't been around?

Sometimes he felt like he'd abandoned his family, leaving the order. It was hard to come to terms that he'd picked an education over living closer to his family and joining the church. Though no one had ever *said* they resented him for leaving, Sam wondered if they did.

After another twenty interminable minutes, the nurse he'd spoken with approached them. Sam jumped to his feet. "Rebecca, have you found out any information yet?"

"Only a little bit. I've been waiting for Dr. Sullivan to give us the okay to accept visitors. After he saw Winnie in emergency, he went on rounds. However, I just got a hold of him and he gave the okay for a brief visit."

"Thank you, that's very good news."

"How is Winnie?" Eli asked.

Rebecca flipped through the papers clipped to the top medical chart she was holding. "She's just been moved to a private room. It looks like she's sustained a number of cuts and abrasions, and some burns to her legs. Her right foot is also fractured."

"Poor Winnie," Eli muttered.

"If you'll follow me, I'll take you both to her room."

Taking a calming breath, Eli nodded. "That would be fine."

Luckily, they didn't have far to go, just a few feet down one gray-checkered hallway, then another couple of yards down a second, this one with blue and green squares. Around them, stainless steel racks and bins lined the walls. The sharp, pungent smell of lemon-scented bleach filled the air.

Finally they arrived. "Here is her room. Number five-forty-one."

Eli already had his hand on the door handle. "Thank you."

"You're welcome. Remember, don't stay long, and don't be too worried if she's groggy. They've given her some medicine for her pain."

Pointing to a brown plastic chair outside her room, Sam said, "I'll wait out here, Eli."

"There's no need. Winnie would be pleased to see you, I think."

In her condition? Sam doubted that. Lately, he hadn't met a woman who appreciated seeing someone new without looking her best. "I don't—"

"Come, now. I don't want to stand here holding the door forever."

Reluctantly, Sam followed his brother in, hoping to stay in the back shadows and then slip out when the two of them got to talking.

But he had a hard time concealing his surprise when he did see Winnie Lundy. She certainly looked very different than he remembered her. Even lying down, she looked tall and lean. Eyes the color of a fading winter day set off ivory skin.

Those eyes widened when she focused on them. "Eli?"

"Yes. I'm here. Sam, too."

Embarrassed, Sam held up a hand.

"Don't stay too long," the nurse murmured once more after checking Winnie's vital signs and slipping out the back door. Sam edged closer. Ready to leave the moment it seemed suitable.

With his usual way, Eli moved to her bedside quickly. "So, how are you feeling?"

"Not so good." She frowned. "My foot hurts."

"Only one?" Eli teased.

"Both." With a frown, she glared at her feet. One was covered in protective gauze and bandages, the other in a temporary cast.

Eli raised his brows and whistled low. "Your feet and legs got the worst of it, I'm afraid. What did the doctor tell you?"

Winnie frowned. "That I'm going to be here for a few days. He said burns are prone to infection, and since I'm going to have a difficult time walking I need to let my body heal a bit here."

"*Das gut.*"

"No, it's not." Obviously agitated, Winnie gripped a handful of white sheet, almost as if she'd like to be choking it. "The last thing everyone needs is for me to be in the hospital. Jonathan and Katie are going to be busy enough."

"I came for Jonathan. Samuel is going to help, too. That's why we have friends and family, *jah*?"

"Yes, but I know you shouldn't be spending your days here either. You've got plenty to do, too, Eli. I know it's planting season."

"*Jah*, those seedlings will wait for no man. I'm gonna go back tomorrow, but I'm sure Katie will visit tomorrow for a bit. And Sam here has promised to keep an eye on you for us all. He's going to visit with the doctors, too. Sam—" He looked around. "Sam?"

"I'm here."

"You look like you were about to leave. Come closer, Winnie can hardly see ya."

Feeling once again like the little brother tagging along, Sam approached. "Hi, Winnie. I'm sorry about the barn and your injuries." To his surprise, she smiled, showcasing the pair of dimples Eli had mentioned.

"Samuel Miller, you are a sight for sore eyes."

Eli chuckled. "I'm sure he'd rather you saw him with good eyes."

Sam couldn't help it. He met Winnie's gaze and smiled, just like they used to do years ago, before they'd grown up and changed. "It's been a long time since we've seen each other. You weren't around when I came to visit my family in the fall."

"I was in Indiana."

"Well, I'm glad to see you. I wish we were visiting under other circumstances."

"I do, too." After a pause, Winnie looked beyond him to his brother. "So, how is Jonathan? Is he hurt, too?"

"I don't think so."

"What about the barn? The animals?"

"I haven't called to get any information. I've been waiting to hear news about you."

"Will you go call?"

"Winnie Lundy, you are as bossy as ever."

"I'm only worried about the farm and my family."

"You should be thinking about healing, don'tcha think?"

"I can't get better until I know how everyone else is. Go call, would you?"

"I will, when I find a phone—"

"You can use my cell phone," Sam interrupted, eager to be back in the conversation. Pulling it out of his jeans pocket, he carefully showed his brother how to dial the number and press send. "You'll have to use it outside, though. Hospitals don't take kindly to people using cell phones in the halls."

Looking determined, Eli nodded. "I'll go call right now. If you're sure you don't mind being left again."

"I'll be all right."

With a start, Sam realized that Winnie thought he was going to leave the room, too. Had she really thought so little of him? "I'll stay with you. That is, if you don't mind."

Pulling the sheets a little more securely around herself, Winnie shook her head. "I don't mind."

Sam sat in the chair next to the hospital bed. "Is there anything I can do for you?"

A dimple appeared. "You mean besides gettin' me outta here? No."

"Did you understand everything the doctors said?" he asked gently. He could only imagine how scared she must be. The sterile hospital was a far cry from her usual environment. "I can speak to them for you."

"I can talk to doctors, Samuel."

"I didn't mean—"

Immediately, regret filled her eyes. "Listen. I am grateful for your help. I imagine Eli is, too."

"I'm happy to help."

"But, surely, you have other things you'd rather be doin'?"

Sam swallowed hard. It was obvious that Winnie felt he'd moved on and now no longer cared very much for the people he grew up with. It was evident in her voice, in the way she looked at him.

Sam had essays to read and five students to mentor at the college, not to mention the usual work on his research programs. But all that paled compared to the look of need in this woman's eyes.

Eli walked back in. "I spoke with Katie's mother, Irene. She said all the animals are safe, and Jonathan is no worse for wear. Only the barn is a complete loss."

Winnie pursed her lips. "We'll have to tear it down and begin again."

"That we will," Eli said. "Irene said Jonathan was pretty upset about it, not so much because of the work required but because your father had built the barn."

"*Jah*," Winnie said with tears in her eyes.

"Jonathan's mighty worried about you. I told Irene I'd call back when I spoke with the doctor, but that Winnie was awake."

"I'm right here, you know. I could tell you how I'm feeling."

Sam looked at Winnie and grinned. "You never were meek, Winnie. Even when we used to play games at school, you always insisted on being in the thick of things. I guess some things never change."

With a quick glance at Sam, Winnie blushed. "Some things do." After clearing her throat, she said, "Eli, come sit down and talk to me. The last thing I remember is the barn exploding."

"That would be the hay catching on fire."

Sam nodded in response. As Eli talked about the excitement of riding in an ambulance, Sam noticed Winnie's eyes drift shut. The ordeal was taking its toll on her, and most likely, the painkillers were making her sleepy as well.

When Eli continued to prattle, Sam touched his arm. "It's time to go."

"You think so? We've only been in here a few moments."

"Look," Sam pointed out. Winnie's eyes had drifted shut.

Eli's cheeks flushed. "All my talking wore her out, I'm afraid."

Giving in to impulse, Sam nudged his older brother. "Yep, you always were a bore, Eli."

As he hoped, humor lit his brother's expression again. "Not all of us have a fancy education, you know." Once out in the hall again, Eli leaned his head back against the cool tiles on the wall. "It's been a terribly long day."

"How about I take you back to my place and you can get some sleep? I'll come back just in case Winnie wakes up."

"You don't mind?"

"Not at all."

"Then I'll take you up on it." He looked around. "Where do you think the doctor is? I want to know what is going on with Winnie."

"I'll check in with him when I get back. Most likely, he's doing rounds or something."

"I suppose." They took the stairs down to the parking area. Moments later, they were in Sam's Ford truck.

Eli might have been Amish, but he had a typical man's interest in all things mechanical. They spent the drive to Sam's place discussing the engine, gas mileage, and other details about his vehicle. Only when they parked in front of Sam's condo did he realize they'd spoken in Pennsylvania Dutch the whole time.

Funny how that came back to him without even realizing it.

"My place isn't much," he warned as he unlocked the door. "It's just two bedrooms, a kitchen, and a place to sit."

Eli looked around with interest. Stepping forward, he pressed a hand against Sam's ancient corduroy couch. "Good enough for me."

"Want something to eat? I have some turkey."

"Turkey's good. Thanks."

Together, they made sandwiches, then ate them with pickles and tall glasses of tea. Now that their immediate concerns about Winnie were abated, Eli took time to fill Sam in on the latest news about their parents and sisters, Beth, Kristen, and Toria. Just the week before, their parents had taken a bus to Lancaster to check on their grandparents. Mamm's parents' health was failing, and though the timing wasn't the best, with planting season just around the corner, the trip had to be taken.

Sam was thankful for all the latest news. He did write to his parents once a week, and tried to visit with the family at least once a month, but that was not always possible, given everyone's schedules. Right as they finished their sandwiches, Sam realized that Eli hadn't filled him in on their brother Caleb. "Is Caleb all right?"

For the first time, Eli frowned. "I don't know. He's been restless and secretive."

"He's seventeen. All boys are like that, especially during their *rumspringa*. I sure was."

"Maybe." Leaning back, Eli said, "I remember you feeling torn. All of us knew it was because you loved schooling so much. Even the bishop knew you had a great mind and were anxious to learn." He shook his head, considering. "But I don't get the same feeling about Caleb, and neither does Mamm or Daed."

"What do you think is going on?"

"Foolishness."

"What kind? Has he been drinking beer? Staying out too late?"

"If it was just that kind of thing, I don't think anyone would notice much. No, his behavior seems different. He's pushing our boundaries."

"What does Daed say?"

Eli raised an eyebrow. "What do you think? Nothing. Our father never shares his worries." Crumpling up his napkin, he added, "And, well, Caleb is their late-in-life child. Sometimes I think they turn a blind eye toward his activities. Far more than when you and I were teenagers."

"Sometimes I wish he'd tell us more. I never know what he's thinking."

"Maybe one day he'll share more. Not yet, though." Stifling a yawn, Eli stood up and stretched. "I best get some sleep. I won't be much use to Winnie if I can't keep my eyes open."

"Don't worry. I'm leaving now to sit with her. And I'll continue to sit with her tomorrow, too, after you go on home."

"You don't mind?"

"It's the least I can do. Use my phone and call my cell when you wake up. I'll give you an update."

"I should probably call the Brennemans, too, and check in again."

"Call all the people you want, Eli. My phone is yours."

"Just plan on me having your bed for the night, brother. That's enough, I think."

After another wave goodbye, Sam walked to his car, wondering why he felt such a need to help. Because of his older, steady brother who had always been there for him? Because Eli always supported him, even when Sam's wants and needs were so foreign to Eli's?

Or was he doing all this for Winnie, who he'd hardly known but had felt instantly drawn to?

After all this time.

Chapter 3

"This place smells like the inside of a *shanshtah*," Katie murmured as they stood in front of what was left of the barn three days after it had gone up in flames.

"I wish it was only the chimney smell that concerned me," Jonathan replied. "Unfortunately, the odor is the least of our worries."

Yes, the air around them most certainly held the scent of ashes, but the pungent odor was nothing compared to the destruction of his barn. Though it hadn't burned completely down, more than half was gone. What remained looked so flimsy that it wasn't worth the risk of keeping. The whole structure was going to need to be torn down, then rebuilt. "I don't know how I'm going to set things to rights," he added.

"Luckily, you don't have to do anything on your own. Both our families are eager to help, as is the rest of the community, English and Amish. We're all praying, too, you know."

"I keep forgetting to count my blessings." Thinking of Samuel Miller's latest phone call, he said, "It is surely a blessing that Winnie is going to be better soon."

"When Anna and I visited her yesterday, she seemed almost like herself."

As he looked around at the extensive damage, Jonathan couldn't help but shake his head in wonder. "It's a blessing that all our animals came through this, too. We didn't even lose a chicken."

"The Lord surely was looking out for us." Katie laid a hand on his shoulder. "He'll help us now, too, I think. And don't forget, we've got each other."

"I never forget that," he murmured as he shifted and turned to pull his wife into his arms. "Your love is my greatest blessing."

Yes, her love truly did warm his heart. On some mornings, when he woke to hear Katie already fussing in the kitchen, humming a tune, he could hardly believe they were now married.

What a whirlwind their courtship had been, too! Less than a year ago he was a lonely widower, who'd gone to Katie's home and asked if her parents could spare her for a time so she could help with Mary and Hannah while Winnie traveled to Indiana.

At first, things had been difficult—neither he nor the girls had been especially welcoming to her at first. But as days turned to weeks, a love between them all had bloomed. Next thing he knew, they were planning a wedding. Now they were a family. Obviously, the Lord knew he needed someone special in his life.

Together they entered the house, which was miraculously undamaged by either the fire from the barn or the water from the fire trucks. As soon as they entered the kitchen, Katie began to bustle about.

He took a seat at the worn table and took a moment to watch her. As usual, she fussed like a busy bee, wiping down already clean counters, filling a teapot with water, then placing it on the gas-powered range to boil, and neatly folding two towels that the girls must have used earlier in the day. Finally, she laid a particularly pleasing cake in front of him. "I made a sour cream cake early this morning. I thought you might enjoy a slice while we make plans."

"And how did you know plans were going to need to be made?" He'd purposely been vague about his worries, knowing she would try to shoulder all of the burdens.

She smiled as she picked up the knife and cut two generous pieces and placed them carefully on plates. "I heard the fire inspectors saying they'd be back today to visit with you. I guess we're going to have a lot to think about."

Biting into the warm, moist cake, he paused for a moment, just enjoying the simple goodness of the treat. After he put his fork down, he said, "I'm worried, Katie. I'm worried about Winnie and the animals and rebuilding and finding the time to rebuild. But I'm also terribly worried about the cause of the fire. The inspector said the culprit was most likely a tossed cigarette. It just doesna make sense. Who would be smoking in my barn?"

A dark shadow flickered across her face as she pushed her plate to one side. "Well, now. That is a difficult question. I'm not sure."

Something in her voice led Jonathan to believe that there was something she wasn't saying. "But you must have an idea, right?"

"Well . . . I might."

"Come now, Katie. Tell me what *you* think. Do you reckon it was maybe an English teen trying to find a place to get away?"

"All I know is that it wasn't me or you or Mary and Hannah."

Hastily swallowing his latest bite of cake, he looked at her frankly. Yes, his *frau* most certainly had an idea about the smoker in his barn. "Who do you think, Katie? I'm out of ideas. I've racked my brain, but for the life of me, I canna think of anyone who would even think of such a thing."

Reluctantly, she looked at him. "Maybe it was an Amish teenager," she said quietly. "Maybe someone was having a little smoke and something went terribly wrong. An accident. I don't think it was an *Englischer* teen. There are many other places to smoke and carry on besides an Amish farm. No . . . I reckon it was an Amish teen. An Amish boy or girl experimenting with smoking."

"That could never happen." No member of the community would lurk around other people's property. Besides, if it was someone who was Amish, he would have come forward and admitted his mistake.

"Sure it could. We Amish aren't perfect, you know. We all make mistakes time and again."

He pushed away his plate. It no longer looked appetizing. "Yes, but . . ."

With a hard glare, she stopped his words. "Oh, honestly, Jonathan. Don't be so naïve. I smoked. I experimented."

She was such a perfect wife he sometimes forgot her dark history. "Well, you're the exception, Katie. I'm sure most Amish *kinner* don't act out like you did."

"Like me?"

"Jah, like you," he fired back. "Your running-around years were difficult—you've said so yourself. Neither Winnie nor I ever did the things you've admitted to doing."

"I thought you said you understood about my past," she said quietly. "I thought you forgave me."

"I have." Feeling frustrated, Jonathan reached for her hand. "I'm not angry with you, I'm just sayin' I don't think an Amish teen burned down my barn."

In a huff, she stood up. "Well, I think differently, not that you seem to want to listen to my views. Now, excuse me while I go tend to the girls' rooms." Like a whirling dervish, Katie jumped to her feet, slapped the cake plate onto a counter with a thump, then swirled toward the front hallway.

He called out to her before she disappeared completely. "Katie, what did I say?"

Her feet slowed. "It's not worth talking about."

"I think it is. I thought you were tryin' to teach me how to be more open. To communicate better!"

When she turned around, Jonathan noticed tears had filled her eyes. "Katie, please talk to me."

"Perhaps you could begin to listen with your ears and your heart. Don't say one thing and mean another."

"I wasn't doing that."

"I think you were. I think you said you forgave me, but you didn't really mean it."

Her words caught him off guard. Had he done that?

Before he could say a word, she spoke again. "Jonathan, perhaps you should do some thinking about whoever did this. The Bible asks us to forgive our sins, even those who sin against us. Are you going to be able to do that? Are you ever going to be able to really forgive whoever burned your barn, put your animals in danger, and sent your sister to the hospital?"

He was prevented from pursuing the discussion by a brief hard rap at the door. "That's the inspector," he said.

A flash of tenderness filled her gaze before she turned away. "You'd best go get the door, then."

After another hard rap, he opened the door to the fire inspector. "Good afternoon, Mr. Grisson."

"Mr. Lundy, hello. Want to come out to the barn? I'd like your opinion on some things."

"I'll be right there," he said quietly, just before he donned his black hat and followed the fire marshal outside. Katie had given him a lot to think about.

And, most importantly, he had a feeling she was right. He wasn't sure if he was ever going to be ready to forgive the person who trespassed and damaged his property.

That was a terribly hard realization to come to terms with.

Sam's cell phone chimed late Sunday afternoon, just as he was about to drive over to the hospital and check on Winnie again.

As soon as he answered, Eli spoke in a rush. "Samuel, I'm calling from the Brennemans'. I am worried about Caleb. Once again he is not here when he's supposed to be."

"Maybe he simply forgot the time. You remember how it was when we were teens," Sam said reasonably.

"No, it's more than that. I told him he needed to tend to his chores, no matter what else he did today. When I went out to the barn, the horses' stalls still hadn't been cleaned."

Now, that was worrisome. Their father had ingrained in all of them the importance of tending to responsibilities. He couldn't imagine Caleb had been taught any different. "Eli, do you think he's gotten into some kind of trouble?"

"I'm not altogether sure." Sounding weary, Eli added, "I was never interested in pushing boundaries like he is. Come to think of it, I was never too concerned with the outside world. And you, you just wanted to go to school."

That was a fair assumption. Learning had been his rebellion, and it had taken up a lot of his extra time. It had been a difficult and tough decision to discuss his desire to focus on learning instead of Amish life. "Learning how things worked was all I thought about. But Caleb isn't like us, is he?"

"He's more secretive—and used to more freedoms. Remember how we always had the girls to look after?"

"I never thought I'd ever be able to go anywhere without Beth," Sam said.

"I feel responsible, too, since Mamm and Daed are visiting our grandparents."

"When Daed comes back, you can speak to him." With a jolt, Sam realized that, indeed, that was how it was going to be. He'd had little to no part in raising Caleb—the boy had been still a child when he'd left home. Though they were brothers, sometimes he felt as if he was little more than a distant relation.

"One night last week . . . he came home drunk."

"All boys do that at least once, I imagine." He'd taught at the college long enough to know a bit of experimental drinking was the norm instead of the exception.

"I wonder . . ."

Sam clutched the phone tighter. "What?"

"It's nothin', just that . . ."

"What, Eli?" Sam was really starting to feel alarmed.

"Lord forgive me for even thinking this, but I don't trust Caleb right now. I'm afraid . . ." He closed his eyes. "I'm afraid he was involved with the fire."

Sam felt as if someone had punched him in the stomach. "You think?"

"I appreciate you not pushing off my fears. Samuel, ever since the fire, Caleb has seemed more withdrawn. He's not offered to go with me to help clean up. In fact, every time I mention the fire, he looks like he wants to escape." He cleared his throat. "Samuel, what are we going to do if it *was* Caleb who started the fire?"

"I don't know." That would be a terrible situation. He didn't know what he would do—or what he would say if Caleb found out that he and Eli suspected him of that.

Both situations would be hard to excuse.

"I won't have a boy of mine lazing around from sunup to sundown," his father called out from the buggy whose wheel he was repairing. "Get to work and stop your lolly-gagging."

David Hostetler hurried out to the barn, grabbed hold of his work gloves, and went where his *daed* had told him to go, to the back pasture. Weeds were threatening to choke the path to the pond creek. It was a sorry, awful job, pulling out weeds, cutting debris, then carting it away. As he tromped out, taking care to not step in the mud, he passed his two older brothers who were almost mirror images of their father.

"What were you doing over there, just sitting around in the sun?" Kenny asked. "Daydreaming?"

"No. I just lost track of time."

"You'd best start remembering or be prepared to be reminded," Anthony said.

Though Anthony was right, David didn't comment on it. Instead, he tucked his head down and kept walking. There was nothing to say, and nothing anyone expected him to say. He was the middle child in a family of eight. He never seemed to stand out. At least, not in any good way.

He picked up his pace. Finally, away from the prying eyes of his family, right next to the cool, trickling waters of Wishing Well Lake, he pulled off his glove.

The burns were painful, the skin raw and blistered. Days in hot stiff leather gloves only served to make things worse. The only good thing about his current chores in the fields were that if he worked his hands raw, no one would question where he got the burns, they'd only tease him for having soft hands, not work-hardened and tough.

But David would welcome that teasing, because it would mean that no one knew what he'd done. After slipping on his gloves, he grabbed hold of the scythe and swung the blade against the tall grasses.

The sting was almost welcome. Anything was better than thinking about the fire.

Chapter 4

"We won't have to delay our wedding, do you think?" Anna Metzger asked as soon as Henry joined her on the front porch of the Brenneman Bed and Breakfast. Gazing toward the horizon, where just a few miles away the Lundy farm was situated, she murmured, "Is it appropriate to say our vows with everyone still recovering from the fire?" Recalling the heartbroken expressions on Jonathan and Katie's faces, she added, "Maybe we shouldn't celebrate such happy things right now."

Henry looked at her with concern. "You sound as if more is bothering you than the troubles at the Lundy farm. Is there a reason you're asking? Do you want to delay things?"

"Not at all. We've already waited so long."

"That we have."

When Henry held out his hand, Anna took it with

pleasure. The moment his fingers curved around hers, she recalled the first time they'd held hands. A spark of awareness had run through her body, making her realize happiness might actually be possible. It had been an astonishing moment . . . for a time, she'd been sure happiness would never find her again.

Now, with his touch, warmth and comfort was in her life. Looking into his eyes, she shook her head. "I guess I just want everyone to be happy."

"I want that, too."

As they stepped down the four steps that led to the front porch, and walked along the neatly trimmed walkway to the surrounding gardens, Anna smiled. "I can't help but be envious of Katie and Jonathan. As soon as they knew they wanted to get married, they went and said vows. It all happened within months."

"They had different circumstances. After all, Katie already was Amish."

"Well, I'm Amish now, too," Anna said proudly. "And I think it is time I got married and was your wife." After entering the garden, she stepped away from her fiancé and wandered down the rows of budding plants. This garden was a tremendous source of pride for her— until she'd come to live at the inn, she'd never tried to grow even a single tomato. Now Henry's mother, Irene, entrusted her with much of the upkeep of the large garden.

When she stopped at a row of fresh herbs, fragrant aromas filtered around them, the smell of thyme, rosemary, mint, and parsley lighting her senses. Unable to stop herself, she knelt down and pulled two pesky weeds. "I feel like I've been waiting forever."

Maneuvering among the rows far more slowly, Henry sniffed a batch of dusky purple lavender, plucked a stray dandelion, then tossed it into her pile. When Anna looked at him approvingly, Henry chuckled. "It's just been a little over a year, Anna."

With a grimace, she attacked two thistles that had the misfortune of daring to bloom in the midst of three heirloom tomato plants. "Just what I said. Forever."

"Hardly that."

"It feels like forever when you're in love."

Pulling her hands back into the comfort of his own, he brushed his lips against her brow. "Oh, Anna. I love you, too. Now, don't worry. I'll make sure we won't delay the wedding. Katie and Jonathan will understand."

She loved it when he told her he loved her—she knew she'd never get tired of hearing sweet things from him, of hearing how much he cared about her. "I hope Winnie will understand, too. When Katie and I visited her, she looked to be healing, but still in some pain."

"Jonathan saw her yesterday. He said she was sitting up in bed."

"That's good. She must be feeling better."

"*Jah*—and listen to this—Samuel Miller called with news again last night. Winnie's physicians reported last night that they will be discharging her soon. Maybe even in a day or two." With a direct look, he said, "Then, of course, we'll need to help her get around with that cast.

I have a feeling she's not going to want a few injuries to slow her down."

Just imagining Winnie attempt to do her usual routine with a cast on her foot made Anna smile. "You're right about that. She'll be warring with her injuries, for sure." As Anna thought of Henry's report, she mused, "So, Sam Miller was there again?"

"Yes."

"It sure is nice he's helping her so much at the hospital."

"It is."

Anna wished she knew more about what was going on between Winnie and Sam. When she and Katie had quizzed Winnie about him, her normally talkative friend had turned conspicuously closed-mouthed. "Have Sam and Winnie known each other a long time?"

"Yes, all of us have known each other all our lives. Samuel and I are the same age, with Winnie just a few years behind. Eli Miller is twenty-eight. Katie is a bit younger than you, just twenty."

"What a time you all must have had."

Henry treated Anna to a rare smile. "We sure did. We were constantly running through chores to play kickball or some such." He paused. "Lately, though, few of us have seen Samuel. He moved on, you know. Though we have lots in common, Samuel chose a different path." A dab of worry appeared between his brows. "I always thought he was happy to be living among the English. I hope Winnie isn't finding his views too strange."

"Well, it's certainly nice he's been so attentive. I know it's eased both Katie and Jonathan's minds to have him nearby."

"Like I said, he's known Winnie for many years."

"But they haven't seen each other much since Sam left the order. Why is he being so attentive? It seems out of place for him to be so concerned with Winnie's health."

"I don't think so. Katie's worrying about Mary and Hannah, Jonathan's got his work at the lumberyard and the cleanup at his place, and Eli's got Caleb and spring plowing," Henry pointed out practically. "Samuel, on the other hand, is right there. Even if he's not Amish, I'm sure he feels just as strongly as he ever did about being near family."

"Well, I'm probably reading too much into things. But I couldn't ignore how Winnie reacted when we brought up how much Sam was visiting. What if something wonderful was happening? What if they're falling in love? Winnie's had such heartache, not being able to find her right partner . . ."

Henry stopped tugging on a dandelion and frowned. "*Lieb?* Between Samuel and Winnie?"

"Don't act so surprised!"

Henry looked at her sharply. "I think smelling all this peppermint has gotten to you. They wouldn't be in love. They couldn't. Samuel's no longer a part of our world and . . ."

"Sure, they could," she interrupted. "Stranger things have happened. Look at you and me."

"I don't fancy being thought of as strange."

Anna looked at him sharply, then grinned as she caught his joke. Feeling better, she continued with her dreams. "I don't know, Henry. Just think, there's poor Winnie, stuck in the hospital with nothing to do. And Sam visits her all the time. Seems like the perfect time to grow a friendship."

"It's the perfect time to wish there was somethin' else to do besides sit in a drab hospital room, mark my words about that."

"Maybe . . . but maybe not."

"Ach. You have your head in the clouds, Anna Metzger. You need to be thinking about your wedding and our life together. Not Winnie and Samuel."

"But what if—"

"Nope. It won't."

As he leaned close to kiss her, Anna smiled. Well, Henry could deny it all he wanted, but Anna knew there was more on Winnie's mind than just injuries.

"Anna?" Henry whispered as his lips brushed her jaw.

"Mmm-hum?"

"Stop thinking and kiss me back."

That, at least, was something she was very sure she could do.

Now that the pain from the burns was subsiding, Winnie felt more at ease. Not only had it been hard to focus on anything other than finding relief, but the enforced time lying on her back had made the hours go by so slowly. She'd also hated being connected to so many tubes. It was embarrassing to have to ask the nurses for help to do most anything.

It had been difficult, feeling so terribly vulnerable.

Now that she wasn't on so many pain medications and her head was clear, Winnie's mood had brightened considerably. She could visit with whoever stopped by in her usual manner.

That was a good thing. She liked feeling in control and being aware of her surroundings, especially in an unfamiliar situation like the one she was in now.

Hospitals most certainly were not the place for her, though everyone had been as attentive as possible. The constant noise outside her door was jarring, as was the pungent smell of disinfectant. In addition, someone came to see her at least once an hour, to check her vital signs or to give her medicine.

At least the people who worked there were nice. The doctor, Dr. Sullivan, was mighty kind, too. He seemed to understand how scared she was, and he not only checked her injuries but stayed an extra moment or two and talked about things.

Now Winnie knew all about Dr. Sullivan's two grandchildren and his love for hiking. They'd begun to talk hiking trails around the area. Winnie had even promised to write him a list of her favorite spots up near Lake Erie. All of this had been much to his assistant's annoyance, Winnie was afraid. The younger Dr. Merchek was a man who kept a strict schedule and doled out smiles like expensive rewards.

Though the other patients she'd talked with complained bitterly about a constant stream of visitors, Winnie had become appreciative of it. Otherwise, she knew she would have caught herself worrying about Jonathan, Katie, and the girls, or wishing she could do something—anything—to try and help them out.

But of course, her only job was to try and get better and listen to what the doctors said.

Restlessly, she pressed the button on the television remote and watched the screen. A pair of women seated on a bright blue couch were talking about their children. One was terribly upset—it looked like no one could comfort her.

When a man in the audience yelled at them, Winnie pushed the channel changer. Oh, but she would never understand why so many people discussed their problems with strangers!

She'd just found a game show when a knock came at the door.

She looked up expectantly. Even a shot would be a welcome distraction from her boredom.

"Are you up for company right now?" came a muffled voice from behind the door.

Her heart got all fluttery. In quick order, she shut off the TV. "Sam?"

Cracking the door open, he poked his head in, his lovely light brown hair a mussed mess as usual. "Yep, it's me again. Do you feel like some company?"

"Don't even ask such a thing! I've just been sitting here wondering what to do with myself." Quickly she straightened the sheets around her waist, adjusted her bed a bit, and vainly wished she'd asked the morning nurse to help her smooth the hair under her *kapp*. Her hair most likely looked like a bird's nest. "Please, come in."

"Wondering what to do with yourself, hmm?" Kind hazel eyes looked her over and twinkled. "You must be feeling better."

"I am. Well, I am, a bit."

"That's good." He smiled as he shrugged off his tan canvas jacket and restlessly pushed back a portion of his straight brown hair that seemed to always want to cover one side of his forehead. "I see you've mastered the remote control. Are there any shows you like?"

Sorry that he'd guessed what she'd been doing, she pushed the black contraption farther away from her. Though he most likely wouldn't care that she'd been watching TV, she felt ashamed that she had done so. "Not so much." Wrinkling her nose, she added, "Much of what they talk about I don't understand."

"Because of the technology? I imagine information about cell phones and iMacs are hard to understand."

"Oh, no, I understand technology. I may not use it, but I'm fairly interested in all those gadgets. No, it's everything else that I find confusing. Yesterday I found three shows on ways to diet and exercise. Woman after woman talked about ways to change. I don't understand why so many people are displeased with the way God made them."

"That's because you see things a little more clearly than most. I'll bring you a book or some magazines next time I visit, if you'd like."

The fact that he talked about coming again made her happy. "*Danke*. I do like magazines, especially the gardening and cooking ones."

"I'll bring you as many as I can hold."

"I'd like that very much. I mean, if you don't mind."

"I don't. Not at all." As he took the chair next to her, Sam said, "I spoke with the nurses before I came in. They said you are doing better." Looking her over, he said, "Are you, really?"

"I am. Now I only have one needle in me, from this IV bag." She held up her hands for inspection, feeling so much freer than she'd felt since she'd arrived at the hospital.

"That is a good thing." He frowned at her arms, decorated with more than one or two purplish marks. "It's a shame you got so bruised, though."

"I'd rather have bruises than more bandages. They'll fade in time."

"Did the doctor tell you any more news?"

"Not anything of use. He reminded me of the fact that I'm going to have a difficult time walking around and doing my chores. He said the bones in my foot are going to take their time to heal." Remembering the conversation, she added, "First I am to be in a wheelchair. Then, if I'm very good, I might get to only have crutches for five weeks."

To her delight, Sam laughed. "I better warn Jonathan!

He already says you hate to slow down. You'll be a dangerous woman in a wheelchair."

"Not so much. Besides, I imagine I'll be slow for quite a while, I'm afraid."

"That's a good thing."

"Maybe."

"It is. And, listen, you must promise to use that wheelchair as an excuse to be a lazybones."

"Perhaps—but that's not who I am—or who I want to be." Winnie tried hard to not think about why she even cared about what Sam thought of her. For the last few years, she'd practically given up on love. When she was a teen, the boys used to tease her because she was so skinny and tall. Later, other boys had complained about her outspoken ways. And though she'd learned to be a bit more patient and to curb her tongue as well, there often seemed to be other areas where she had felt lacking.

All of it had taken a toll on her confidence.

Samuel shifted, propping one brown suede boot on a metal rung of her fancy electronic bed. Quietly, he murmured, "So, who do you want to be?"

"Just myself, I suppose. That's enough, *jah?*" She hoped he wouldn't hear the lie in her voice. In truth, she wanted far more than the person she was. She wanted to be married and start her family. She wanted the things she'd always yearned for but never seemed to be able to grasp.

"It's definitely enough. You're *glikklich*, did you know that?"

"Why would you say I'm lucky?" His comment surprised her almost as much as his use of Pennsylvania Dutch.

Sam resituated himself, flopping an elbow up on a knee. Somehow he always managed to look completely relaxed—even in such a stark hospital room. "Me, I've never been that happy with just myself. I always have had too many goals, I suppose."

"Such as?"

"Oh, nothing worth mentioning right this minute. It would put you to sleep."

"You'd never put me to sleep."

When his eyebrows rose, she felt her cheeks heat and thought quickly to save herself from embarrassment. "I mean, I've been given so many medications, it's hard for me to sleep."

"That's to my benefit, hmm? Now I don't have to worry about keeping your attention."

When he flashed a grin, she smiled, too. Winnie tried to convince herself that the only reason she was smiling was because she wasn't sitting alone anymore. The job was fairly tough to do. Sam Miller conversed with the easiness of a person who was confident with himself and his world.

That confidence made her feel completely giddy and a bit off kilter. He looked at her the way she'd always hoped a man would. The way Malcolm, her pen pal in Indiana, never had.

But he is not here to see you. He is here to check on you as a favor to his brother, she reminded herself.

As the silence between them lengthened, she became more aware of how close he was sitting to her. Of how much she'd been thinking about him without meaning to.

Only a brisk ding from the nurses' station down the hall broke the spell. "You can tell me about your dreams. I'd find them interesting. What are some things you'd like to change?"

But Sam still looked uncomfortable. "Nothing today." Before she could respond, he spoke again. "Now, no more about me. I'm supposed to be asking you the questions."

Well, she could be stubborn, too. "I refuse to answer any more questions." Remembering a bit of advice her mother had once relayed to her, Winnie said, "Tell me about your life with the English, Samuel."

Leaning back in his chair, he looked at her a little more closely. She met his gaze and felt a little spark of something special pass between them.

Awareness?

She knew what it was—it was the feeling she'd hoped to feel with boys as a teenager. It was the zing she'd ached to feel for Malcolm but never had. Now, here it was, unbidden and bursting with surprise, and there wasn't a thing she could do about it.

Oblivious to her thoughts, Sam shifted again. "There's not so much to tell." He shrugged. "You know most everything. I work at the agricultural college."

She was interested in more than just his occupation, but beggars couldn't be choosers. "Come now, Samuel, there's a lot to say about that job, I imagine. What do you do there?"

"This and that. I teach. Mentor students."

Oh, getting him to talk was like pulling teeth! "What do you talk to the students about?"

"Their futures." With measured words, he added, "English kids have so many options I think that sometimes they don't know what they want. I try and help them focus."

His statement caught her attention. In a way, she couldn't help but feel envious. Oh, she'd never had huge desires to accomplish great things. But it did sound intriguing to have so many opportunities at her fingertips. And to even have someone with experience to guide her, why that sounded mind-boggling. "Are you successful? Do they . . . focus?"

Samuel laughed, a deep, rich sound that floated through the air and lodged in her heart. "Sometimes. Not everyone's future is easy to figure out, you know."

"I imagine. What else do you do besides work with students?"

"I spend a lot of time in the fields and gardens, experimenting with soil composites and fertilizer." His voice warming, he said, "Lately, I've been trying to promote our Amish ways to everyone else. Too many people want to substitute science with what works. I don't always trust the results, you know?"

"Do people listen?"

"Sometimes. Organic produce is fairly popular right now. People are interested in our natural ways of insecticide and our practice of composting." Folding his hands around a knee, he said, "Just the other day, we studied how earthworms break down soil and help root expansion. Oh, sorry. I forget that not everyone is interested in worms and dirt."

"I am." But in spite of her best intentions, she yawned. "I mean, I'm interested in your take on things, especially with other people's interest in the Amish. Their curiosity makes me smile. So, our old ways are new now?"

Chuckling, he nodded. "That they are. But some would say that is how things always have been—people are adopting techniques that were always there, just forgotten."

"I've noticed that at my shop. I've met many people who now are appreciating the smooth lines and fine workmanship of master craftsmen."

"I'll have to visit your shop when you get better."

"It's not mine, of course, but I do enjoy working there."

"What else do you enjoy? Gardening?"

"I do. Not like you, but I do like getting my hands dirty and producing something. I'm not much of a person for cooking or sewing, but I do enjoy a day in the garden."

"So you garden and work at an antique shop."

"Yes. And you work and . . . do what?" she prompted, wanting to know more. Sam intrigued her, pure and simple.

A shadow fell over his eyes. "I work and read mostly. Hike and bike. Every now and then I watch a movie."

"I've only seen a few movies. One time we stayed in

a hotel and my parents let us watch *Cinderella* on the television. I saw a few others when I went over to an English friend's home."

"Maybe I'll bring a movie for us to watch tomorrow."

"I'd like that, if you have the time." She took a chance. "That is, if you don't have a date or something."

He visibly started. "A date? No. I, um, don't date much."

"I'm surprised." Samuel Miller was a handsome man.

"You shouldn't be." A ruddy blush colored his cheeks. "I . . . I sometimes wonder how I fit in, if you want to know the truth. A lot of the women I meet are from different backgrounds. Sometimes I feel like I am speaking *Deutsch*, our views are so crisscrossed. They think my ways are old-fashioned and quaint."

"I heard some women don't even go to church."

"No, they don't. Some have far different values than I do. Even though I left the Amish, I don't think my heart did."

"That's a terrible place to be," she said softly. "I would imagine it would be hard to straddle two worlds."

"I'm not trying to straddle, just fit in. But I wouldn't say my path is 'terrible.' It's difficult, but it is the path I've chosen. I chose to leave the Amish in order to further my education. Because I chose to leave, I must also live with the consequences."

"But don't you wish things were easier?"

Samuel considered her question for a moment before shrugging. "Sometimes. But, Winnie, truthfully, I don't pray for things to become easier. Instead I pray

for patience. God never promised us an easy life, and I
don't think I need an easy life—just one I can feel good
about."

"I hear what you are sayin'. And you're right. Even in
the Amish community, people have struggles." Taking a
chance, Winnie dared to reveal a bit more about herself.
"Last year, I wrote to a man for quite a time. I thought
he and I might have a future one day. But when I went
out to Indiana to visit him, I found we didn't suit each
other after all."

"And you were disappointed?"

"I was. I . . . I never told my family, but I knew as soon
as I saw Malcolm that I'd never fall in love with him.
There was nothing about him that struck my fancy. But
I tried to pretend there was a possibility." Winnie felt
her cheeks heat. At the moment, she would have given
most anything to run out of the room. Never before
had she admitted how hard she'd tried to make things
work with Malcolm. It had been difficult, indeed. "After
three weeks, I gave up."

"Three weeks is a long time to give someone!"

"It was. But I was so determined to make something
happen." She shook her head. "In the end, it was no
good. It was like trying to put a round knob in a square
hole."

"I hope one day you find your match."

"*Danke.* I hope you will one day find your match,
too."

"If we're lucky, we'll take that big step one day. I just
hope when we do, the path won't be too painful."

"We'll hope and pray." Winnie forced herself to look anywhere but directly at him. She was afraid if she met his gaze, he'd see what she was trying so hard to conceal. Pointing to her feet, she grinned. "I've been learning that sometimes even when our paths aren't always easy, one survives. And sometimes, it is worth all the hardship."

"That's good advice." His lips twitched. "As long as it doesn't involve a broken foot."

"I'll let you know if my foot's pain is worth it." She blinked as he laughed. And finally, gave in to the pull that was happening between them. An invisible, tenuous bond held them together. She felt it as much as she had felt the instinctive knowledge that Malcolm would never be for her.

For a split second, she spied hope and a yearning that matched the feelings in her heart.

Winnie forgot she was sitting in a hospital bed with needles and bandages over her. She forgot how unhappy she'd been. How much she'd wished things would change and that she be given an opportunity to do something new with her life.

All she seemed to be able to think about was the man sitting next to her. How his hair was streaked with gold from hours in the sun. How his shoulders and arms looked like they could hold the biggest load of wood with ease. She noticed the calluses on his fingers, and the lines around his eyes that had nothing to do with age and everything to do with laughing and living.

But even more importantly, she noticed the things that had nothing to do with looks. His sun-streaked hair hinted of his love of the outdoors. The calluses and muscles showed he wasn't afraid to carry burdens. The lines on his face proved he wasn't afraid to live.

But as her fancies settled down, Winnie slid back to reality with a thump. He wasn't Amish. It was too late for both of them. It was now too late to even dream.

Clearing her throat, she said, "I'll look forward to those magazines and a book. Thank you again for offering to bring some reading material."

His expression clearing, Samuel nodded as he stood up. "Like I said, it is no trouble. I'll bring them by tomorrow. And that movie I promised?"

"I would enjoy that. A special treat, indeed."

Backing out of the room, he nodded. "I'll go, then."

"Yes. I'll see you tomorrow. Goodbye, Sam."

When the door closed and the room felt too big, Winnie pretended it was only her foot that was hurting.

Chapter 5

David had never meant to start the fire. All he'd been doing was trying his hardest to make smoke rings. He and two other boys had seen some English teenagers making perfect circles in the air outside the Brown Dog Café. When David had seen how impressed his friends had been, he'd become determined to make them, too.

They were much harder to make than he'd thought.

That night, well, he'd been so intent on spying those rings in the moonlight, he hadn't realized that he hadn't been extinguishing the cigarettes like he should.

At least, he supposed that was what had happened.

But once that first spark flickered, then flashed into flames, he'd hardly had time to do anything but back away in a panic—the blaze got so big so quickly.

But still, even then, he'd stayed nearby. After all, he

knew he was at fault. The right thing to do would be to alert the Lundys and help get all the animals out of the barn.

But all he could think about was what his *daed* would do when he found out.

When he heard Jonathan Lundy's shout and the frightened shrieks of the horses, he'd felt relief. Jonathan would take care of everything. And so he ran farther into the shadows. He wanted to help. Honestly, he wanted to do whatever he could, but it was surely too late.

Besides, it seemed as if his feet were running faster than his mind could work. Like lightning, he'd run across the back fields, the tall grasses whipping against his knees like miniature reminders.

When he got home, his *daed*'s kerosene lamp glowed from the window of his parents' bedroom. He'd let himself in just as he heard the familiar thump, thump of his father's thick-soled shoes echoing through the darkness. He knew what his father was going to do—he was going to ride out to the Lundys' and give assistance. Most likely, his well-honed sixth sense had alerted him to a fire nearby.

That's what his father always did—the right thing. He'd never had patience for people who didn't follow rules. He didn't believe in gray areas. No, things were stark in his father's world. Either a person was right or wrong. And if someone was wrong, that was usually unforgivable.

He'd hardly had time to hide in the shadows before his father had mounted their mare and rushed to the farm.

And then the next morning, when he heard Winnie was in the hospital and that the whole barn was ruined, it was too late to say a word.

What was done was done.

How could he confess what he'd done? No one would understand his reasonings anyway. He hadn't meant to set the fire. He hadn't meant to run and hide. But he had. He didn't understand why things had happened.

Now he couldn't help but wonder if this was God's way of punishing him for smoking.

He'd decided right then and there never to smoke again. He hid his last carton and lighter from sight. When the time was right, he'd take it into town and toss it in a trash can. He didn't dare dispose of anything around the farm. He was too afraid.

But now David couldn't sleep. Something told him that things still weren't right. They would never be until he admitted all his wrongs.

But every time he thought of the expression on his parents' face, he dared not say a word.

Truthfully, there was little he could do now. What was done was done. Now he just had to hope and pray that no one would ever find out. If his father ever discovered the truth, he'd be horribly angry. So angry David was afraid to tell him.

But what he did still shamed him.

* * *

"Thank you all for coming. I know I need your help to make these difficult decisions," Jonathan began, looking toward Henry Brenneman and his father, John, Eli Miller, and Marvin Kropfs, the bishop of their church. "I spoke with the fire marshal and he assured me that their investigation is complete. They've called the fire an accidental one, that was set by a stray cigarette."

The other men looked at each other in consternation. The bishop's expression hardly flickered—it was almost like he hadn't heard a thing.

But that was his usual way of listening—impassive. Stoic.

Jonathan wondered what was going through their minds. He'd seated them all at the dining room table, where they could see each other equally around the oval and take notes if needed. But as the moments passed, Jonathan began to doubt his instincts. Maybe he should have asked Bishop Kropfs for a more formal meeting at another location?

Maybe he should have just said nothing and waited for someone else to bring things up?

Finally Bishop Kropfs spoke. "Jonathan, if the police and fire investigators said their work is over, does that mean they no longer need to come nosing around here?"

"I believe so. We can rebuild and move on." Quietly, he added, "It doesn't look as if someone was meaning to do harm . . ." His voice drifted off. He wanted to give whoever had done the damage the benefit of the doubt.

He wanted to concentrate on moving forward instead of looking backward, but the positive, optimistic words felt stuck in his throat.

The truth was, he felt bitter and angry inside. He wanted retribution. He wanted someone to be punished for the destruction and danger caused.

"Accidents happen, Jonathan," the bishop said with a shrug, looking at Henry's father meaningfully. "Perhaps it was God's will."

Jonathan knew what that shared look meant—the two older men thought he was acting a little too rash and foolishly.

Maybe he was.

But, for the life of him, Jonathan couldn't think of a single reason why the good Lord would have wanted his barn to burn to the ground.

Though, of course, it wasn't his place to question the Almighty. But still, the Lord had given him a mind, too, and he was intent on using it. "I realize that the Lord has His ways, but there are signs that it might have been someone in our community who set the fire. Accident or not, the fire was a terrible thing."

"We were right lucky Winnie wasna hurt worse."

"Only by the grace of God did we get the animals out and Winnie to safety," Jonathan agreed. "However, now I find myself unable to sleep. I think about Katie and Mary and Hannah. What would have happened if my girls had been here? What if the fire had spread more than it did? I could have lost my house." Haltingly, he added, "I could have lost my girls."

Henry whistled low. "But you didn't. Come now, *freind*. Don't dwell on what didn't happen."

"I'm having trouble only looking at the bright side. Too much was in danger."

A new awareness entered John Brenneman's expression. "I hear what you are saying . . . I, too, have been plagued by 'what-ifs.' After all, I, too, have a daughter who could've been caught in the fire. But . . . that doesn't change the fact that Winnie is all right, your animals are okay, the girls and Katie are unharmed, and your house is fine. We shouldn't go borrowing trouble."

Frustrated by the other men's inability to read his mind, Jonathan shook his head. "John, you are right, but that is not what concerns me. See, I'm wondering what I should do about the culprit. Should I give the police permission to try and figure out who started the blaze, or should I just let the investigation fall and move on?"

Bishop Kropfs sipped from his coffee, and obviously finding it cold, frowned and pushed it away. "Cigarettes are not against the law. How could anyone even begin to figure out who did such a thing? That investigation sounds impossible."

John nodded as well. "Monitoring the English is not something we should be worried about. Besides, who could it be? I couldn't help with any ideas. I know many of the English, but not their habits."

Jonathan sighed. Obviously, he was going to have no choice but to share all of his worries. "Katie suggested that it's more likely to be an Amish teen. I think she might have a point."

"C-certainly not," the bishop stammered. "No member of our group would do such a thing."

As the other men looked just as horrified, Jonathan hastened to explain himself. "While at first I was shocked, now the idea makes more sense to me. My place is familiar to everyone in our community—but not to outsiders. After all, there's no reason for an *Englischer* to be sneaking around my land, just to have a smoke. There're many other places that would be far more convenient."

"English teens still do sneak around, though. Even English parents don't smile upon teenagers doing such things." John waved a hand. "Most likely there was beer or wine or something hidden in your barn, too. Or, it could have been a pair of teens." He raised his brows. "Put that way, your barn would be a far sight better spot to play around in than a parked car."

Henry chuckled. "*Daed*, the things you say. Sometimes you still surprise me."

"I'm old but not *deerich*," John replied with a wink.

Bishop Kropfs chuckled. "No, you have never been a foolish man, John."

Choosing his words carefully, Jonathan said, "While I agree that my barn is a secluded spot, I still don't think it is a likely place for English teens. And, the police didn't find any evidence of liquor bottles or cans. I think we need to consider the idea that it was one of our members. An Amish child doesn't have as many options for foolishness. It really does make the most sense."

"I'm afraid I have to agree," Eli said, looking a bit worried. "It would be wrong to not imagine that someone in our order made a terrible mistake the other night. We all remember feeling our oats, so to speak."

"Even if it was an Amish teen—which I doubt—I'm not sure why you called us together," the bishop said.

Jonathan's throat went dry. Without so much as raising his voice, it was obvious that their bishop was not pleased with the proceedings or the thread of conversation. Katie's dad was starting to look uncomfortable, too.

Slowly, he looked each man in the eye and finally got around to the real reason he'd sought their company. "The fact that it could have been a member of our community concerns me greatly. If a teenager did cause such an accident, it bothers me that he or she hasn't come forward and admitted his responsibility."

"That is troublesome," John murmured.

It was finally time to admit the thing that was bothering him the most, even if it didn't make him feel proud. "I, personally, don't know if I'll be able to move forward without knowing who did this."

The bishop peered at Jonathan over his half-moon spectacles. "You could, with God's help."

John Brenneman chimed in. "If it was an accident, it shouldn't matter who caused the damage."

"*Jah*. You need to forgive, Jonathan," the bishop muttered, his voice laced with impatience. "You need to *bayda*, to pray and ask for guidance."

Jonathan struggled to keep his expression as neutral as

the others'. At least, thankfully, Eli and Henry weren't saying too much. It would be even harder if the both of them were feeling the same way.

He chose his next words with care. "I would like to forgive whoever trespassed on my land and did so much damage. But how can I if the person responsible hasn't accepted any blame? If the person hasn't even asked for forgiveness?" Frustrated with the whole situation, he pushed back his chair and braced his hands on the thick oak tabletop. "Someone put everything I love in harm's way and hasn't even bothered to step forward. It eats me up inside."

"It would bother me, too," Henry said.

"I'm afraid I will not give my blessing to your investigation, Jonathan. What's done is done." The bishop pushed back his chair and looked ready to leave.

Every time Jonathan closed his eyes, he felt as if the fire was ablaze once again. The all-encompassing rage and terror of those moments, when he wasn't sure if Winnie was all right. His fear that all the animals would burn to death. In his heart, he knew he would never be able to accept the situation and put it behind him without answers.

Even if it went against the basic tenets of their beliefs.

After a lengthy pause, the bishop proclaimed, "I suggest we accept that we might never know who trespassed on the property and move on. Whoever did this will surely be feeling guilt, mark my words. And, of course, judgment is not ours to give, but rather our maker's."

The other men nodded. Reluctantly, Jonathan did as well, but the decision didn't sit well with him. He knew forgiveness was one of the tenets of their community. But still, he found he could not simply accept the fact that someone had trespassed, accidentally burned down his property, and almost killed his family and then got away.

Long after the men left, Jonathan stood outside and stared at the remains of the barn. Plain and simply, he was angry about the damage. He still felt as if a frog was in his throat every time he thought about what could have happened to his sister.

And while he could accept an accident, he surely didn't know if he could accept a lie for the rest of his life. As of now, he knew every time he spied a teen looking sheepish or secretive, he would blame him.

And surely, that wasn't right either, now was it?

"Jonathan, you're still out here?" Katie asked as she walked out to stand beside him. Staring at the charred remains of the building, she folded her arms over her chest. "Are you planning to join us inside anytime soon?"

"Maybe." He would go inside if he could shake the anger and sense of helplessness that coursed through him every time he glanced at the remains of the barn. Being around his daughters while filled with such bitterness wouldn't be good at all.

"Maybe, hmm?" Instead of sounding perturbed, Katie just seemed amused. "I'll tell Hannah that, then. I'm sure she'll understand that her *daed* doesn't know when he's going to tell her *gud naught.*"

In what had become a habit, Jonathan reached for her hand. Very sweetly, she slipped hers in his and held on tight. As always, her palm felt cool and smooth and reassuring. So ladylike and feminine, but strong, too.

Remembering how hard it used to be for him to trust, he took a chance. "I'm having a time accepting the bishop's decision."

"What was it?"

"We're supposed to simply rebuild and let the Lord take care of the rest. Katie, I don't know if I can do that."

Instead of replying immediately, she released his hand and walked over to the burnt remains of the barn. With a loving hand, she ran a finger over one of the few planks that was completely whole. "This has been a special place, hasn't it?"

"What do you mean?"

She turned to him. "Oh, Jonathan, I know it has to bring back memories of your father, and your grandfather, too." She raised a brow. "Doesn't it?"

"Some." A lump formed in his throat as he thought of all he'd lost in a few hours' time. Saddles were gone. His father's finely honed bridle. His grandfather's ax.

No, he hadn't lost memories, but he had lost the tangible evidence that people important to him had existed. He'd lost items close to his heart—items he'd one day wanted to hand on to his daughters or a future son.

The barn's destruction made him feel loss similar to when his father passed away, after his long battle with cancer.

Picking up a charred board, Katie examined the dark shadows marking the wood before easily breaking it in half. Blackened splinters sprinkled the ground and her skirts right before she loosened her grip and let the pieces fall to the ground. "I also see reminders of how I used to feel." She turned to him, her vibrant blue eyes seeking his. "If it was an Amish teen who did this, then he or she must be feeling fairly terrible. I, personally, felt guilt for years for the lies I once told to both my English friends and my family."

"What are you sayin'? That you would have liked to have been caught?"

"I'm not certain." She shrugged. "But I do know that while we can break the past and try our best to toss it from our life, it's not always that easy." With a small smile, Katie opened her hands, revealing black stains on her fingertips. "Even after pushing away the damage, we're still marked."

"Yes, but your hands can be washed."

"It's not as easy to remove tough stains as one might think, Jonathan." Stepping toward him again, Katie murmured, "For both your sake and the teen's I am glad you are not going to simply drop what happened."

"And if we don't find anything right away?"

"I don't want to go against the elders' wishes, but maybe it wouldn't be a bad thing to do a little guessing and questioning on your own. It's your right, after all. This was your property."

"I don't want to go against the Bishop."

"I wouldn't want you to. But I don't want to see you miserable either. I think it might be a mistake to assume that just because there is fresh wood in this place that the past can be erased."

"I'll think on that." There was so much to think about, his head was spinning.

"In the meantime, perhaps it is time to come inside? There're two girls who would love to spend some time with you."

He took her hand again and held it firmly as they walked away from the burned remains. Away from the doubts to the certainty of all that he had . . . a wife and two lovely daughters. A home and a place to go home to. That, indeed, gave him comfort.

Chapter 6

"So, tomorrow is the big day, right?" Sam asked when he entered Winnie's hospital room. For once, he actually looked like he was coming from his job at the college. He held a thick leather satchel in his right hand and had on a blazer.

"Yes. I am going home tomorrow. I am terribly anxious to leave." Gesturing toward his fancy jacket, she said, "I guess you've been at work?"

"Yep." He made a face. "I had one meeting after the other. First with the department chair, then with a couple of prospective students who wanted to know more about the agriculture program. That's why I couldn't stay too long yesterday. I had a lot to prepare for."

"I understood." She'd needed that time to herself anyway. She'd spent hours thinking about their relationship, struggling to remind herself that there was little between them other than a matter of convenience for a short time. Sam lived and worked near the hospital. She, Winnie, had just happened to be nearby for a time. After tomorrow, their friendship would fade away again, just like it had years before.

That wasn't a bad thing. No, it was just how things were.

"I know you are a busy man."

"I hope you believed me when I said I had a lot of work to do. I really couldn't get out of it."

She didn't appreciate his tone. "I'm not a child, Samuel. Nor backward." He winced but she couldn't help but let him hear the displeasure in her voice. "I might not have gone to work in a college, but I still can understand responsibilities."

"I didn't mean to act as if you didn't."

Now she felt self-conscious. "I'm sorry. Sometimes my tongue runs away with me."

"Can we call a truce? I brought you something." He held up a flat plastic box.

Winnie played along. "Now what might that be?"

He smiled broadly. "It's a movie. *Singin' in the Rain*."

"*Singin' in the Rain*? I've never heard of such a thing. Most times we try to dodge the rain, not sing in it."

Looking almost boyish, Samuel popped open the box, then pulled out a silver disc. "You, Winnie Lundy, are in for a treat. People say that *Singin' in the Rain* is the best musical of all time."

She wasn't even sure what exactly a musical was. But still, seeing a movie was indeed a treat, and one she would likely be grateful for in the years to come. "Plug it in, then."

He chuckled. "Say, play the movie, Samuel."

She obediently complied. "Play, Samuel."

Just as he inserted the disc into the player, Nurse Brenda came in with a bowl of popcorn. "Here's your movie treat," she said, beaming.

"Oh, *danke*! I do love popcorn!"

"Have a good time, you two," the nurse said as she walked back out the door.

Holding the bowl in her lap, Winnie smiled. "That was nice of her."

"It was. I asked her to pop up some in the microwave for us. Can't watch a movie without that."

Winnie couldn't help but stare at the contents in the bowl with a new distrust. "I've never had microwave popcorn. Is it safe?"

Humor filled his hazel eyes. "As safe as watching a movie, Winnie."

And with that, he pressed play, sat in the chair next to her, and grabbed a handful of popcorn just as a tall man in funny old-fashioned clothes started talking about being a movie star.

Winnie couldn't help it, she was enchanted. She'd only seen a few other movies, and those had been with an English friend back when she was eight. Never had she seen a movie with such singing and dancing!

She found herself munching the popcorn and sharing smile after smile with Sam, laughing at the blonde's voice. Every so often, she'd ask Samuel a question about the movie's plot or characters. He answered each one like they weren't silly at all.

And when their hands touched while grabbing a handful of popcorn, Winnie pretended not to notice how much even such a simple touch affected her.

All she knew, was that long after Gene Kelly and Debbie Reynolds looked into each other's eyes and kissed, long after Sam had put the movie back in the case and departed, long after the smell of popcorn was replaced by the scent of antiseptic . . . she still remembered exactly what it had felt like to be completely happy in Samuel Miller's company.

"I am very grateful for all of your help these last few days," Winnie said to Brenda the following morning. "I have much appreciated all you've done for me."

"It was no bother."

"I'm sure it was. When I first got here, I was in sad shape."

"You certainly are doing much better now, I'm pleased to say." Brenda briskly moved around the room in her squeaky sparkling white tennis shoes, picking up cards and rearranging items quickly and efficiently. "I've liked getting to know you and learning more about your kind. You're my first Amish patient, you know."

Winnie would have taken a bit of exception to Brenda's phrasing of "her kind" except that now she knew Brenda well enough to understand what she meant. During the five years that she'd worked at the hospital,

Brenda had told her about patients from many different countries that visited. She loved learning about different cultures and traditions.

As Brenda watched Winnie carefully smooth her dress's fabric around her waist, she frowned. "Don't these pins that hold your dress together ever stick you?"

Winnie chuckled at the question. "Not yet. You learn as a young girl to fasten them carefully."

"Your hair looks all neat and tidy."

"I'm glad of that. It's felt like a mess of tangles."

"It's pretty. Why, it's the silkiest hair I've ever braided. Long, too."

"I told you we don't cut our hair."

"Well, you look fetching now that it's neat and tidy under your *kapp*."

"Brenda, you sound almost Amish!"

"Danke!"

"Oh, Brenda, I will miss you." Impulsively, Winnie hugged her nurse, who looked at first taken aback by the burst of emotion, then a little teary-eyed.

"Don't forget to take care of yourself, you hear? The burns are out of the danger zone, but the skin will be tender." Waving a finger, she added, "And go easy on that foot. There's a big difference between sitting around here and hopping around at home."

"I don't think I could get much done, even if I wanted to." Gingerly, she got into the wheelchair the orderly held for her. Brenda was about to hand over her bag full of belongings when Sam and Eli bolted through the door.

"Are we late, Win?" Eli asked, his face red and splotchy.

"Almost. What took you two so long?"

Sam held up a hand. "Don't let him lay a bit of this blame on me. I was at his house early this morning but he wasn't ready."

"Cow has colic."

Brenda wrinkled her nose. "You're talking about a real cow, right? Like one that says 'moo'?"

Instead of looking abashed, Eli seemed anxious to share his story. "Oh, you bet. She's better now, but it was touch and go for a time."

"She's a stubborn heifer, that's for sure." Sam chuckled. "She's worse than a child about taking her medicine."

Eli grimaced. "Far worse. She kept stomping her hooves and bellowing every time Caleb ventured near." Sharing a look with his brother, he added, "Though now that I think about it, I don't think Caleb was too sad about that."

"He wouldn't be," Sam stated. "He's a master of dodging chores."

"Like you would know," Eli retorted.

Winnie held a hand up in protest. "Stop, you two! You're here now, so that's all that matters."

"That's right," Brenda added with a grin. "All that matters is you're here for Winnie's big departure."

"*Jah*, and I'm ready, too."

To her surprise, Sam crouched right down next to her, bringing with him a sharp, clean, heady scent that she couldn't ignore. "You look ready. It's good we didn't wait a moment longer."

She had no desire to look anywhere but at him. Feeling like a teenager, especially with Brenda watching with interest, she fought off the flutter of nerves that were threatening her composure. "Yes. I would have flown the coop and you two would have had to search the countryside for me."

"I don't think you would've gotten very far, hopping on one foot." Eli frowned at his brother. "Get up, Samuel. You're blocking everyone's way."

Slowly, Sam stood up. Then, their procession started forward. The orderly pushing her, Brenda walking by her side, Eli now holding her belongings . . . and Samuel keeping everyone company.

Funny how he seemed to be the only person she was aware of.

Winnie looked from Eli to Sam and tried to pretend that one of them didn't affect her like Sam did. But the truth was that every time Sam Miller was in her presence, there seemed to not be enough air in the room. Her breath ran short, and her pulse raced a bit more than usual.

Brenda winked her way. "Sam and Eli, I best remind you both that Winnie here needs to be treated like a lady of leisure."

"I'll make sure of it," Sam said.

"What's a lady of leisure?" Eli muttered.

"A woman who sits around a lot," Sam explained.

"Ah."

As the orderly and Brenda bantered back and forth, Winnie met Sam's gaze. "Thanks for driving me home today."

"It's no problem. I am sorry I'm late."

"You're not. I just got released."

Eli grunted. "There's a lot of traffic today, Win. It's going to be quite a while before we're back home again."

She looked Sam's way as they continued their way down the hall, its pungent antiseptic scent almost making her eyes water. "I hope we won't ruin your whole day?"

"You won't. I decided to take a few days off from school. I have some vacation days coming."

Eli looked at his older brother fondly. "He's going to help with the plowing and planting."

"Really?" Winnie looked from one brother to the other. Since she'd known the Millers, she'd never known Eli to ever ask for help or for Sam to come out and assist. "Is that the only reason?"

"Eli also explained how Jonathan and Henry sometimes lend a hand, but there won't be time with the Lundy barn needing to be rebuilt. And, well, Jonathan also told me that you've got a follow-up appointment in a few days' time. When Katie said she was going to hire a sitter and a driver to accompany you, I thought I'd just stay out your way and take you then."

"That's mighty nice of you. A most generous use of your vacation."

"It's what I want to do." He sighed. "Plus, well, Caleb's been around less than usual. It's starting to be that no one can count on him for anything. Eli told me that last night Caleb went out and didn't show up until almost midnight. I'm beginning to really regret my parents' long trip north, especially since it's during Caleb's *rumspringa*. He doesn't always want to listen to his brothers."

"That will pass soon, I imagine."

Winnie felt a bubble burst inside of her. For a moment, there, she'd been sure Sam was staying nearby to see her. But, surely, his reasons were far better. After all, he'd left their community. She needed to remember that.

Chapter 7

"And then, of course, McClusky told everyone to behave themselves in his store. That caused a commotion, I tell ya," Eli continued as Sam drove the three of them along the narrow, hilly lanes that made up the Amish community. After checking Winnie out from the hospital, they'd gone through a drive-thru for burgers, then started for the Lundy farm. And along the way, Eli had become a chatterbox, relaying neighborhood news with the exuberance of a gossipy maiden aunt.

"You know how McClusky is," Eli said, continuing. "Not much happens around here that he doesn't know about."

"Uh-huh." As Sam slowly curved the steering wheel right onto an unmarked street, he tried to remember who McClusky even was. But there was no use asking Eli to clarify things. Ever since they'd left the city and driven southwest toward the Amish communities, he'd become determined to fill Sam in on every momentous—and not so momentous—occasion that had happened over the last six months.

There'd been quite a lot of occasions. Sam appreciated the update. Truly, he cared about the people in this area very much but, nevertheless, felt removed, as if the people Eli were speaking of were characters in a story.

And though he'd been the one to leave, Sam felt uncomfortable about it. And a little guilty. He wasn't part of the Amish community anymore. This place was based on close family ties and sacrifices. Their parents both worked hard to see all their children's physical and emotional needs met. He felt selfish to have only thought of himself over the past couple of years.

"Don't forget to turn left at the Johnsons' place," Eli cautioned. "It's the house with the three flowering pear trees, Samuel."

Quickly Sam tapped the breaks and veered left. When Eli started up again about the day the trees were planted, Sam peeked in the rearview mirror.

Winnie was still sleeping. Her head listed to one side, her lips slightly parted. She looked peaceful.

For much of the drive, she'd dozed off and on. Sam couldn't help but glance her way every now and then. During his visits to her bedside, the two of them had begun to converse enough that he felt more comfortable with her than with any other woman of his acquaintance.

Winnie wasn't afraid to have opinions. She was smart, too, and he appreciated that. During their visits, she'd entertained him with stories about her friends and her new job at the antique shop. But unlike Eli's annoying chatter, Sam had been charmed. He enjoyed seeing the community through her eyes.

Likewise, she seemed to enjoy hearing stories of his job and students, so much so that he wondered if she secretly wanted to continue her education.

He fought a yawn as Eli prattled on. Oh, he enjoyed hearing about the community. And, he dearly loved his older brother. But sometimes Eli simply forgot that his life was far different. It was like Eli assumed Sam could step back into the community as if he'd never left. It wasn't quite so easy. He'd changed. He was different— and in some ways maybe not for the better.

Instead of the lifelong friends and relatives in Eli's world, like Jonathan Lundy and Henry Brenneman, Sam's circle of friends was far more wide and varied. Though he got along with them fine, some of their beliefs challenged all the things he'd held dear.

In addition, while much of Eli's activities revolved around the family's needs, Sam's focus remained steadily on himself and his work. He spent hours a day working on research grants, student curriculums, and developing new and innovative methods for growing. Some were fascinating and challenged his brain in all the ways he'd hoped they would back when he dreamed of learning everything he possibly could. Other problems felt so insurmountable that he longed for dull, everyday conversations like the ones he was having.

None felt as personal as Eli's struggles with Caleb.

So why was his mind drifting?

As he downshifted and passed a black buggy, he found himself looking for the driver the same as Eli, just in case they found a familiar face.

Maybe he hadn't changed as much as he thought.

Ten minutes later, they pulled onto the Lundys' driveway. When Sam saw the destruction of the barn, his mouth went dry. Next to the pretty white-board house, the blackness of the building was startling.

He turned away from the damage just as Katie and her girls came out to greet them.

Groggily, Winnie sat up. "We're here already?"

"We are, sleepyhead," he said, his heart melting a bit at her half-closed eyes.

Eli pulled open Winnie's door and carefully helped her slide to the edge of her seat just as Katie rushed forward, pushing a wheelchair.

Winnie groaned. "I don't need that."

"Sure you do. We borrowed it from the Johnsons'."

Winnie tried not to let her pain show by biting the inside of her cheek. Their busy morning had jarred her body something fierce. Tender skin under bandages stung and her leg ached painfully. Moving around was sure different than sitting in a hospital bed all day!

Katie kissed her cheeks. "Winnie, I'm so glad you're back. It's been terribly quiet without you."

"Aunt Winnie, I lost a tooth!" Hannah exclaimed, impulsively reaching in and hugging her tight. Though she did her best to hide it, her whole body jumped in agony.

"Careful," Sam called out before Eli or Katie could say a word. "Your Aunt Winnie might be out of the hospital, but she isn't all better yet."

Hannah stepped back and blinked quickly, obviously fighting tears.

Mary, her little seven- year-old shoulders squared and resolute, stepped forward. "Here, Aunt Winnie. Let me help you."

"We'll be careful with her," Hannah murmured by Mary's side, her expression contrite.

Sam's cheeks colored. "I know. I, um, didn't mean to snap."

Though she was in a wheelchair, Winnie did her best to smooth things over. "Sam, it's fine. Girls, I missed you, too. Let's go on inside, shall we?"

Visibly gathering her wits, Katie nodded. "Yes, let's go in." With the girls' help, she pushed Winnie's chair along the smooth path toward the kitchen door, where no stairs interrupted their way. Sam picked up her bag and walked beside Winnie, his presence feeling as solid and comforting as it had in her hospital room.

When they entered the spotless kitchen, Winnie breathed in the appetizing aroma and smiled. "Katie, something smells mighty good."

"We made you soup, Winnie! Pronto Potato Soup," Hannah cried out. "There's vegetables in it that Mary cut up."

"That's my favorite. I'll look forward to tasting it."

"I've got your bed all ready for you, Winnie," Katie said. "Let's get you settled, then I'll bring you some tea. Or would you rather have soup right away?"

"I most certainly do not want to sit in bed. I'd fancy sitting in the *Sitzschtupp* and enjoying a nice cup of tea, if you don't mind."

"That's a *wonderbaar* idea! We can show you our quilt!" Mary said.

"I canna wait to see it."

Hannah pulled on her skirt. "We can show you our new fabric, too. It's yellow and purple. I love purple."

Winnie laughed. Oh, their enthusiasm was so good to see. She'd been so lonely in that sterile hospital room. "I love purple, too."

Katie frowned. "Perhaps it would be better not to wear your aunt out—"

"They're not wearing me out in the slightest. I welcome the company—the days were long at the hospital. Though I did have Samuel's visits to look forward to, I did get mighty lonely."

Katie raised her brows. "You looked forward to seeing him?"

"Well, yes." As Sam's cheeks flushed, Winnie stumbled over her words. "I mean . . . I mean, he was so kind."

"I was glad to visit," Sam said. "Like I said, I work nearby."

Winnie rushed on. "Yesterday he brought me a movie to watch. And popcorn."

"Now isna that somethin'?" Katie murmured.

"I wanna go in the hospital now, too!" Mary exclaimed.

As Hannah chimed in, Winnie felt as if she was an awkward teen again. Sam looked uncomfortable and Katie looked as if she was doing all she could to mind her tongue—but had an awful lot to say. "Um, like I said, it's good to be home."

"Care for some tea before you get on your way, Samuel?" Katie asked.

"No, it's time I got goin'," Sam replied. "Eli and I were planning to talk about some growing techniques before we go out to the fields tomorrow. And Caleb is hopefully waitin', too." With a disgruntled expression, he added, "Eli says he hasn't been tending to his chores. I want to try and help persuade him."

When Katie and the girls left to get her some tea, Winnie found herself alone with Sam again. Now that they were back in familiar surroundings, she felt awkward and shy. Their differences seemed even more apparent than ever—as was the fact that things were changing.

There'd be no more movies or long talks about their pasts and dreams to look forward to. She'd heal up and continue helping Katie and Jonathan, and Sam would go back to his life among the English.

Once again, she would be the old maid. The woman who'd found a future in a job instead of with a man and family of her own. She tried to tease to cover up the lump in her throat. "Thank you again for everything, Samuel. I'll always be grateful for your time."

"It was nothing. Perhaps I—"

"Samuel, you ready?"

"Yes." Sam took a step toward Eli, to where he was waiting by the door. "I suppose I'll see you in three days' time. When I drive you to the doctor."

"I'll look forward to it." She tried to keep her voice even, to not betray how happy his offer made her. "I mean, that is, if you're sure you can spare the time."

"I told you I could. I didn't lie."

"I know."

They shared a meaningful look. One of humor and of melancholy. Winnie felt that same curious jolt between the two of them. It was getting more and more of a struggle to pretend she didn't wish their circumstances were different.

Then Katie and Eli walked Sam away, out of her life.

Sam was just about to walk out the door when Katie stopped him. "Samuel, before you leave we would be grateful for your advice."

"About what?" Sam asked.

"Jonathan and Katie think it was most likely an Amish teen who set the blaze," Eli explained.

Katie continued. "The elders recommended Jonathan not do anything, but that's tough advice for him to follow. We might do a little investigating on our own." Looking somewhat guilty, she added, "I know we're not supposed to, but I feel that whoever did this needs to take responsibility. Winnie was badly injured."

Sam wasn't sure what he could do, but he had a feeling he'd feel just as strongly about wanting to do something—anything to feel like he was a part of the solution. "Any idea why someone would do such a thing?"

"No."

"Then how are you—"

"We might ask around a bit." She shrugged. "I'm hoping it merely was an accident. But even if it was, someone needs to apologize, don'tcha think?"

A strong sense of foreboding encompassed him. He'd been so wrapped up in his feelings for Winnie, he'd pushed aside the fact that the Lundys' barn had been set on fire. With care, he said, "Do you suspect anyone in particular?"

Katie nibbled on her bottom lip. "No one in particular . . ."

"Let's not mention any names. It would be foolish to make rash guesses," Eli inserted quickly.

Sam turned to him in surprise. What was that about? "Who are you thinking of, Eli?" Though they'd discussed Caleb's flighty ways, surely Eli now didn't imagine he was the guilty one?

"No one."

"I don't have anyone specific in mind," Katie said with a sigh. "Eli's right. I don't want to start pointing fingers. But . . ." Her voice drifted off.

"Something needs to be done," Sam finished.

Eli nodded. *"Jah.* Something surely needs to be done."

"It's too hard not knowing what happened," Katie added with a shrug. "And, well, there's always the worry that whoever started the fire could start another one."

A cool shadow passed through Sam. His brother knew something. Katie was worried more than she'd let on.

Was there more to all of this than he'd imagined?

Once again, Sam realized how many ways he'd cut himself off from the Amish community. He'd forgotten something that was basic to their way of life—they weren't backward or ignorant about the ways of the world. Instead, they *chose* not to adopt certain lifestyles of the current society.

They still had problems and gossips and differences with each other. Kids still didn't think ahead. People still made mistakes. This world wasn't completely sheltered and perfect—no, in some ways, it was just as filled with flaws as any other society.

He'd forgotten that.

After the men had gone, Winnie watched her sister-in-law slice a thick wedge of zucchini bread then carry it to where she waited. Still warm from the oven, the scent of the spiced treat made her mouth water. Oh, it was so nice to be home! "Katie, this looks wonderful *gut*."

"I thought you might be ready for something fresh and homemade," Katie replied with a smile. "How was the hospital food?"

"Not so bad. I wasn't especially hungry anyway."

"Your burns are healing?"

"Oh, yes. They're much better. My foot is, too. In fact, the doctor said he might have released me yesterday, but he wanted me to stay off my feet as much as possible for another day."

"We'll make sure you stay off of them now, too."

"That's not necessary. I'm tired, but otherwise fit. I can't wait to go to work, both here and at the store."

"We'll see what your brother has to say about that."

"Catch me up on all that I've missed. Do you really fear it was someone in our community who started the fire?"

"I don't know for sure, but it's my feeling. Nothing else makes much sense. The English have many places to smoke—it's not even looked down upon all that much. In our community, however, that would be a different story."

Winnie frowned. "I hate to start naming kids, but I can't but help to think of possible people."

Lowering her voice, Katie murmured, "I've even suspected Caleb Miller."

Winnie felt as if someone had punched her in the stomach. They suspected Sam and Eli's brother? "Really?"

"He lives within walking distance," Katie pointed out. "Not all the other kids do."

"I suppose." Caleb had changed some over the years—and it was clear both Eli and Sam were worried about him. But to imagine him responsible seemed farfetched. "I'm sure this has been bothering Jonathan as well," said Winnie. "Have you scheduled a raising?"

"Not yet. Actually, I think he's been wondering if it would be possible to do the barn raising near Henry and Anna's wedding in May. We'll have lots of friends and family in for that."

"Many hands will make the work better."

"He doesn't want to steal Anna's and Henry's attention, though."

Sipping her delicious tea, Winnie nodded. "I wouldn't want to do that neither. Anna's waited a mighty long time for this day."

Katie nodded, delicately nibbling on her bread. "She has. She never said a word, but I got the feeling she was disappointed that Jonathan and I got married so quickly, even though everyone knew she had to do things in her own time." Wiping a crumb from her skirt, she looked to Winnie. "So, are you going to tell me about Samuel?"

"There's not much to tell."

"I think maybe there is." Grabbing a cloth, she smoothed it over the fine wood of the oak table. "I've seen you sneak a peek at him a time or two."

Her sister-in-law's statement embarrassed her. "I look at everyone, Katie."

Katie stopped dusting and frowned. "Don't get your feathers ruffled. I'm just stating what I've seen. Though Samuel is six years older, I recall that more than one girl was taken with him when we were all in the same schoolhouse."

Winnie remembered that, too. Just as she remembered how confused she'd felt when she'd learned that he wanted to move away from all of them. "Now it doesna matter what I think or what I notice. He's not one of us anymore, Katie. That's all that matters."

"That's true. Yet . . . it is a shame, though."

"Yes." Winnie wasn't ready to share her thoughts, but

they were there, perched on the edge of her tongue, plain as day.

Looking her over, Katie narrowed her eyes. "I think there was something between you two. A spark."

Winnie knew there was. She felt lit up like a lightning bug whenever he was nearby. But that didn't make her reality any different. He was not for her, and couldn't be.

And she was so tired of disappointment. For whatever reasons, she'd never been drawn to any of the men in her order. And her visit with Malcolm had only made her dreams for love and marriage seem unattainable. Malcolm had been so self-centered and full of himself. They'd have whole conversations about his family, his goals, and his dreams . . . and never once would he ever consider that she might want something, too.

Now, of course, she'd become attracted to the absolute wrong person. If she didn't stop daydreaming about Samuel Miller, all she'd be doing would be setting herself up for a good cry. Again.

Chapter 8

"Where've you been, David?" Caleb Miller asked as he raced to catch up.

David shrugged. "Around."

"Not very around." Caleb huffed a bit as they ran down a slope near the back of the Lundys' land toward Wishing Well Lake. "You weren't at McClusky's on Saturday or with everyone at the Brown Dog on Friday night."

"I've had chores and stuff," David said, hoping that would explain away his hands. They still looked raw and hurt. He'd taken to dodging most everyone who would notice, not wanting to risk giving an explanation.

But Caleb had been persistent and hard to resist. Since the weather was especially warm, they'd both decided to go fishing, and maybe even take a dip in the lake. Their chores were done, the sky was robin's egg blue, and they had three hours until twilight, when it would be time to rush home for dinner and to feed the animals.

After they hopped a freshly painted fence and walked past a group of dairy cows, Caleb added, "I looked for you at Sunday's singing."

He bent his head down so his friend wouldn't realize how much his words affected him. He didn't have many friends, and if it wasn't for Caleb, most likely no one would have noticed him missing. "I just didn't feel like goin'."

As was his way, Caleb accepted the reason without thinking about it twice. "Well, you sure missed a lot of talk."

"What about?"

"The Lundys' barn, of course."

He clenched his hands, glad Caleb wasn't looking at them. "What are people saying?"

Caleb didn't glance at him as he pushed aside a clump of long grass and led the way to the banks of the lake. "No one is any closer to figuring out who started the fire, but Jonathan's going to try and figure out who did it."

"Why?" he asked in a rush. "It was an accident."

Caleb stopped and looked his way. "Why would you say that?"

"I don't know. I mean, I thought that's what everyone was saying."

Caleb pulled out his fishing pole and opened up a jar filled with a good dozen night crawlers. "You're right. The fire inspector said arson is usually done a different way. Anyway, there're rumors that Jonathan Lundy might be going against Bishop Kropfs's wishes. No one knows what to think about that." After a good long pause, he said, "It's all kind of scary soundin', don'tcha think?"

He was so scared he thought he'd start crying like a baby. No one went against the bishop. Well, no one he'd ever heard of. "Why . . . why do ya think Jonathan is so determined?"

"My brothers were talking about it last night. I stood in the next room and listened. Basically, Sam and Eli say that Jonathan can't forgive the people who did this because they won't admit their mistakes." As if Caleb had just been talking about his math facts, he shrugged and pushed over the jar of night crawlers. "Take one and bait your hook. We ain't got all day, you know."

Dutifully, he pulled out a thick worm, stuck it on the hook, then cast off. "You know, maybe whoever started the fire never meant to do it."

Caleb rolled his eyes. "Of course the person had a reason."

"It could have just been an accident."

"Yeah, but if it was an accident, whoever did it would have admitted to it, don'tcha think? Jonathan Lundy would've gotten mad, but the person would have been forgiven."

"Sometimes it's not that easy."

"You're making it a whole lot harder than it has to be. It's our way to forgive—even if saying it and hearing it ain't easy."

"But—"

Caleb screwed up his face. "David, why are you quarreling about this? Whose side are you on anyway?"

"No one's. I'm . . . I'm just surprised someone would go against the bishop's wishes, that's all. My father says we're always supposed to mind our elders."

"Even when they're wrong?"

Especially when they're wrong. That's what faith was, right? But, as usual, he didn't say anything. He didn't dare go against Caleb—not when Caleb was his only good friend.

And, well, everyone liked Caleb Miller. If David got on his bad side, life would be even harder. "Never mind. Let's just fish, Caleb."

"Yeah. Sure."

Only the thought of hooking a big fish, big enough for Caleb to tell others about, gave David hope. That and the thought of how good fried catfish would be at supper.

"Just a little bit farther now," Henry Brenneman whispered in Anna's ear. "Careful now, mind the rock."

"Mind the rock! Oh, now that's quite a phrase for you to be saying, especially since I can't see a thing at the moment." Chills raced through her as he chuckled low and sweet against the nape of her neck.

Reaching out behind her, Anna reached for his hand. When his capable fingers curved around hers, she held fast. "It wasna necessary to blindfold me, you know. I would have gone wherever you wanted to guide me."

"I think differently."

She smiled even though she couldn't see his shining eyes. But even blindfolded, Anna knew he was pleased as punch. All morning he'd been staying close by her side. After they served guests, he'd invented a half-dozen reasons to stay in the kitchen far longer than normal. Why, he'd even helped her shake out the entryway rugs, something that he usually never ceased to avoid. Henry wasn't one for dust flying in his face. "So where are we going? And what is the occasion, please?"

"If I told you, it wouldn't be a surprise."

"Exactly!"

"Not one more word. Settle down, Anna. Just a few more steps. Trust me."

She did. She trusted Henry like no one else. With that in mind, she stopped fussing and put her hands in his and trusted.

Still holding one hand and taking comfort in the other that rested on her shoulder, Anna trudged on. Oh, the ground had never felt so rocky and difficult! Though her feet were encased in sturdy shoes, she still felt off kilter.

"Stop."

"Blindfold off now?"

Instead of replying right away, he merely slipped his fingers around the cloth and loosened the knot behind her head. "What do you see?" he whispered, his mouth close to her neck.

She blinked several times to allow her eyes to adjust.

And then she noticed the stakes on the ground. "Is this for our home?"

"It is." Eagerly, he pulled her along, showing her where their bedroom, kitchen, and family rooms would be. When he slowed to a stop, he stomped his foot. "And this will be our front porch. Anna, within a year, we'll be greeting the morning sun from this spot."

She turned in a circle and then turned again, this time spinning fast enough that the air flew up under her skirts and belled them out. She giggled at the thought of behaving like a schoolgirl. But that's what she felt like! Free and in love and happy. "It looks perfect, Henry."

Suddenly the emotion of all they'd been through caught up with her. "We're so blessed."

Triumph in his eyes fell away as he looked at her more closely. Reaching out, he gently wiped a tear away. "Why are you crying?"

"I don't know. I guess because for a while I thought all of this was never going to happen. I've been wondering why you never mentioned where you wanted to build."

"I've been too afraid."

"Afraid of what?" This was news to her. From the time she'd first moved to his home, Henry had always acted confident and assured.

"You, if you wanna know the truth."

Anna was dumbstruck. "You're not making any sense."

Stepping to the side, he reached for her hands. When

he held both securely within his own, he said, "Anna, you've given up so much. Sometimes, I know it's been particularly hard."

"It has, but I expected some things to be hard—they would have to be, don't you think? I mean, honestly, Henry, I was used to microwaving popcorn and zapping frozen dinners. But . . . but that doesn't mean my old ways were better. It's just taken some adjustment . . . and I have adjusted."

"I know you miss your music stations on the radio," he said, showing Anna that he'd truly listened to every story she'd told him about her past life. "I know you liked watching your soaps, too."

She fought a smile. "Believe me, I'm perfectly fine not watching *Days of Our Lives.*"

"I'm just sayin' that I wouldn't have been shocked if you had changed your mind."

"Changed my mind—Henry, did you really think I could just up and leave you?" Anna didn't even try to contain her surprise. After everything they'd been through, she would have thought Henry was the last person in the world to doubt her love for him.

"I didn't think you would do something without thinking, but I could imagine that one day running your own home without any electricity might be terribly hard." He cleared his throat. "I've never taken your efforts for granted, Anna. You've given up a lot for me."

"I've gained more than I gave up," she said, knowing that words could never completely describe the peace she'd found with the Amish, the confidence that now surrounded her because she knew she was not alone—she was walking with the Lord. "I told my mother that yesterday when she came out to visit." Slowly, she added, "And, you know what? I think Mom is realizing that. No longer is she worried about me missing credit cards and cell phones. She's thinking about how happy I am, and how secure and comfortable I feel with you. How our love is the most important thing to me."

"I'm glad you two are talking more."

"Me too." Anna didn't know if she and her mother would ever completely put past arguments behind them, but she did think that they'd reached an agreement. She'd even stopped complaining about Henry's Amish life and how unsuitable he was for Anna. Sometime during the last year, she'd seemed to understand Anna and Henry were a good match. That it was their differences that complemented each other, and made each of their rough edges smoother.

Anna was truly grateful for her mother's change of heart. "Oh, Henry, I can hardly believe we'll be married at the beginning of May."

"May is not a long way off at all."

"No, though sometimes it still feels like a lifetime."

Reaching out for her, he murmured, "Sometimes, I think that, too."

His pronouncement made Anna very happy.

Sam had never minded getting dirty. That was a good thing, since at the moment, he was knee deep in mud and manure. He and Eli had been plowing and prepping the soil for the spring alfalfa crop over the last week, and while he didn't necessarily mind it, he had a very good feeling that he'd never get the earthy smell out of his clothes ever again.

Two rows over, Eli caught sight of his face and laughed heartily. "You look like you've been rolling in mud and came up the loser."

"I feel like it."

"In another day or two we'll be done and the soil will be better for our effort."

"That doesn't mean I won't be happy to be clean for a bit, though."

"You city types," Eli teased.

Eli chuckled again, then got back to work, carefully raking the soil with as much care as if he was handling baby chickens.

Sam did the same, though his mind kept drifting to other things, such as the people in the community. Most of the conversations he'd been part of had centered on the Lundy farm.

He liked Jonathan Lundy and was eager to help him repair his barn. Jonathan had a good job at the lumber factory and therefore could only work on Saturdays. A group of men—Sam included—had decided to help dismantle the building. Next would come a month of Saturdays in preparation to rebuild, culminating in a barn raising.

"Is Jonathan still thinking about raising his barn around the Brenneman wedding?"

"I believe so. May is a *gut* time to work. The weather

will be warmer, and most of the planting will be done. Lots of men will be there to lend a helping hand." Straightening for a moment, Eli said, "It's a shame you won't be here for that."

"I'll try."

"Really? I thought you had to get back to the university."

"I do, but I want to do my part."

"You already have. No one will expect so much from you."

That bothered Sam more than he was willing to admit. Maybe because it was so true. No one here had ever accused him of not belonging, or for wanting to follow his dreams. Instead, they seemed to take his appearance in their lives the way they'd taken his leaving, with a shrug and a prayer that God had a plan for each of them.

Now that he thought of it, his English friends didn't treat him much differently. They were cordial and easy to work with. They respected his intelligence and his work ethic. But had they ever reached out to him in order to deepen their friendship?

More importantly, had he ever done that? As Sam felt his muscles expand and contract with the motion of his raking, he thought he never really had. No, more likely, he was constantly torn between two worlds, precariously balancing the views and values he was brought up with and the modern norms.

And there were quite a few modern conveniences he had enjoyed very much. Such as ESPN. He loved watching sports on television. He enjoyed baseball games and had become a fan of the Indians. He liked watching the college basketball games and rooting for the underdogs.

But was sports on TV all he needed?

"Let's clean up now, the sun's beginning to lay low."

"All right."

Sam walked his path, looking around with a sense of pleasure as he did so. His body felt worn, his mind free. He looked forward to a good meal and a solid night's sleep.

Those were the things that mattered. Not ambition and research papers.

Chapter 9

"Oh, would you look at that?" Sam said to Winnie as they passed the Oberlins' farm. "Benjamin's got a new pup. Think he's going to be a good farm dog?"

Winnie turned just in time to see a speckled dog with popped up ears tagging alongside Ben and his plow. She chuckled. "He'll be good if he learns to mind the horses. Ben's got a team of four out today. That's a lot of hooves for one small *hund* to look out for."

"I betcha before long that dog is going to be taking a rest in the sun and leaving the hard work to his master."

"I imagine so." As the farm faded from view, she turned her attention once again to Sam. He'd been kind enough to offer to drive her to the doctor that morning. And though he said he didn't mind the errand, she still felt a bit guilty. The trip back and forth to the medical center was sure to take the better part of a day. "I hope Eli could spare you today."

"He can, I promise. We've been plowing and preparing the fields since I arrived. We are both happy to take a break."

That was yet another thing she liked about Sam. No matter what, he seemed to have a pleasant disposition. She'd rarely heard him ever complain. "I'm hoping to get some good news today."

"I hope you will. It looks like your skin is healing."

"I'll have some scars, but it's a small price to pay."

"That's the right attitude, Win. Good job," he added, sounding very much like the teacher he was.

The traffic got thick. She was still nervous enough around the large tractor trailers to fall silent so Sam could concentrate on the many vehicles around them. But every time there was silence, she found herself thinking about how their lives might have been if Sam had never left.

Moments later, he pulled into a parking place. As he unbuckled his seat belt, he grinned at her. "Now, don't you go running off without me, Winnie Lundy. Your brother would have my hat if I didn't insist you sit in your wheelchair."

Her cheeks heated at his gentle teasing. "Go on with you now, Samuel. I don't have all day."

But underneath her gruff words, she held these moments close to her heart.

A few days later, Winnie's ears were filled with jubilant shouts. "They're here! They're here!" Hannah shouted before racing Mary down the hall and jerking the door open with a flourish.

"Careful now, Hannah," Winnie called out, but her warning was ignored. Not hard to understand, since it was she who was stuck in the wheelchair, not her nieces.

Winnie sat quietly and listened to the three Miller men enter and get greeted with a round of excitement. It was hard to tell whose voice was whose as a chorus of "Hi, Sam! Hi, Eli! Hi, Caleb!" rang out.

As Katie joined them and conversation flowed, Winnie slumped as she continued to listen. Being in a wheel-chair surely prevented her from being in the thick of things.

Slowly, she wheeled herself to the edge of the family room, so she could peek into the kitchen just enough to catch a bit of what was going on. Anything was better than seeing nothing.

After stomping their boots clean on the grate out-side, the men finally came in. While Eli merely waved a hello and Caleb made a beeline toward the tray of vegetables and dip laying on the counter, Sam walked toward her. Winnie noticed that same amused look that always seemed to lurk behind his eyes. "How is your foot today?"

Looking at her cast, Winnie shrugged. "The same. I can't wait to get this cast off. I feel like I'm a prisoner. All I can do is watch from the sidelines." She winced then as she heard herself. "I'm sorry," she said quickly. "I sound like a petulant child. I know you didn't come over here just to hear me complain."

But instead of being taken aback by her clumsy words, he sat down on the tile in front of the bare fireplace. "I came over here for meatloaf and mashed potatoes, if you want the truth."

That admission brought her out of her pity party and made her laugh. "Samuel, you came to the right place. Katie is a right fine cook."

He pushed stray locks away from his forehead. "So, what have you been doing?"

"Quilting. Katie and I are making a wedding ring quilt for Henry and Anna. And, well, the girls are working on place mats for the couple."

"I figured you wouldn't be restless for long."

"I have been, but I'm trying not to let it get me down." She shrugged. "I like being busy."

"I like that about you."

"Well, you must like all Amish women, then. We all do a fine job of keepin' busy."

He chuckled. "Winnie, one thing's for sure. You are sure to never run out of things to say."

Once again, her penchant for speaking her mind made her feel self-conscious. Winnie swallowed and tried to pretend she wasn't moved by his attention. But, just as when they'd been in the truck together, she was. Still conscious of his gaze settling on her, she pushed the conversation along.

"So, what is new with you?"

"I got a new teaching assistant to help with labs. Her name is Kathleen and she's sharp as a whip."

"Kathleen?"

"Yep." Sam's eyes shone as he continued. "You would get a kick out of her, Winnie. She asked more questions than anyone I've ever met. And she carries around enough books for three people."

In spite of her jealousy, she was intrigued. "Why so many?"

"When I asked, she said they were more useful than her computer! She's going to keep me on my toes, I tell you that. Some days I feel like I can hardly keep up with her, she's so smart. Yesterday afternoon, she questioned the validity of one of the experiments we were working on. That led everyone into a rousing discussion. Two boys almost started yelling."

"It sounds exciting." But, really, his words brought forth a feeling of doom. In her world, she felt as confident and smart as anyone else. But in Sam's college world, she felt like a *dummkopp*—a dunce. When he started talking about scientific methods and organic compounds, she was completely lost.

Sam just kept talking, lost in his musings. "It was incredibly exciting. It's moments like that when I remember why I got into teaching. There's nothing like a group of interested, active minds."

"I'm sure they like you, too."

"They will, until I grill them over the reading and question all of their methods and theories. Then I have a feeling they won't like me very much." He chuckled. "Having to justify a hypothesis is a difficult task to perform."

Once she filtered out all the fancy language, Winnie got to the heart of the matter. "Test-taking is part of learning, *jah*?"

Sam blinked, then smiled at her with dawning respect. "Of course, you're right. I forget just how sensible you are, Winnie. And forthright."

In spite of her best intentions to keep emotionally distant, Winnie was pleased. Rarely did people praise her for being sensible. In the past, most men she'd been interested in had preferred a more dreamy type of woman. They'd viewed her blunt way of seeing things as unfeminine. Of course, the only schooling she'd had was in the one-room Amish schoolhouse that he had been in, too. Like most other Amish, her formal schooling had ended at fourteen. After that, she'd focused on other important lessons, such as how to keep a good home.

"Sam, what are you doing?" Eli called out.

"Talking to Winnie."

"Well, come on over here, wouldja? Jonathan was just going to tell us about his plans for the new barn."

"You better go, the plans are exciting, to be sure," she said quickly when he hesitated.

"Okay." Standing up, he grasped the handles of her chair. "I'll push you into the kitchen. That way you won't have to be here by yourself."

"It's okay. I can move myself, and well, I've heard plenty about the barn plans. Go on."

As soon as he was out of sight, Winnie rested her head against the padded fabric of the wheelchair. Oh, but he made her heart race, he was so terribly good-looking. She liked the way he was interested and seemed to care about so many things. There always seemed to be a hint of mischief lying beneath his eyes, like he was thinking of so much more than he ever spoke aloud.

No, there was nothing plodding and quiet about Sam.

Once, at the hospital, she'd noticed a pair of women looking at him with interest. One had whispered to the other. After a moment, they'd both giggled. Winnie could only imagine the interest he inspired among the women at his college.

That new Kathleen was probably smitten with Samuel, too. Valiantly, Winnie decided that was good. After all, he would be a fine husband for some woman.

The door opened again. Moments later, the welcome voices of Anna and Henry joined the throng. To her pleasure, both Katie and Anna soon left the kitchen and joined her.

"We couldn't take that conversation a moment longer," Katie said as soon as she sat down. "Plans and more plans. Those men are excited about every nail!"

"Henry's acting as if it is *his* dream barn they're fixin' to construct! These men are planning for it to be double the size and twice as sturdy."

"It's too bad Sam and Eli's parents aren't here," Winnie said. "They'd help settle everyone down. Mr. Miller always has been the voice of reason."

"I don't think even Mr. Miller could settle this talk down," Katie murmured. "Eli can't seem to stop talkin' about a bigger tack room, a work shed, and even a storage area for the house." She paused. " 'Course, a storage area might come in handy. There's never enough space in the kitchen."

"Don't get roped in," Winnie advised. "If you give those men any encouragement, they'll never stop the plans."

"Like they would even think about listening to us."

Anna rolled her eyes. "What do we know anyway?"

Katie puffed up her chest. "Nothing about barn building, only about keeping a home."

"And we all know that is nothing like organizing a fine barn."

Unable to stop herself, Winnie erupted into giggles, and her friends joined in. "Soon enough, the men will be having to help us with wedding plans. I'm so glad you aren't going to delay the wedding, Anna."

"I am, too, though I've been concerned about doing the right thing." With a worried look at Katie, Anna murmured, "Are you sure you don't mind a celebration in the middle of so much chaos? I feel awfully selfish."

"No one would accuse you of being selfish, Anna," Katie said. "You've put a lot of your own needs to the side time and again. It's time to put yourself first."

Anna's gaze softened before murmuring, "Henry's worried about the timing of the wedding, too."

"He shouldn't worry, and neither should you," Winnie said. "Whether you get married or not, it won't change what already happened. Now we'll get to have something to look forward to."

"And we need a celebration soon," Katie said. "Too much doom and gloom will only keep us up at night."

Anna looked at Katie. "Your mother said the same thing."

Katie chuckled. "More and more, I fear I am sounding like my mother. Who would have ever thought!"

Anna turned to Katie. "How is Jonathan holding up?"

Katie paused. "I think the mystery of who started the fire is bothering Jonathan more than he lets on. His heart and mind want him to forgive and forget, but how can he if no one claims responsibility?"

"Maybe we can help?" Anna ventured.

"How?" Winnie asked. "I don't know who we would even talk to."

Katie nibbled her bottom lip for a moment, then spoke. "Winnie, remember how we used to go to the Weavers' home for singings?"

"*Jah*. They were a wonderful couple." Looking at Anna, Winnie explained. "Often a family will host singings for the community's teenagers on Sunday evenings. It's a time for young people to get a chance to be together and have fun."

Anna scowled. "And what do singings have to do with us?"

"I think we ought to host a few singings and visit with the kids a bit. We might learn something," Katie said practically.

Winnie's eyes danced. "It will be like we are playing detective."

"That could be dangerous," Anna warned. "Whoever set the barn on fire has got to be feeling guilty. Plus, what will we do if we do find out who did it? Tell the authorities?"

Katie sighed. "I haven't thought that far ahead. All I know is that it's hard to forgive someone who hasn't sought forgiveness. And I think Jonathan needs that." Katie shrugged. "Besides, he doesn't have time to ask questions of people. He's working at the lumberyard, and at tearing down the barn."

"Henry is busy, too. We've had a lot of guests at the inn."

"Eli's got planting and Caleb to watch," Winnie added. "And Sam . . ." Winnie stopped, feeling self-conscious, especially when Katie looked at her curiously.

"Yes?"

"Nothing. I was just going to say that I'm sure Sam has a lot to do, too."

"Of course he does. He's busy with things at his college. And his own life—right?" Anna said the last as a question.

"Yes. Well, I mean, I suppose." But wouldn't it be wonderful if he wanted to stay with them? Wouldn't it be something if his life was right there in their community, too?

"Sam is a good man," Katie said slowly, but with a tone edged in steel. "I'm glad he's been so helpful. But he's not really one of us any longer. We can't expect him to drop everything and help us build a barn."

No matter what happened in the future, Winnie knew Sam had become a part of her world. Again. "He may not live here with us, but I know he still cares. It's not like he is shunned."

"That is true," Katie agreed slowly. Without even trying to be subtle, she glanced over her shoulder toward the kitchen door. "And he did stop by today. That is new."

After glancing at the door as well, Anna turned to Winnie, her eyes narrowing with speculation. "He sure is a handsome man, isn't he?"

"I only have eyes for Jonathan, but I do have to admit that I've always liked his sunny personality," Katie said.

"He's been a good brother to Eli and friend to Jonathan, visiting me like he did in the hospital."

With a mischievous smile, Anna said, "Are you sure he only visited you for his brother?"

"Of course."

"Oh."

And Winnie felt bad. After all, she knew exactly what she was doing—shutting out her friend. But it couldn't be helped. She couldn't entertain the feelings in her heart.

There wasn't anything anyone could do.

Winnie had finally fallen hard, and now that she realized that there was nothing she could do in order to make things better, she was going to have to resign herself to a life alone.

Perhaps she would soon find greater value in her work, or in simply being an aunt instead of a mother.

But she didn't think so.

Chapter 10

Everything was going too fast. The rumors and talk were snowballing into a big heap of trouble that couldn't be escaped.

And David had surely tried.

But there was no avoiding the talk and gossip. Everywhere he looked, people were speculating about the cause of the fire and how the Lundys weren't about to give up. Jonathan's struggle to forgive whoever had started the fire was a cause of much discussion.

Men and boys alike were finding it hard not to take sides. Some thought Jonathan was right to have dug in his heels like he had. After all, someone had to take responsibility for the fire, it was the right thing to do. Others thought Jonathan had lost sight of the Bible's teachings and of the *Ordnung* as well. Compassion and forgiveness were qualities to be proud of, not something to be ignored when the timing wasn't right.

It had been hard to stay out of all the discussions, but he had done his best.

And still, David's hands wouldn't heal. Sores had formed on his burns, stinging and scabbing. They made the most menial tasks an effort and filled with pain. Almost every night, he'd taken to soaking his hands in warm water, hoping and praying for the skin to mend. But it was as if the Lord wasn't listening to him . . . or perhaps He was making him pay for his lies and secrets.

"David, you done cleaning the stalls yet?"

No matter how hard he tried otherwise, David always found himself flinching the moment he heard his *daed*'s rough voice. "Yes."

"Come over, then."

After putting aside the rake and removing the soiled hay from the premises, he rushed to meet his father, who was looking at him impatiently.

"I don't know what is taking you so long these days. And let me see those hands of yours."

Dutifully, David held out his palms, concentrating on keeping his face expressionless as he flattened them out. But oh, how they ached and burned.

To his surprise, his father looked concerned. "They are in a bad way. How come they are so ripped up? What did you do?"

"I don't know."

"Sure you do. No one hurts hands like that and doesn't know what happened. What did you do? The truth, now."

The truth. Oh, how his father loved asking for honesty.

But everyone in the family knew from experience that the only truthfulness Amos wanted to hear were words that didn't upset him.

But . . . David also knew the Lord wanted him to speak of the truth, too. Maybe if he finally admitted what happened, his hands would start to heal, and the sleepless nights that plagued him would be a thing of the past.

"David?"

"I . . . Well, you see . . ."

"Stop your sputtering. Speak like a man."

Here was his chance. If he'd been braver or smarter or more confident, David knew he would have seized the moment and told all. But he was afraid of his father. He didn't trust him. Too many times, he'd met with a sharp comment or quick hand for speaking without thinking.

Now David made sure he never did that. Quickly he made up a story. "I was mending one of the back fences and cut my palms on the barbed wire. It's nothing."

Reaching out, his *daed* gripped his hand and looked at it more closely. David's pulse raced. Was it obvious that the sores were from burns not cuts?

"Did your mother look at them?"

"No. There was no need. I'm fine."

After eyeing his face another long moment, his father pointed to a basket laden with baked goods. "I want you to take that basket to the Lundys' for your mother."

"What?"

The burst of surprise earned him a sharp look. "I said, take that basket to the Lundys', and be quick about it. Your mother has been in a charitable mind. She's been baking for Jonathan and his family morning, noon, and night. Go take it over now."

Slipping on his straw hat, David nodded, then hurried to comply. He'd just picked up the basket and started toward Palmer, their sorrel, when his father's voice cracked through the quiet. "And David?"

"*Jah?*" He didn't turn around.

"Don't be so foolish with the fencing again. I'm to be needin' every available hand to help with the planting. You should know better."

"I learned from my mistake," David murmured. "It won't happen again."

David couldn't believe he was at the Lundys' again. In the broad daylight, the burnt cinders of the barn made him feel terribly ill and queasy.

"David Hostetler?" little Mary Lundy called out from the front porch. "Is that you?"

"Where's Katie? I mean, your *mamm*?" David still sometimes had to remind himself that Katie Brenneman was Mrs. Lundy now.

"She's inside. Go on in."

David stared at the shut door. To him, that door seemed to symbolize everything that he'd been trying to do—put up as many obstacles as possible so he wouldn't have to face the consequences.

Mary scampered off her chair and with a swift turn

of the wrist, flew open the door and raced inside. After a second, she peeked out again. "You comin' ain'tcha?"

"*Jah.*" Once in the kitchen, the heavenly aroma of baked ham and stewed apples floated over him. "Mrs. Lundy, I've a basket for you from my *mamm.*"

"She's such a dear." Katie slipped the basket on the counter, then linked a hand around his elbow. "I just baked a ham. How about a snack?"

Though the ham did smell enticing, he couldn't leave fast enough. Pushing his hat back, David shook his head. "No. *Danke*, I've gotta get back."

Her eyes widened at the sight of his hand. "Whatever happened to you?" She reached out and snatched a hand before he could even think. "Oh, my! You have an infection!"

"I'm fine."

"I think not. Come here by the sink and we'll try to doctor you up a bit."

"I don't want—"

"She likes doing things her way," Mary chirped up. "You'd best just let her do it."

"Mary's right," Katie said as she pulled out a hand and guided him closer. "Now, come here, and let me see if I can help."

David thought his heart would stop beating when Katie clasped his right palm, clucked over the swollen areas, opened a jar of ointment, then gently rubbed some over each wound. "How did you get so hurt?"

He claimed the same lie. "Barbed wire."

"This is *gut* medicine for burns, but I think it will help cuts, too."

Before he could say another word, she pulled out a clean strip of linen and hastily wrapped his hand. "Keep them wrapped up, David. It will hold off the infection."

"Yes."

After doing the same with his other hand, she spooned another bit of ointment into a leftover jelly jar. "Put this on morning and night and your cuts will be better in no time."

Backing toward the door, he said, "I've gotta go." Turning, he fled the confinement of the Lundys' kitchen as quick as his feet would take him.

And had the bandages off well before he unsaddled Palmer.

Sam made the drive from Eli's home to his college campus in under an hour, which felt like a minor miracle. Sometimes the traffic on I–71 got so congested it reminded him of a colony of ants, with everyone simply marching along.

After parking in his assigned spot, he nodded to a few students he recognized around the central fountain, bypassed the library commons area, and hightailed it into the agricultural building.

However, there was nothing otherworldly about the commotion that greeted him once he walked to his department's offices.

"Hi, Professor Miller!" Zach, one of his students who

worked in the office, called out. "I'm taking a message, but I'll be off the phone in just one sec."

"No problem." Standing in front of Zach's desk, Sam found that he needed a moment to adjust to the noise and commotion. Phones rang, music blared, and everywhere he looked students were standing in twos and threes and talking as loud as possible.

Once, he used to find the activity and noise energizing. Now, especially after spending the morning with his Amish friends and family, all the noise and lights seemed annoying. Almost unnecessary and distracting from what was really important to him.

With a click, Zach set down the phone. "Sorry"—before Sam could say a word, the student rushed on—"Professor Miller, this place has been going crazy. And you've gotten so many messages and papers, there's hardly an empty inch on your desk."

"I was only gone a week. I couldn't have that many messages, surely."

"You do. Once more, everything's been slowly falling apart." Lifting up a stack of slim yellow papers, Zach frowned. "First off, you've got about twenty-five messages to return, not to mention all the notes here from students wanting to speak with you."

"Any reason why?"

"They want to know if you've graded their latest quizzes."

"I haven't."

"Don't tell them that, they're nervous wrecks," Zach said, clicking open a screen on his computer.

"I'll tell the kids they're going to have to wait a few more days. I've had some family commitments."

That stopped Zach's fingers. "I've never heard you mention your family before."

"Well, I have one," he replied wryly.

"I'm sorry how I sounded. It's just that I've never heard you speak of your family. Do they live nearby?"

"About an hour east."

"Is everything okay?"

"Yes, they um, just needed a hand. A sister of a friend was in the hospital and they needed a translator. And someone to look after her."

"A translator?"

"Yes. My family is Amish."

"Amish? Like the old-fashioned people?"

Thinking of how well Eli was juggling spring planting, helping with the Lundy barn, and looking after Caleb by himself, Sam chuckled. "You'd be surprised at how forward thinking they can be."

"You know what I mean. I mean, don't they wear hats and white caps and long skirts and ride around in buggies and stuff?"

"Yes." It made Sam uncomfortable to hear his whole family's way of life reduced to funny clothes and transportation methods. But, well, that's part of why he'd always been reluctant to tell people he'd grown up Amish, wasn't it?

Zach turned completely his way, work forgotten. "So, a translator, huh? What do you guys speak?"

"We speak English."

He waved a hand. "Come on, Professor. You know what I mean. Don't they or you speak another language, too? Dutch?"

Well, obviously he was going to have to talk about this, even if he didn't want to. "The Amish speak Pennsylvania Dutch, but it's a derivative of German, not Dutch. But everyone learns to speak and write in English as well." Before Zach could ask any more questions, Sam said, "I'll go get busy. Sounds like we don't want to get any further behind."

"No, we don't." Zach looked at him curiously, then shook his head. "So, what do you want me to tell the people who call this afternoon? Are you scheduling visits and taking appointments, or would you rather Kathleen handled the bulk of them?"

"I'll see students. Kathleen's bound to be ready for a break." Approaching the students milling around outside his office door, he said, "Sorry, guys, I don't have the quizzes graded yet."

"Can't you just tell us how we did?" one asked.

"I mean it—I really haven't had a moment to grade anything. I had some family commitments to take care of."

The same blank stares met him that Zach had used just a few moments ago. "You all go on, now. I'll post the grades as soon as I can."

With a few grumbles, the students turned and walked away. "I didn't know Professor Miller had a family," one whispered.

And that was the problem, Sam realized. Over the

last few years, he'd been so intent on his work, he'd done little else. Now he was paying for it.

Suddenly feeling overwhelmed, he unlocked his office door and turned on the light. "I'll be in all afternoon and tomorrow," he turned and said to Zach.

"I'll pass that on." Finally looking mollified, Zach added, "Do you need anything, Professor?"

"Sure. Order in a couple of sandwiches and soda when you get time, okay?"

"Italian club?"

"Sure," he replied as he wandered into the sanctity of his office.

But it didn't feel homey at all. Instead, it felt like it often did on Fridays, when he was anxious for the weekend to begin. The room felt small and confining. Dark and claustrophobic. Utilitarian and serviceable. Its lack of window made him feel like he was working in a glorified janitor's closet.

What was even more vexing was the idea that he'd been happy here for quite a while. Correction—he'd been trying to make himself happy here. But perhaps that had been like trying to fit a square peg in a round hole.

He'd just sat down when the phone rang. Instead of waiting for Zach to screen the call, he picked it up himself. "Miller."

"Professor, I'm worried about my internship," Andrew Thrust said in a rush. "No one's contacted me yet."

"I'll look into it. As far as I know, they haven't made any decisions yet. I'll call you next week."

"But what if they don't accept me? I need this in the worst way."

"I know. Hang in there, Andrew. What's meant to be will happen."

"Oh. Um, well thanks, Professor. You're the best."

He'd just hung up when the phone rang again. Now he was feeling a little bit sorry for Zach. No wonder the guy was looking so ragged. "Miller."

But instead of another question or demand, it was the sweetest voice ever on the other end of the line. "Samuel?"

"Winnie. Hi." He didn't even try to hide the concern he was feeling. "Is everything okay?"

"Oh. Yes. I had just heard you left this morning. I um, wondered if you made it back all right. I hope you don't mind my calling on the telephone."

"No. I don't mind at all." Actually, her concern made him smile for the first time all day. It had been a long time since anyone had worried about him and let him know it so transparently. It had been even longer since he'd felt so pleased that someone cared. "I just walked into my office a few minutes ago. The drive was not a problem at all. Where are you? I know you can't be calling from home."

"I'm actually at the Brennemans'. Mrs. Brenneman was kind enough to let me help out at the inn today. I'm helping with some mending and ironing. It's one of the few things I can do while sitting down."

"I'm glad you're not alone." He'd been coming to realize that Winnie was so self-sufficient, it was unlikely that she'd ever make an issue of being bored or lonely. But she still would feel those things.

"I'm glad, too. I'd like to feel helpful and not a burden for a change." After a long pause, she chuckled. "I'm sorry, it just occurred to me that you must be terribly busy, and here I am, chattering on about nothing. I'll let you go."

He hadn't thought she was chattering at all. And, in fact, he found the pleasant way she had about speaking calmed his nerves and lifted his spirits. It put everything in perspective. Just hearing her positive approach to responsibilities made him rethink the dozen things on his to-do list. Perhaps now he wouldn't look at them as simply burdens, but opportunities. "I'm glad you called. Perhaps when I come back to help Jonathan with the barn we'll see each other again."

"Oh, yes. When will that be?"

"In a week or two, I'm thinking. But if Eli needs more help in the fields, I might come back sooner."

"I'm glad. Oh! I mean, it will be nice for Eli to have that help, you know."

How long had it been since he was around a woman who didn't even try to hide her feelings? "I think it will be nice, too."

"Well . . . I best get going."

"Thanks for calling, Winnie. I'll visit you when I go see Eli."

"Yes. Well, *dats gut.*"

After he hung up, Sam found himself staring at the phone, and wishing that he was sitting across from

Winnie instead of just being surprised to hear her voice.

Her words were so full of expression. She had no need to hide her emotions. It made everyone else seem too guarded.

He hoped she really was healing as well as she said she was.

"Professor Miller," Zach called out, bringing back reality. "Aaron Knight is on the phone. Can you meet with him now?"

"Sure. Tell him to come on over." He might as well do his best to adopt Winnie's attitude and be thankful for his work. After all, it would keep him busy until he could see her again.

Chapter 11

"Were we just as boisterous and noisy during our sing-ings?" Winnie whispered to Katie as they watched the crowd of teens congregate in the front of the Bren-neman's Bed and Breakfast. "I don't remember being so rowdy, but maybe we were."

Katie grinned. "Oh, we were."

As one boy told a joke and the rest of the assemblage roared in laughter, Winnie frowned. "Truly? I seem to recall being more circumspect."

"You weren't." Loud laughter mixed with taunts and jokes as the kids went about building a bonfire that Henry was loosely supervising. Katie leaned closer to be heard. "However, I will admit that they seem to be gettin' louder with every passing minute."

"Do they seem too loud?" Anna asked as she walked over to join them. Eyes dancing, she said, "They don't seem bad, just like they're having fun." As one girl visibly flirted with a brown-haired boy, Anna chuckled. "It all looks pretty tame. When I think of the things I was doing at sixteen and seventeen, I feel like cringing. I wasn't at friends' houses either."

"Where did you spend your free time?" Winnie asked. Though Anna didn't speak about her English life too often, Winnie enjoyed hearing stories about the things she did.

"Anywhere there weren't watching eyes. Friends' cars. Movie theaters, parks." Her eyes lit up. "Shopping malls. Oh, I loved to go shopping."

"These kids are doing that, too, sometimes you know. Remember, most have started their *rumspringa*," Katie said.

"I betcha kids are the same, no matter where they are," Winnie mused. "I went to plenty of these singings and all I seem to remember is feeling the need to yell and laugh and be as loud as possible. Ach, what a time we had. I'd forgotten how special it was."

Anna frowned. "Now, here's something I've been wanting to ask, but haven't had the nerve. If it's called a singing, how come I don't hear any music?"

"Oh, Anna. Sometimes people sing, but mostly singings are just an excuse to have a good time with everyone. In the fall, there are bonfires and hay rides. Winter brings sledding and ice skating in the moonlight. Spring and summer, long walks and picnics."

Anna shook her head. "It sounds like fun. It's too bad more English teens aren't as satisfied with such wholesome pursuits."

"Don't let the clothes fool you," Winnie warned. "These teens are feeling the same things any other teens in America are . . . restless."

Katie crossed her arms over her chest. "Which brings us to our reason for being here. Who do you think is our likely smoker?"

Winnie scanned the crowd, but to her eye, no one looked any different than they usually did. "No telling by standing here. I suppose it's time we all went out and mingled. We'll only learn by asking questions."

Anna raised a brow. "And hope someone mentions setting fire to your barn?"

"Try not to be that obvious," Katie said before stepping down the stairs and joining a group. Within seconds, she was chatting up a storm with all the teenagers, looking for a moment no older than the teens surrounding her.

"Boy, she's good," Winnie said.

"That's Katie. On the outside, she looks to be the easiest person in the world to know. So sweet and merry, too. I always pity the person who assumes there's not much more to Katie than pretty cheeks and beautiful blue eyes."

Winnie chuckled. "I may not have her eyes, but I've got crutches and an injury to play up. And you, Anna, have the best thing of all to discuss."

"What's that?"

"The most perfect topic in the world for a crowd of teenagers who ache to be in love—a wedding!"

Anna beamed. "That's right! I do."

They mixed in with the kids. Sure enough, the girls did enjoy speaking with Anna about wedding plans.

Before they knew it, though, everyone was also interested in her past life. A few kids asked questions about high school and college, about malls and movies and things of the outside world.

Anna answered readily, and then to Winnie's amazement, she started talking about how she'd tried smoking when she was a teen.

Winnie kept a sharp eye on everyone's reactions. But no one seemed either particularly interested or surprised by Anna's revelations. The girls just shrugged and asked instead about rumors they'd heard of people piercing their belly buttons.

But then, just as they were about to give up their pitiful efforts of detective work, Winnie noticed one boy looking at Caleb Miller in alarm. It took a moment to place his name. He was quiet, somewhat shorter than most others, and usually stayed in the background during gatherings. But his strawberry blond hair triggered a memory and she knew at once who he was—David Hostetler.

All Winnie knew about the family was that there were a great many *kinner*—eight or nine, and that Mr. Hostetler was terribly determined to embrace only old ways. He'd always seemed strict, too. Winnie had rarely seen him laugh or make jokes like her father often did.

Just as she decided to walk over to see why David

looked so ill at ease, two boys asked for more lemonade. Moments later, David was gone.

David walked as quickly as he'd been able to the back field. As soon as he'd felt safe, he crouched down and tried to catch his breath, but it was hard, he was shaking so badly. Katie Lundy knew. *She knew.*

Otherwise, there's no way she'd have asked the questions she did.

"David, are you okay?" Caleb Miller asked. "You raced out of the gathering so quick—like, I thought you were gonna get sick or something."

"I'm fine. I just had to be by myself for a second."

When Caleb's eyes widened and he backed up a step, David fumbled over his words again. "I mean, I didn't know anyone had seen me leave. But you can stay, if you want."

Around them, the earth smelled fresh and new. Freshly plowed. Alive and rich. Much of the dark rows looked the same as their farm. And because he knew just how hard it was to keep things looking good, David walked toward the edge of the land. Once safely on the side, they both sat down.

"So, what's wrong? You look like you saw a ghost."

"Nothin's wrong. I just didn't like how Katie was staring at me."

A line formed between Caleb's brows. "Like how?"

"Like she knew something bad about me."

"What would she know? And who cares anyway? All we're doing is bein' kids."

"No, this was different. I think she was staring at me because she thought I did something wrong." With a sinking feeling, he was sure everything in his life was about to fall apart. "She's going to go make up something to my father and I'm going to get punished."

"You need to stop worrying and get out more." Caleb laughed. "Why were you staring at her anyway? I thought you liked Krista."

"Krista wasna paying attention to me. She's all eyes for the older boys all of a sudden."

"Well, if Katie was looking our way, I bet it was because she remembered how I used to follow her around like a puppy. That's my secret," Caleb said, tucking his chin to his chest for a moment. "I used to fancy myself in love with her."

"She's old."

"*Jah*, but she's pretty."

"She's a lot older."

Caleb shrugged. "Not that much. Anyway, I never thought anything would happen between me and her—I'm just saying that I used to have a little crush on her."

Taking a chance, David murmured, "I think she knows I've been smoking."

Caleb's eyes widened. "Truly? Why do you think that?"

"I saw . . . I saw her looking at me while Anna was talking about all that."

"About what?"

He could hardly say the words. "About when, you know . . . the barn burnt down. The fire officials said it was from someone smoking. When she looked at me, it was like Katie Lundy knew I'd been doing something I wasn't supposed to." He swallowed hard, wanting to also tell Caleb about how she'd doctored his hands, but didn't dare. If Caleb knew the truth about him, he'd tell on him, for sure.

"Well, we know you weren't the one who started the fire, so what does it matter?"

"I'm afraid she's going to say something to her husband or to my parents."

"That's not too bad, is it?" Caleb shrugged. "Who cares if she did think you were smoking anyway? I know even my brother Eli tried it once or twice, and he's practically perfect. I don't know about Samuel, but I betcha he's done all kinds of things out there among the English."

"You don't know what would happen if my father found out. He'd be really mad."

"Hey? Why are you so worried? You stopped smoking anyhow. I heard you tellin' the guys how you didn't care about smoke rings no more." He paused, looking at him more closely. "At least, I thought you stopped. Didn't you?"

"Sure I stopped." Suddenly, he knew he had to ask for a favor. "Caleb, I stopped, but I still got the cigarettes and stuff. I don't have a safe place to throw them out. Would you mind if I gave them to you?"

Caleb lifted a hand in protest. "I don't want all that. What am I gonna do with them?"

"My *daed* hardly lets me go anywhere. And there're eight kids in my house. I'm never alone. Not like you." Thinking quickly, he said, "I was hopin' that maybe if I gave you my lighter and pack of cigarettes you could get rid of them for me."

Caleb bit his lip. "I don't know . . ."

"I wouldn't ask you if there was anyone else." Oh, he was so ashamed. "But there isn't. Would you take them from me? I could drop them over at your house tonight."

"Tonight?"

"Yeah. Sometimes I sneak out."

"Then you get rid of it."

"You can't just toss those things in a field or something. They've got to be gotten rid of somewhere away from here. Like McClusky's store."

"I don't know."

"It's been weeks since I had any free time to go to Mc-Clusky's. I've got no one else to ask, Caleb. Please say you'll do this."

A strange look fell over Caleb's face. "Sure," he mumbled in a rush, his eyes now darting around like he was nervous to be seen with David. Uncomfortable. "Go ahead and give them to me."

"When? Later on tonight?" Thinking quickly, he said, "We can leave now and I'll give you the lighter."

"No. By the time the singing's over, my brothers will be looking for me."

David was so eager to get those things out of his life, he pushed a little more. "Tomorrow night?"

"Ah. Yeah, sure." Caleb stepped away. "I'm gonna go now." A new look shone in his eyes. Worry and trepidation. Fear.

"I guess I'm just acting crazy." David tried to smile, but he knew it came out sickly. He'd pushed too hard and now Caleb distrusted him. "I'll walk back to the party."

Caleb's eyes cleared. "Okay." Bumping his shoulder in a friendly way, Caleb added, "When we get back, I dare ya to go over and talk to Krista and her friends."

"She won't want to talk to me."

"Sure she will. If you hadn't been so worried about Katie Lundy looking at you, you would've seen her interest. Come on, why don'tcha? The singing's almost over. If we wait much longer, we'll have to wait a whole 'nother week to make plans."

"You go first."

"All right. My *daed* said I could start using the courting buggy. I mean to use it for courting, too."

Their pace quickened as they walked toward the others.

But though his pace was strong and purposeful, David still couldn't stop shaking. He hadn't liked how Katie Lundy had looked at him, and worse, he was scared to death of facing the reality of what he almost did. He'd almost admitted to Caleb that he'd been in her barn.

Caleb nudged him. "Come on, don't keep standing

over here by the tree, looking like you're trying to hold it up. There're too many pretty girls over here to talk to. Let's go see if they want to go walking with us."

"I'll be there in a minute."

Suddenly Caleb looked worried. "Some are looking at us. Come on, David, I don't wanna go over there by myself."

"I mean it, go ahead."

"I hope you figure things out soon," he said over his shoulder in obvious disgust. "I'm going. If Krista goes out walkin' with me, don't be mad."

"I won't."

Caleb didn't wait another moment. Sure enough, he sauntered over to the girls, all full of smiles. Before long, one of them was walking by his side, gazing at him in happiness.

Caleb had it so easy. He was good-looking and strong, and a whole year older. His family laughed, and he even had a brother who was smart, so smart he became a professor or something.

David Hostetler was none of those things. His body didn't seem to want to grow. He was flustered around girls.

He hated his life at home.

All he had was the ability to make smoke rings.

And now he couldn't ever tell another person about it.

"You're looking mighty dreamy-eyed, Anna," Irene Brenneman said when she found her on the porch two evenings later.

Anna started. "I'm sorry. My mind went wandering."

"Thinking about the wedding?"

"Yes. And the fact that my parents will be coming to visit for two days."

To her surprise, Irene joined her on the top step, moving the bowl of sugar snap peas Anna was shelling. "I'm looking forward to getting to know your parents better, Anna. Each time they've visited, I've come to see a lot of them in you."

Anna liked how Irene had phrased that. She liked imagining that she'd inherited good qualities from her parents, despite the fact she'd chosen a lifestyle drastically different from theirs. "They are nice people. Good people."

"And you are a wonderful girl."

Irene's compliment warmed her heart. Henry was a fine man, and Anna imagined Irene and John had harbored their share of doubts about Anna's suitability for him. "They might be a little demanding. They aren't used to this lifestyle."

"Then they came to the right place, hmm? We are, of course, a bed and breakfast. We cater to all sorts of English. Don't worry so. John and I will make them welcome."

Anna slowly turned to Irene. "Are you sure you're okay with me marrying your son? After all, my past—"

"*Jah.* I am sure."

"But perhaps you should know—"

Irene cut her off again. "I don't need to know more than I do now, Anna. We all have checkered pasts. Even me."

"Even you?"

With a hint of humor, Irene's eyes sparkled. "Well, some pasts might be a bit more checkered than others, but what's important is what is between you and the Lord. It all comes back to the Lord, Anna."

Pulling the bowl closer, Anna murmured, "I'll get these beans done for supper."

With a sigh, Irene pulled herself up to her feet. "I suppose I must get to work, too. I've hired two girls to come help me clean today. Watch out for them, will ya? I don't want to see them yakking away in the guest rooms when there's woodwork to be oiled."

"I'll keep a close eye on them, for sure." Digging her hands into the cool nest of beans, Anna grabbed another pod and broke it cleanly.

And as she thought about Irene's words, and how God was looking out for all of them, even in the darkest of days, she reflected how much better she felt. How much more at peace she was living the Amish ways. It was like she was made for this lifestyle all along. And all the hardships she had gone through in the past were directing her to this place, and the man that she loved.

Closing her eyes, Anna said a prayer of thanks. Yes, things were so much easier when she remembered she wasn't alone. And never had been.

Chapter 12

Now that she wasn't in so much pain, Winnie was settling into her old routines. Though she was anxious to go back to work at the store, she didn't mind helping Katie with the girls and the housework as often as she could.

Now, as they were working on Anna's wedding ring quilt, Katie seemed particularly thoughtful. Winnie had quite a few thoughts of her own—mainly about Samuel Miller, so she didn't mind the quiet in the least.

But Katie broke the peaceful moment before Winnie had even needed to thread her needle more than once. "You know, I can't help but think about the fire. No matter what I do, my mind keeps drifting back to that."

"I don't know if hosting the singing helped much. Do you?"

Biting her lip, Katie shrugged. "Only time will tell."

Winnie leaned over the fabric and concentrated on making straight, even stiches. Recalling how most of the teenagers hadn't been especially eager to speak with them, she said, "Goodness, Katie, I don't know why we thought the teens would tell us anything."

"They were friendly."

"That is true. But it's not like they were eager to go about telling us any deep, dark secrets." With a touch of sentiment, Winnie imagined things weren't so much different now than when she was their age. Teens were rarely in a hurry to seek out the advice of someone older.

"I guess not. But I might understand their problems more than they think."

Winnie nodded. She knew of Holly, the English girl Katie'd befriended during her running around time. Though Katie hadn't spoken of it much, Winnie knew Katie had once fancied an English boy, Holly's brother.

"There wasn't anyone who you thought acted suspiciously?" Winnie asked.

"The only one was David, who I know hangs around Caleb quite a bit. Do you know him?"

"Only the family. They keep to themselves."

"That David's a strange one. Kind of timid and nervous." Chuckling, Katie shook her head. "Forget I even mentioned him. He's too nervous to do anything without his parents' permission. Gosh, when I was talking to him about our plans for the barn raising, he looked scared to death. I don't think he's very handy with tools either. He hurt his hands on some barbed wire something awful."

"I guess we'll just have to keep thinking, then," Winnie said as they drifted back toward working in silence.

After all that worrying about how to discover the fire starter's identity, Winnie came across a clue a few days later—when she least expected it. It was there in the buggy next to hers—mixed in with a canvas bag of groceries and a basket of dry pinto beans. A carelessly tossed package of cigarettes.

She looked around. Whose buggy was this? As she used her crutches to peer a little closer into the buggy, she heard footsteps crossing from Sam McClusky's general store to the parking lot.

"Winnie? Miss Lundy? Is something wrong?"

She started. Turning away from the evidence, she met the golden-hued eyes of Caleb Miller. Oh, dear. Had Katie been right? Could Caleb really have been the person who'd started the fire?

What should she do now? Tell Eli?

But what if Eli didn't even know Caleb was smoking? Surely it wasn't her place to tell him! Yet . . . he and Sam had done so much for her brother and Katie. Wasn't it her duty to let them know what she'd seen?

More distressing, what if they did know something but were choosing to keep it secret?

"Winnie? You look kind of funny. Do you need to sit down or somethin'?"

"No, Caleb. I'm fine," she lied. "Sorry my mind drifted. I, uh, just saw something that reminded me of my past."

He cocked his head to one side. "Really? What did you see?"

She couldn't blame Caleb for his surprise, she was having trouble at the moment thinking of a single memory that would have anything to do with his buggy. But still, it was time to come up with an excuse!

"Yes, I, uh, saw your basket of dried beans and was remembering a time I cooked them for Jonathan and the girls. They were truly verra bad. Jonathan was sick for a whole night, I tell you that." There. Now he would look into his basket and realize what she'd seen. He'd be flustered and tell her why he'd been smoking. And, more importantly, what happened the night the barn burned.

But instead of looking guilty, he just smiled. "That must have been a terribly long time ago."

"Not so long."

When she made a point to stare at the basket again, Caleb glanced at it, too. For a moment his grin faltered as it was obvious they were both staring at the exposed carton of cigarettes.

Furtively, he reached a hand in through the open back window and not-so-stealthily tried to cover them up. Winnie kept her expression wide-eyed and innocent. It would be better for Caleb to offer an explanation instead of her pressing him for one.

But still, she didn't look away when he met her gaze sheepishly. "I guess I shouldn't even try to hide them, should I? You going to tell my brothers?"

"About the beans? Or . . . about what else was in that basket?"

"You know. The cigarettes."

"You shouldn't be smoking, you know." Oh, she half expected lightning to burst out of the clouds above her, she sounded so very prim. Still, she waited. Waited for him to admit that he'd been in the barn.

Waited for him to tell her he'd made an awful mistake.

"I know." He shrugged. "They aren't mine anyway."

"Come now, Caleb."

"I'm tellin' the truth! A friend of mine—well, he's kind of a friend—he all the sudden said he didn't want them anymore but couldn't get rid of them at his place."

"Who is this friend?"

"I don't want to say. Anyway, he passed them on to me. I kind of forgot about them."

"Really?" She doubted any such "friend" had given Caleb the cigarettes. No, he'd just been caught.

"Really." His eyes blazed, daring her to doubt him. "I didn't want them, but my friend made me take them in order to throw them away. I didn't feel like I had a choice." He paused. Looked at her with wide eyes. "Have you ever felt like that?"

She nodded. Of course she knew. Everyone faced situations like that. When she'd gone to Indiana to see Malcolm, she'd known right away that he wasn't the one for her. Yet she stayed. It would have been most embarrassing to admit such a mistake . . . when she'd begged and pleaded to go for weeks beforehand. Of course by then Katie and Jonathan had fallen in love, so her going to Indiana had served a purpose in the end.

"My parents aren't home right now, you know," he said quickly. "They're in Lancaster. All that's home is Eli and now Sam, and I don't know what they'd say. I'd just rather they not find out, you know?"

"I understand. It's one thing to have to answer to parents, another when it's an older brother."

"They say things like they understand, but they're different than me. Neither of them ever wanted just to goof off for a little bit."

"Instead of worrying about who I'm going to tell, I think you should tell me the whole story."

He kicked the wheel of his buggy, causing his horse to snort in annoyance. "What do you mean? They're just cigarettes—not drugs. I wasn't doing anything too bad."

Winnie treaded carefully. "You know . . . sometimes accidents can happen. Things can happen when we don't even mean for them to."

Caleb bit his lip. "I know that."

What did he know? "So, where has this boy you know been smoking?"

"I don't know."

"Are you sure? Maybe he's been sneaking around. At night? Maybe he's been going to other people's places?"

"I don't—" His eyes widened. "What are you asking?"

"Nothing," she replied, back-pedaling fast. She'd wanted Caleb to confess to his part in the fire, not rely on her to coax it out of him.

And what if she was wrong about everything?

"Never mind. Like I said, I promise I won't tell your parents."

"Danke," he said with a nod, then turned away.

Well, she wasn't lying—she wasn't going to tell his parents a thing. But she was going to tell Eli. He needed to know what his brother was doing.

And even if it was all innocent, it wasn't her place to guess what needed to be done.

Pointing to the smashed box of cigarettes, he mumbled, "I'll get rid of these soon."

"The sooner the better, yes?"

Caleb didn't answer.

Sam couldn't deny it, he couldn't stop thinking about Winnie Lundy. Every time he'd been in her company, he'd found himself sneaking glances at her every chance he could get. He found her smooth black hair intriguing. And those dimples delighted him just enough to want to encourage her to smile as often as possible.

He liked her spunk, too. Sam knew more than one woman who would not have bounced back from injuries as well as Winnie Lundy did. No, she was no meek miss.

Yes, he'd thought quite a bit about Winnie, and about living Amish while he was back at home. Helping to plow fields and put into practice some of his agricultural theories had been a treat as well.

As had being close to Caleb.

But then he'd gone back to his real life. He slept in his apartment, watched ESPN, and worked nonstop. But nothing seemed the same.

Yes, he'd seen her that time he went to the Lundys' for meatloaf. He'd also talked to her when she'd called.

But it wasn't enough.

And though his feelings for her worried him, he found that he didn't want to push her away from his thoughts. No, he liked thinking about her. Liked seeing her. And he needed to see her again. Needed it as much as heirloom tomatoes needed good fertilizer.

Free from responsibilities, on Saturday morning he drove back to the small area of stores in the outskirts of Peebles and found the antique shop where Winnie had recently started working again.

After parking in the gravel lot around the corner, Sam walked in, then felt like a bull in a china shop . . . or what he was—a large man in a flowery, cramped jumble of breakable items.

The place set his teeth on edge.

Then he spied her. A wrinkle had settled in between Winnie's expressive eyes as she counted a bunch of tiny porcelain thimbles on the counter in front of her. Yet still . . . she looked as pretty as ever.

Her head snapped up when he knocked into a rickety picture frame. "Sam?"

"Winnie," he said, just as calm as could be. It was a pleasure to watch the range of emotions cross her expression. She went from harried to shocked to pleased to . . . he wasn't sure what. The wide-eyed expression on her face was definitely something he would always be glad he saw, it was almost comical.

Oh, Winnie Lundy lightened his day just by being herself. He was terribly glad he'd decided to come see her.

Finally, she spoke. "Is everything all right?" Lumbering to her feet, she scanned his face. "Are the girls sick? Katie?"

He motioned for her to rest herself. "Everyone's fine, Win. Sit down, now, before you hurt your foot."

"Then why . . . why are you here?"

Of course she would ask the obvious. That was Winnie's way, no mincing words for her! Feeling vaguely embarrassed, he answered her. "I just thought I'd pay you a visit today and maybe see if you would have time to go to lunch." Yes. Lunch. Food was always a good idea.

Even in the dim light, Sam noticed her cheeks pinken. "Oh. I'm sorry. I . . . I brought my lunch."

"Oh." Was that how it was, then? He'd mistaken their burgeoning friendship to mean far more to her than it did? "Well, then, I guess I'll just look around, then."

She opened her mouth, shut it, then nodded.

He was left to wander around the place and try not to knock into things. He felt like a clumsy fool.

From the back room, an elderly lady spied him and approached, her gray dress almost fading in with some of the washed-out upholstery of two sofas. "May I help you?"

"No. I, um, was just looking around."

A gleam flickered in her narrow eyes. "For something special, perhaps?" She picked up a monstrous china pear. "Fruit makes nice gifts."

He couldn't imagine a worse item to receive. "Surely?"

"Oh, yes. It's not something one would buy for oneself."

He was stuck in the conversation and he couldn't get out. "*Jah*. I mean, yes, I can see that."

Winnie blurted, "He's with me, Madeline."

"Ah." Sizing him up, the small woman looked him up and down. "Perhaps you came here looking for something special after all, hmm?"

"I only stopped by for a moment." He backed toward the door.

"You don't have to leave right away, Samuel," Winnie said.

"Oh?" There'd been a hint of sweetness in her voice. Maybe things weren't as awkward as he'd feared?

He shifted his weight for a moment back and forth, then was thankful when the owner shuffled off toward the back and they were alone again. He looked for something to say. "So, how's business today?"

"Slow."

"Oh. I'm sorry."

"I don't mind too much, not really. It's my first day back and all."

"I thought you were going to try and rest." Remembering how stern the nurse's instructions had been, he murmured, "You should've listened."

"I have been resting. But it was time to go to work." Winnie slowly got to her feet. "Madeline?" she called out. "Would you mind so much if I took a break?"

As quick as lightning, the lady poked her head out of the back room again. "No. Take your time, Winifred. Be careful, please. Don't want to knock over the merchandise."

Sam stepped forward. "I'll be glad to help you out of here." Anything to leave the claustrophobic environment!

"Danke," she murmured.

Now that he felt in charge again, Sam curved a hand around her waist before she had time to move away. "Make your way slowly, and I'll be here for you in case you fall." Lowering his voice, he murmured, "I'm far more worried about your neck than ugly fruit."

Winnie fought off a giggle. Then she concentrated on fighting off other feelings—such as the tingle she felt from Sam's hand around her waist.

Or how special she'd felt when he'd said those wonderful words. *I'll be here for you.*

As she felt the heat from his hand coax through the fabric, making her warm and toasty, she hopped a little bit faster through the mixed up maze. "I don't know what we're going to do when I don't need your help anymore."

"Hopefully, we'll think of something."

His voice was gravelly and sure, not teasing at all. Which, of course, made her even more jumpy and lightheaded. Winnie hobbled forward, knocking into a pair of baskets and a wooden hand-carved train. "Oh!" Perhaps she should've gotten her crutches.

Out from nowhere was his steady presence again. Keeping her safe and secure. One hand gripped her waist, the other righted the baskets. "Easy, now."

"I'm not usually so clumsy."

"I know." Lowering his voice, he murmured, "You're not clumsy, Winnie. Not by a long shot."

There was something in his voice that made her look at him quickly, but Sam's expression was almost serene as he curved one hand around her elbow to help her exit the building and make their way down the cobblestone path. "Want to sit for a moment?"

"Sitting sounds wonderful—*gut*." In no time Winnie was on a wooden park bench by Sam's side. "It is *shnokk* here, don'tcha think?"

Sam's eyes widened. "Cute? Well, hmm. Yes, I suppose it is."

As usual the charming town was bustling and busy. All around them, shoppers and tourists were chatting, eating waffle cones, carting boxes of fresh Amish baked goods, and talking on cell phones.

Though no one was rude enough to try and photograph her, Winnie was particularly aware of her dress and how obvious their differences were as she and Sam sat side by side.

Since he was saying nothing, she murmured, "I, um, I'm sorry if I seemed discourteous when you first entered. I was just surprised, is all."

"No, I should've warned you that I was thinking about stopping by."

Remembering his hurt expression about passing up lunch, she said, "And lunch—going out to lunch would be mighty nice. Another time."

"Yes. Maybe another time."

He sounded so doubtful; she did her best to be encouraging. "If you're out this way again, lunch would be a treat. If . . . If you'd still care to um, eat."

"I imagine I'll want to eat lunch another day."

Now that she finally saw his smile and heard his humor, Winnie relaxed. "Tell me a story from your week, Sam. I want to get back to how we used to be. I don't care much for this stilted, strained conversation."

"Gladly. Would you like to hear about my parents' latest letter? It seems that my grandparents' health has really improved. They'll be starting home before too long."

Relaxing against the back of the bench, Winnie nodded. "I'd love to hear about your family, Samuel."

And so, Sam talked. Winnie listened, but also daydreamed at the same time. And, against her better instincts, she wondered what a future by his side could be like. If it was even possible.

Because at the moment, Winnie didn't know if she'd ever felt happier than she did right then—sitting in the sun with a broken foot, all while talking about families and work and nothing at all.

Perhaps God really did answer prayers.

Chapter 13

Caleb kicked the milk pail. As his thick-soled boot hit the metal brim, fresh milk splattered everywhere, speckling the packed earth underfoot and the sides of the thick fencing with white dots.

For one startling moment, the three Miller brothers stared in disbelief at the terrible mess.

"I didn't mean to do that," Caleb said.

"I'm sure you did," Sam replied. "Otherwise you wouldn't have launched your foot at the pail." Looking their little brother up and down, he added, "I sure am glad I came out here this weekend to help some more. Eli shouldn't have to deal with your tantrums on his own."

"I am not having a tantrum."

"You are certainly not doing anything good. I have to tell ya, Caleb, I expected more from you."

Caleb puffed up a bit, definitely in a huff. "Well, I expected to be trusted."

"We don't always get what we want, now, do we?" Looking as mad as a hornet, Eli pointed to the milky mess. "You're going to have to clean every bit of this up, and sanitize the bucket, too. We don't have time for such *dumhayda*, such foolishness. We have work to do, don't you remember?"

Scowling, Caleb said, "Of course, I remember. All I ever do is chores. It's you two who seem to find time for other things."

Sam had had enough of the tantrum. "Such as?"

Crossing his arms over his chest, Caleb replied, "Things like sneaking around and watching me."

Eli shook his head. "I wasna sneaking, Caleb."

"Oh, yes, you were! You were watching me and talking to Winnie Lundy about me—and thinking things. I canna believe you thought I would knowingly burn down the Lundys' barn."

"No one has accused you," Sam pointed out.

"Sure you did. Well, you were going to."

Eli groaned. "Caleb—you shouldn't have been listening to other people's—"

"You shouldn't have been saying such things!"

"Enough." Sam knew it was time to try and bring a bit of calm into the situation. It wasn't going to be easy. Ever since Caleb had overheard them speculating about his involvement in the fire, things had gone downhill fast. "We all need to calm down and talk this through."

"I don't want to." Bright red splotches of anger formed on Caleb's cheeks. "I wish Mamm and Daed were here.

They'd tell you how wrong you were." His chin lifted. "They would."

Eli glared. "I wish they were, too. Because then you probably wouldn't have pulled half the things you've done this spring."

Back went the obstinate look. "Like what?"

"Like staying out late. Lying about your where-abouts."

Kicking the ground, Caleb said, "I don't want to be ganged up against."

"Then don't ruin a day's milk, *bruder.*"

"Look. I know I made a mess. But, that doesn't mean I set fires."

Eli leaned his head against one of the stable doors. "You are not listening."

Grabbing Caleb's shoulder, Sam gently squeezed. "Just listen, will ya? You can't live your life in separate lanes, like on the hills around us, Caleb," Sam cautioned. "Things don't move on their own, parallel. They mix to-gether, influencing each other. Your actions of late have cast doubts. We didn't blame you, but I'd be lying if I said we didn't feel like we needed to ask you about the fire."

"And we were going to," Eli said.

"Only after I heard you talking about me."

Eli sighed. "This discussion is the reason I was reluc-tant to ask you about things. I was worried you'd get all hotheaded."

Turning to Sam, Caleb's eyes filled with tears. "Sam, I thought you liked me."

"I do."

"Then why won't you believe me? I promise I'm not lying."

Sam's heart broke as he pulled his kid brother in for a hug. No, they hadn't handled this conversation well at all. Neither he nor Eli had a woman's knack for tact. Winnie would've known what to say. And well, Caleb was right. Their parents were far better at dealing with conflicts. They did have six *kinner*, after all.

Nestled against Sam's chest, Caleb's body shook. "You did say things could be separate. Like how you were Amish in your heart even though you went out into the world."

This time it was Sam who felt Eli's curious glare. Now, though, Sam was beginning to realize that "separate" wasn't how he could live his life after all. Slowly, he spoke, verbalizing his thoughts the moment they became clear in his mind. "I was wrong."

"What?"

"I wanted to learn when I was your age. I wanted something different than what I already had. And it made me feel ashamed. No, it wasn't driving cars or smoking or staying out late. But it was different, and I wanted it badly. Mamm and Daed understood my feelings and let me go live with the Johnsons. I was so relieved."

As he caught Eli's interested gaze, Sam realized that he'd never shared these inner feelings with his older brother either.

His desire not to hurt anyone's feelings had backfired.

Instead of creating an aura of peace, it had only instilled a fair amount of distrust and confusion.

Thinking back, Sam felt driven to confess everything completely. "Being away from here was hard. As I studied for my GED, I tried to cling to our ways and still fit in with all the *Englischers*. I stayed in my clothes, hugged my beliefs tightly. But then . . . I began to feel too different. I wanted to learn so badly, I put that first and began to adopt some of the Johnsons' ways." With a helpless shrug, he added, "It was easier to get along."

This time it was Eli who did the reaching out. With a pat on his arm, he murmured, "Do not be so hard on yourself, Samuel. You were only sixteen, after all. That's not so old. And everyone likes to fit in."

Sam shared a smile with Caleb. "*Jah*, Caleb. I was only sixteen."

Caleb looked at him suspiciously. "What's that smile supposed to mean?"

"It means that at sixteen, I, too, thought I knew so much. But sometimes I still made mistakes, just like I do now."

"Back then, what did you do?"

"I prayed. I clung to my belief in Christ. But I let the conveniences influence me, same as anything else. I moved on, away from our ways."

"But you're a fancy *Englischer* now—a college professor. Everyone says you're a smart man and is proud of you. Why do you think you did something wrong?"

"Because I tried to live my life in a narrow path,

thinking I could have everything if I only looked straight ahead, never side to side. But that was a foolhardy thing to do. We're all connected to each other, Caleb. The Lord lets us live in communities because we need them. For too long, I tried to excuse my behavior by thinking that it was okay for me to ignore some of our rules, because the Lord had gifted me with a strong desire to learn."

"And a really large brain."

Eli chuckled. "But now you think you are not fitting in?"

"Now I see what I have given up to reach for my dreams. I haven't been here for you, Caleb. I haven't been here for Eli or our parents." He also hadn't been around for Winnie, and had a feeling that if he had had her steady, bright influence, his world might have run more smoothly.

Eli cleared his throat. "Caleb, since we are now certain you did not start the fire, I have a terribly important question to ask you."

Those golden eyes of his blinked. "Yes?"

"Do you know who did?"

After two eternal minutes, Caleb nodded slowly. "I think so. But I don't know why."

"You need to tell us who. Jonathan Lundy needs to know the truth."

"First—I've gotta ask you something."

"Yes?"

"Would either of you mind if I only told Jonathan?"

Sam was shocked. "You don't want to tell us?"

"No."

Eli scowled. "You don't trust us now?"

"I trust you, but I know this friend of mine trusted me." Looking away, he said, "I know I need to betray his confidence. But if I'm going to do this, I'd rather only tell the one person who needs to know."

"And it's not us," Sam said with a knowing look to Eli.

"Are you mad?" Caleb asked.

"No. If I'm honest, I'm right proud of you," Eli replied. "You, little brother, have just grown up. Do you want me to take you to Jonathan's tonight, or do you want to go on your own?"

With a new resolve in his features, Caleb shook his head. "I'll go on my own. Now that we've talked . . . I think I'm finally ready to accept responsibility."

Sam looked at Eli and felt as old as the hills. "We'll be here waiting, then. Waiting and praying."

"But first," Eli said with a raised brow. "First, it's time to clean up your mess. Yes?"

With a sigh, Caleb reached for the bucket. "Yes."

"I am thankful you could come help me with this work, Caleb," Jonathan said to the teen when he'd shown up late in the afternoon unexpectedly. All he'd said was that he wanted to help with the barn for a bit. Guessing that far more was on his mind, Jonathan nodded, slipped on his work gloves and led Caleb to what was left of the pile of burnt lumber.

Now, as they worked hard together, Jonathan prayed

that he and Caleb would eventually get to the real reason for his visit. And that he would listen with a bit more patience and tact than was his usual habit. However, his insides were raging and impatient. All he wanted to do was let loose of the crazy mesh of emotions that had been rolling inside of him from the moment he'd heard the first snap of burning wood.

Pulling out a partially burned board and tossing it into the scrap pile with a grunt, Caleb merely nodded.

"I am going to need a lot of help prepping this area, especially if it is going to be ready for the barn raising."

"What are you going to do with all the wood?"

"Burn it. Not much else it's good for."

With a sideways look, Jonathan added, "You know, it's a terrible shame that this even happened. All from someone's carelessness."

Caleb's hands stilled. "Mr. Lundy, that's why I came here. I need to talk to you about that."

"Oh?"

"See . . . well—are you sure you need to know who started the fire?"

"I think I do. While I'm putting the Lord firmly in charge of things, I feel a need to know. A need to understand." He glanced Caleb's way to make sure he was listening. "See, it looks like a spark from a cigarette created all this destruction. Something so small changed everything in one minute. Right while I was sleeping. I pulled my sister out right about here." He pointed to the spot where the barn's doors used to lay. "Caleb, if the Lord hadn't put me here, she might have died. It's hard to come to grips with something like that."

Caleb swallowed. "What do you mean, come to grips with?"

"To realize that through someone's honest mistake, my sister could have been taken from me."

"But it was just an accident."

"But we need to take responsibility even if something was unintentional. Though I'm ashamed to admit it, it's these things that keep me up at night. I'm trying to forgive, but my heart isn't ready until I have someone to forgive."

"What are you going to do?"

"I'm going to keep hoping and praying and watching. Maybe one day I will know who was responsible."

Caleb picked up another two boards and laid them on the pile. When he picked up another piece of wood, a good portion of it crumbled under his fingertips. As the black ash flew to the ground, the boy looked troubled.

"Careful, now," Jonathan said. "This looks like just wood, but there's nails and things around here. If we're not careful, we're going to get cut."

"I've got gloves on." The boy held up two hands to prove his point.

"Gloves don't protect you from everything. That's why the Lord gave us a mind, don'tcha think? We need to use it every now and then."

"Jonathan . . . if you do find out who burned your barn, what are you going to do to him?"

"I don't know. Talk to him, I suspect."

"That's pretty dumb. Talking doesn't help."

"It might help me, though." He caught the boy's eye. "I'm thinkin' if someone is able to come forward and talk to me about the fire, about what happened, it might help a lot. A conversation can be pretty powerful." With a shrug, Jonathan lifted another board and added it to the pile. "Of course, we both know that no one has come to talk to me. I wish that wasna the case, though."

"Maybe the person was scared."

"I suspect he was. Or *she* was. Of course, I was scared too, that night. Ach." With a grimace, Jonathan pulled a nail out of the thick leather of his glove.

"Did you get hurt?"

"Not badly. Just a prick."

Caleb visibly tried to measure a smile. "I heard that we're supposed to be real careful with the boards. There might be nails and such."

"I heard boys are supposed to watch their mouths around their elders." Jonathan found himself also doing his best to temper his smile.

"I'm trying."

Patting the boy on the shoulder, Jonathan murmured, "So, is that what you wanted to talk about?"

"Kind of." Caleb closed his eyes for a moment then with a lost, helpless look, murmured, "I think I know who set the fire."

"Who do you think it might be?"

"David Hostetler. He's been acting nervous and such. He also handed me some cigarettes and asked me to get rid of them. He acted like he was scared to even touch them." Golden eyes watering, Caleb said, "I never wanted to tell on him, but my brothers started thinking that it might have been me."

It took every bit of effort for Jonathan to keep his expression neutral and easy. For him not to start peppering Caleb with a dozen questions. "I'm sure that bothered you."

"It did. Verra much. I'd rather be in trouble for the truth, you know? Only the truth can help sometimes."

"I think you're right about that." He held out his hand and shook Caleb's. "I'll keep this to myself for a bit. I appreciate you coming here and telling me."

"I hope it was the right thing."

"I know it was. No one ever promised that the right thing would always feel good. Sometimes the right thing just lets you sleep at night."

After Caleb left, Jonathan walked out beyond the remains of the barn, away from the house. He needed a moment to come to grips with what he'd just learned.

So . . . David Hostetler.

He always liked the boy. He felt a bit sorry for his home life. He was such a shy, timid thing, too. In his heart, Jonathan figured if it had been David, he must have been scared to death.

Frightened.

Alone.

That knowledge caught Jonathan off guard. He'd been hugging his anger to his chest like a shield. And consequently, that anger had prevented him from thinking about how anyone else might have been feeling. That knowledge shamed him.

It was time to *fagebb*, to forgive. And, he realized, the Lord was asking him to do something harder, too. Instead of waiting for someone to take the blame, he was going to need to reach out to David. Reach out and lend a hand. And hope it was the right thing to do.

Chapter 14

"It was kind of you to pick me up after my doctor's appointment again," Winnie said to Samuel after he helped her navigate her way from the medical building and into the large cab of his black Ford truck.

"You should have asked me to come pick you up from home and take you here, too," he chided as soon as he moved into the cab beside her and buckled up. "I would have been happy to do that."

"It was no bother hiring a driver. I don't want to take advantage of you." She'd also been hesitant about spending so much time alone with him. The feelings she had for Samuel Miller seemed to become stronger with each passing day. And though she could envision a life with him one day, she still wasn't sure if he was on the same page, or just helping out a family friend.

"You're never a bother, Win."

Winnie shifted in her seat. It was a somewhat jerky

move, what with the new cast on her foot. But hopefully, it wouldn't be on for much longer. The doctor had examined her most recent set of X rays and proclaimed her to be healing nicely. Her new cast was smaller and lighter and now allowed her to bear a bit of weight on it. "I'm so happy to be more mobile," she said.

"I hope you don't overdo it."

"I won't. Besides, I'd rather have sore arms from hopping around on crutches than continue to feel isolated. I didn't care for that one bit."

"I bet you didn't. I can't imagine you ever being happy to sit on the sidelines."

"That would be me, for better or worse."

"Now that you've gone to the doctor, where would you like to go now?" He grinned. "I am at your mercy."

Winnie blinked. Oh, when he said things like that, he almost sounded like he was in a courting frame of mind. But she knew he wasn't really. Playing it safe, she said, "I don't care. We can just go home, if you'd like."

"I'll take you home." He paused. "I have to make a stop first, though. Are you in a hurry?"

"Not at all." He smiled at her blunt answer, right about the time when she wished she'd have learned to watch her boldness.

"I have to stop by my office, but then I was hoping you might like to get a bite to eat."

A smarter woman would be more watchful of her heart. But no matter what her brain might be telling her, she couldn't ignore her heart—being in Sam's company made her happy. "Yes, let's go to your office. I've been curious about your place of work."

"All right, then." With a few turns, Sam pulled into the parking lot in front of a wide array of red-bricked buildings. "This is where I work. There are some benches outside; I can walk you over to one while I run to my office."

"Is your office on the second floor?"

"No, it's on the first."

"Then, I'd like to go inside and see what you do."

"It's not fancy," he warned.

"Good. I'm not fancy either." She felt deliciously warm when he smiled at her joke.

Looking a bit awkward, Sam finally nodded. "All right, then. Off we go."

He helped her out of the car, then led the way. Students were everywhere. Two girls looked at her curiously, then walked on the grass so she could continue on the sidewalk. Winnie gave them a friendly smile.

Everywhere she looked, Winnie spied something new and interesting. Each building they passed was constructed of dark red brick, black-trim framed windows. Matching black doors marked each entry.

Gardeners had been busy. Flower beds of cheery begonias and brightly colored petunias decorated the spaces between the buildings. And then there were the statues. Every few yards, another bronze figure dotted the landscape. She stopped in front of the one closest to them. "Who's he?" she asked.

"I don't recall exactly. He's one of the founders of the school. There are statues all around the campus."

"It's a remarkable place," Winnie murmured. Everyone looked so interesting and studious. "This is where you went to college, yes?"

"Yes. They gave me a full scholarship." Looking around fondly, Sam stopped for a moment. "I'm glad you're here, Winnie. For somehow I've started to only think of this campus as my place of work. I forgot all about my first impressions."

Sam clasped her elbow as they approached the two wide cement stairs that led up to the main doorway. "Have a care, now," he murmured as she struggled to find just the right place to position the ends of her crutches.

He hovered around her, making sure she was stable, then curved an arm around her side to help prop open the door.

When they went in, Winnie caught a glimpse of two bulletin boards before being ushered into a musty-smelling office.

Right away a voice greeted them. "Professor Miller?"

"Afternoon, Zach." With a smile, Winnie turned to the man. But for a moment, she couldn't help but stare at him. He had multiple piercings in his eyebrows and one circular silver loop on one of his lips. But what was most surprising was his hair—it was a short, spiky bright red—the color of watermelon in July.

To her surprise, he was staring back at her with just as much curiosity and interest. "Who are you?"

"Winnie Lundy."

"Hi. Hey, I like your hat."

"Thank you." Cautiously, Winnie touched her *kapp* to make sure all her hair was still neatly in place.

Sam stepped in between them, breaking the inspections. "Zach, Winnie is a friend of mine from back home. Winnie, please meet Zach Crawford. He helps me try and keep this place organized."

"Hello," she said, nodding her head.

Zach darted a look of amusement toward Sam. "Did you grow up with Professor Miller?"

"*Jah.*"

"*Jah?*" A smile passed over Zach's face. "I love your accent. So, you two are friends, huh? What was he like as a kid? Super smart? A know-it-all?"

"I'm not sure what a know-it-all means, but he was always terribly *shmeaht*, I mean, smart. Even when we were in school together."

"No kidding? I didn't think you two were the same age."

"Oh, Samuel's older, but we Amish have many grades in one building."

"Like in the olden days, huh? Was it hard to—"

Sam rapped his knuckles on Zach's desk. "That's enough questions for now, don't you think?"

"Oh! Yeah, sure." Nodding toward Winnie's pale cast and crutches, Zach said, "Hey, I'm sorry about your leg."

"*Danke.*"

"How'd you break it? Driving a buggy?"

"Zach . . ." Sam's voice held a warning. Winnie wondered what, exactly, he was warning his assistant about. Because they were speaking to each other so much?

When she looked his way, she understood. "I'm sorry for all the questions," he said with a concerned expression.

"I don't mind." When she turned toward Zach again, she was amused to see him now leaning on the desk, his chin resting in his hands. His attention was focused on her, and his expression was filled with honest curiosity, not anything mean-hearted.

"I hurt my leg in a fire," she said. "A bad one."

"No way." Zach's eyes widened. "Where was it? Your house?"

"Oh, no. It was in our barn, in the middle of the night. I hurt myself trying to get some goats out."

"Wow! I never met anyone who raised goats."

"They're *gut* pets, I'll tell you that. But they are ornery and eat most anything."

"I've heard that. My cousin raised pigs. Now, they do eat everything. My cousin Jamie said they got out and ate a whole Jell-o salad. Their noses were bright red!"

Winnie chuckled. "Zach, a *pikk's naws*, I mean a pig's nose would be a snout, *jah*?"

"Oh. *Jah*."

Sam rolled his eyes. "I only came in here to check on some things. We won't be long."

But Zach didn't seem to care about his schedule at all.

"There are some notes for you right here," he muttered, before turning back to Winnie. "How did you put out the flames? Blankets? Buckets of water?"

"Ach, no! The fire trucks came, of course."

"I didn't know you all used the fire department."

"Oh, sure. We Amish use the fire department, just as anyone. We've all helped put out fires, too. We like to help each other, you know?"

"That's nice." Pointing to her leg, he said, "But you still got hurt?"

"Yes. A board or somethin' knocked me out and my *bruder* Jonathan had to pull me to freedom. The whole episode was scary, I'll tell you that."

Sam threw up his hands and walked away. "I think I'll bow out of this conversation while I can. I'll be right back, Winnie."

"Have a seat," Zach offered, not looking dismayed in the slightest by the way Sam had spoken to him. "Would you like a cup of tea or a glass of water?"

"Yes, *danke*."

Zach looked delighted to hear her speak. "*Danke*? Does that mean thank you?"

Sam poked his head out of his office door. "It does. Winnie, you don't have to drink anything."

"I can speak for myself, Samuel. It is my leg that's hurt, not my mouth."

His own straightened into a thin line. "Obviously."

Oh! Why was he acting so strange? Was he nervous for her to find out things about his life at the university . . . or for Zach to find out things about his past?

Zach brought her a glass of water, which she sipped on just as the phone started ringing and a crowd of students blew in the door.

And *blew* was exactly what their arrival seemed like! The group of four boys and three young women were loud and boisterous, and moved in a pack. Each one was wearing a combination of shorts and T-shirt, some with big, clunky sandals . . . others with tennis shoes.

With barely a look in her or Zach's direction—who was on the phone and writing down notes anyway—they rushed toward Sam's door.

And then Winnie got a real opportunity to see what Sam's life at school was really like. Without even a pause at the threshold, they scampered through the opening and almost without drawing a breath, peppered him with questions.

Across from her, Zach turned away and started typing something on his computer, still talking on the phone. The kids, obviously vying for immediate attention, just kept getting louder and louder. They shot questions Sam's way that Winnie didn't understand.

It all sounded very foreign and yet exciting. Winnie sipped her water and just listened to the commotion around her. Just as Zach lowered the phone, it rang again. The door opened and shut, and more students wandered in and out. Somehow they'd all known that Professor Miller had arrived and were obviously glad to see him.

Sam, for his part, seemed to treat them all with

the resigned patience of a put-upon big brother, offering advice and instructions with humor and a touch of steel.

Now she understood the choices he'd made. A college setting was where he belonged.

After a good thirty minutes, Sam ducked out of his office again, looking sheepish. "I'm sorry, I never intended for this to take so long."

"I enjoyed sitting here and watching everything. It's lively."

To Sam's dismay, Zach let out a bark of laughter. "It's always this way when Professor Miller is here."

"Why is that?"

"He's a popular professor. Always has time for the students, which they really appreciate. And he's so amazingly quick and smart. He reads all the latest journals and studies and can analyze their pros and cons really fast."

"That's wonderful—*gut*, Samuel, *jah?*"

"Zach's making more of me than he needs to." Carrying a satchel stuffed with a bunch of blue packets on one shoulder, Sam bent down to help Winnie with her crutches. "Let's get you on home."

"Hope you'll come back and visit, Winnie."

"*Danke*, Zach. I'm sure I shall. It was good to meet you."

Zach was still beaming when Sam escorted her slowly out the door. After negotiating herself down the stairs with Sam wrapping a hand around her waist in case she lost her bearings, she turned to Sam. "This was fun."

"I'm glad you visited. Would you still like to grab something to eat before we head on back?"

"Sure." As she approached his truck, she wondered what his life was going to be like years from now. Would he ever find a woman who would make him happy? Would he one day settle down here, forever?

The thought of Samuel once again having a life she was not a part of made her blue. She'd miss him something awful.

When he opened his truck door, she gratefully accepted his help getting in.

"Winnie, are you okay?" he asked just before he closed her door. "You look like you're about to cry."

"Oh, it's nothing. I was just thinkin' about how different our lives are."

"Not so different, not really. Inside, I'm still the same Samuel Miller you used to play basketball with."

"We're different enough. I'm Amish. You are not."

A muscle in his jaw jumped. "That is true."

Winnie's outspoken nature got the best of her again. It hurt too much to keep everything she was thinking inside. "Sometimes when I think about you gettin' married and staying here, away from our community, it makes me sad, Samuel."

For a moment, he looked stunned. Finally, he spoke up. "The truth is, Winnie, when I think about that, I get sad, too."

"Truly?"

He nodded. "But see, inside, in my heart, I just

don't see myself getting married here. It's not going to happen."

Not going to happen. His pronouncement felt like a crushing blow. He wasn't thinking about marriage? Ever?

And here she'd thought she'd come to mean a lot to him. She'd completely misread his feelings—and she'd done just what she'd been trying not to do—imagine the two of them with a life together.

"I actually have been . . ."

But she'd heard enough. "If you don't mind, I think we better get on home. I betcha Katie could use some help watching the girls."

"Don't you want to get some lunch? We could talk some more . . ."

"No. I'm not too hungry. And . . . I'm kind of tired, too."

"Did I say something to upset you?"

Oh, she yearned to tell him everything. How she'd been thinking about him so, so much. How she desperately wanted things to work out for them, one way or another. But at the moment, it was terribly obvious that could never happen.

"Of course not. You've been a wonderful *friend*, driving me around. I'm grateful for your friendship."

"All right, then," he murmured, not looking too happy.

Winnie pretended to sleep the rest of the way home. It was easier than pretending her heart wasn't breaking.

She couldn't deny anymore that she'd really begun to hope that they might've had a future together. For a little while, she thought maybe they had a chance. Instead, all that happened was that she'd gotten her heart broken again.

Chapter 15

Sam didn't understand what had happened. One minute, Winnie was excited about visiting the university and his life. The next, she was talking about him being married. When he'd tried to ease her worries, she'd just looked hurt and disappointed.

"She was near impossible, Eli," he complained, practically the moment he walked into the kitchen.

Looking up from his plate of baked chicken, canned fruit, and carrots, Eli looked confused, "Who is?"

"Winnie. I don't know what she wants." He held up a hand to stop the incoming question. "And before you ask if I asked her, I did. Asking for her to explain herself didn't help."

Pulling his plate toward him, Eli grunted. "I see."

"Do you?" From the moment Sam had entered Eli's home and interrupted his supper, he'd been talking up a storm. What a change from their usual routine. Now it was Eli who was doing the nodding and Sam who was pacing and running his mouth.

Eli pushed back his chair and walked across the kitchen to wash his plate and neatly set it in the drying rack. After that, Eli pulled open the back door and led Sam outside.

Together they walked out toward the edge of one of the fields. Sam shared a smile with his brother when they saw their accomplishment. In the fading sun, rows and rows of freshly tilled soil lay before them. It had taken days of hard work to prepare the land for planting, but now it looked beautiful to Sam's eyes. There was something about land that had been cared for that gave it a special look. Healthy and fresh.

He breathed deep, enjoying the scent of freshly tilled soil. Yes, it was a strange scent to enjoy, but it smelled wonderful to him. It was why no matter how much schooling he'd done—he needed the land as much as it needed him.

"So, Winnie Lundy's got your heart. That's an interesting thought."

Looking sideways at Eli, Sam commented, "You know, I never actually said that."

"Come now, Samuel."

"All right. Yes, I suppose she does have my heart, but there's nothing I can do about it."

"Why's that? She'd make any man a wonderful-*gut frau.*"

"She would, but . . . I'd have to move back here. Do you think the Lord really guided me to all that learnin' just to travel back here?" To Sam, that seemed kind of a waste of time, though he supposed that was putting things a little harsh.

"But the two of you would make a good go of it. Perhaps she's your reason to come back to us," Eli stated practically.

"Everything isn't so easy. I'm a college professor, remember?"

"I haven't forgotten."

Something in the way Eli said that made Sam wonder if maybe he'd concentrated too much on his job over the years and not enough on family and relationships. Feeling defensive, he murmured, "My work at the college is important to me. I can't help that."

"I know." Together they walked slowly back to the house. "Perhaps we could speak to the bishop. Maybe he would let you still work, at least sometimes. Then you could have Winnie and your college."

But that seemed wrong. It would be selfish to try— he'd be putting his schedule and needs before his family's or his faith.

Besides, Samuel knew that attempting to juggle both worlds and his job and the needs of a wife wasn't an option. The life on campus was too worldly, and seemed to be getting more so each day. Students came to college full of excitement and information about the newest, fastest ways to do things. In spite of his best intentions, he'd gotten caught up in their excitement.

In contrast, the restrictions of the Amish way of

life would make a daily transition difficult at best. He could make himself sick by trying to do justice to each facet and most likely would never please both groups.

No, he'd have to quit his job and find something else.

But then would he be happy? And what about all the time and work he'd put into things? "I wish I was more like you, you know."

Eli looked taken aback. "Never wish that. You are the smartest man I know."

Sam felt humbled by Eli's honesty. He knew his brother didn't speak those words lightly. He, like their parents, had valued Sam's desire to further his education. "I might be book smart, but you are far smarter in the ways of the world."

"I'm only trying to do what is best today and leave the rest up to God. He'll guide me—and you, too, if you let him, Sam."

"I'm trying."

Eli started heading back to the house, pausing before he stepped in the door. "I think you need to talk to the Lord more than me. *Stop*, Samuel. Stop rushing and planning and doing and driving. Stop and pray and listen."

When had been the last time he'd prayed for longer than a minute or two? When had been the last time he'd sat in silence and used the time to contemplate his wants and needs and what the Lord wanted him to do?

In a daze, Sam wandered back into the house to his mother's *Sitzschtupp* and stood still for a moment, just taking time to look around. The walls were freshly painted a creamy white. An oak plaque decorated the area above the fireplace, listing his parents' marriage and each child's birth. On the opposite wall a large quilt hung. Its vibrant red, blue, and black triangles never failed to catch his eye and imagination.

To his dismay, Sam now realized yet another reason why the Amish didn't have televisions and radios and computers. All that noise and business was distracting.

Slowly, Sam relaxed against the smooth wooden back of the *shokkel shtool*, the rocking chair that rested to the right of the fireplace, and closed his eyes.

Please Lord, he prayed. Please help me find myself.

And though he never talked about it much, moving away from his home and community had been trying. Though he still found solace in the scriptures and privately held fast to his prayers and his personal relationship with the Lord, many other activities in his life had taken some adjusting to.

And, for better or worse, he had also celebrated them. He liked taking advantage of modern conveniences. Sometimes he thought he wouldn't be able to get through his day without his cell phone, yet alone his computer. If he left all that, he would be forced to give it up.

He'd also be putting a barrier in between himself and the outside world again. Oh, sure, he would keep his friendships, but he knew in his heart that they'd all soon drift apart. It was only natural to do so. They'd have different interests.

And then there was his education and his love of learning. Would he ever be able to turn his back on that? It seemed like it would be difficult to face himself or the Lord if he did that. Hadn't the Lord given him a wonderful mind to put to good use? Wouldn't it be a mistake to ignore his gifts?

He wasn't sure.

"Lord, I'm feeling afraid," he said aloud. Finally daring to admit what was in his heart. "I'm afraid to hope for a future with Winnie. I'm afraid to ask her to leave the order. I'm afraid to give up my current way of life."

Worse, Sam distrusted this new surge of emotions he was feeling. He'd become used to knowing what he believed and walking forward. He felt four years old again. In his sturdy brother's shadow, he sometimes felt as if he would never measure up. How could he, really? Eli always made the right thing look so easy.

He'd happily settled into the farming way of life as did their parents and grandparents. While not perfect, Eli had always seemed determined to do his best—and most of the time, that was certainly good enough.

Sam, on the other hand, had always somehow managed to fight his expectations. He still was struggling with doubts.

He was startled from his trance by Caleb. He rushed into the *Sitzschtupp* with a flurry of motion, like he always did, but this time it didn't seem to be his usual restless spirit guiding him. His eyes were red, like he'd been trying not to cry. Obviously hearing Caleb's clunky steps, Eli rushed in, too.

"Sam? Eli?"

"Caleb, what is it?" Sam asked.

"I need help from both of you."

Eli set his open palm on their younger brother's shoulder. "Of course. Sit down and we'll talk."

Sam vaguely recalled how their mother had always offered them a hot drink when they were upset. "Do you want some hot chocolate?" Eli snapped to face him, his look conveying his confusion. Sam simply shrugged. "Anything at all?"

Caleb shook his head. "I just need you both to listen."

"That's what we're doin'," Eli said.

Caleb raised a hand. "I mean to say . . . would ya hear me out before saying anything? I need to talk and be heard, not lectured."

Sam let Eli take the lead. And, as usual, he did not disappoint. Eli said, "Now what is it? Are you still worried about the fire and your friend?"

Sam liked how Eli deliberately didn't try to push Caleb.

Caleb nodded. "When we talked, I didn't want to tell you any names. I told you and I told myself it was because I trusted my friend—and I only wanted the person who needed to know to know. But now I'm starting to wonder if I'd made the wrong decision."

Sam looked at Eli, who shrugged. "That's a very important change. What brought it on?"

"When I spoke with Jonathan, his manner reminded me of our *daed*." He looked at both Sam and Eli. "You know how Daed doesna say much but you know he always listens? How no matter what he loves us and cares?"

Sam nodded. That description fit their father well. "Yes?"

"Jonathan's manner reminded me of how different my friend's father is. He's verra different. My friend never talks that way about his parents. He's afraid to make mistakes. He's afraid to talk to his *daed*. And now, I'm afraid to talk to him because I told on him." Their brother's eyes filled with tears again. "Now he has nobody."

A dozen thoughts filled Sam's head. There was no simple answer to ease Caleb's worries. But when he looked toward Eli, Sam relaxed. As usual, Eli didn't look flustered at all. Instead, he was patting Caleb's slender shoulders.

Then Eli spoke. "Let's pretend no one ever cared about who started the fire. What would you think then? Would keeping the secret be okay?"

"I don't know. It feels like a terribly hard burden."

"Did you chat with the Lord and ask for His help?"

"No."

"You might want to consider doing that, Caleb. Sam and I were just talking about how much He helps us . . . when we admit we're only mortal," Eli said.

Eyes wide, Caleb turned to Sam. "Praying helped you?"

"More than I can put into words," Sam said.

Eli winked. "That is sayin' something, wouldn't you agree? Our brother always seems to have words on his tongue I don't understand." Squeezing Caleb's shoulder, he said, "This time, I don't know how to advise you. I think you did the right thing. Lying and pretending you don't know something won't make problems disappear."

"But what happens when my friend finds out I told? He's going to be so mad."

"I guess he'll either be mad at you or will let you try and explain your reasons. Either way, know that I'm proud of you."

Caleb blinked. "You are? After everything I told you?"

"Of course. You're my brother."

Warily Caleb looked to Sam. In the pit of his stomach, Sam felt the same way. "I love you and am proud of you, too." Taking a risk, he said, "Caleb, at the moment, you and I are facing some big problems—too big to face by ourselves. I've been wondering where I belong. You've been wondering who to side with. We need to not forget that the Lord is always with us. We need to involve Him in our worries and fears. If we offer ourselves, He will help."

"You think?"

"I know." With a smile, Sam waved a hand. "God provided us with each other, yes? I don't think that was happenstance."

Later that night, after Eli and Caleb had gone to bed and he only had the cool evening for company, Sam reflected on how peaceful he had felt advising and being advised by his family. It was something he hadn't truly experienced in years. And he missed it.

He knew without a doubt that the Lord had been at his side, guiding him. Caleb needed him, and Eli was offering his support and opening up to him. He felt as if he'd just stepped into where he needed to be, for the first time in years.

Suddenly, all of the doubts he'd held on to about his place in the world became clear as day. This was where he belonged. Their tight-knit community, with all the friendships and gossip and worries, was as much a part of him as the hair on his head. He'd been a fool to try and distance himself from that.

It was time to return to his family and to his community. Now he just had to find a place to fit in.

He decided to wait to speak to Winnie about his new revelations until things had gotten organized. No sense in worrying her until he could offer her a future.

But oh, he was looking forward to a future with Winnie. For the first time in a long time, everything felt right.

Chapter 16

After tossing and turning for hours, Winnie gave up sleeping. She put on her robe and slippers then carefully hobbled down the hall by the light of the moon still resting high in the nighttime sky. Oh, but it did feel freeing to only need one crutch.

With a few well-placed rests and a sturdy oak banister for support, Winnie left the stuffy confines of the house and found refuge in the cool comfort of the front porch. Instead of choosing a rocking chair, she claimed the top step, just as she had for what seemed all her life. It was her favorite spot to find solace.

And that was what she most definitely needed at the moment. Her thoughts were too chilling and worrisome. She'd fallen in love with a man she didn't want to love. Well, with a man she was *afraid* to love.

She didn't know what to do. So she did what her mother had taught her, so many years ago. She prayed.

Closing her eyes, she said the Lord's Prayer, spoken from her heart, each verse speaking to her soul. Though sprawling fields reminded Winnie that she was only one of God's creatures in the vast world, she still felt as if He was listening for her.

"Dear God, help me know your will," she whispered into the still, starry sky. "I feel so alone and confused."

Asking God's will was really all Winnie felt she could do anymore. After all, the last few weeks had most definitely been in the Lord's hands. She could not think of another explanation for why she was led to Sam—a man she'd not spent much time with until recently.

And the Lord had most definitely seen to it that they'd meet. She and Jonathan had both remarked how odd it was that she had been the one to break her foot and sustain burns when he'd been in and out of the burning barn so many times.

The hospital was near where Samuel worked. And because Sam's brother Eli was good friends with Jonathan, Samuel had felt honor-bound to visit her.

A nonbeliever might have called that a coincidence, but it was too much of a coincidence for her. No, God had meant for her and Sam to cross paths once again.

Winnie just wasn't sure why.

Was it to strengthen her faith? To give her a trial like so many women and men in the Bible?

If that was His will, well, Winnie had to say that she was sorely disappointed. She already did love the Lord and intentionally sought His guidance on a daily basis.

The recent turn of events felt like a cruel joke.

"Lord, I know I'm Amish. I love my family. I love my dear nieces. But I know I've fallen in love with Sam, too. I don't understand why You brought us together when You knew that love would be wrong."

As her words flew into the air and seemed to dissipate the moment she said them, Winnie closed her eyes and tried to listen to a reply.

But—as she was afraid would happen—no reply seemed to be forthcoming. Frustrated, she spoke again. "What do you want for me to do? Leave everything I know and love?"

A dawning awareness flew through her. Was that His will? That she leave the order, too?

Perhaps Samuel needed an Amish wife in an English world. He needed her values and their common ways.

Plus, it wasn't like he'd strayed too, too far from their way of life. Yes, he had adopted many English ways, but he still believed in their sense of community, their faith, and their rules, despite bending a few of them.

Yes, that had to be it. She and Sam hadn't met again so he would leave all his accomplishments and join her. No, they met so that she could be his partner and helpmate. So she could be the person who knew and understood him in a community where so many did not.

The thought of shouldering that responsibility scared her. She didn't know if she was ready to leave everything she'd known to be with Samuel.

As the cool night air fanned her face, Winnie reflected some more. Perhaps leaving her own kind to be with Samuel was what love was? Didn't love mean putting another's needs before your own?

In her other relationships with friends and family, she'd always been the type of woman who noticed what wasn't right, noticed qualities in other people that she wished could be changed. She noticed flaws in appearances and flaws in character. Katie had commented more than once that her outspoken ways sometimes hurt people's feelings.

She'd certainly had a time with Malcolm's absent-minded ways toward her. She hadn't liked being taken for granted. Hadn't liked not being appreciated.

Now that she was wiser, Winnie knew she'd been realizing that Malcolm hadn't loved her any more than she'd loved him. In each other's company, it had been necessary to think about other things and other people, because what they had was never special at all.

With Sam it was different. From the time she'd seen him in the hospital, he'd struck her fancy. She'd thought about him for hours. She imagined what future conversations would be like and reviewed what past conversations had included.

And though things weren't always wonderful between them, they were exciting. And she appreciated their differences. Yes, she accepted Samuel Miller just the way he was. And she was grateful when he accepted her that way, too.

She was in love, and was willing to do whatever it took to be with the person she loved. She'd waited too long to find this. At the moment, it meant accepting that he needed to be with the English. That his students and his research were important to him. She could make sacrifices for him, then.

Standing up, Winnie felt almost joyous. Despite the fact that she still had to convince him that marriage was the right path for them. But she now knew she was willing to make this sacrifice for him.

Though it would fair break her heart.

Because, she realized as she opened the door and stepped inside the house, while Samuel had left with his family's blessing, she would not be seeing the same acceptance.

He'd left before he'd taken the vows of the Amish faith. Before he'd joined the church. She would be leaving after.

It made all the difference in the world. He had been loved and always accepted.

She would be shunned.

Suddenly, it felt as if everything was crashing down once again.

As tears pricked her eyes, Winnie limped to her room. "Oh, dear Lord, You certainly know how to bend us to your will, don'tcha? I hope You will not leave me. I have a feeling I am about to need You more than ever. Please stay with me, no matter where I am. No matter who I am. Please know that I only want to follow Your will, and I want to honor You by being the best woman I can be. At the moment, I really do believe that the best thing for me is to be with Sam."

There was no turning back. She was frightened and nervous of her decision, but also felt curiously lighter. Even if nothing ever happened between her and Samuel, at least she knew that she'd prayed about her feelings and her actions, and felt at peace with her decisions.

Now that the decision was made, everything seemed almost easy. The first thing Sam did was speak to Bishop Kropfs.

After discussing things for quite some time, the bishop sat back and stared at him boldly. "Samuel, are you sure about this? You seem to be making these decisions hastily."

"I would agree that to most, these decisions do seem rushed. But I have prayed long and hard about them. And I'm seeking your guidance as well."

"If you leave your life at the college, what are you going to do?"

"I'm hoping to do two things. I'd like to buy some of the land that's adjacent to the family farm and use some of the methods I've been teaching about to increase crop productivity, but I'd also still like to teach some, too."

Bishop Kropfs's brow rose. "Teach who?"

"I'd like to offer farmers in the community some training. And, if you don't mind, I'd like to still teach at the college. Not on a daily basis, but perhaps as a guest lector a few times a year."

"That has a nice ring to it, I'm thinking. And if it's only every now and then, perhaps it won't be too difficult to manage," the bishop added, obviously warming up to the idea. "You could hire a driver, I suppose."

Sam figured relying on other people to get him around might be the hardest adjustment of all. He'd have to learn to depend on others. "I would like to be able to continue teaching. But, I'm also willing to listen to your advice. And, I'm wondering if you all will be able to forgive me for leaving."

"Forgive you for what?"

"For leaving the faith. For trying things out on my own."

"There's no shame in that, Samuel. Everyone has to step out and experience things. We're proud of you. I promise you that. We will discuss this and do some praying, too." He looked up. "I must say I'm surprised. I thought you were happy with how things were."

Sam chose his words carefully. "I was happy. And, I think I could be happy there for the rest of my life. But lately I've been starting to realize that just having a good career wasn't enough. I need all of me to be fulfilled. Only by marrying in my faith and living my life the way I grew up will give me the sense of peace I've been yearning for."

"We will give it some thought, Samuel."

"*Danke*, Bishop."

After the conversation, Sam went back to the campus to meet with his school's administrator. That discussion was far harder.

"I don't understand, Sam," Bill Ames sputtered. "You've been extremely successful in both the classroom and in the research department."

"I've enjoyed being here a great deal. I don't know if I can explain my feelings other than that I think it's time I went back to my family."

"But aren't they only an hour or two away?"

They were a world apart in other ways. "Yes."

"What are you going to do?" Bill raised an eyebrow. "Do you have plans to go to another university? If so, I feel I have a right—"

"It's not that." Feeling suspiciously like a lad in trouble, Sam figured he had nothing to lose. "Bill, the thing is, there's a woman involved. She's Amish."

"But you are, too. Right?"

"No. We Amish don't join the church until we feel compelled to. I never joined. But I'm ready to join now."

"Couldn't this . . . this woman just come out and live with you?"

"I will not ask her to. Her faith and family are as important to her as breathing."

"But she could. I think you should speak with her."

"I've made my decision. Though, I have asked the Bishop if I could come back as a guest lecturer at times."

"Is that right?"

Sam could feel himself blushing. "I know it's a lot to ask. But I am only following my heart and soul."

"I am starting to realize that. Well, this is going to

cause me no small amount of problems. We've already made up the schedule for the fall semester. We've assigned classes to you. Students have signed up."

"I know, and I am sorry about that."

"But not enough to change your mind?"

"No. I'm afraid not."

A dimple appeared in his boss's cheek. "So you're leaving everything for love, huh? When some of the girls hear of this, they're going to swoon."

Sam sat down with a chuckle. "Hopefully, things will work out. I haven't talked to Winnie yet."

"You're taking a leap of faith, then."

"I guess I am," he said with some surprise.

Bill stood up and shook his hand. "I truly do wish you the best of luck. If you find the opportunity to be a guest lecturer, let me know."

"You'd allow me to do that?"

"Without a doubt. I hope that woman knows how lucky she is. There're not many who would be willing to switch careers and lifestyles like you are."

"If you knew Winnie, you'd know that she'll tell me what she thinks, for better or worse," Sam said as he walked out the door.

To his surprise, he felt lighter and freer than ever.

Chapter 17

"Have you heard the news?" Katie asked as she entered the *Sitzschtupp*.

"News about what?" Winnie looked up from the wedding ring quilt she was working on. To her dismay, it had taken a broken leg to finally gain the patience needed to complete a project.

"About Samuel Miller, of course. Everyone is saying he's moving back."

Winnie dismissed the gossip with a smile. "That's not news. He's been back for some time, helping Jonathan with the cleanup of the barn and helping Eli with the spring plowing and such." Honestly, sometimes Winnie was sure her sister-in-law loved to make mountains out of molehills.

"It is far more than that, Winnie. He's moving back, for good. He left his college and everything. At least, that's what I heard he talked to the bishop about it."

Katie shook her head. "This is surely a season of change. That barn burning has set off a series of events I never would have dreamed."

Startled to find her hands shaking, Winnie pushed the material to one side, not even caring that some of it fell to the floor in a wrinkled heap. "I can't believe Sam would do something like that. He loves his college."

Looking mighty satisfied to have finally gained her sister-in-law's attention, Katie folded her arms over her chest. Somewhat smugly she added, "Perhaps he's found other things to love."

"Nothing you're sayin' is making any sense." Winnie knew her voice was flustered, but she didn't care. "I think we should wait to speak to Sam himself before we go speculating on his future."

"Suit yourself, but I know I'm right. I heard all this straight from Mr. McClusky at the store this morning. He'd heard straight from Lydia Hershberger, who heard from the bishop. It's a fact, Samuel Miller is coming back."

"My word."

Katie rushed over and hugged her tight. "Oh, Winnie, I'm so happy for you."

"Stop talking like that, wouldja?" She was too nervous for so much teasing!

"Surely you don't have to be so cross."

"I'm not trying to be bad-tempered. I just don't want to hear any more talk and gossip about Samuel."

"Do you want me to leave, then?" came a voice from the doorway.

Winnie whipped her head toward Sam—toward that voice she'd know anywhere. "I didn't know you were here."

"Jonathan let me in." With a gentle smile, he stepped closer. "So, may I come in, or would you rather I leave you alone?"

Katie beamed. "Of course, Samuel. Come sit down."

Winnie just stared. She felt helpless and out of control, like she was stuck in the center of a tornado. Gingerly, she got to her feet, anxious to at least be able to face him that way. "How much did you hear?"

"Enough."

"You shouldn't have listened."

"I couldn't help it. Your conversation was pretty important. I sure didn't want to interrupt."

"Still—"

Katie cleared her throat meaningfully. "Honestly, Winnie. What is wrong with you?"

"Nothing." It was just she was terribly embarrassed.

Samuel came closer, now standing mere feet away from her. "I was hoping we could have a conversation—not an argument."

"Yes. I . . . I've been wanting to talk to you, too." However, inside, she felt as if everything was off kilter.

"You could talk now," Katie said, all smiles.

"I'd like to talk. Privately." Winnie sent a meaningful glare Katie's way.

Katie finally caught the hint. "I think I'll go upstairs. I'll take the girls, too."

"Thank you."

Sam's gaze turned guarded. "Winnie? What is going on with you?"

"Not as much as with you, I'm coming to find out," Winnie replied, feeling somewhat shaken up inside. Her heart seemed to be beating double time.

"What is that supposed to mean?"

"It means that I've just discovered that you intend to stay here. That you intend to join the church."

Samuel took a chair. "Please, Win, let's sit down and talk things over." When she did as he asked, he surprised her once again by reaching for her hand. "Here's what I've been thinking. I thought maybe that way we could maybe try courting a bit. I met with the bishop and I think I've got everything arranged."

"To do what? Quit your job?"

"Well, yes."

The tears fell, and she didn't even try to hide them. "But why?"

"Because I can't be all things to everyone. I chose you."

"Really?"

He squeezed her hand. "Yes, really. What are you upset about?"

"Sam, I've been wantin' to talk to you, too. To tell you that I would leave the order for you to be happy. I've been praying about it, and I think I would make a mighty fine professor's wife. If . . . if we came to that."

He stood frozen. "You would have done that?"

"Yes, if that's what would have made you happy."

"But, Winnie, I never even considered asking you to do such a thing. The outside world is so different."

"Maybe. Maybe not. We would have each other, and you would be happy. That was going to be good enough for me." Glaring at him, she chided, "Unfortunately, you didn't even think to talk to me about it. You didn't care enough to seek my opinion."

"But you have it wrong, Winnie. It wasn't that I didn't trust you. Or that I didn't care about you. See—I wanted to surprise you."

"You certainly did that." She wanted to unbend, but she still felt a bit foolish—and dismayed. Perhaps they should take things more slowly?

"Winnie Lundy, I'm not giving up on us. I aim to court you."

Looking at their hands, at their fingers linked together, Winnie knew she'd never felt more breathless. Never felt so happy. Never felt so confused. Slowly, she looked up at him. "Why?"

"Because I can't help myself," he said simply. "Whenever I think of my future, I now imagine you in it. And here is the place for us. This community. Among the Amish."

"You wouldn't miss your university?"

"Not as much as I would miss you." He almost smiled.

So did she. Perhaps their foolishness was over. Now that all their obstacles were being removed, they would finally be able to concentrate on just the two of them, and how they felt about each other. "I would miss you, too, if you went back to the English."

Then it seemed only natural for her to reach for his other hand. It felt only right to link her fingers through that hand, too.

To simply just appreciate how much Sam had come to mean to her.

"So, may I call on you again soon?"

"Yes. As long as you announce yourself instead of lurking around doorways."

He tapped his head. "I'll try and remember that."

And then he was gone. Giggling like a schoolgirl, Winnie fell back on the couch. For the first time in a long while, she felt pretty and fresh. Wanted. It was a right *gut* feeling, indeed.

Chapter 18

David couldn't catch his breath. His chest hurt something fierce and his lungs burned, like a pile of hot coals were sitting on his chest, weighing him down, preventing him from moving.

The worst had happened. Jonathan Lundy had found out the truth.

Just a few moments earlier, Jonathan had shown up by his side at the lake and boldly stated that he knew David was the one.

The person who'd set fire to his barn.

And now all the air inside of him seemed to have left.

"David, surely you're not going to pretend you didn't hear me. Don't you have anything to say?"

"Ah . . . yes." In the space of two heartbeats, David slowly managed to meet his gaze. Those crystal blue eyes that had always seemed so patient and sad, especially after the first Mrs. Lundy had died, looked nothing like they usually did. Instead, the man's pupils looked like ice, like the depths of the skating pond come March, when the top layer was so thin you could see underneath it.

He gathered himself together. Looking back down at his boots, so scuffed, on account they'd been his older brother's, he murmured, "There's nothin' to say." He winced, automatically flinched when he heard his words out loud. This was about the time his pa would have backhanded him for speaking at all.

But instead of looking even more angry, Jonathan sighed. "So it's gonna be like this, is it?"

"Like what?"

"Like you pretendin' you don't know what I'm talking about and like me pretending I'm not hurt." Looking across at the stillness of the pond, he shook his head sadly. "To tell you the truth, I'd kinda hoped things would be different."

David had hoped his secret would stay hidden forever. That he'd never be having this conversation. But it was finally time to face his punishment. "There's nothin' to talk about. I burnt your barn and never told no one."

Around them, clouds filled the sky. Within the hour, rain would come, treating the tiny seedlings in the fields beyond to a much needed drink of water. Cooling things off for a bit.

"I suppose that's how things could be described." Turning away from the water, Jonathan faced David again. "Is that how things happened exactly? All of a sudden, you got a bee in your bonnet to harm my family?"

David couldn't help it—he flinched. But he didn't try to defend himself. There was no defense.

Jonathan's eyes narrowed. "Well? You want me to be guessin' again? All right. So, you reckoned you wanted to kill my horses?"

David bit his lip to keep from talking.

"You wanted to go to jail?" An eyebrow raised. "You wanted to hurt Winnie?" He leaned forward just as David tasted the sharp metallic hint of blood. "Is that it? For some reason, you're upset with my family? Is that what happened?"

"No . . . I . . ." How could he answer those questions? He felt so helpless. What excuse could he possibly give?

"All right, then. I suppose we have the answer." Roughly, Jonathan grabbed him by the collar. "Come with me. We'll go down to the sheriff's office and I'll press charges. You tried to murder me and my family when we haven't done anything."

"No!"

Miraculously, Jonathan's iron grip eased. "No? Then what happened? How did that fire come to be? Talk, boy," he whispered. "You've got nothing to lose and only the truth to gain."

"The fire was an accident." Tears started to fall. His voice cracked. He struggled to breathe as everything that he'd tried so hard to hold in threatened to fall, to break apart, to burst through him. "I promise, I never meant for it to happen, I never meant to harm the horses."

"Ah."

But now that he'd set his tongue in motion, it appeared in no great hurry to stop. The words rushed out. "Please believe me—I would never mean to hurt Winnie. Or you. I didn't mean to. I was tryin' . . ." He struggled to talk. "I was trying to . . ." He couldn't say it.

Jonathan pushed. "Trying to what?"

To David's surprise, Jonathan reached out and took hold of his hand. As if he felt David's scars, he gently turned his palm over and examined the rough, angry skin that was taking so very long to heal. Clicking his tongue he said, "I don't know if it makes things any easier, but the Lord already knows the truth."

"If He knows, He doesn't care. I asked Him to make everything better. He didn't."

"Our Lord can't verra well go putting burnt barns back together, can he?"

"I asked him to guide me to know what to do. To help me. He didn't."

"He guided you here, to this conversation. That counts for something, I'm thinkin'."

"But He grants miracles in the Bible."

"David, it's my belief that some miracles are small. The love of a family member. The beauty of a sun-filled day. See, He grants us miracles even when we don't deserve them." Jonathan released his hand and crouched in front of David just as the rain started to fall all around them. "Jesus already knows our sins but loves us anyway. He already knows our sufferings, our weaknesses, our dreams, and he loves us anyway," he said again. "Always. No matter what."

"You really believe that?"

"With all my heart. There's some good in that, don'tcha think?"

David had never thought of the Lord already knowing things. In a way, it did make him feel better. To not have to hold secrets anymore.

But why, then, hadn't he already gotten in trouble? "Why hasn't God punished me?"

Jonathan looked him over. "Maybe He already has. You look like you've been carrying a heavy burden all on your own. Perhaps it's time to share some of that weight. Please talk to me, David. If you didn't mean my family harm, tell me what happened that night. I need to know. And, I have a feeling, you might need to share the story."

Whether it was Jonathan's words, or the way the man's hand was curved protectively around his own, or the light cleansing rain falling from the sky, David finally felt able to talk. "I should first tell you that I don't have too many friends. I don't know why." When the older man said nothing, only nodded, David continued.

"Sometime back, some boys had gotten hold of ciga-rettes and were selling them. I took some money that I'd saved and bought a few packs and two lighters. For the first time, the other boys looked at me like I fit in."

"And so you started smoking?"

"*Jah.* At first, I was no good, but then I got better. When a few others started talkin' about some *Englischers* who could make smoke rings, and they talked like they admired that, I decided to try and make them, too."

Instead of glaring, Jonathan merely looked reflective. "I imagine those would be difficult to make."

"I got pretty good at it. But I wanted to be real good, so next time I saw everyone I could show them." Oh, his pride and vanity had cost so much.

"And did you?"

David shook his head. "No. That night, I went to your barn. It's not too far from our house, you know. Plus, the loft doesn't have any windows. No one would see the sparks of the cigarettes in the night."

"And so there you were."

"Yes. I was tryin' to make smoke rings. I could just make out their forms in the dim light peering up from the windows below. I was trying so hard, I hadn't put out one of the old cigarettes so well." He swallowed. The sparks, the memories, were as vivid as if they'd happened hours instead of weeks before. "When the hay caught on fire, there wasn't anything I could do. I tried to stop it. There was a horse blanket, I tried to smother the flames, but they just seemed to eat up the fabric instead of be hindered by it."

"And you burned your hands."

David looked at his palms. "I did. By then, there were flames everywhere. It was too late." Daring to look at

Jonathan, David murmured, "I promise, I tried to put out the flames, but it all happened so fast."

"I know."

"At first I was going to wake you up, but I heard you yelling. And then I didn't know what to do. I was too afraid to come out of the shadows. So . . . I ran."

With a heavy sigh, Jonathan stood up. "It's a blessing you weren't hurt. Things would have been verra bad indeed if you hadn't gotten out in time. Oh, David. What would have happened if you had died in the fire?"

David had never thought of that. It had never even occurred to him to think about what would have happened if he had really gotten hurt.

It had never occurred to him to be grateful for anything.

Surely the Lord hadn't spared him for a reason. But, the Lord never did things without a purpose. Did He?

Continuing the story, he murmured, "I jumped from the loft just as the flames spread and your horses started screaming. I meant to go get them, but then I heard you coming and . . . and I was scared." As two tears slid down his cheeks, he whispered, "I was so afraid."

"I would have been afraid, too," Jonathan said softly. After a moment, he said, "And then, you went home?"

"I did. When I got there, my *daed* was already getting ready to go to your place. I knew he'd never forgive me if he knew what I'd done. If he knew I'd been careless and a coward. If he'd known that I'd run. So . . . so I hid. When he left, and the house was quiet, I washed up the best I could, got into bed and pretended to sleep."

"Only pretended?"

"All I could hear in my head was the roar of the fire and the horses screaming." Lowering his voice, he confessed, "When I closed my eyes all I could hear were my faults. That's still all I hear."

With a weary expression, Jonathan nodded. "Now I know the truth."

David wiped his cheeks and tried to prepare himself for what had to come next. They had to tell his father. Next, of course, would be to tell the authorities.

His voice husky, Jonathan asked, "Have you prayed for forgiveness?"

The question surprised him. "No."

"Maybe it's time you did."

"I . . . I will."

Jonathan gazed at him again, his eyes almost looking regretful. "I think you'll feel better for that."

Perhaps it was Jonathan's own sad expression that gave him strength—perhaps it was hearing that God already knew what he'd done. But from somewhere deep inside, David finally found the strength to do what he'd wanted to from the moment the first piece of hay ignited.

Closing his eyes, he spoke from his heart. "I am sorry, Jonathan. I will do whatever I can to help make things right."

After saying the words, David found he could breathe again. The horrible burden that had been suffocating him seemed to have lifted. With that weight lifting, he felt almost normal. He opened his eyes. The world around him was still the same, but it seemed brighter. He felt stronger, too. He'd done it. He'd followed the Lord's will, he'd faced the worst, and was prepared to accept the consequences.

Jonathan sighed. Then, to David's surprise, he stepped forward. Holding out his hand, he gently shook David's. "I accept your apology."

And then he turned and walked away. Around them, the fine droplets created a kind of hazy mist, blurring their surroundings. The haziness seemed to fit the moment—it blurred everything, which was how David was feeling.

What was going on? Surely after everything that had occurred, Jonathan wasn't just gonna leave? After a slight pause, David rushed after him. "Jonathan, *Mr. Lundy*. Wait. Please."

He stopped. "Yes?"

"What are you gonna do now?"

Still without turning, Jonathan replied, "I need to get back to work."

"I mean . . . I mean about me."

Slowly, he faced David again. "I expect you might help out with the barn raising. There's a lot to do and I'll need every able man."

"But—"

"Don't even think of getting out of it. Even men with hurt hands can contribute. I expect to see you with your family."

"But what about the authorities?" he sputtered. "What about my father? Aren't you going to tell on me? Don't you want me to be punished?"

"To be honest, for days and weeks, I have sought vengeance. I wanted someone to blame. I wanted to be able to understand why such a thing would happen to *me*." He rubbed a hand along his beard. "See, I was only thinking of myself, I'm afraid. You know I lost a wife. I thought surely that was enough pain for a man to bear. The fire was terribly hard for me to understand."

"I see."

Jonathan shook his head. "No, I don't know if you do. I didn't want to forgive, but after hearing your story, I realized I have been wrong. See, sometimes, accidents happen." Looking out beyond David, he murmured, "Fear and pride can take over in a heartbeat. It can make even the best of us do terrible things. Making you hurt more will not make me feel better."

"But I did a terrible thing."

"David, what happened *was* terrible. But you didn't do it on purpose. It was an accident. You've apologized to me. That is enough."

"But my father—"

"You've discussed things with the only Father I care about. He is the one who guides my life. He is the one I have to answer to. Because of that, I am satisfied."

Jonathan stepped away, then, after turning and spying David standing there, did something truly amazing, he stepped closer and pulled David into a hug. "You will be all right, David. The next time we see each other, all will be good. I promise you that."

David could only nod as tears slid down his cheeks, mixing with the mist. Sometime during their conversation, he, too, began to realize that there was only one Father in his life as well. That although his own family situation wasn't as he'd hoped, he could bear it, because it was only a temporary circumstance. Soon he would be a man with his own family.

And one day he'd be in the eternal kingdom, and that would be the nicest place of all.

Chapter 19

Instead of going back to the house or to work, Jonathan took a detour and drove his buggy along some of the small, windy roads that had connected various plots of land with each other—and had for generations.

The crisp air held a touch of warmth behind it, reminding him that time, as always, moved on, no matter what the circumstances.

That thought had never felt more true. His conversation with David had been revealing, indeed. But, if he were honest, it was also God's whispers in his ear that had been the most telling. During that hour, Jonathan had never felt closer to the Lord, never more open to His will.

Lost in thought, he slowed Blacky's pace. When the horse restlessly bobbed his head, Jonathan parked the buggy to the side, near a thicket of fresh spring grass that the horse could easily munch on if desired.

Then he got out of the buggy and walked a ways up. Scanning the horizon, he could just see the faint outline of the Brenneman Bed and Breakfast. To the other side, he could see the shadows of the Hostetler barn.

Jonathan knew the family well—it was impossible not to know all the surrounding families well, their community was so tightly knit. And while his had never been a perfect life, Jonathan had always known that the Hostetlers' circumstances were difficult, indeed.

They were not well liked.

Oh, Jonathan figured he could have tried harder to reach out to them. They all could have tried harder. But Amos Hostetler was a somewhat difficult man, without humor. His wife was cowed and meek to the point where it was difficult to have even the most simple of conversations. Their children—all eight of them—were good enough, but a little standoffish. Jonathan's Mary had put it best—they weren't good playmates.

Rumors had circulated that perhaps Amos was too hard on the children. Some blamed his farm's continual financial problems for Amos's short temper.

Jonathan had a feeling that Amos was just that way.

And empathizing with David—hearing the admission in his voice, seeing the fear and resignation as he told his tale—was like a blow to his belly. Jonathan felt that nothing positive would be accomplished by involving David's father.

When the Lord had guided him, whispered in his ear, Jonathan had suddenly known what to do.

It was time to forgive.

He'd been so caught up in his anger, so determined to seek justice, that he'd neglected to realize that there were other feelings and viewpoints involved.

Seeking retribution from David and his family would not bring his barn back. It would not erase the all-encompassing fear that had engulfed him when he'd worried about Winnie.

When he'd been afraid for his animals' lives.

The memories would still be there. And perhaps that is what needed to be. Those memories were strong. Not only of the bad things, but of the good things, too. Of how all their neighbors pulled together and offered support.

Of how his boss Brent was offering to give him the wood for the barn, and offered to shut down the mill for a half day so everyone could help. That was a gift greater than he could have imagined.

So was the gleam of hope in David's eyes. Jonathan had no doubt the boy would help build the barn as much as he could. He also knew that the guilt and weight of his actions would be with him forever.

But perhaps the memories of Jonathan's forgiveness would be there as well. And perhaps that forgiveness would ignite a new flame in his heart and lead David to be the man he wanted to become, instead of the one he thought he had to be.

Winnie looked, then looked again when she saw who was driving up the long, winding road to their farm. The buggy was definitely Eli's, but the form in the front seat certainly was not the lanky body of Eli Miller.

Who could it be?

She was even more curious when the buggy horse sidestepped a bit near a patch of bushes. Something had spooked it, and the driver was having a difficult time finding his bearings.

Or so it seemed.

"Who's that?" Hannah asked as she came to stand beside Winnie at the front window.

"I'm not sure." As she'd done more times than she could count, Winnie picked Hannah up and sat her on the kitchen counter. "Someone's comin' in Eli Miller's buggy, but I don't think it's him."

Hannah scrambled to her knees as she peered out. "*Jah*. It don't look like Eli."

Mary joined them. "Isn't that a courtin' buggy? Eli doesn't drive that around, does he?"

"Not for some time." Glancing at her niece in some surprise, Winnie said, "I'm surprised you knew about courtin' buggies."

"I like them. They're prettier, don'tcha think?"

"I do." Winnie always enjoyed riding in the fancier, sleeker buggy with its open top. It was far more enjoyable than the sedate, closed-in buggy. Staring at the driver again, she murmured, "Could that be Caleb?"

Little Hannah clapped. "Oh, I hope so! I like Caleb."

"That man's not Caleb," Mary stated without a bit of doubt in her voice as the buggy approached. She squinted and pressed her nose to the windowpane, creating a smudge that would need to be washed off with vinegar. "It looks to be Samuel."

As the buggy stopped and the driver alighted, Hannah held out her arms for Winnie to help her down. After Winnie complied, she ran to the door and scampered down the front steps before Winnie could say a word. "Samuel!" she cried, loud enough to startle all the animals in the barn.

In a moment's time, Mary joined her sister.

Sam greeted both girls with friendly hugs, then helped them climb up to the bench of the buggy; they so obviously wanted to try out the seat.

This time it was Winnie who wanted to press her nose to the pane and watch more closely, because she certainly did not want to miss a moment of what was happening.

If she wasn't mistaken, Samuel Miller was dressed Amish and had just arrived in a courting buggy. "What in the world?" she murmured. Stranger things had happened, but not for some time.

When the girls got off the buggy, Mary turned to the window. "Winnie! Winnie, come out, why don'tcha?"

Winnie knew her cheeks were likely blazing red. She was mighty thankful neither Jonathan nor Katie were around to comment about that. But still, she waited.

"Winnie? Winnie!" Hannah sung out. "Come on!"

Well, it looked to be out of her hands now. "I'm on my way," Winnie murmured, though she knew no one could hear her. Carefully, she made her way through the kitchen and did her best to meet them, glad that she hardly needed help anymore.

In a flash, Sam was up the steps, stepping behind her and gently closing the door. She could hardly do a thing besides stare at him.

He seemed to be enjoying every bit of her surprise. "Hi."

"*Gut-n-owed,*" she said formally.

Hat in hand, Sam looked amused. "Good afternoon, to you, too."

Darting a look at Mary and Hannah, she was pleased to see they were off playing with their dog near the garden. Since this was one of their favorite activities, she wasn't worried about them. Not near as worried about them as she was about her beating heart!

The only thing to do was to offer Samuel something to drink. "Would you care for some lemonade?"

"I would." Already walking to the kitchen door, he motioned for her to sit on one of the many chairs decorating the front porch. "I'll get it."

She sat. Not because she needed the rest for her foot, but because she couldn't believe what was happening.

In no time at all, he was back with two glasses in his hands. After passing her one, he sat down next to her. "This drink is a blessing. It sure is hot."

"It is most pleasant—" Oh, she couldn't do this. "Why are you dressed Amish?" she blurted. "Why did you arrive in a buggy? In a courtin' buggy, of all things? What is going on?"

"It's like I told you the other day. I'm going to join the church."

"Yes, but I didn't think you would do it so suddenly. Where's your truck? Your Ford?" She'd liked his shiny black truck. She'd always thought he looked right fittin' in that bold vehicle.

"I sold it."

Lemonade sputtered everywhere. "Samuel Miller, you start talking this minute. When do you plan to be baptised?"

"On Sunday."

"Are you sure you don't need more time to consider things?"

"I'm positive." Then, sheepishly, he grinned as he lifted one leg. "Well, I might need more time to get some proper clothes. The pants are Eli's and they're mighty short."

Turning serious, he said, "Winnie, now that my decision has been made, I'm anxious to return to the community. I've missed my family. I've missed our community and the strength and comfort it gave me. And, then, there was a certain mouthy dark-haired woman with the prettiest dimples I ever saw. I've started thinking about her quite a bit."

Winnie couldn't believe her ears. This was really happening. All the feelings she'd been trying to stifle unsuccessfully could now be brought to light. She could begin to hope again.

"I still hate to think of you giving up everything."

"I'm ready. When I was younger, it felt as if my brain

was too big for my head. All I wanted to do was learn and learn and ask questions. I was never more sure in my life when I asked my family to let me go study. I needed to learn as much as I needed to breathe."

"And then?"

"I followed where I thought the Lord was guiding me. I was sure there was a reason he made me so smart. I felt it would be wrong not to see where it all led me." After a sip of lemonade, he continued. "I loved going to university. I loved the challenge. But, Winnie, there's more to me than this brain of mine. And, there's more in my head than just a desire for knowledge. I want family and love and my faith."

"I know you love your family. I've never doubted that. I don't think anyone has."

Looking almost boyish, Sam tilted his head. "Oh, but you're going to make me say this, aren't ya? All right, I will. I care for you, Winnie."

For once, Winnie couldn't think of a single response. Her lungs felt out of breath, like she was struggling for air. For so long, she'd longed to be loved. To have someone in her life who cared about her . . . and who she cared deeply about.

For some time now, she knew that person was Sam. But she didn't want her love to cause him regrets. She didn't want him one day wishing he'd never left his English world.

Sam's hazel eyes glinted. "Don't make us wait, Winnie." He leaned forward, bracing his elbows on his knees. "Don't make me wait another day for you to be my girl."

The childish expression made her smile. After all, they were two adults in their twenties. Hardly star-crossed teens.

Yet, being his "girl" sounded awfully right. But still, scary.

"I . . . I don't know." Truly, she was still trying to get her head around the fact that everything she'd hoped for was coming true.

"Do you want to take things slow? We can do that, if you'd like."

"I would like slow, if you don't mind."

"I don't mind at all. You are worth it. And the life I want with you is worth it, too."

Oh, so was he. After all the past disappointments in love, Winnie now knew it had been the Lord's way of preparing her for this relationship—the relationship with Samuel that she could rely on for the rest of her life.

She'd needed those trials and tribulations to be strong enough to start a life with Samuel. She needed past experiences so that she'd be wise enough to understand Sam's feelings when he talked about his past. He stood up. "So, Winnie Lundy, would you care to go for a ride in my borrowed courting buggy?"

Winnie couldn't help it, she laughed. "I'd love to, but I'm not certain you need an extra passenger just yet."

With a grimace, he said, "I forgot horses have minds of their own."

"I'm just teasing you. You'll get the hang of things again soon. But I'm sorry, I canna go. I'm watching the girls for Katie today. She's over with Anna, helping with some wedding things."

He finished his lemonade, sat it on the wide planks of the porch, then stood up. "Maybe tomorrow? In the afternoon?"

"I'm working until four o'clock. If you come over after dinner, I'd love to go for a ride."

Almost shyly, Samuel Miller smiled. "Then I'll be back."

Winnie could only nod as he stepped down the stairs. He waved goodbye to the girls, and then coaxed Eli's horse on his way again.

If that don't beat all. She had a beau. A fine man, too. Samuel Miller.

Chapter 20

From the porch, Winnie felt a great sense of satisfaction and excitement as she watched the men bond together in work teams and the women carry overstuffed baskets toward the shade of the oak and walnut trees.

Today was a special day, indeed. With God's help—and everyone else's—by nightfall they'd have the makings of a new barn.

"Well, those men are certainly as busy as can be. We best not stand here too much longer. We'll be sproutin' feathers when we have important work to do," Irene Brenneman said. "We need to plan where all the ladies are going to put their dishes."

Winnie pointed to the dining room, where the long oak table was covered with an assortment of quilts. Since Katie was busy trying to tend to everyone, Winnie was doing her best to plan the logistics. "I'll direct the ladies and the food here on the table. They can leave their baskets with quilts and dishes near the trees." As two children skipped rope nearby, Winnie winced, just imagining how difficult it would be to stay organized with so many children underfoot. "And, I think we should encourage the *kinner* to go play on the other side of the house near the garden."

As the hours passed, Winnie noticed the men falling into place, each doing what they did best. Jonathan instructed groups, John Brenneman double-checked supplies, and Brent, Jonathan's boss at the lumberyard, explained how he organized the lumber. Finally, with much good humor and teasing about who was the strongest, the barn raising began.

Voices and music rang out, children scampered and laughed in the vibrant green fields, and the scents of hearty food and sawdust filled the air.

For all the hard work, it was great fun.

All the while, Winnie did her best to stay near the construction, all in hopes of catching a glimpse of Samuel.

She wasn't disappointed. Whether by design or chance, she saw quite a bit of him throughout the morning. His smiles and nods in her direction were worth all the knowing looks and teasing glances from the other women.

Finally lunch was served. After a quick, silent moment of prayer, Winnie took her place at Sam's table and brought over plates of chicken and bowls of potatoes.

"*Danke*," he said, when she brought him a festive-looking gelatin salad.

"You're welcome," she murmured with a smile. Even though she'd done no part of the meal except to serve it.

It was customary for the women and children to eat after the men had their chance. When Winnie took Sam's spot, she hardly noticed what she put in her mouth—all she could think about was how handsome he'd been. How the same yet different he seemed around the other men.

How smitten she was with him. A warmth filled her. Could this really be her future, a life working side by side with such a generous, giving, handsome man? It all seemed too good to be true.

"Winnie, if you're not too tired, we've got a good amount of work to do, if you're done sittin'," Irene called.

"I'm not tired, my leg feels fine." She hopped up. "I'll be right there."

Just as the sun set, a shadow fell across the front porch. The barn frame was up. Families began to take their leave, gathering sleepy children and sparkly clean food containers.

Jonathan, Katie, and the girls were inside getting the girls ready for bed.

Winnie sat on the front stoop in the shadow of the new structure and breathed a sigh of contentment. The day had been a busy one, but most gratifying. Barn raisings were always a pure example of their way of life. She was never so proud to be Amish. Once more, she knew she'd be counting her blessings for many days to come.

She was just about to do that when yet another shadow fell over her—this one far smaller. Ah, yet another blessing, indeed. "Samuel. I thought you had already left."

"Without telling you goodbye? I wouldn't do that."

"The barn, it looks *gut, jah*?"

His tawny brown hair was still damp from when he washed up. As was his habit, he brushed it out of his face and looked at the structure. "It's a fine building. I don't think I'll ever be able to look at it without remembering this feeling of accomplishment. I'm pleased with it."

"You should. It's a right beautiful barn. My brother is so pleased."

Sam smiled as he dropped down to sit next to her. "Have I told you today how glad I am to see you're back on two feet?" Sam said, his eyes twinkling in the way that made her heart melt.

"Not half as glad as I am. I was thinking those crutches would always be my companions." Carefully, shaking her right leg, she said, "Though I have some scars, I feel like I did before the fire."

"The scars are a small price to pay for being healthy again, I think." Pointing to the new barn, he said, "This building kind of feels like my life right now. Though the old structure has gone away, the memories will always be there."

"And in its place?"

"In its place is something new and fresh. Supported by many strong hands and hearts."

"That's a fitting description, I think. Samuel, I am mighty glad you decided to come back. I would have become English for you, but I don't know if I'd have ever fit in the way you would've needed me to."

"I think you would have done all right, but I'm glad I'm the one who did the changing."

"You don't think you'll have regrets?"

"No. Especially since the bishop felt I could still teach at the college a bit." Flashing a smile, he added, "Like the fire in the barn, what happened was unexpected, but now that time has passed, I see that it was not all bad."

He held out his hand for her to take. "With the Lord's help, I think we'll see in the coming years that it will prove to be the right thing."

She placed her other hand over their joined ones and squeezed gently. Oh, she never wanted to let him go! "I know what we have is the right thing, indeed."

"May I come by tomorrow?"

"I'd be terribly sad if you didn't."

"That's it? No exceptions or rules or circumstances?"

"Like you, I feel new again. Being hurt in the fire taught me to count my blessings more. I'm going to count you as my greatest blessing."

Slowly, Sam lifted her hands and gently kissed her knuckles. Winnie didn't even try to pretend that she didn't feel a rush of pleasure from his touch.

She would never have dreamed that she'd spend a full

week in a hospital with burns and a broken foot. And even more, that it would all lead to finally thinking of marriage.

Funny how so much of what she used to worry about didn't bother her anymore.

"You know, one day, we might look back at all this and laugh."

Still looking at their joined hands, Sam said, "About how we met?"

"About how the Lord really does have a plan. And that His plan is both wondrous and true."

"And never ceases to amaze."

Winnie looked up at him and smiled. "I've fallen in love with you."

"And I you." Slowly, Samuel Miller leaned close and gently brushed his lips against hers, and then kissed Winnie again.

Right there, on the front stoop of her brother's home. In the shadow of a freshly built barn, where all things seemed possible.

Epilogue

"*Gude Mariye*, Anna!" Katie called out from the doorway. "It's time to wake up, and to be quick about it, too! I canna believe you are sleeping so late on your own wedding day."

"Late?" Anna peeked out of the covers, then groaned. "It's barely light out. What time is it?"

"Five. Come now, there's much to be done." Looking a bit shamefaced, Katie said, "I know it's early, but I'm fair to bursting with excitement."

As usual, Katie's enthusiasm was contagious. Sitting up, Anna looked fondly at the woman who had once, long ago, been just a good friend. Now she was about to be her sister.

Henry!

"Have you seen your brother yet?"

A sweet, knowing smile filled Katie's gaze. "I have."

"How's he doing? Is he *neahfich*?" Oh, she really hoped

he wasn't. If he was apprehensive, perhaps that meant he really regretted everything. Or was having second thoughts?

"He looks nervous, indeed."

"He does?"

Katie broke into a broad grin. "But not for the reason you're thinkin'—it's because he hopes everything will go okay."

"Oh. Well, I, myself feel extremely happy! I'm finally getting married."

"I'll be happy when you get out of bed. It's time for breakfast. People will be arriving in just a few hours and we've much to do before that. There's a bit of baking that still needs to be done."

The ceremony was supposed to begin at eight that morning. During the ceremony, they'd sing hymnals from the *Ausbund*, have scripture readings, and read passages from the *Ordnung*. They wouldn't be fully good and married until noon. After that would be a wonderful chicken dinner and pies.

She pushed the covers away and stepped out of bed. "All right. I'll get busy. I better get my parents up. It will probably take them the whole time to get ready."

"You're wrong," Katie said with a smile. "Your *mamm* beat me up! She's helping my *mamm* and Rebecca sort through the plates and such from the wedding wagon."

Anna knew she shouldn't be so shocked. Anna had forgotten but was reminded, time and again over the last year, of the many good qualities her mother had in abundance. She was earnest, had a desire to please, and above all, she had an infinite love for Anna. And Anna loved her, too.

Though she wasn't quite the baker Irene was, she could certainly make fine pies and other baked goods. She also had a knack for planning large events—whether they were English or Amish. With Irene's blessing, she helped organize tables and count linens—no small task for a guest list of over two hundred people.

"I'm glad she came," Anna said. "I should go visit with her."

"That's a *gut* idea, I think," Katie murmured.

Anna's bridal gown was a new dress of light blue. Though without adornment, it looked special to her eyes—perhaps because the brand-new dress symbolized so much. Now, though, she ran downstairs in yesterday's dress, a plain gray one which she'd been taken to wearing when work or chores would be especially consuming.

The group in the kitchen looked up in surprise when she appeared. "Up already?"

"Katie made sure of it."

Irene chuckled. "How about some breakfast?"

"Thank you." Though her stomach was in knots, Anna knew it would be wise to eat a hearty meal. The rest of the day would be spent visiting with the great number of people who had traveled to spend the special day with her.

After Irene prepared a plate of fruit, eggs, and toast, Anna's mom brought it to her. "Here you go, honey."

Anna patted the seat of the chair next to her. "Will you sit with me, Mom?"

"Of course." A pretty, familiar smile she loved passed over her mother's expression. "How are you doing?"

"I'm excited."

"I'm glad. It's a special day. Henry is a good man. You chose well, Anna."

Anna knew that had cost her a lot to say. When Anna had first fallen in love with Henry, her mother—rightfully—had doubted her motivations. But during the past year, it had been her mother who had made all the changes. Now here she was, helping in the kitchen to prepare a feast that was most likely very different than the wedding and reception she'd dreamed of hosting for her daughter. "Have I told you lately that I'm glad you're my mom? You've been a wonderful mother to me."

Her mother blinked. "You've forgiven me for not trusting you to know what's best?"

Anna nodded. "I shouldn't have held a grudge. I'm sorry it's taken me so long to accept your apology."

Her mom wiped her eyes. "I'm proud of you. You've made a wonderful life here for yourself."

A wave of relief and happiness passed over Anna. Finally, it seemed as if everything was right in the world. In her world, the only place that mattered that morning.

After breakfast, all the women got busy making casseroles and baking two more pies. Anna was happy to see that her mother didn't mind in the least doing so much work. In fact, she looked to be enjoying the cheery banter of all the women surrounding them.

Two hours later, from the corner of the kitchen, Katie cleared her throat. "Anna, I can't hold my tongue a moment longer. You must go get ready! The ceremony will start before we know it."

Her mother stood up and held out a hand. "I'd like to help, if I could."

Grasping it, Anna smiled. "I'd love your help. Thank you."

Henry and Anna's wedding ceremony was wonderful-*gut*, Winnie thought. She liked seeing all the English there, at first looking a bit awkward, then settling in and enjoying the ceremony with as much care and sentiment as everyone else.

Winnie had always thought there was something magical about hearing and seeing the old rituals come to life and remembering vows spoken before.

Across the aisle with all the men sat Sam. He was sitting next to Eli and Caleb. If she hadn't been looking for his muscular form, she might have had to look a bit harder, he blended in so well. Now it felt as if all their pasts hardly mattered. Only the present and their future goals were what counted.

Right before she was set to join the other women as they prepared all the food, Sam caught her. "Got a minute?"

Winnie knew she'd spare him any amount of time. "Sure."

"The wedding was a good one, don'tcha think?"

"I do."

"It got me thinking . . ." His words floated away as a group of neighbors nodded in their direction before moving off.

When they were alone again, Winnie said, "What got you thinking?"

"I'm hoping we'll be as happy one day, too. I mean, I would be happy if you"—he stopped, obviously looking impatient with himself—"oh, Winnie, I'm not doing a good job of this am I?"

"I'm not sure. It depends what you're trying to do."

"I know we've been courting a bit, and that you wanted to take things slow, but well, I'd like you to marry me soon. If you would like."

Well, there it was. Her proposal from Samuel. It had happened. Just like that!

The words were much like she expected but the moment was like nothing she'd ever imagined. She felt giddy and pleased . . . and at peace.

Winnie felt right. "Well, now, I think you're doing just fine."

"Then, what do you say?" Samuel looked her over, his beautiful hazel eyes brimming with emotion. "Do you have an answer?"

Reaching out for him, Winnie took his hand. "Oh, Samuel. For such a smart man, you can sure be *deerich*, so foolish! Of course it's a yes. It's always been a yes for you. Always."

If they'd been alone, Winnie guessed they might have kissed. Instead, surrounded by so many who loved and cared for them, he just smiled.

Across the lawn, she caught Katie's eye. When Katie raised her brows in question, Winnie nodded.

Then, when Katie let out a little squeal, Anna looked up. After sharing a glance with Katie, Anna turned to Winnie and grinned.

Yes, it was a special day for all of them. A day to remember and hold close to their hearts for a long time to come. A day for brides and engagements . . . and futures to plan.

And oh, what wonderful things were surely in store!

Giving in to temptation, Winnie spun in a circle and laughed. What wonderful things, indeed.

Shelley Shepard Gray

SHELLEY SHEPARD GRAY is the beloved author of the Sisters of the Heart series, including _Hidden_, _Wanted_, and _Forgiven_. Before writing, she was a teacher in both Texas and Colorado. She now writes full-time and lives in southern Ohio with her husband and two children. When not writing, Shelley volunteers at church, reads, and enjoys walking her miniature dachshund on her town's scenic bike trail.

BOOKS BY
SHELLEY SHEPARD GRAY

FAMILIES OF HONOR

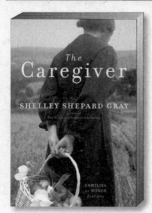

THE CAREGIVER
978-0-06-202061-1 (paperback)

A chance encounter changes the lives of a young widow and a broken-hearted man. While they try to forget each other, neither can disregard the bond they briefly shared.

THE PROTECTOR
978-0-06-202062-8 (paperback)

Ella Troyer feels bitterness towards the man who bought her family's farm once her father passed away. What she does not know is that he secretly hopes Ella will occupy this house again . . . as his wife.

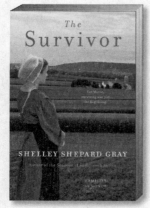

THE SURVIVOR
978-0-06-202063-5 (paperback)

In the final book in the Families of Honor series, young Amish woman Mattie Troyer has healed from the cancer that nearly took her life . . . but can she find the man who can mend her lonely heart?

SISTERS OF THE HEART

HIDDEN
978-0-06-147445-3
(paperback)

WANTED
978-0-06-147446-0
(paperback)

FORGIVEN
978-0-06-147447-7
(paperback)

GRACE
978-0-06-199096-0
(paperback)

SEASONS OF SUGARCREEK

WINTER'S AWAKENING
978-0-06-185222-0
(paperback)

SPRING'S RENEWAL
978-0-06-185236-7
(paperback)

AUTUMN'S PROMISE
978-0-06-185237-4
(paperback)

Visit www.ShelleyShepardGray.com and find Shelley
on Facebook for the latest news on her books!

Available wherever books are sold, or call 1-800-331-3761 to order.